THERE IS A LAND

A LIBÈTE LIMYÈ MYSTERY

TED OSWALD

This is a work of fiction. Names, characters, organizations, places, events, and incidents are either products of the author's imagination or are used fictitiously.

Text copyright © 2015 Ted Oswald.
All rights reserved.

No part of this book may be reproduced, or stored in a retrieval system, or transmitted in any form or by any means, electronic, mechanical, photocopying, recording, or otherwise without express written permission of the publisher.

Lyrics to *Come join us, come on, you'll see where we are* and *I must give the good Lord thanks* are taken from *When the Hands are Many: Community Organization and Social Change in Rural Haiti*. Copyright © 2001 by Cornell University. Used by permission. All rights reserved.

Ebook published by Kindle Press, Seattle.

Amazon, the Amazon logo, and Kindle Press are trademarks of Amazon.com Inc., or its affiliates.

Print book published by Dispatch Publishing.

ISBN-13: 978-0-9886005-3-9

ISBN-10: 0988600536

Cover design by Corrigan Clay

To my parents

PROLOGUE

There was a Land.
And in that Land was a Boy.
And in that Boy was a Seed.

They come in a time of fear.

In this year, 1994, hope has already stood up to be counted, named itself, and been dashed. The elected government is toppled and scattered as its army turns yet again like a sharpened spear on its own people.

In this month, September, the retaliatory embargo against Haiti continues to make its markets seize and crops fail to flow down the mountain trails or up from the valleys and into the cities.

On this day, the twenty-ninth, reports of foreign troops arriving on the island's shores begin spreading throughout this part of the country.

And on this day, in this month, in this year, the Son comes up the mountain.

He walks slowly. Not because he is tired, or lazy, nor because a heavy load presses upon his ever-broadening shoulders. It is because the day is beautiful.

The Sun's face is hidden by thick, painterly clouds. Birds loop and dive, reveling in their easy flight. The earth is wet with merciful rain.

And despite all that is wrong with the world, in this moment, all is well with the Son. He sings songs to himself and plots stories to share, for in these lyrics and words he can forget things as they are–dismal, dire–and dream of what they might be. Infrequent rain means sparse crops, yes. Disease has claimed some from his family who dot these mountains. Hunger, always present, gnaws from within. But he, this Son, has a spirit made to soar.

When the two jeeps approach bearing men clad in green and holding guns poking out at all angles, his singing stops. He slips to the side of the mountain path, and a cloud of dirt envelops him. Seeing these dark men, these paramilitaries, who come to boss and pry and take, is not uncommon. But he does not usually see so many, not all at once. He tries pushing thoughts of the dark men away, but they linger. He lays his eyes on the green of the valleys below, on distant trees so small they blend into a quilt over the land, on the Artibonite River sliding among them like an aqua serpent. He returns to his lyrics and musings, but it is no good. The fear has slipped beneath his skin.

His gait stretches. His pace quickens.

The path from here to home is long. He tries to buffet his fears with thoughts of the curvy girl he likes, the heft of a harvesting blade in his hand, his sister near their kerosene lamp as he delights her with tales. His keen eyes take in much when he wishes them to, and he takes these raw observations and spins them into legends that make the world feel bigger than the mountaintop upon which he passes his life.

When he comes upon the first *lakou*, a collection of neighbors' ramshackle homes, it is silent. He sees curtain doors sway in the breeze and pots left to sit over dying cooking flames. It is as if everyone from the smallest child to the oldest man has hidden as part of a game.

The fear burrows deeper yet. Those jeeps, those men, those guns; they have claimed him. The Son can resist no more. He runs.

He takes to the cornstalks on the hillside, as he's been warned to do by his father. His *papa* is a local organizer and leader with the Lavalas Party and had helped sweep President Aristide into office, the same president who was swept out not long after. He is a good man, his father. He speaks of *jistis* and *demokrasi* as if they are familiar friends, bodied and breathing and coming to take up residence on their mountain. His father is a hero for his vision, and his mother, much loved by all, has helped as much in bringing them here. When news of the coup came, so did violence. Jistis and demokrasi were quick to flee. His parents were not.

Threading through rocks and spare trees, the Son slides up the hill to gain a view of his family's house and yard. The sight is surreal. He sees the dark men enter and leave his small home, throwing the family's chairs, mats, bowls, rice, and seed stores into a pile. He watches them hoist the family's goats, pigs, and roosters into the jeeps. He gasps at the sight of his father and mother–on their knees, guns to their heads–watching this emptying of their lives with tears.

Where is his sister? The fear, now at his throat, makes him double over. He forces himself to rise, to look at their possessions, licked by growing flames, and looks away over the stalks of corn and beseeches the mountains and valley, the sky and everything in it, to end this moment.

The Son watches as the men drag his father to the closest tree, a *mapou*. They produce a noose and toss it over a branch.

Suddenly his father is up, dangling, and dying. As the men let his suffering stretch out, the Son's mother cannot help but scream. Half of the dark men train their guns on her. Half aim their guns at his father.

The sky shatters.

The foul cracking sounds bounce from slope to scarp and back in cruel, hollow echoes.

The Son's gaze falters. He falls low among the rocks and roots. He trembles, bile churns in his stomach, creeps up his throat, and out.

And with these murders, the Son, this boy, becomes a man.

• • •

Death surrounds. The cost of living, they say.

Many deaths mean little when the dead pass and the wide world fails to take note.

Other deaths are grand in significance, marking the stop of one thing and the start of another. They are premature reapings, and their sadness staggers.

You might think these deaths are the former. But you would be wrong.

These deaths on a quiet mountain in Haiti are a long-term loan taken out by Fate. Though the victims will be mourned by few and forgotten by most, they have shaken the foundations of what is, so that at just the right time and just the right place the course of things might change–irrevocably, impossibly, and for forever.

PART I

I lift up my eyes to the mountains—
where does my help come from?
Psalm 121:1

Deye mòn, gen mòn.
Behind mountains, there are mountains.

THE PROPHET

Kouri pou lapli, tonbe nan gran rivyè.
Run from the rain to fall in the river.

There are souls lingering in these woods, these hills, these mountains.

The black, brewing storm keeps the Moon's light at bay, barring it from the good it might do. Candle flames dance until a powerful gust rises up, extinguishing lights throughout the land. The dark hides what it hides. Until the broken girl, soul and all, must flee.

I would do

She thrusts herself against the tree, hoping the others had not heard the twig snap, the branches rustle, her breathless curse. Her mind, unstuck in time, careens between past fear and present danger. Convinced that if she stalls, if she does not move, she will die.

Her eyes dart from left to right. She scans the field of trees before her and their monstrous tangles of limbs. *Nothing there.*

I would do anything

No sound. No light. But then, a flash fills the wood, a crash steals her gaze.

Is it them?

The drops are heard, then felt, filtering down through the foliage above. Her senses are lost in the new downpour. She shields her eyes, a futile effort to keep the falling water from claiming her sight. Shuddering in the cold, she hazards a deep, long breath. *Did I beat them?*

Another flash. The fleeting light gives a glimpse of three shifting forms. Prowling in formation and oblivious to the sheets of rain, they move straight ahead. Straight toward her.

She snaps back behind the tree and stifles a whimper. Her body trembles with a power previously unknown, claimed by the thought of their fangs entering her flesh, rending her apart. Such a horrible end! Teeth clenched, she looses a wordless, aspirated prayer.

She reaches for her remaining shoe–the other lost in her sprint through the woods–and flings it as far as she can.

She watches. Hopes the beasts will run away and afford her a moment to sprint the opposite direction. But they are not taken in. They have her scent. It is now just a matter of how to best claim her.

I would do anything for you

She steels her mind, pushing the wisps of words aside with the branches that hover before her. Sodden, she pulls her book bag from back to front, unzips it, feels around, and sobs in frustration. Was it gone? Had she lost it?

Her desperate fingers close.

This is it then.

Just as she'd been taught, she pounds the flare's cap. It bursts into flame and smoke, bathing Libète and the beasts in a light both flickering and red.

The light flashes. Red. A warning.

— We're coming back on, Gerry says.

Libète pushes Jak, who sits next to her, and laughs at the boy's just-told joke. He smiles too. They are dressed in their best, though none of their listeners can see them.

They put on their headphones and squint to take in their pale reflections in the glass between them and Gerry. Libète sits taller than the boy, but he is catching her up. Her plaits glisten in the studio's low light.

— You look ridiculous, she mouths, pointing out the headphones swallowing Jak's head.

— So do you, he mouths back. His smile is wide.

They each feel a hand on their shoulder to still them. Libète turns. Stephanie frowns, but the girl sees a smile itching at the corner of the woman's mouth. Libète pats her guardian's hand reassuringly and swivels in her chair.

Gerry speaks. I want to welcome you all back, dear listeners, for this special New Year's Eve program . . .

With a deep breath, Libète exorcises the last trace of playfulness. Her face is set. The restraining hand slides away. She fixes her eyes on Gerry as he greets the audience, smiling at her through his words. She nods back, sitting straight as a pole.

— For those just joining us, we have two special cohosts with us to herald in 2014, some of the boldest voices of a new generation, Libète Limye and Jak Alcide, two children–

— Young adults, Libète corrected.

— . . . refined in the brutal crucible that is Cité Soleil–

— Among many kind and loving people there, she added.

— ... who have given us an example of courage beyond their years through their activism.

Libète offered a small bow in her seat. Thank you for the kind words, *Mesye* Gerry.

— Thank you, Mesye Gerry, Jak parroted as he slid his flat hands from the shallow desk before him to his lap. Wet palm prints remained, soon vanishing in the studio's cool.

— By now many of you are familiar with this pair's story, Gerry said. Based on the YouTube video's view count, it's likely you've even watched as these two stood and accused the villain Jean-Pierre Benoit of conspiracy to kill a mother and child and lead a prostitution ring.

Libète piped in. And I'll remind our dear listeners that this ... *man*, if I can even call him this, has skirted the law and still walks among us innocents, as free and careless as the day he was born.

— And be that as it may, Gerry answered, I must confess that at the end of another long and hard year, I tire of discussing Benoit and our broken justice system. We could cover such things all day. But on this evening, on this New Year's Eve, I'd rather discuss Haiti's hope–which to my old and tiring eyes, appears to be its youth. It appears to be you, Jak and Libète, and your work.

Jak spoke first. Oh, our work's really not that special–

Libète slapped the back of Jak's head. Our work is not only *special* – she gave the boy a cutting look – it is one of the most vital social movements of the last decade in Haiti. A comprehensive youth congress to organize Cité Soleil and demand full social, economic, cultural, civil, and political rights for the underclass. Jak and I are honored to be the original conveners and delegates of this democratic congress.

— And you have a large rally planned for Independence Day tomorrow, no?

— *Wi*. Yes. That is correct. We will mark it as a day of independence from unjust markets that rob us of our dignity, from an abusive political system that makes a mockery of the word democracy. Tomorrow is a day for us to gather and focus on what makes us poor, and to then rejoice over what makes us rich!

— A tall order! Gerry gave a patronizing laugh, though Libète didn't mind. I, as one of the old guard in this fight, look forward to hearing more! So in this next half hour, to pass the torch and begin tomorrow's celebrations today, I'll hand over the microphone to these childr–*young adult*–hosts. They'll be taking calls from you. And these two–well, maybe just Libète–have let me know that all topics are on the table. Gerry poked at the control panel before him. First caller!

A small yellow light on a sound board before Jak turned green.

— Wi, hello? the voice said. Am I on? A squawk of feedback followed, making the children cringe.

— Yes, dear friend and caller, you are on, Gerry said impatiently. Please, turn your radio off in the background.

— Oh, yes. Of course, of course. They heard the caller, an elderly man by the timbre of his voice, shuffle off. On the way back to the phone, they could hear him clear his throat and spit. Libète smiled at Jak.

— Children, the gentleman said, I understand you have made a commitment to justice?

— That is right, dear sir. It is our birthright and lives' pursuit.

— And then why does it not bother you to do a grave injustice by slandering one of our most successful and generous businessmen, Monsieur Jean-Pierre Benoit? Does it not bother you that the tiny bit of notoriety you now exploit comes from dragging his good name through the mud with these tired, baseless accusations? Have you no shame?

Gerry cut off the call with the flip of a switch.

— Ah, I'm sorry for that. We screen our callers, but bad eggs can't always be avoided. He cast a glance over to the show's producer to his left. The man gave a shrug.

— It's all right, Libète said. We mustn't silence debate. The Truth defies all silencing. Right, Jak?

— Um. Right.

— Unfortunately, in this battle of accusations, Benoit's attacks go beyond just the verbal. He employed thugs and murderers to do his dirty work before, and he does so now. As we came into the studio this evening, there were protesters outside. Threatening us, and the radio station. Pull their pockets inside out and you'd find a few goud from Benoit's bank account deposited there. No matter the amount of money, no matter what Benoit might do through his minions, here is the thing he still doesn't understand: he cannot kill the Truth as long as we are willing to speak it. Yes, his example is yet another mockery of our laws, but we have already seen that our esteemed *prezidan-pou-lavi* Jean-Claude Duvalier walks about the streets of Port-au-Prince unconvicted by the courts. This is the ultimate insult to those who suffered in his regime's grip! Why should we expect that Benoit, an amateur villain next to Duvalier, would face justice unless we, the sovereign people, hold Benoit to account?

Gerry was smiling widely. Libète, the strength with which you speak! At what, age fourteen?

— I turn fifteen tomorrow.

— Ha! I should simply abdicate my place behind the microphone to you. Anything to add, Jak?

— No. Yes. I . . . I mean . . . no.

A frown slipped across Gerry's face. Every tap of the host's index finger signaled his disappointment. Stephanie patted Jak on the back and whispered, *It's okay.*

— Next caller, then. Who are we speaking with?

— I'm called *Madanm* Honoré. I have seen the video taken the night you children confronted Benoit. Of course, the police officer–what was his name?

— Dimanche, Libète said.

— Wi, Dimanche. He is at the center of the camera's attention. But we hear your voice and see you two small children standing up. This officer, the one who arrested Benoit, I've wondered what's become of him. In a way, he is an equal hero, *non*?

Libète and Jak looked to each other. Libète could not speak this time. Jak filled the gap. Of course he's a hero. All I ever did was figure out what Benoit's crimes were. Officer Dimanche, he is the one who took my thoughts from the air and made them action, as only an adult could. Without him, there would have been no attempt at justice.

— And he is gone, Libète added sadly. For speaking truth, he was silenced. Fired from the police. Forced into hiding. That's all we know.

A lull settled over the studio. Mesye Gerry began to speak, but Libète cut him off.

— I thank you for posing that question, Madanm. We must all remember Dimanche and those like him who stand up for what is right and true and suffer for it.

— But you fear not? Gerry asked.

— Our voices protect us, Jak said.

— It's true, Libète said. Here we are, three years later, without incident, *because* we stood up. The more well-known we are, the more protected. If harm comes to us by one hand, the same hand points straight back to Benoit. And we have counted the cost.

— We have counted the cost, Jak echoed feebly, as if a well-rehearsed refrain.

Stephanie began to pace at the back of the room. Her face was tight and impassive.

Why does she let us do these shows if what we say makes her so nervous? Libète sighed, returning her attention to Gerry.

— Dear listeners, let this be a sobering call to you–*pran kouraj*, take heart! To Libète and Jak, know that you are not alone in the struggle! Gerry cleared his throat. All right. Next caller.

— Am I on? came a hissed whisper.

— Yes, mesye, you are–

— I say this for the world. I only have a moment–

— Slow down, mesye, please–

— *Take this down!* The children looked at each other. Terror accented every syllable of the man's speech.

— Dear listener, what is–

A loud crash and thud was heard in the background.

— Write this down! 2563–

Libète scrambled, trying to pull a pencil and paper from her book bag.

— 3214-3149–

— Mesye, you must slow down–where are you? What's this number–

— 2563, the caller said. He began repeating the entire sequence, 3214–

Two explosions were heard, gunshots, rendered almost comical in their smallness through the tinny phone receiver. A gasp followed.

— Mesye? Are you, mesye, are you all right?

Muffled footsteps followed. The phone clicked silent.

Gerry attempted to redial the caller. Mesye? Are you there?

Libète had only the first few digits committed to paper and cursed herself. Her wide eyes jumped from Stephanie, who stood with her hand clasped over her mouth, to Jak, who sat with his hands to his temples as he mumbled. Libète ripped off her headset.

— Did you get that, Jak? Did you get the numbers tucked away in your head?

His eyes opened, full of dread.

He nodded slowly.

The dogs creep closer.

Libète screams, trying to frighten them, waving the red, sizzling light in her hand. Though adrenaline courses through her, she feels impossibly weak. The rain falls over her in torrents.

— Get away! she shouts. Get away! she whimpers.

Their eyes reflect her light. As do their teeth.

She shifts the flare to the opposite hand and stumbles backward. Leave me alone! she cries.

Voices shout in the distance. The beasts' owners, the more vicious animals, are nearly upon her. She turns to run, and one of the dogs rushes after her. She thrusts the flare out as a weapon, jamming it into the dog's face. It gives a brief cry. The other dogs pause, and Libète does not wait a moment longer.

Go.

She shot off again, running straight into a dense cluster of trees in hopes of slowing the dogs' pursuit. With both feet bare, every step brought shooting pain from the rocky soil and fallen branches.

The flare's light helped her slalom the trees. The dogs grew closer. They nipped at her heels, and their growling, huffing, and barking played in Libète's ears. She wagged the flare behind her, praying it might keep them at bay.

She slammed into a tree. Her knee plowed into the trunk, and it felt like it was punctured by a branch's stub. But there, ahead, she saw it: a break in the darkness. A clearing! She threw herself forward.

Dear God, protect me!

But it was not a clearing. As a lightning bolt slashed the sky, she reached the tree line and crossed, realizing what it was: a ledge, and a swollen river below. The water caught the lightning, reflecting it back with cold menace.

Her heart stopped.

The two remaining dogs bounced around her now, closing in as they cut back and forth to block an escape. Libète stepped back tentatively toward the edge, stifling a cry. She broke a toe or two in her sprint, she is sure.

Bondye, Bondye, Bondye...

The flare trembled in her hand, its power waning.

Faced with divergent paths shooting out as branches from a bough, how does she decide which to follow? Chance a dash toward the hungry dogs and the hands of the sinister forces who had unleashed them? Or leap blindly into the rushing river?

But there was no choice. Not anymore. With reason stifled, free will and fear stripped away, instinct was all that remained.

Libète threw the flare at one of the dogs and stepped from earth into air, plummeting into the dark water below.

Stephanie saw fit to stop the interview. Libète did not argue.

The trio leave Gerry and his technician and rush to Stephanie's Land Rover parked in the station compound.

Stephanie unlocks the rusting vehicle and glides into the driver's seat. Jak opens the back door and slides to the other side to make space for Libète. They buckle up. The seatbelts provide a fleeting sense of security.

— Are you two all right?

Silence is their reply.

— Dear Lord, that was horrible, Stephanie says. Jak nods, biting his lip. Libète only gazes out the window.

Stephanie turns the key, but the engine is reluctant to turn over. *Come on, Tòti*, she huffs. That was the Land Rover's name, christened by Jak because it was slow, green, and ancient, like many tortoises. With a new and brimming sense of danger, Stephanie finds these features less endearing. Stupid hunk of . . .

Stephanie waits a moment and tries again to no avail.

Libète's eyes floated to the sliding gate ahead. The radio station was part of a larger compound, right off Delmas Road, one of Port-au-Prince's main thoroughfares. The crowd of protestors who had assembled before the show had swelled, but hired security–a man with a shotgun–kept the gate locked and his finger hovering near the gun's trigger. Libète slid her window down to listen to the crowd's chanting.

She had grown used to being cursed in public. *Aba Libète*, a popular one, meant "Down with Liberty." Small protests were routine these days, as regular as the Sun trading places with the Moon. They didn't affect her, but she hated how the protesters' threats made Jak retreat into himself.

She inclined her ear and listened more carefully. This was different.

— Libète, put that window up. You don't need to hear that.

— But Steffi–listen!

They heard cheering. Any curses were drowned out by praise. By applause!

— A counter protest! Jak exclaimed.

In the hour since they had arrived at the studio, more people had come out to quiet the voices for hire!

— Ha! Libète smiled. *Benoit loses again.*

Stephanie tried the engine again. It grumbled and finally turned over, unhappy to be ripped from the afterlife.

— We need to get out of here, Stephanie said, shifting into first gear. Tòti lurched toward the gate. I just wish we didn't have to pass through this crowd . . .

— The good half will keep us from the bad half, Libète said definitively.

The guard unlocked the gate and slid it back. Jak noticed that the watchman's bald head was covered in beaded sweat. Libète wore a wide smile and waved as Tòti inched through the thicket of people. There was pounding all over the car, and Stephanie let her horn blare.

Hands reached in through Libète's window, and she shook them with aplomb. *Kenbe fèm!* she called. Hold strong!

— *Libète!* Stephanie shouted. Get that window up!

— But they're friends!

— Now!

Libète muttered while turning the window's handle.

— Libète, watch out!

A knife slid through the window. Jak tried to follow his shout by springing across the seat, but found himself trapped by his seatbelt's webbing. Libète struggled to focus on the blade. She reeled back as the knife's owner pounded on the window.

— You watch yourself, you little bitch! he shouted. You watch yourself! We're coming! He was young, and his features were contorted in fury. Libète unclasped her seatbelt and scooted across the seat, into Jak.

In a blur of motion, a large hand reached around the thug's face and yanked him backward. The knife slipped from the window, and the thug disappeared among the crowd. Libète breathed only through her nose, her chest heaving as her hand grasped blindly until it clasped Jak's.

Stephanie began shouting as she sounded endless short honks. Tòti, finally extricated from the crowd, careened onto Delmas Road.

— *Dear Lord!* Stephanie cried. Did they get you?

No reply came.

— Answer me!

— N-non, Libète whispered. No. I'm okay. I think.

— Jak?

— Me too.

— *Bondye.* She exhaled as slowly as she could and palmed her forehead. Should we still even go to my family's party?

Libète looked to Jak. His face was set with fear. She let loose her grip of his hand and puffed her cheeks before taking a deep breath. Patting him on the shoulder, she cleared her throat. But of course! We're safe now, she said. We're safe, she repeated, as if to convince herself.

Libète swims poorly.

She struggles to keep from sinking below the river's surface.

Breath comes with a struggle. The current is strong, and the water just cool enough to deaden her muscles and shock her lungs. Libète finds herself losing against the swift water that fills her nose and mouth. She paddles to break the water's ceiling and take in air.

An eddy carries her into a hard bank and knocks out her breath. She sinks back under, choking violently.

This is the end. The thought registers with a surprising calm.

The end. A peace beyond understanding descends on her, and through the layer of water she glimpses, or maybe only senses, a familiar presence.

Libète grasps for what seems like a leaf-covered arm extended toward her and collides with a half-submerged tree.

Silence lingers over the dining room. It is trespassed against only by the sounds of forks scraping dishes, knives piercing steaks, chewing, and swallowing.

— I suppose the evening's events have cast a pall over our little party, Moïse Martinette said. The old man took a swig of wine and swished it about his mouth. He looked down his glasses around the table, taking in his daughter Stephanie, his son Laurent, his guest Remi and, at the opposite end of the polished mahogany table, Libète and Jak.

Libète met Moïse's eyes. He was as grim and imperious and august as ever. She gulped hard and choked on a bite of meat. Drowning it with a swig of fizzy La Couronne, she forced out "*Wi*."

— It was horrible, Stephanie declared flatly. A man killed on air.

— This new danger. This violence at every turn. Haiti is relapsing, said Remi.

There was resignation at the aired opinion. Laurent looked at Remi and used his tongue to pick at a steak fiber caught in his teeth. He finally chortled and swallowed a draught of wine. Remi laid his silverware flat.

— Relapsing into what, pray tell? Laurent asked. He rested his elbows on the table, the sleeves of his tailored dress shirt rolled up.

Remi, still in his suit, lifted his napkin to wipe around his goatee. Where we were only a few years ago. Assassination. I mean, threatening a girl with a knife for speaking her mind? Political intimidation. Endless corruption. It's a downward spiral.

— But what gives you the right to make such pronouncements?

Remi waved off Laurent. Just because I live in the US doesn't mean I can't give an opinion. You and I both went abroad for our studies, Laurent.

— Ah, but one of us stayed on the other side.

— Laurent, calm down. He's a guest, Moïse interrupted. Leave this bickering behind.

Laurent puckered his lips and poured himself another glass of wine. But Father, surely I can say what I will, no? We can't silence debate, can we? Your words, Libète, from the radio show, no? To silence me would be a *crime*.

Libète cleared her throat to speak.

— The Truth defies all silencing, Jak blurted. That's what she said.

— *La Vérité!* Ah, yes. Ha! Is that with a big *V* or little *v*?

— The big one, Libète hissed. *Oh, how this man tests my patience. If he wasn't a relation of Steffi's* . . .

— Why don't you let these things rest for now? Stephanie said without losing her composure. She placed her hand on her older brother's wrist. Tonight is a celebration, no? A new year on the way? Her eyes pleaded.

Laurent looked at her blankly before turning back to Libète. I've heard your "truth," my esteemed guest, and I find it lacking.

Stephanie rubbed her temple and sighed.

— Heard it many times before, Laurent continued. On the lips of my students, ever so naive, decrying the way things are. Neo-Marxist mumbo jumbo. Progressive claptrap. Religious pandering. It's as dated as Jesus's cross, Marx's corpse. He paused, then smiled. Obama's hope.

Libète clenched her teeth. You ridicule our struggle? Jak's and mine? Our organizing?

— Dress-up theater, Laurent said.

— Back off, Laurent, Stephanie said.

— You're no better, Steffi. Haiti's poet laureate who pens a couple of angsty verses about changing the world. Writes a few stories. Your solutions to our society's ills?

— What's come over you? Leave this alone, Remi said. Stephanie looked to Moïse at the head of the table, imploring him to intervene.

— Am I the only one ready to say that this world is broken? Laurent asked. Just simply, irredeemably broken? To be able to look down at this mess of ours and see there's no fixing it?

— I know what's true, Libète said. I've seen it. I know it.

Laurent replied with a roll of his eyes. What do you *really* know?

— Love. Love is true. And I know myself. What's inside me.

— Ha. Ha ha! You claim what the greatest minds have sought and never found.

— Great minds and empty hearts go together.

— To *know* yourself, *ti fi*? Laurent broke from his French to utter "little girl" in Kreyòl. The words stung. Laurent proclaimed, Be wary all, when we're guided by the truth of fourteen-year-old girls!

— Even if I don't know myself, I certainly know what *you* are. An ass! Libète said, pointing her fork at him.

Moïse chuckled at the name-calling. Stephanie and Jak nervously played with the steamed vegetables on their plates. Remi watched Laurent slack-jawed.

— Only you could take a terrible evening where we've all been frightened out of our minds by what took place over the radio and *choose* to make it worse, Remi said. To see noble actions and challenge them as empty! You, Laurent, *you* are a frightened little boy without an ounce of this girl's courage!

— Ah, *ad hominem*, the refuge of the feeble-minded and limp-tongued. Don't worry. At least you two have company. Not knowing who you really are, Laurent said, turning back to Libète. It's as common as cholera these days. All the same, I know *what* you are. You're a symbol. But dear child, before life sweeps you away, remember that symbols bleed and break just like the rest of us. You'll learn soon enough that the call to do something simply for the sake of doing something accomplishes *nothing*. Just talk to those past generations of true heroes who have struggled valiantly and squandered much. My esteemed father, perhaps?

— Laurent! Moïse finally bellowed, slamming down his hand. Enough. This is beyond good humor.

Laurent raised his hands, and his palms faced the company. Forgive me, father, he said with great sobriety. I know not what I do. He chortled.

— You've always pushed when you should have pulled, Stephanie said under her breath. Taken instead of given. She crossed her arms.

— Always, Remi added.

Laurent's face soured into a sneer. The wine, it speaks too much. He crumpled his napkin and pushed out his chair from the table. Will you excuse me, dear guests? Today has been *quite* the day: a sad punctuation mark on another pathetic year. And I . . . I have a cigarette that must be smoked with utmost urgency. He stood to his full height and strode toward the door.

— Laur-*ent*, Stephanie said, halfheartedly. Don't do this. He paused at the dining room's arched exit, inclined his head, and pushed forward.

— He's never made good dinner company, Moïse said, stirring his rice with his fork before taking a small bite.

• • •

— Aw, I hate those intellectuals. Like having a PhD permits Laurent to be a prick! All talk, all criticism, nothing useful! Blah, blah, blah.

— Elize had a Ph.D., Jak said.

— Elize was *different*, Libète said, reflecting on her departed mentor. A different breed from *him*. Bleh!

The two leaned against the veranda's railing and looked down from Boutilier on Port-au-Prince below. The Martinette estate was practically palatial, gleaming white, and stunningly lit. The puttering of the electric generator that made their evening possible could be heard coming from whatever corner in which it was tucked away.

— Moïse is nice enough, Jak added. He was a professor.

— He's the same, as far as I'm concerned. Just sitting there. Taking it all in through those wine-lidded eyes.

— He's written some good books. Steffi's let me read them. I think you'd like them. He's against the state of things. Very antiestablishment.

— Look around, Jak. Someone living in a place like this, allied with people like *us*?

— Well, Steffi respects him. I won't judge him.

Libète arched an eyebrow. Maybe Steffi is the same. Growing up in a home like this. There's no way to avoid having privilege infect you.

Jak stood up straight. Watch yourself, Libète. You know better.

She looked away and scratched the stone with her half-bitten fingernail. Jak was right, of course. Her life had been transformed the day she met Stephanie, just as Stephanie's was changed when the Martinettes took her in decades ago. *I'm sorry,* Libète said. *Today hasn't gone like I thought it would.*

He looked back down on their city. *You were wonderful–on the radio.*

Libète flashed a smile. *I was, wasn't I?* She rested her elbow up high on Jak's shoulder and listed into him as she'd done since they were small. She let her eyes furtively slip down to the other end of the veranda where Remi and Stephanie talked alone. Moïse had retired after another glass of wine. *The conversation,* he had said, *has been too vigorous for me.* He had bid them *bonne nuit.*

She watched Stephanie laugh and sway, her winning smile on full display; Stephanie did not usually allow herself to be so unguarded. She reminded Libète of one of her school peers shamelessly flirting. Libète didn't like the association.

Jak stood straight as a sentry at Libète's touch, proving a willing prop in Libète's eavesdropping. She noticed he smelled of citrus, a cheap cologne he'd adopted as of late. Though he had grown taller, his slight build and short stature seemed fixed, as though his sole chance to thrive had come and gone. His bad leg had kept him from most sports, leaving him to exercise his mind. In that regard, Libète had found, he remained unmatched.

— *What do you think of Remi?* Libète said, still stealing glances. The children had only seen him twice before, both times around the holidays when he returned from the US to visit his family in Haiti. Jak shifted Libète's elbow and peeked at Stephanie and Remi as well. He caught a whiff of Libète's hair, and its sweetness stopped him cold. He forced himself to pay attention to the adults and noted their postures that were so open and friendly. He unconsciously copied Remi's pose.

— He seems like a *bon nèg*, Jak said, a good guy. *A lawyer who actually cares about justice*, Steffi called him. He seems a rarity.

— Not that stuff. I mean, what do you think *she* thinks of him? Do you think they . . .

— It's obvious, wi?

Libète smiled, but her smile drooped, giving way to sadness. What's happening, Jak? To us?

Jak sputtered. With a shock, he pulled back, straightened his tie. What do you mean?

— Laurent, I hate to say it . . . but was he right? What *are* we doing? Who are we?

Jak sighed, immeasurably relieved at her question's turn.

— We're . . . where we are.

— But in a place like this? Eating like queens and kings with lawyers and poets and intellectuals, up in Boutilier? So far from Cité Soleil, from tent cities, from the real world . . .

— It's only a meal. You don't lose who you are, what you've experienced, just because of what's on the surface.

She sighed, recalling how this day had begun in a not-so-unordinary way. She awoke at her boarding school. Ate a full meal. Studied, even though it was a day off. Forced herself to pray. Served at the hospital. Played football. Then was whisked away by her guardian to be featured on a nationally aired *radio show*? She was somehow a public figure leading a mass of disaffected, slum-dwelling youths in between school hours? It was unreal.

— But when you wade into privilege enough, doesn't it make you something else? she asked.

— I can't say. I look at you and see, well, you.

— And I look at you and see you.

They both smiled.

A phone rang, shouting for attention from the other end of the veranda. It was Stephanie's ringtone. Libète saw the faces of the two reunited friends dampen, like a cloud bank crowding out moonlight.

Steffi's face fell as she answered.

Something's wrong, Jak said. The children approached warily, mirroring Remi's concern.

— What is it? Remi mouthed. She held up a forceful finger. *Gerry*, she whispered. She strained to listen to the torrent of Kreyòl pouring from the phone.

— *Wi, dakò, wi, wi . . . Orevwa.* She put her phone down.

— What's wrong? Libète said.

— We need to go.

— Tell us what's wrong! Libète blurted.

— That was Gerry. The studio was broken into. Ransacked. A group of thugs. Gerry's producer – she shuddered – he was beaten to a pulp. The assailants wanted the tapes–

— The tapes? Of the show?

— But there were none. No recordings to give. They don't keep them.

— But why would anyone care about that show, grisly affair such as it was? Remi asked.

— *The Numbers*, Libète and Jak said in unison.

THE LAND, DARK AND CLOSE

Jan ou vini se jan yo resevwa ou.
The way you come is the way you are received.

Komisyon pa chay.
Messages are not burdens.

He watches her from the woods.

Gawking, listening, stretching his neck. Prowling into the light with the grace of a vulture two days out from its last meal. The man steps closer.

He is so very, very still. Facedown. Or is it a she? the watcher wonders. Her hair is uncovered, closely cropped. *Definitely a she*, he decides. She is out under the blazing Sun and full sky. Her bare feet still touch the water. Her deflated book bag lies next to her. He sees the dirt and rock of the river bank scattered where she crawled and notices that her torso does indeed rise and fall, rise and fall.

He slips close and takes her bag gingerly, his eyes locked on her as he rifles through its contents. A soggy bread crust. Clothing. A drowned composition book with pages and pages of slightly blurred ink that mean nothing to his illiterate eyes. A mostly punched blister pack of pills.

He is not happy. This take is nothing, nothing at all.

He spreads the bag open once more and puts his head in deep, like a showman between a lion's jaws. He recoils, dropping it all. Could it be? he murmurs aloud. He reaches in again and extracts a pigeon with a small band around its sagging foot. The creature is dead.

The man throws the bird into the water. Too far gone to eat, he says under his breath.

A loud bray arises, and the man leaps into action, shushing and cursing and shushing the beast.

And then comes the groan, from the ground, from the girl. She stirs.

He moves quickly, taking the bag, then dropping it, then grabbing it again, then preparing to run and make an escape. She makes another sound, a curious one. Sneezing? Sniffling?

This girl, who has clearly cheated death, is awake. And crying.

The man is struck. Vulture no more, he puts the bag down definitively, and approaches the girl.

He reaches out to touch her, wondering momentarily if his touch might break her. When he grows closer, he makes out the faintest of words escaping her chapped lips, repeated over and over as if in dazed prayer:

Dieudonné, she sounds, *Dieudonné,* she sounds, *Dieudonné,* she sounds, *Dieudonné . . .*

They leave the Martinette home immediately. Though the clock creeps toward midnight, all hope and enthusiasm for the new year and its new beginnings are vanquished.

With the hosts already asleep, the three exchanged hasty good-byes with Remi and the house staff and began the long, lonely ride down the winding mountain road. The air they shared in the rickety Land Rover was heavy. Steffi, though tired, drove at the frenzied speed of her thoughts. Jak somehow fell asleep. Libète looked at him jealously.

The radio caller.

Libète rested her head against the window, feeling its dull vibrations rattle her skull.

Killed, for . . . what?

Tòti's illuminated dashboard clock clicked past midnight.

Numbers? Of all things, a life lost over numbers?

The digits were spoken in a breath and then . . . gone. What purpose was a message if its meaning went unexplained? As far as she was concerned, the caller's death was for nothing. This saddened her greatly.

Wan road lights streamed past as they reentered the city. Others who had left parties and clubs in the hills were also descending back into the world, the real one, full of tent dwellers in between collapsed structures, roaming youth, and finally, the sea of glinting tin-roofed shacks: Cité Soleil, her home.

Everything beyond Cité Soleil's boundaries was so unnecessarily complicated. In Cité, she spoke about compassion and love, rattled off proverbs like a sage, criticized selfishness, and railed against power. *Raising the consciousness*, as she called it, came so very easily. Outside Cité's thirty-four sections, cynicism crept in. It sucked the hope and power right out of her words until even she doubted.

When they reached St. Francis Boarding School, Stephanie flicked the headlights on and off, and a night watchman, their grizzled friend Véus, stirred. He pulled open the tall iron gate. His shotgun hung tiredly from one hand.

Stephanie pushed Tòti through the gate's threshold.

— *Bonswa*, Madanm Steffi, Véus said through a smile missing a few teeth. A long night, eh? He gave a wink.

The flirt, Libète thought. *He has no idea all that's on our minds.*

— Good night to you as well, Steffi said, forcing a smile. Mesye Véus, I'm pleased to see you, but some bad things have happened. I will explain more tomorrow when I return. I need you to show extra *prekasyon* these next few days. The rally is tomorrow. Make sure these two are protected, you hear?

Véus straightened up at the charge.

— Anything for you, Madanm. No harm will come while I'm on watch. He gave a humble salute. Steffi nodded gratefully and pressed the accelerator.

— Ah! But wait! he said. There are more gifts left for our *Ti Pwofet*!

This was his pet name for Libète: the Little Prophet. She perked up. Gifts! Give them to me! Libète shouted from the back seat.

— Manners, Libète.

— Sorry, Steffi. Mesye Véus, I would greatly appreciate it if the items left in my honor would be turned over to me.

Véus grinned again. But of course. A card, it looks like, and a bag of *dous makos*.

Steffi rolled her eyes and let a chuckle escape her lips. The goods changed hands, and Libète began to slip her hand into the bag to tear off a piece of the sticky-sweet candy.

— Not now, Libète. Save it for tomorrow.

Libète opened her mouth to protest but decided it was not the time.

— *Mèsi*, Véus. We appreciate you.

— My pleasure, my pleasure . . .

As they idled in the courtyard between dormitories, Jak and Libète popped their doors' locks.

— Are you sure you two are all right here?

The children looked at each other before turning to Stephanie and nodding in unison.

— This is home, Jak said. This is safe.

— That's right. Happy Independence Day, Steffi.

— And happy birthday to you, Libète.

The girl grinned. Why, thank you, thank you very much.

— Maybe we can go somewhere else for the rest of the school holiday, get away from all this heaviness? Stephanie said. Maybe the house in Jacmel?

— That would be lovely, Libète said.

They slid out the sides of the Rover and waved as Stephanie reversed out of the school grounds.

— Quite a night, Jak said. Libète gave him a quick hug. I'm glad I had you there with me through it all, Jak. You keep things sane. He smiled, grateful his reddening cheeks were hidden in the dark.

They split off, Jak to the boys' wing, Libète to the girls'.

The dormitory was quiet. It was a large chamber with bunk beds lining the walls and usually housed girls from ages five to eighteen in its different sections. The majority who boarded were on scholarship from distant parts of the country, and most of them had left for the holidays. The poorest had already returned after Christmas celebrations for the consistent meals. Libète crept down the rows of bunks. She had no desire to stir the girls and recount the night's events, decidedly more bitter than sweet.

Other students lived in the neighborhoods surrounding the school and streamed in each day for classes. Because Jak and Libète were orphaned and still refused to live with Stephanie outside Cité Soleil, Stephanie had lobbied the administration to secure them bed space in the dorms. Leaving school grounds at night was strictly against the rules, but Stephanie was a gifted advocate: her resolve, spiced with kindness and unselfishness, often prevailed. Special dispensations were common from the teachers, school staff, and old headmaster.

— *Libète?*

— *Is that you?*

— *She's back! Libète's back!*

Those in the bunks weren't as asleep as they'd seemed. Clapping broke out. Libète smiled, giving up on her attempt at silence. *They waited up for me!* She soaked up the claps like rain on parched earth.

— Hey! Hey, you all! Quiet down! shouted the night matron from where she slept in an adjacent room. There's trouble for the next one I hear who makes a sound! Big trouble!

The applause cut, but the girls' voices now traveled like wisps throughout the stuffy room.

— *Bon travay!*

— *You were great!*

Libète landed with a satisfied thud on her bunk.

— *Mèsi! Thank you all!*

She smiled. *More bitter than sweet.* The story of her life.

—You really were wonderful, came whispered from the bunk above Libète's own. A thick hand extended down.

Didi. Her bunkmate and friend. Libète reached for the hand and gave it a loving tug.

— Thank you, *kè mwen.* My heart. Libète's lips were not prone to such sentiment, but kind Didi merited it.

— You're welcome, *cherie.* What are you bringing back this time?

— A treat. Here, I'll give you some–

— What do you think I am? I brushed my teeth! Save them for tomorrow. I'll enjoy the wait.

— Quiet down! the matron called. *Silans!*

Libète stifled a laugh. They were opposites, she and Didi. Where Libète was lithe and comely, Didi was pudgy and homely. Libète would curse an offender with a blue streak, while Didi would offer a blessing. *Probably why we fit together so well.*

She put the dous makous in the gap between her mattress and the wall so that the matron wouldn't happen upon it, and took out the card. This need not wait.

Libète strained her eyes in the low light streaming from the night matron's room. With a finger's slide she tore the envelope and pulled out a greeting card. It had two brown, cartoonish children with big, exaggerated heads as they held hands. *Bon Aniversaire,* it read, a birthday greeting.

She smiled, unfolding it to read the rough script inside:

Stay away from the rally, she whispered aloud, surprised. *Enemies are close.*

The girl awakens in the most unusual of states.

There is sweet singing there, the lone voice of a man rising up against the sounds of clanking metal and burlap rubbing against burlap.

But there is another sensation, more pressing: her body, contorted into the most undesirable of shapes.

Her sight comes next, but all she sees is her arms dangling in an indecipherable tangle of shadows upon the ground. She feels as if the Sun wraps her in a hot blanket.

There, in her memory's haze, she recalls a heavy truck charging past, kicking up dirt and fury and making her cough, and children, children who sang sweetly.

Then there is the rhythmic *bump, bump, bump,* and her body's rise and fall. All of these sensations are noted before her final faculty slots back into its proper place: her speech.

— What are you doing to me? she mutters.

The singing stopped, the bumping stopped, they stopped.

— Ah! So you're alive? the man said, a genuine question. He stepped close, but she only saw oversized work boots and frayed trousers, dirt embedded in their seams.

He was curiously upside down. Or rather, Libète finally realized, she was.

— Release me! she rasped, her voice's volume unable to match her command's desired strength. She tugged against the ropes that held her folded in half, over–*what is this thing?*

A tail whipped her face like she was a trespassing fly.

A donkey. The beast was spurred by her thrashing, and her kidnapper tugged hard at a sisal harness to keep the ass in place.

— Calm down! Calm down, you idiot!

— Don't call me that!

— I speak to the *bourik*, you silly girl!

— Why am I tied? What are you doing with me? Adrenaline coursed through her, inflaming her senses, cutting through the fog. Untie me, you pig!

He punched the donkey's front quarter hard, and it finally settled. She still had not seen the man's face.

— Fine. *Fine!* he shouted. But I won't let you ruin me! I won't let you steal my peace! He slipped his fingers to a top knot that secured her body to the beast. *What rudeness . . . what ingratitude,* he grumbled.

With one final pull at the knot, she was free. She slid off and hit the ground, hard. The road's dust went everywhere, into her hair, eyes, and mouth. Rolling, she pulled herself away from her captor and the beast's indiscriminate hoofs. Her limbs proved unresponsive, but she tried to stand nonetheless.

I must escape. I must get away.

She stood and staggered one step, another, before crashing again on the ground. Her broken toes brought her sharp pain.

— Be careful, be careful, you stupid girl! Slow down!

— Don't you touch me! she snapped. Don't you come near!

Her vision blurred, from the heat or exertion she did not know. The floating forms before her soon coalesced into the singular vision of an old ass and an old man.

The various fragmented details finally came together. He stood there with a straw hat. His pursed lips were surrounded by budding stubble and a growth under his chin that was so wild and uneven it could hardly count as a beard. His tank top was soiled and stretched and ripped, and displayed his ribs and the tight skin of lean arms. His donkey was weighed down with large packs strung together. The beast gave a little kick, like it was relieved to be rid of Libète's dead weight.

The man clicked his tongue. You're not well.

— Where... where are my things?

— Your bag?

— My bag.

— You know, you're rude. He said this as he rummaged through a pack on the donkey's back and withdrew her book bag. Here I am with Saint-Pierre and we take you from the edge of the abyss and trouble ourselves to carry you up this mountain.

— I didn't ask for your help, she barked. I didn't ask for–

She paused. *Did he say mountain?*

Turning her head, she gasped. Before her was a vast panorama she had not yet glimpsed. They had left the river and valley and were on a mountain road, and she saw only a vast range of patchwork green and brown mountains.

He threw the bag to her, and she failed to catch it thanks to her unresponsive arms. She tried again, picked it up, and undid the zipper.

— What's... uh... in the bag? the man asked, as innocently as he could manage.

Libète's features curled together. Don't act like you didn't open it. She looked inside. Her face softened and a tear crept to her eye. The bird, she said. What happened to him?

The old man slit his throat with his finger. Libète stiffened. Have any water? she asked.

— A little.

— Give me some.

He *tsked* but did not refuse her. He handed her a corked glass Coke bottle. She reached into her bag and extracted the sheet of pills, popped one of the bulky things into her throat, and swallowed with a gulp. She threw the bottle back to him from where she sat. Rising, she took a moment to test her legs and lungs.

— Which way to Dieudonné? Libète said.

He pointed up the mountain. Where did you think I was taking you?

Her mouth twisted, trying not to let her confusion show. I didn't know Dieudonné was up on a mountain. I thought it was somewhere below. Near the ocean.

— I know these mountains well, the families in them well, and the only Dieudonné I know lives that way, higher up.

— What? What do you mean? Families? No, no, you don't understand. I'm looking for a *town*, a place called Dieudonné.

— And I'm telling you, in this part of Haiti, there is no such town. Only people. Dieudonné, it's the name of a family, I tell you, a *family*. The one to which Saint-Pierre and I were carrying you.

With this, her eyes widened. Her mind seized.

Libète collapsed again, for with this new blow, hope died.

She stays in bed late, only pulled from the undreaming void of sleep by a blunt prodding on her arm.

Libète shields her eyes and squints, blocking out the light of the risen Sun.
— Happy birthday, Libète, Didi says with a smile.
— Ugghh. She rolls over, forces her head beneath her pillow. What time is it?
— It's *late* o'clock. We let you sleep in, but we're running behind. The others have been knocking on the gate all morning, waiting for your instructions.

Libète slept the night before, but fitfully. Her perverse birthday card and the night's events had left her mind uneasy as she scaled suppositions and rappelled conclusions. Funnily enough, among the horror of threats and mysterious numbers and the dead man at the other end of the phone line, it was Laurent's condescending words that continued to trouble her the most. Exhaustion had finally descended like a fog on the mountains of her mind and claimed her.

— Come on, come on, come on, Didi said. There's not time for this. We need to get ready. Besides, I have something you'll enjoy. She brought a bowl from behind her back, the scent of its steaming contents filling the air.

— That's - Libète pulled the pillow from her face and squealed - *joumou*! She claimed the squash soup, a New Year's standard forever linked in Libète's mind with her birthday, and used the spoon wading in the bowl to scoop up her first bite. You made this?

Didi smiled. Jak did. Got special permission to use the kitchen.

— Mmm. He's a saint.

— He is. Didi sat on the bed, the mattress sagging under her added weight. Eat as you go, Libète. There's much to do.

• • •

Libète slipped in spoonfuls as she flitted about the wing getting ready. In the bathroom, she stood behind a plastic curtain, taking a bucket shower while Didi rattled off updates.

— The banners are all finished and up on site. Tomas told Adonis and Adonis told Gesner. Pastor Formètus has the sound system set up at the stage. They've already got the music playing, and each section's runner is knocking on doors, getting their people out. MINUSTAH is there, along with some police, but staying inside the law enforcement section as requested.

Libète poured cool water over herself, watching it splash around her feet on the orange tile floor. Any problems besides those gun-toting idiots being there?

— Eh. Well, Garcelle is complaining. Again. She wants ten minutes for her speech rather than five.

— She would, the little *demagog*. We agreed on five. She doesn't get a minute more.

— I told her you'd say as much. Leaving out the demagogue part.

Libète smiled. She and Didi had a bond that had little to do with the mere fact their beds were welded together. Both were originally from far away, Libète from remote La Gonâve and Didi from Hinche, the capital of the *Centre département*. The year prior, when Didi arrived at the school, she had been teased mercilessly for both her weight and, unexpectedly, for her keen intelligence. Libète put a stop to that, and they became fast friends.

— Hey... how do you know all these updates already? Libète asked. I thought you hadn't been outside the school yet.

Hearing the *boop boop* of a cell phone's buttons being pressed answered her question.

— Have you been texting with *my* phone? Hide that! Libète said. Student phones were considered contraband.

— Don't *worry*. Everybody's been out of here for ages.

Another splash. I can't believe you let me sleep so long.

— Jak told me about last night. You needed the rest.
— Towel, *s'il-vous plaît*. Libète reached from behind the curtain. Didi obliged, putting the rag in her hand. I've still got to decide what to wear!
— Cheri, why all this worrying? Didi said. I picked out an outfit and had Claudette iron it. Your gray suit, blue top.
Libète poked her head out from the stall's curtain with a megawatt smile. Kè mwen, you're simply the best.

• • •

Stomach full, deodorant applied, hair up, makeup on, jewelry in place.
Libète sighed, looking herself over in the wing's one full-length mirror. She was composed. She was lovely. She was ready.
— We're late, Libète! Even for you!
— I'm coming! Libète rushed to her bed and reached into a locker beneath. She pulled out her red book bag and stuffed her notebook with her talk's notes inside it. She grimaced at the sight of the cryptic birthday card and put it in to show Jak. The gifted sweets went in too. *Just in case.*
She took a fleeting glance in the mirror as she walked past and paused. *I look so old.* Her eyes were the same, though. She tripped back through time to worse days, hungry and lonely ones, passed under a tent with a body in revolt against puberty. *Look at me now.* She spun around. Libète's wardrobe had benefited from Stephanie's tasteful eye and open wallet. *But the eyes, they're the same no matter what.* She saw Didi's reflection join her own. Her friend wore her church clothes, but couldn't hide their restitched seams and crooked hem.
— You look good, Libète said, meaning it. Didi looked away. You do too, she replied. Aw, don't forget! Your pill.
Libète nodded soberly. She took the capsule from Didi's hand, popped it in her mouth, and took a gulp of water from Didi's proffered glass. They did not speak of it further.

As they stepped into the yard, they spotted Jak sitting on a planter under the shade of a moringa tree, absentmindedly tapping his heels on the ground. He was dressed in navy slacks, a pristine white shirt, and a striped tie–the same ensemble from the night before.

— Let's go, Jak! Libète shouted, signaling with grand, sweeping motions as if he were the reason they were late. He hurried over as best he could, hobbled by his leg.

— Thanks for the soup, she said, giving him a peck on the cheek as she strode on toward the front gate. Jak reached up to the spot her lips had touched.

— Come *on*, Jak! Didi said, pulling him along. He nodded slowly, his thoughts trying to catch up.

— Véus, Libète said, open up.

He stepped out of his concrete booth, leaning on his gun like a cane. He looked ashamed. I . . . can't do that, Libète.

— What? What the *hell* are you talking about?

He signaled with his head to the other end of the yard. On the second level, leaning against the wrought-iron railing, were two unfamiliar men: one was young and black, the other old and white.

Yon blan. A foreigner.

The blan surveyed the three youths. He stood erect in an emerald guayabera, his hands clasped behind his back, his eyes shrouded by a pair of sunglasses, his balding head blanketed by wisps of white hair. The man behind him had bulging eyes and an isosceles face with a chin that narrowed to a seemingly impossible point. The white man adjusted his belt and licked his lips as though he was preparing to speak.

— *Children*, he intoned in English.

— *Timoun yo*, said the black man, his apparent interpreter.

— What do you want? Libète spat back in Kreyòl, shielding her eyes against the Sun.

— Are you – he looked at a clipboard – Libète Limye?

She frowned. Non, she said. My name is Sophia Jean-Phillippe. It was a spur of the moment lie, mixing her deceased mother's name with that of her favorite Haitian footballer. The blan's eyes, still hidden behind dark lenses, bored a hole in her.

— My name is Mr. Brown. I am your new headmaster. Libète slouched. The Haitian man parroted Brown's words in Kreyòl. And I do not appreciate games, he said coolly. The other man interpreted again.

— Well, we're on our way out, Libète said.

— No, you're not. My office. Now.

The Sun is gone, and the sky covered by a ceiling of cumulus cloud.

Libète sits atop the donkey. The man had said little to her for most of their climb, looking over his shoulder occasionally to glimpse her, the poor creature she was. Her eyes are vacant. He knows consolation is not his strong suit and does not attempt it.

— We are not so far now, not far at all, he says, his voice trailing off. He bites his lip. His hips and back cry out from the long day. They are nagging reminders that he is old, and failing. He steels himself. If he is to be master of anything in this life, it must be his limbs.

He passes the time singing a bit, and asking things, but they are all rhetorical dead ends, the kind of thoughts dressed as questions he would often ask Saint-Pierre, the donkey.

— *The air, it's heavy today, no?*

— *What a mountain we're climbing, eh?*

— *It will be good to lie under a roof tonight, yes?*

For a man so accustomed to living half his time without conversation, the quiet unnerved him greatly. He often regaled Saint-Pierre with stories—the same stories, time and again—but the beast always maintained his same obstinate silence. *The donkey and girl have a similar way about them*, he thought.

He soon began to talk about himself, for as with many men, this was a much-favored subject.

He told her of his life spent near the water, breaking rock, sifting through earth, all to uncover something precious within it all. I'm blessed. I have a sense, you see. I can *feel* where the metals are, how they wish to be found by me, wish to be mine. They call to me. *Sa a se yon kado. Ki Bondye te ban mwen.* This is a gift. From God.

Libète offered no reply.

He told of his extraordinary strength that had been sapped because he'd proven too boastful about it. He shared that he was irresistible to women, evidenced by the twenty children he had peppered about the countryside. And, as if to help explain the seeming impossibility of the latter, how his good looks had been stripped from him because of this infidelity.

— He gives and he takes, you know. Bondye. Gives and takes away . . .

Libète still gave no answer, no matter the claim. He could tell she listened, though. He had saved his greatest tale for last.

— I'm blind, you know.

Libète inclined her head, and the man thrilled at this. *Ha! A breakthrough!*

— Completely blind, he said. I can't see a thing.

— That's ridiculous. Libète couldn't help herself, the harsh words so easily slipping from her lips.

— Non. No, no, no. My vision was clouded by the Good Lord himself. He has never restored it.

— But you can see. Clearly. Clearly you can see.

— But I'm telling you, I can't! A testament to his power, I suppose. I can sense all without my eyes.

— Prove it.

— But I have already, haven't I? I walk and move and sense everything. But without my eyes working. If I understood how...
— I don't want to hear it. Please, stop with these foolish, stupid stories, mesye... mesye...
She huffed. What *is* your name? With all of your blabbering, I know all about your bastard kids and present ugliness, but I don't even have your name!
— Ah, ah, ah! He was smiling inwardly. *Such progress I'm making!* You are so right, my dear. Saint-Pierre and I, we don't use names so often, the two of us! It is Dorsinus. Dorsinus Flavoril.
— Well, be quiet, Dorsinus. I don't need your nonsense.
— But–
— I said I want my silence.
— I'm tryin–
— *Silans!*
— But we've arrived! We're finally here!
Libète looked around, taking in her surroundings. The mountains were dark and foreboding. She could see rare points of lamplight throbbing in the dark, marking the lay of homes on the mountainside.
— Foche, he said. You have stumbled from darkness into light.
— It's still dark.
— Not if you could see as I do! The people, they are good here. They light the land, burning like those little lamps, but brighter! She looked at the man, who was taken by his surveying of the hills. Though I am not at home here, he said, I am home.
Libète's shoulders sagged. *Home.* Such a thought, such a wonderful one, seemed to let her breathe deep and long.
But this, of course, wasn't her home. She had none, not anymore.
— Come. We must reach Dieudonné.
They continued up, passing one lakou yard lined with cacti followed by another, until they left the road and stepped upon a narrow side path. Even Saint-Pierre's spirits seemed to lift from treading this coarse, famil-

iar earth. Dorsinus began to hum a melody. His steps quickened and the weariness of his joints seemed forgotten in this final stretch.

— There it is, he said pointing. A lone house stood by a lone tree. Man and animal pushed forward, but Libète cried out.

— Wait! He turned to her, noticing her unconsciously clutching the sides of her capri pants. Dorsinus felt his heart sink. *What does this girl carry?*

He tugged at Saint-Pierre's lead. All will be well, Dorsinus said, encouraging her gently.

There was stirring within the house, and a voice. Is that–is that you, Dorsinus? came a call.

The man thrilled at the recognition.

— Ha ha! What good ears you have, Magdala!

The sheet entrance swung open, and a woman, tall and thick, thrust herself through. He moved to hug her, but she dodged the hug. Hands to yourself, old man! She patted him on the back and laughed heartily. How is the old saint? She pointed to the ass.

— He's well, he's well. His face clouded. He removed his hat. There's something else, though. *Someone* else.

— Oh? She looked about. The dark kept her from seeing the girl slumped on the beast's back.

Dorsinus tried to summon the girl's name to his lips, but realized he had not yet learned it. Girl, he called to her. Come close.

Libète slipped off Saint-Pierre, cringing as she took painful steps forward. She stood silent before them, eyes downcast. The woman's brows leaped up. Who is this? One of your own?

He shook his head. Someone I found. She... asked for you.

Magdala's eyes traveled from the man to this stranger and back again. Can she speak for herself? Is she okay? There was softness there, a genuine concern. Still, Libète could not look up and meet the wide, caring eyes.

— *Eske ou byen?* Are you well? Magdala asked. *Kijan ou rele?* What are you called? She extended a warm hand to Libète's chin, coaxing her head up to allow their eyes to finally meet.

Stilling her trembling lips, Libète looked straight into Magdala's face. My name? My name is Sophia.

Jak squirms in his seat. This unnerves Libète tremendously.

— Relax, Jak, she growls. *Tout byen.* All is well.

— Why should I relax? At least when Mèt Valcin was headmaster I didn't have to watch my back all the time! He even *liked* me. The first day with this Brown and we're on his bad list.

— Stop *worrying*.

— He's right to worry, Didi says.

— Bah! Libète crosses her arms and looks away.

Mr. Brown and his interpreter were still outside the office. Libète assumes they do this to intimidate her, Jak, and Didi. It only makes her angry. *These fools are making us late!*

In a sense, this was her fault. Libète had seen the last headmaster, a man, dismissed from his post after she had uncovered certain... improprieties. The school had been without a head teacher for the past month, leading to lax discipline and general ease around campus before the holidays. It had been wonderful. Now, seeing this Mr. Brown come onto the scene, the nagging proverb came to mind: *Dyab ou konn pi bon pase dyab ou pa konn.* The devil you know is better than the devil you do not.

— You two aren't in trouble. I'm the one who lied and gave him the stupid false name.

— Libète, open your eyes! This has nothing to do with that name.
— Then because we got the other headmaster fired?
— You've forgotten?
— *No.* Of course I haven't forgotten... She grimaced. Aw, forgotten *what?*
— Last night. The dead man on the radio. The station raid! The Numbers! Libète, something is very wrong. Terribly, terribly wrong...
— What do you mean, Jak? Didi asked.
— I went to the computer lab, tried to do some searches to figure out what the Numbers might mean.
— And?
— Well, nothing. I didn't find anything. But the man on the other end, he *died* for them. We have to be careful.

The birthday card resting in the bag on Libète's lap suddenly felt like it weighed a hundred pounds. She sighed as she produced it from her bag.

— What's this? Jak said, holding it up for him and Didi to read. He read the inscription. Libète could see his whole person deflate.
— Where did this come from? Didi asked.
— It was one of Véus's two deliveries last night.

Jak shook his head. You've not been threatened for months. Not here. Not like this.

Libète shrugged. It's nothing. Didi retreated into a nervous silence.

— This is a real danger, Jak said. We do things, say things, and people get hurt. They *die.* We've seen it before. Even the man with the knife last night–

— He was just some hired thug, Libète sneered. And we were protected by the People! Just as we'll be today. No one could get to us. They're our shield, Jak.

— *This is no game.* We aren't wandering around collecting bottles in the reeds. Even that meant corpses...

Libète cringed at the memory of Claire and Ti Gaspar, mother and child, caked in mud and blood, wrapped together in death. Memories of the two were always with her, but the details were harder to recall. Maybe because the vicissitudes of time brought new troubles, or maybe because that was simply how memory worked, insulating one from past pain.

— Aw, Jak. *Jak, Jak, Jak.*

The boy thrust her reaching hand away. Don't treat me like one of those kids who look up to you, Libète. *Don't.*

She forced a smile but resented him, his worry, and his fear.

By the time Mr. Brown and his Kreyòl voice, Charles–it turned out he had a name too–entered the room, the three children were sitting in morose silence. Brown let his weight slide into the executive leather chair behind his desk and flipped up his sunglasses' lenses to reveal normal glasses beneath. His flat gray eyes were just as unsettling as the dark lenses had been.

Libète glanced around the office, noticing it had already changed since the new headmaster's recent arrival. Haitian ephemera–flags, pictures of founding fathers–had been replaced by American counterparts. *So many white men with wigs.*

— Just look at you all, Mr. Brown finally said. Though the accent was unidentifiable to the children's ears, his words rolled with a southern lilt.

Charles began to interpret, but the headmaster cut him off with a curt wave.

— I have no patience for your nonsense, no patience at all.

— But Mesye Brown, Charles said in English, they can't understand what you say.

— I know. I want them to be unnerved.

Libète and Jak looked sidelong at each other. Libète cleared her throat and spoke. Mr. Brown, you know we study English at this school, no?

Brown's jowls sagged and his face flushed. He shifted his lumpy body. I see.

Silence settled, but for the ticking of a clock.

— Well, all of what I said still applies.

Charles opened his mouth to speak, but when everyone else in the room glared at him, he shrank back.

— Why is you unhappy with us? Libète's comprehension was decidedly better than her spoken English.

— I listened to your radio... *performance*. You are bringing unwanted attention to yourselves. As far as I'm concerned, I have been placed in a position of authority to protect you and your fellow students. We do not need thugs rallying outside to cheer you on, nor for you to become wrapped up in intrigue that gets a man killed.

The way Brown spoke was so genteel, so patronizing, so soft that it unnerved Libète more than anything.

— With the respect that you deserve, we didn't ask for this attention.

— I have to disagree. I've heard your story. I know what you're about; you're troublemakers.

— For good reasons, Mr. Brown.

— I don't care about the *reasons*. I care about educating the children here. I care about lifting up this community through its instruction–

A phone buzzed from Didi's bag, and Mr. Brown's eyes snapped to it. You have a phone? Of your own? Take it out.

Didi reached in and withdrew it with a trembling hand. It's... it's–

— Mine, Libète said. I keep it for emergencies.

— You know phones aren't allowed.

She stripped it from Didi's hand and slid it across the desk, muttering, *Revèt pa gen janm rezon devan poul.* Mr. Brown looked to Charles, who seemed to inflate at the opportunity to interpret. "A roach is never right standing before a chicken."

Mr. Brown set his lips straight, weighing his words. I want to tell you, there is nothing keeping you at St. Francis.

— What do you mean? Didi is on a scholarship. And our school fees are covered by a... what is the word? Money... that is put to the side.

— A trust, Jak murmured.

— Yes, a trust. That our guardian, Stephanie Martinette, pays our fees from.

Mr. Brown tapped his finger a few times on the desk. That's not at all what I mean. Nothing *entitles* you to stay here. Your small tuition fees are not worth the trouble they bring. He said it so apologetically it took a moment to grasp his meaning.

— What are you saying? Jak blurted, sitting up straight. We are to go? To leave? The boy shuddered. This school was his home, his entire life. This was a threat that cut deep. Libète set her jaw. For her, not so much.

— No more trouble. That is all I'm saying. Bring this nonsense to an end. For the school's safety. And for your own. Now go.

THE ONE WHO RAN

Pye pa gen rasin.
Feet don't have roots.

After bathing, Libète slumps on the packed dirt floor and draws her legs close to her body. Her eyes are adrift and unfocused. The room is dark but for a flickering flame illuminating two mats and walls lined by narrow shelves filled with pots, plates, and mismatched mugs.

Magdala observes Libète silently from the shack's door. The woman's heart, already a fragile and tender instrument, cracks at the sight. You say she asked for *me*? she whispers.

— She did, Dorsinus replies at full volume, chewing with his mouth open. He scoops more cooked yams from the plastic plate Magdala had given him, popping the leftovers into his mouth. A similar plate sits before Libète on the floor, untouched.

Magdala shakes her head. She pulls Dorsinus outside, out of earshot.

— She told you nothing of herself?

— Not a word. Not even her name, until you asked.

The woman moves to join the girl on the ground, but hesitates; her clean nightgown would suffer for the act of solidarity. She drops anyway, lowering her head to try to meet Libète's empty gaze. *My dear Sophia–*

Libète flicks up her head and meets Magdala's eyes with a hard stare.

— How is it that you've come to be here?
— Dorsinus.
— But how is it you've come to me? To know my name? To ask for me?
— I was told.
— Told?
— Told.
— But by whom?
— I cannot say.
— You don't know who?
— I know who.
— You can't remember, then?
— I cannot forget.
— Then tell me.
— I cannot.
— How can you expect me to take you in without knowing a–
— *Souple. Please.* There is new strength in her voice, but Magdala sees the gloss covering over Libète's eyes. They drift, taking stock of the shadows that tremble as though tortured by the light.
— For your good, Madanm. For my good. Please. I will be gone before long.
— Before long, you say?
Libète's head dips.
Magdala withdraws. Dorsinus smacks as he chews. She scowls at the man, who shrugs it off and chases the starch with a small cup of water. Magdala looks at the sky, starlight beginning to poke through parting cloud.
— You can stay, Magdala says, over her shoulder.

• • •

Libète laid awake in the dark, covered by a thin blanket to shield against the night's cool touch. Thoughts flickered, stoking her mind's fire. A far drum beat, ghostly and faint. She could not tell whether she imagined its dull sound.

Magdala could be heard breathing from across the room, and Dorsinus's snores could be heard from outside–where he slept beside his friend, the ass.

Libète sat up, drawing her knees to her chest. Moonlight slipped between ramshackle boards. She reached for her bag. The zipper chattered as she opened it, bringing a torrent of memory that took her breath.

How funny the power of the small to herald the enormous.

She bit her lip to stifle a whimper, and then, with her eyes squeezed tight, mouthed silent words.

Such loss.
Such pain.
All comfort you take from me.
When did you cease giving?
You have won, you know.
And we are finished.
I am broken, I am broken, I am broken, I am broken . . .

She opened her eyes. Her words were empty, aimed at the inscrutable, the distant, the absent. To a god no longer known.

Her soul had been darkened. Her mind polluted. With her heart's every beat, anger rippled throughout her being.

Libète shuddered. *I will not cry.*

She reached into the bag and took out the pills.

She palmed one before swallowing it without water.

She laid back down on her own mat. There would be no sleep for her. For among all the things that weighed upon her, one of the heaviest was that only five pills remained.

Libète storms out of Mr. Brown's office, bag slung over her shoulder, leaving Jak and Didi behind.

— Libète, *wait!* Jak hollers. She is down the corridor, now the stairs. He tries to follow, but his leg fails him. Didi hangs back, her head held low.

— Of all the... how could... getting my phone taken! Libète shouts. Today, of all days!

— She didn't mean to! Jak said. How could she have known it would ring?

— How are we going to get to the rally? She slapped the back of one hand into the palm of her other. Steffi was waiting for our call!

Jak's brow creased. You would think she'd have come already...

— She was probably the one who called! Libète held out her arms. Ridiculous! If we walk, we'll miss the whole thing! My *own* speech! I've spent days on it! What good is a congress without its president?!

— It's a *congress*, Jak said. It's not *about* the president.

— Bah!

— The others are capable, Jak reassured. It isn't about *us*, is it, Libète? It's about the community. To celebrate *it*. To celebrate everyone in *it*.

— But–how can they–without–ah! She pounded on a wall. *Damn it!*

He was right, of course. *As always.* She took three deep breaths, collecting herself.

— I'm sorry, Didi whispered. I'm sorry. It was an accident.

Libète stepped toward Didi and looked her hard in the eye. Libète hugged her. I know it's not your fault. It's that fool, *Mistur Bro-wn*, she said, in her best attempt at a drawl. I'm the one who's sorry. I could never blame you, not for a thing, my heart. Libète kissed her on both cheeks. Whether we make it or miss it, all will be well. Maybe we can at least be there for the march.

After her speech–which would have been exemplary–and the resulting applause–which would have been interminable–the march was what Libète anticipated the most.

They rushed to the school's gate. We need out, Libète called to Véus. He had watched their argument and reconciliation unfold but stepped out from his booth pretending to have seen and heard nothing.

— What's this, now?

Libète gave a grand gesture from left to right, as if to part the Red Sea's waters.

Véus shot out of his chair. I'm sorry for all that with Brown.

— No time for apologies. Libète repeated the sweep. You can do so later. Let us go!

He nodded. But I wonder about the wisdom of–

— There's no need to worry, Didi said. We'll be back before dinner.

Véus squinted. It's just that Madanm Stephanie, well, she raised the alarm last night. We're at threat level red here, you know!

Libète's jaw dropped. Véus. *Please.* Just open the gate. There's no danger in going to the fields today. We'll be surrounded by people. *Our* people. Any villains who mess with us will have a battle on their hands.

He sighed and took his keys from his belt in a jerky, stubborn motion. He grumbled as he undid the door-within-a-gate's padlock and chain.

Didi went through first, and then Jak. Libète followed, but at the last second poked her head back in the door.

— Oh, and Véus: a question. Who left those gifts yesterday?

— Why do you ask?

— Uh, I want to tell them thank you. If I see them.

— It was two merchant women. Both unknown to me. One old, one young. Again, I ask. Why?

Libète bit her upper lip. No reason, she said coyly. Letting on about the note would ensure that Véus locked them away for good.

55

— Got any more of that dous makos? Véus asked, his eyes lighting up.
Libète smiled, rubbing her belly. It's all gone, sorry to say!
He gave a small, dutiful bow.
He's a good man. She decided she would give him a piece later, should any happen to make it through the day uneaten.

They awaken to shouting.

The argument's participants are some distance from Magdala's shack, its sentry tree and lonely privy, and the long, worn, dirt path that leads down to Foche's main road. Its volume grows. Those shouting are approaching.

Magdala rises to peek out between the doorframe and sheet, only to pull herself back a moment later. Libète assumes it is for modesty's sake. The woman is still in her nightgown, her hair carefully wrapped. But as the woman changes into a work dress, the girl sees wariness tugging on her features. Magdala utters clipped prayers as she flits around the room, so preoccupied she doesn't even acknowledge her guest.

There's something else going on here. Libète changes into her one other set of clothes: T-shirt and jeans. It reminds her of her flight and all she has escaped. *All I've left and lost . . .*

The voices outside reach new heights.

Libète sighs. This new day has worries all its own.

She tied her headscarf, long and blue, over her stubby hair only now starting to grow again. She stirred from her place on the floor and went to the sheet, stepping outside. *Magdala knows who's fighting.* The woman had settled against the wall opposite the door, her hand to her mouth, eyes clenched shut. She sounded as if she were crying. Libète noticed

Dorsinus outdoors, already awake, reclining on the ground against his burlap saddlebag. He lowered the brim of his hat and hummed, whittling away at a piece of wood in his hand. Unfazed by the approaching fight, he was fashioning what looked like some kind of fowl. She thought she heard him *tsk tsk tsk*.

The morning Sun flooded her vision, and it demanded her obeisance. Libète refused to pay it heed. She shielded her eyes and instead followed the sounds to the source of the commotion.

A struggle was underway. The words had become wrestling. Two figures had locked their arms and bodies. One, the larger, was dominating.

She gravitated toward them.

Moving toward conflict, despite all that had happened in the past week, was odd. Maybe some peacemaker's reflex, or a product of her curiosity. She did not run, nor rush, but stayed light on her aching toes. The shouted words grew more distinct.

— Get your hands off me!

— Give back the *kòb*!

To her surprise, they were not men, merely grown boys.

— The money is gone! You hear me! The speaker was tall and thin, his muscles coiled and sinewy. The smaller one ripped himself away only to lunge back and land a punch squarely on the other boy's jaw. The recipient reeled back.

The one who delivered the blow was only slightly shorter. Despite his contorted features and hunched body, she could see he was particularly handsome. Seeing an opening, the taller boy leaped on the other and grasped him in a chokehold. The smaller tensed, struggling in vain. He soon stilled, humiliated.

The two remained there, their bodies heaving as they gasped for air.

— I've told everyone already! the victor said. The money. It's gone!

It was only then the victor glimpsed Libète. She stood on a berm, looking down at them, her face inscrutable but for eyebrows that slanted in a subtle show of disapproval.

The one on the bottom spat another curse. The victor bent toward the loser's ear and whispered words, low and calm.

The victor released the other and stood to full height. He looked into Libète's eyes. He had a round face and head, hair growing unkempt, and clothes both dirty and worn. She thought she saw shame in his eyes. He turned and jogged off.

It was all so curious.

The loser rose and dusted off his clothes. He watched the victor slip away, and Libète saw his fists tighten and forearms tense. He spun and gasped at taking in Libète.

— Who... who are you? He stuttered the question as if speech was a forgotten, foreign thing.

She looked away from him. I'm... Sophia.

He took an unconscious step toward her. His frame, his well-set features, his intense eyes: the way every piece of him fit together so very well made her blush.

— You... you saw that? All of that?

She nodded. The loser looked crestfallen.

She felt her hand tugged, her arm pulled. She jumped. It was Dorsinus.

— Come along, the old man said with surprising sternness. Libète obliged, glad to be pulled away from the young man and his piercing eyes.

— I'm Prosper, he hollered feebly. Prosper, he repeated.

Dorsinus and Libète trudged up the path back to Magdala's home. Her senses now regained, Libète retracted her arm from the old man.

— Don't you touch me, she said crossly.

— Byen, byen, byen. He let go like he'd just touched a live wire. But come away from all that business. We must pretend it didn't happen. For Madanm Magdala's sake.

Libète followed, feeling Prosper's curious eyes still upon them.

— What do you mean, for her sake?

— The one. He's her son.

— The one who lost?

Dorsinus looked back over his shoulder and shook his head. Of course not. He clicked his tongue. The one who won. The one who ran. He pointed. Félix, he said. The one who *is* lost.

She tried to steal a glance. Magdala's son was now in the distance, all of a few inches tall, moving up a hill, soon to vanish behind its crest. *Félix*.

She wondered if this one also sneaked glances over his shoulder, back at her. What did he witness when their eyes met? Did he see her for who she *was*, or for who she is?

The one who ran, Libète repeated. *The lost one.*

The rally's jubilation climbs to the sky. The children hear the crowd while still a mile off from the football fields that host them. They quicken their pace.

There was no better place to play football, no better place to watch matches unfold, than the Centre de Tri de l'Athlétique d'Haïti. Set toward the northern boundaries of Cité Soleil, it had joined disused fields together and transformed them into sports pitches. The complex was proof resurrection was real. Here was grass and turf. Here were hot meals for youth. Here were rules and sensible consequences for their breaking. Here was *order*. A picture of what life could be.

The perfect place to host their rally.

The sports club was the progeny of Robert "Boby" Duval, a former national football player and another victim of the Duvalier dynasty, Haiti's dictatorial presidents. In 1975 he had been tossed into Fort Dimanche, a notorious prison. Many who entered disappeared forever in its bowels, but others, like Duval, were merely tortured and eventually spit back up. Duval transmuted this experience and became a human rights activist. L'Athlétique d'Haïti came into being sometime in the nineties.

— Hurry it up, you two! Libète calls to Jak and Didi. We're not far now!

The plan for the day was simple: gather at the fields, and from there the march would begin. They would head en masse to the large industrial complex that housed Global Products S.A., Benoit's factory that produced cheap T-shirts for rich people an ocean away. Such sweatshops offered jobs, but their substandard wages enriched their owners and mired the workers in subsistence poverty. The youth congress leadership decided they would march from one end of the huge complex's front wall to the other seven times, decrying it as *"Jeriko"* and demanding that the factories–pillars of dehumanizing global capitalism–fall. This had been Libète's idea.

Many would already be at the pitches for early Independence Day matches. Others would come for the live music and performances and stay through speeches meant to challenge and provoke, and, at their best, trigger the youths' imaginations.

Violence had surged in Cité Soleil in 2012 and continued up to the present. Armed robberies increased, murders boomed, gangs again divided the community. It could be dangerous just going about daily business. This was ruinous for a people living hand-to-mouth. The year 2014 would be different, Libète resolved.

Libète had founded the youth congress with Jak and Didi a few months before, dreamed up in between the tedium of classes spent mastering *le subjuntif* and solving for x and y.

The congress was inspired by Haiti's legislature–not as a model of success, but rather its complete lack. They decided another form would have to do. Delegates were selected from different youth organizations and schools, two from each of Cité Soleil's thirty-four sections. Though they as founders were only fourteen years old, members as old as nineteen had been willing to join and follow their lead. Each was expected to organize the youth within their own communities to fulfill the congress's aims: service and protest. In doing so, members lifted up the community with literacy classes, by cleaning the streets, with beautification and tree planting, and in arts with a social message. In just four months, they led with low-cost initiatives that had begun to bond Cité Soleil's fractious zones together.

Stephanie had offered to set up meetings with foreign NGOs. While many delegates appreciated the prospect of outside funding, Libète, as chief moderator, staunchly opposed it. *We do this ourselves*, she had said. *We show that Haitians can solve Haitian problems.* Between the business with Benoit, the congress, her voice on the radio, and coverage in newspapers, she was revered in Cité Soleil–a public figurehead when Jak and Didi, lesser-known, had contributed just as much. But these two believed in her as a leader and president of the congress and did all they could to support her.

— Wait up, Libète! Jak called.

Libète frowned.

The trek to the fields felt interminably long to Libète. Jak's leg slowed them as it always did, broken and set poorly back during *douz* . This was how January twelfth was known, a shorthand used to sum up the horrors of the day in 2010 when the earthquake struck–and all that followed. He and Libète had both nearly been murdered in the days preceding douz by the man who had killed Claire and Gaspar, the mother and child Libète and Jak had found on the outskirts of Bwa Nèf, their neighborhood. Libète had been spared physical injury at his hands, but Jak was not so lucky. His twiglike leg had been wrenched and ruined, much like his relationship with Libète, whom he had blamed for all his woes. Like the leg, the relationship was mended, but not quite as it was. Not so innocent as before.

— Sorry, Jak. Libète slowed and let him and Didi catch up.

Didi was also not what one would call fast. She moved at a contented pace, eager to laugh and joke rather than reach the place to which she was going–destinations were never as pleasurable as the trip. She did impersonations that were wickedly on point, and she could bring Jak and Libète to a halt, doubling them over in laughter with her takes on their least-liked teachers. After just one encounter she had already mastered Mr. Brown and his false sweetness. The levity helped Libète check her impatience. Having these two anchors to slow her tendency to dash off every which way was good for her.

On mild days in Cité, when the streets were calm, the trio would go to the football pitches to watch afternoon scrimmages. Their celebrity meant an entourage of younger children often tried to tag along, but those minutes and hours were much-coveted private moments where the three could laugh and be at ease and the trappings of school and national prominence could be stripped away. Where they could simply be themselves. Be children.

When they arrived at the fields they took up a place at the back of the crowd, in the stands, which offered a view of the whole assembly. To Libète, it was majestic. There had to be at least two thousand people there, maybe more. Even the media had shown up–a few cameramen stood at the stage. Sweeping her head from left to right, she took it all in. She felt an unexpected calm. She had greater ambitions, dreamed of crowds twenty times this size, but still felt a contentedness in this momentary anonymity, a sense in her spirit that humility, despite her ways, was a good thing.

Garcelle, long-winded and opinionated, was still at the microphone, giving her speech that had undoubtedly gone well beyond its allocated five minutes. Libète didn't even care.

At the opposite end of the stand, Libète was pleased to see Rit and Therese, who had been some of her most hated neighbors from her early days in Bwa Nèf. She waved to them, and they waved back.

Others in the stands started to notice Libète, Jak, and Didi. Murmuring broke out, first sweeping the stand before spreading further. Eyes began turning, and Libète demurred from the attention, outwardly at least. Inside, it fed her.

Suddenly, from the stage, Marco, the delegate from Cité Boston, pushed Garcelle aside. Make way for the prezidan!

Garcelle was none too pleased. Libète signaled self-effacingly–*no, no, I couldn't!*–but the rising applause pushed her on. She soon had her book bag slung over one shoulder and was withdrawing her notebook and speech. She started toward the stage and noticed that Jak and Didi remained in the stands.

— Come with me, she mouthed, giving a beckoning tug of her head.

— No, he said. That's okay.

— Didi?

— I'm fine from back here. Go for it, my heart. Libète turned toward the stage.

— Wait–where are those sweets? Didi said. I like a good snack with my show. Libète smiled, extracted the bag from her pack, and threw them to Didi.

Libète made her way to the stage, and the crowd parted down the middle. She took to the microphone as Garcelle sat down with her arms crossed. Libète smiled, straightening the sheets of paper. They were unnecessary security. She had her speech written on her heart.

— My friends, it is a good day to see you all. A good day to gather! To remember what this day means for us. Independence. Freedom. These are powerful! They take us back to the days before the earth beneath our feet was claimed so very wrongly by those who enslaved its people, its resources, and those who they later imported, our forbearers . . .

Didi mouthed the speech along with Libète. She had heard it many times in recent days. She turned to see Jak rapt, a broad smile on his face. There was much betrayed by that look; his was no simple admiration. She looked down sadly at the sweets in her lap.

— But my friends, we must realize that this independence has been in jest. A fraud. How can we say we are free when we are enslaved by systems that thrive off our misery? We are shackled by poor jobs. Guns carried by foreign troops who police our ground. Charitable organizations that give less than they take. A government that cows to the mandates of foreign countries rather than us, the sovereign people.

Already the crowd was caught up in her words.

— How long? Didi whispered to Jak abruptly.

— What? he asked, pulled from his reverie. What do you mean? His eyes were still fixed on Libète.

— *Depi kilè ou te renmen li?*

He looked at her, shocked. How long have I – he gulped – *loved her*? That's a-a silly question. He looked down, rubbing his hand on his kneecap. A silly question, he repeated. Absurd.

Libète's words continued echoing over the field, but their meaning fell away to this pair.

— She is my best friend, he said, like my . . . like my sister.

— But you've never had a sister, Jak.

— Still–what a thing to ask, Didi!

— It's all right, Jak. It's obvious, I think. Obvious to everyone. Everyone but her.

— Really? Jak was horrified at the thought.

They sat in a new quiet, their attention only slowly returning to Libète's speech.

— As we fight and struggle, I want you to know something: I will die for you. Would you die for me? Maybe we don't need to give our lives, not entirely. But to find true freedom, real independence, we will need to sacrifice, just as our forbearers threw off their chains. To die to ourselves. To our selfishness. To the desire for revenge that grows from petty slights as well as serious wrongs.

Jak touched Didi's arm, squeezed it. His face was set in earnestness. Her own heart leaped a bit.

— Thank you, he said. For telling me. I must be more careful not to let it show.

She gave a sigh and a tight-lipped smile. Wi, she echoed quietly, careful not to let her own feelings show. She reached down to the bag and tore a piece of the sweet, popping it into her mouth.

— So stand with me, Libète proclaimed, in protecting one another, in being willing to lay down your life for that of your friends, maybe even your enemies. This is the only way–

Libète craned her neck. There was shouting now, rising from the stands. She tried to speak louder, but some incident had stolen the crowd's attention. All eyes turned from the front of the proceedings to the back. Libète swallowed her words. Her own searching eyes landed on Jak, his face set in horror, before she noticed that Didi was laying on the ground, writhing.

CHACHE LAVI

Chache lavi detwi lavi.
Looking for life destroys life.

Magdala is quiet much of the morning after the fight between her son and Prosper. Libète had observed her from a distance, while seated under the shade of the nearby mapou tree. The woman moves deliberately between tasks: boiling noodles for breakfast, putting water out for her fowl, washing Libète's dirty clothes. Now she roasts coffee beans before grinding them down with a mortar and pestle for the market. Her pounding echoes the drumming Libète heard in the distance the night before.

— Madanm, can I help you?

Magdala looks up, cocks her head, blinks. She returns to her work. Magdala's mind is clearly elsewhere–Libète notices she crushes the coffee beans too much.

Dorsinus already knows comforting Magdala is beyond him. For once, Libète wishes he would speak. She wishes to *understand*.

She approaches him as he gives Saint-Pierre some leaves and dried corn stalks to chew.

— What happened here, Dorsinus?

— Eh? He too was trapped inside his head. He simply muttered, Dark things, dark things.

— But what?

He held up his hand to silence her. Dark things have come, dark things are coming.

Libète suddenly wondered if she was safer with this bunch than the vicious dogs and their owners.

She sat behind the shack on an old stump used for extracting cane juice, watching the Sun rise higher and illuminate this new, foreign land. A mother hen strode before Libète, searching for food as its chicks trailed close behind. Libète needed to be away for a bit, to hear her own thoughts, to plan rather than react.

They might not be far off...

She shuddered.

Anger and fear grabbed her again, shook her, and seeped through cracks in her heart. She tried to control them and the crowding, terrible memories they brought. *In... out*, she breathed. *In... out*, she told herself. She closed her eyes, trying to still the swirling memories, but found herself swept away:

Bullets slipping through night-covered flesh
Faces ghoulish, color twirling fast
Silent Didi laid out, empty, flat

She rubbed at the bridge of her nose, quelling the tears before they could well up, trying again to plug the breach through which the memories poured.

In, she breathes...

Endless farewells, tortured good-byes
Water below, above
Cycle's ceaseless spin

... out, she exhales.

Dieudonné. I reached them. I'm safe, she tried to reassure herself. *I'm safe.*

For now, a prickly voice not her own added from low and deep inside her.

Libète's hand trembled as she slipped off her headscarf, letting sunlight massage her scalp and rub into her skin. She was grateful for the Sun above: it was the only thing familiar here.

Taking in her body helped defy the past and ground her in the moment: *here, now.* Her broken feet, wrapped toes, and ashy knees; her clothes just barely concealing her shoulder's unsightly scar from the bullet wound suffered those years before. She was glad she was spared seeing her face's sad reflection and her eyes devoid of fire.

She longed to be the version of herself that existed in days gone by–elegant braids, lovely clothes, even modest jewelry passed on to her by Stephanie. But it wasn't just the external things. She longed for the inner adornments that had also been abandoned these past long months. Her courage. Her certitude. Her faith.

Shit. She ran her hands through her short hair. Her scalp itched terribly.

She looked to the mountains, Haiti's natural towers. Her vantage point offered the same vistas as the prior day's climb up the country road, but now she was closer to the fields and saw the narrow terraces where every inch of arable land was cleared for planting. Even tiny bits of earth where only desperation could cause anyone to expend seed. Small, dark shapes dotted the landscape. They were people, of course, cultivating the land, cooking near homes perched on hazardous roads, all with their own worries and fears and families.

What if . . .

She looked to the distance. She could see the glint of a blade, a row of people working a single square of the patchwork earth.

I could . . .

She viewed them dispassionately–they were not her fellow neighbors, not friends. No, simply objects of curiosity to be studied, their lives stores of facts she might need...

— Sophia, is it? The question made her jump.

— Wi? she sputtered, shielding her eyes to look up and take in the asker's face. *Prosper.*

— I don't know you, he said. You're not from here.

It was a dumb thing to say. So very obvious. She simply nodded.

He wore a cap now, and long shorts that nearly met the tops of his well-worn rubber boots. His shirt seemed nice for passing a day in the fields; that appeared to be where he was going, attested to by the machete extending from his hand. She cringed at memories of young men in Cité Soleil with their own blades, sharpened for decidedly different ends. His lip was split and swollen from the fight.

— When did you arrive? he asked.

— Last night. Libète's mind raced. With Dorsinus, she added. *How much can I share?*

— Are you one of his?

— His what?

— His children.

She swallowed hard. She hadn't concocted a reason for being in Foche. Only a name. She'd need more than that!

— No, she said. We're not related. She cringed inwardly.

— And your home, then? Where are you from?

Nervousness pricked her skin. *This must stop.* Before she gave up any information and committed herself to a lie too difficult to keep. Is asking questions all you can do? she said.

Prosper gave a lopsided grin. *Mwen regrèt sa.* I won't ask another. He rubbed the back of his head. You, uh, want me to show you around?

— That's another question.

— *Let* me show you around.

Libète thought of Magdala and Dorsinus, trapped inside their own heads. They were more troubled by Félix–the boy who ran–than this one, who had picked the fight. If her pursuers closed in, she needed to be prepared. *To know the land. Where to hide. How to escape.*

She exhaled. *Dakò.* It's agreed.

Prosper smiled, but quickly banished it from his face. He proffered a hand to help her up, but she stood without taking it. She winced.

— You're hurt?

The weight on her toes did give her pain, but it was bearable. She walked toward the footpath without a word. Prosper caught up with her.

— Th-this is my family's plot, he stammered. One of them. My father, he died a few years back, so my mother and I are responsible for it now. He used his finger to trace invisible boundaries around its perimeter.

— How can you tell where it stops and starts? The crops – she pointed to them with a weak twirl of her wrist – they just run one into the other.

— We've been on this land for generations. Have small plots like this all over the place, here and there. High up, down low.

Libète crouched and saw small green buds poking through the dirt. Are these, what, beans?

Prosper tutted. Beans? Of course not. Where did you say you're from?

She had not. The fact was she and her mother had had a small garden on the island of La Gonâve, but that had been in low, inland forest. Goats had been their livelihood. Memories of planting, tending, and picking were distant, burned up in the heat of years passed in Cité Soleil.

— I'm from far away, she said plainly. Her look turned icy. He turned away slowly and cursed himself; nothing he said seemed to come out right. He pointed down the mountain, toward the homes below. What about Foche?

— We passed through the town, but by night. I saw very little.

He came behind her and stood close, closer than she wanted, and used his arm to draw her attention to the mountainside. *He must have cleaned since the fight. For me.* He smelled of fresh citrus, and that made her think of Jak. Tears rose in her eyes.

— Down there is the new capped spring, and that big piece of land around it is the common plot. There's the *legliz*. It's our church and meeting hall. And the *tonel*–did you see it on the way in?–used to heed the spirits. That open ground over there is for when there's market, and when there's market, Foche is a different place. Every Monday and Thursday. People come from all over. They did even before the new road was built. But now, with it so much easier for trucks and motos to come and go, the market is double, even triple the size. All because of the road.

Libète cocked her head. Who built it?

— The government.

She chortled. You're joking.

— No! It's truth. I swear! Foche, it's an important place now. We were struggling, even just two years ago. *Move tan yo,* the Bad Times, we called them. There wasn't much rain. Crops didn't grow. When rain did come, it came like a flood. Washed out paths, the soil, all our seed. But now things are better. The new road lets our food go down the mountain, reach the cities. Lets us bring in fertilizer, more seed. Lets us take loans and pay them back. Foche, it's like new.

To Libète this sounded like a recitation of often-heard propaganda. She turned away and looked it all over again. Steep inclines with ridges formed a natural crescent that wrapped around Foche. She could see clusters of small huts and shacks not too far off the main road. The road traced the shape of the crescent except where it forked, not far from where Libète and Prosper stood.

— But build a two-lane road to the top of a mountain village? For a few *peyizan* farming their plots? Incredible. *Imposib*, she said to herself. When she turned to Prosper again, his jaw was clenched.

— We're *developing,* he snapped. An example of progress. For all the countryside. That's why they rewarded us.

Her eyes traveled over his shoulder, tugged by something distant creeping up the mountain. It was dark and alien, like a roach, and rumbled up the road.

A truck, she realized. It was uncommonly large.

Prosper continued, as much for his own sake as for hers. The road, he said, that's an outside accomplishment. But this land, you see all these beans, this sorghum and cowpeas? Growing so well? That's *our* biggest achievement.

The truck was close enough now for Libète to see MACK emblazoned across its rattling grill. To hear the engine's roar, observe its covered bed and deep black exhaust spinning up and into nothing. Libète hated it instantly.

— It's my mother's biggest achievement, this land, Prosper said. She's a leader here, you know. A *grandon*, a big land owner. He chuckled to himself.

— What's so funny?

— Except she doesn't own the plot. We *all* do. So we're all grandon now. She pulled the community together to make it happen.

Libète cocked her head. Her eyes lit up with a hint of genuine curiosity.

His lips split in a smile. He had finally said something right!

— We realized that if we farmed the corn together, made a crop for ourselves rather than for selling outside, we could protect ourselves by having our own seed supply.

— Yeah?

— Yeah. A university gave us the seed to start, once my mother got everyone to agree on pulling the land together. Ever since, we farm it all, grow our own food, store seed for our own plots. We're bosses of our food. Our own *lives*. He held out a guiding hand. Step back.

They moved away from the road's shoulder and planted their feet in the plot's dark earth. The truck lumbered past, shaking the ground and raising dust. Prosper cupped his hand over his nose and mouth. Libète did the same.

The truck reached the road's end and came to a large iron gate. *Curious.* Libète shielded her eyes to get a better look. The gate was painted brown and built into the earth. It lay in a cut in the ridge; whether it was a natural formation or carved or blasted from the rock, Libète couldn't tell.

— What's that? Libète asked.

Prosper shrugged. It's a gate.

— What's *behind* it?

— The other side of the ridge. A small plateau. Nothing really. The trucks come occasionally, bring supplies. For *syans.* Science.

The gate opened and a man came out. Though the scene unfolding was far away, she saw that the man wore a dark uniform and had a dog on a lead. The sight of the creature made her shrink.

— The university people, the ones who gave the seed, Prosper said. They're studying rocks.

Libète took it all in silently. The truck entered. The gate closed. She frowned.

This made little sense. Her eyes traced the road back to their feet.

— The road. It splits there, turns into a trail, goes by Madanm Magdala's and up over the hill.

— Wi.

— What's up there?

He made a dismissive wave. Nothing.

— Surely something.

— Just an old fortress. French. All broken down.

— A fort? Really? She shifted her weight. Her own fort in Cité Soleil–nothing more than an abandoned store shot to pieces–had always been a safe place to retreat. *Maybe just what I need now.*

— Can we see it? she asked.

— No, no. You don't want to see that. That's the other reason the road was built. *Moun andeyo*, outsiders. They care about visiting that kind of thing. History. Just rocks on top of rocks.
— But I do want to see it.
— Maybe another time. The path is difficult, your injuries . . .
— All the same.
— It's, uh, beyond Foche. None of us go near it. No. Nothing there.
She stared at him.
Prosper sighed then huffed, puckering his lips. He picked at dirt beneath his thumbnail. That's where *he* lives, he said, a streak of bitterness running through the words.
— He? Who do you–
It hit her.
— Magdala's son? Félix?
He bobbed his head.
— Why were you fighting with him this morning?
He didn't answer.
— Did you start it, or did he?
Prosper's face clouded. He did. He started it all.
— Why?
— Félix is a *vòlè*, plain and simple.
— A thief? What did he take?
— What did he *take*? Thousands of goud. Prosper held out his palm and tapped his other index finger into it to accent his words. The community's money, saved up. Every year, we gather here in Foche for a feast, on New Year's Day. We all work together during the year, saving and scrimping, pulling our belts tight, putting enough *ti kòb* together for the big day when we don't have to work in the fields. We don't have to answer to anyone. We all just eat together, enjoy life. It's a day where we stand face to face with each other and know we're human beings, not animals. The money was entrusted to him, put in his care, and he took it. But he didn't just take the money; he took our *dignity*.

Libète had touched a nerve, that much was clear.

— Why is he free, then?

— My mother, Prosper sneered. He breathed deeply to calm himself. She's the only reason. If we had our way he'd be strung up to a tree. But she's a good woman, I'm telling you. Better than most of us.

— Was he returning to Magdala's home this morning?

— Who cares? He's not to step foot in Foche during the day. I was just going to our field. My mother said not to get into anything, but when I saw him . . .

She started to walk toward the fort.

He grabbed her arm. I'm not going out there. Not while he's there. He has to answer for what he's done and he will this afternoon, in front of the whole community.

Her eyes flashed. She ripped her arm away. Thank you for the tour, she said under her breath. I'll be going now.

She heard him fume, and felt some guilt–he had been kind. But friendship–with anyone–was out of the question now.

The road continued quite a distance. It dipped and wound and peaked. Farther on, the road led to the foot of another hill where a mass of stacked, weather-worn stone lay. But as she turned around, she saw that the fortress was not what was so grand about the site. The view from this side of the ridge let her see endlessly, toward the heart of Haiti.

— *The Central Plateau*, she murmured. Flowing through it was the Artibonite River. She had seen it up close, at ground level, but from such heights it was beautiful, like seeing a long-told fable come to life.

A sound grabbed her attention: a faint clicking. She slipped behind a boulder, forcing herself to the ground. Her shuddering made her cheeks puff and teeth rattle. She peeked around the rock ever so slowly.

She faced a goat.

She let her head sink, cursing her jumpiness.

— Come along, Bobby, a voice said. She recognized the speaker–it was Félix, trailing a small trip of goats. The goat before her gave a short bleat and jumped off his rock, scampering off to rejoin his family and goatherd. When she was sure Félix was on his way, she looked over the edge of the rock and watched him. He moved slowly, as though his limbs were tired from carrying a heavy burden.

She looked again across the vast plateau. The vision that had instilled wonder a moment before now seemed oppressive. She was all alone. Yes, separated from all that haunted her, but also from everything she held dear.

St. Sebastien's Hospital is quiet, except for the wailing.

Libète stares at a wall and the aged photograph adorning it. The Central Plateau seen from the air. *Beauty in a dire place.* She runs her toes along the tile grout. Her face is streaked with tears she doesn't bother to wipe away. Beside her, Jak stares at nothing as he runs a circling hand over her back.

It was meant for me.

She looks to the observation room, its door ajar. Didi's mother's cries escape and fill the crowded ward. Libète lifts herself from her chair and drifts toward Didi's room.

Back under the Sun, at the sports field, when Libète had realized what was happening–Didi on the ground, people crowding around–she had leaped from the stage, tearing through the sea of spectators to reach her friend. The poisoned sweets lay on the ground with Didi.

I should be on that table.

So many of Libète's memories are vested in these tiles, tucked away in the cracking stucco, rising up among the ward's rafters and vaulted ceiling. Memories of life preserved, happy reunions, meaningful service, death most cruel. Libète blinks them away.

Bondye, do a miracle.

A lone light illuminates the scene in the observation room. Didi's mother and father keep watch beside her bed. The mother, large and round like her daughter, rattles with sobs. Her father holds his head in his hands.

Bondye, hear my prayers.

Didi had been near death when she was brought to the hospital.

Bondye, take me instead.

Now, hours later, Didi's hope and optimism and joy are gone. She is gone.

Bondye, Bondye, Bondye...

Libète weeps fresh tears while standing outside the room. Under Sister Françoise's supervision she had learned how to assist at the hospital. The Belgian nun was the primary physician and called Libète a *ti infimye*, a junior nurse. Libète could monitor patients as they took a cocktail of pills to treat TB. Monitor blood pressures. Change IVs to rehydrate patients with cholera. It might have been unorthodox to allow Libète this latitude, but the marginal hospital was always short of hands, and Libète had two. *Blessed hands*, Sister Françoise had called Libète's as the girl's fingers helped tie drifting souls to their ailing bodies. Libète looks now to her hands' tensing muscles and sneers. Didi did not need a junior nurse. She needed a real doctor like Sister Françoise, and Sister Françoise was gone on a rare trip for the holidays. *If only she'd been here...*

The hospital doors swing open, and Mr. Brown enters.

Libète wants to scream at him. *Out! Out! Don't you profane this holy ground with your presence! You haunt the school, those classrooms, those walls; that's your domain. Not here! Not this place!*

— Good evening, he says softly.

— Bonswa, she says.

He looks in on his dead pupil, mutters something. Looks at Libète, thrusts his chin toward the corner, once, twice. She and Jak follow him and sit. Libète looks to the wall, clenches her skirt's hem. Jak looks at the man.

— You're all right. His tone peaks at the end of the last word but she doesn't know if it's a question or statement.

Jak shakes his head forlornly. No, we're not.

— What happened? Brown says as he removes his glasses.

Libète will not answer. Jak does. Sweets, he coughs up the word. Poisoned. Left for Libète at the school.

Brown nods several times. Any idea who left them?

Jak's answer was silence.

— I'm sorry. Truly sorry about this whole mess–but I hope you've learned your lesson.

Libète nearly retched. *What?*

— You're reaping what you sowed.

She was out of her seat, standing inches in front of Brown, her hands balled. Jak lunged between the two and pushed her away.

— Who are you? she spat. Who the hell says such a thing?

Jak clapped his hand over her mouth.

— I am responsible for the school. His voice remained calm. For the protection of its students. My first days at this job and you bring this, this–*shame*–on us all.

Her eyes widened. She pushed against Jak's restraining grip, but he held her tight.

— Do you have any idea what a dead child means? Brown asked. How many parents might take their kids away? How the money from donors will just – he made a sucking hiss – dry up?

— You, you *beast!* What kind of monster, what kind of ass, what kind of–

— You must come back with me. To the school. Right now.

— I will *not*.

Didi's father poked his head out of the doorway, trying to understand the commotion interrupting their grieving.

— Come back, or you will be immediately expelled, Brown said. Both of you. Finished.

Libète met Jak's worried eyes, closed her own. A new tear fell down her cheek, and she pinched the bridge of her nose. She grabbed her book bag and stormed out of the hospital, but not before catching the hard, blame-filled stare of Didi's father.

Libète had wandered the trails after parting with Prosper and leaving the vista behind. She had not trespassed closer to the fort–she had no desire to speak with Félix–but instead followed the dirt road back toward Magdala's home.

She cursed herself for the fear that had gripped her–terrified by a goat! But it was not merely a goat–it was those snarling dogs, the pursuing men, and the bitter separations they had hastened. She had already faced so much in her few short years–why could she be made to tremble so easily now? So much that thoughts could scarcely form? So that her legs felt like flimsy reeds? Where did this weakness come from?

She hid among kayimet trees lining the road until the waves of anxiety crashed and dissipated. She inspected her dirt-covered feet. Her splinted toes hurt, yes, but there was more than that. Sharp rocks had torn the soles of her feet. She already had two fresh cuts joining those sustained the night before. Her calluses from padding about Bwa Nèf barefoot had clearly softened in the years since she'd adopted shoes.

Soft singing filtered down the road. Libète watched a lone woman pass by, a girl really, with a bulging belly. Libète's mouth dropped. Despite her very pregnant state, the girl carried a woven basket brimming with sweet potatoes on her head. Sweat dotted her hairline. She sang a simple melody to herself that sounded improvised:

> *Why is it left to me?*
> *No one here to help*
> *Like a one-fingered hand*
> *Oh! Oh! Oh!*
> *Falling to me*
> *Falling to me*
> *Always, always, it always falls to me*

Libète watched her disappear down the mountain.

When Libète finally rose, she stayed off the road. She strode through the fields, careful where she stepped. She tried to recognize the budding plants, but she hadn't cultivated anything for seven years. Carrots were obvious, as were beets and cabbage. She began to notice where adjoining plots stopped and started. Some were carefully laid out in cultivated rows. Others looked like seed had been scattered and left to grow where it might. In one plot she saw weeds springing up all over, a cancer choking out life from the beans they were overtaking. Her fingers itched to set to work pulling the intruders up. The size of the plot was overwhelming and the weeds many. She resigned herself and went away.

As she continued along the ridgeline, her eyes explored gingerly and observed the different types of strata and soil. She noticed a large gash in a rock face. She stopped. *That might do.*

Upon closer inspection, the crevice was five inches across at its widest, and dark inside, so that she couldn't gauge its depth. There was a natural outcrop at its top that would shunt rainwater away. *Yes, this could work.* Hovering her hand at its threshold, she hesitated before sliding her fingers in. Her right hand and forearm were soon enveloped by the rock. She pushed deeper.

— Beware of that crack!

She jumped at the voice and jerked her arm out. Two men were walking toward her. She noticed dampness at their armpits and down their chests. Bunches of newly slashed green sugar cane rested on their shoulders. They stopped and watched her, and she eyed them.

— *Poukisa?* she finally called. Why?

— A man's hand is trapped in there. We had to cut off his hand to free him.

Her left hand unconsciously began rubbing at her other wrist. They continued to watch one another without speaking further.

They were so similar in size and shape, the pair had to be father and son. The older looked like a version of the younger that had aged decades in an instant. He was gray and wore a sweat-stained trilby on his head. The skin of his face sagged, though his muscles were taut and defined. He held a hoe with the cane stalks while his son carried cane on one shoulder while grasping two *koulin* blades, each longer and thinner than machetes. The son was dressed like Prosper and had a nervous quality that made him look wispy and sad.

She gave a meek nod as she left them, limping back down the hill toward Magdala's. Despite the old man's admonition, the scar in the rock wall did not leave her thoughts.

When she was in view of the house, she heard Magdala call out.

— I thought you'd left with Prosper. Magdala was still busying herself, this time pulling pebbles from rice in a shallow basket on her lap. She would not look at Libète directly. Betrayal underscored her words.

Libète came close. No–I just went for a walk with him. He showed me Foche. We . . . had an argument. And he left.

— If not for that boy's mother . . .

Libète stood there, biting her lip.

— You're back, then? Magdala said.

— I'm back.

— That's good. Magdala gave a sad smile, relieving Libète. Magdala's hands returned to their searching, and her mind to its heavy thoughts.

Dorsinus was not to be seen. Only curled flakes of wood from his whittling lay where he'd been overnight. She glided over to Saint-Pierre, who was so very still, so very bored. The ass was tied to the mapou tree by a fraying rope, really just a few strands of sisal. He surely could have broken free if he wished to escape. Instead he stood there, dutifully, as his tail occasionally flicked at flies.

She stepped close to meet the beast's deep brown eyes. They seemed unflinching, and empty of will. She patted down his neck. She coughed twice, which startled Saint-Pierre, and she covered her mouth. *Both of us are tied to this place, non?* she whispered, regret tinging her smile.

Saint-Pierre said nothing.

Libète's mind involuntarily dipped again into her well of fears.

Engine's growl before fierce roar
Fire, white and hot
Counting breaths before death

Pulling herself back into the moment, she found herself gripping Saint-Pierre's rope with all her strength. She moved inside, out of the beastly Sun, looking to busy her hands so that her mind might not wander.

She decided to tidy what she could. She swept the shack with a small hand broom before noticing the small plate of spaghetti and ketchup, kept safe from flies under a red plastic cover. A glass of water had been left as well. Magdala had prepared them for her. *I'm an ingrate, leaving without a word this morning.* She sighed. She ate. She slept.

A bell rang, reminiscent of the one back at school in Cité Soleil. Its location was indistinct as the sound echoed. She rose and looked outside, wondering if she had perhaps imagined the ringing like the distant drums the night before. By now the Sun was in retreat and the shadows stretched long, awaiting their chance to blend into dark and run free.

She saw Magdala descending the hill, and the fear of being left alone claimed her.

— Madanm Magdala! Can I come with you?

The woman cocked her head. She wore a nice dress, a mellow blue. *One probably meant for church.* But it was only Wednesday. With that Libète remembered. *Félix's sentencing.* Magdala nodded. Libète, rubbing her eyes, set off to follow.

They walked along the road, Libète staying behind the woman as they passed homes and followed the sound of the bell. Some neighbors stared. Others looked away in displeasure. Yet others turned away out of something else–compassion? Libète hated the looks, all of them, until she realized they were directed at Magdala.

— What shall I be to you, Madanm Magdala? Libète said abruptly, out of nowhere.

— What's that?

— I must tell others who I am. Why I am here. They will ask, I'm afraid.

— The truth, Magdala said absently. Why not just tell the truth?

— Ah, but the truth–I told you–it's no good. For you or for me.

Magdala mumbled a few words. Libète realized her mind longed to be elsewhere, wandering the hills, maybe. Not ready to confront what they were plodding toward.

— What if I'm a visitor? Libète said.

— Yes, a visitor . . .

— A family member? Maybe a niece?

— A niece. That would be nice . . .

They walked without speaking for some minutes.

— I'm sorry to hear about Félix.

The woman's shoulders sank. I'm sorry too.

— Do you want to talk about it?

THERE IS A LAND

She shook her head. Libète was grateful. There was solace in things left unsaid, and in that solace, a bond.

After ten minutes they approached the church that housed the sounding bell. The structure was deep and wide, built of spartan gray block and sheathed in rusted tin.

They climbed a small hill and stood off from the threshold. The inside of the church looked dark, like a mouth ready to consume them.

Magdala took a deep breath. Let's go in, Sophia. My niece.

She put her arm around Libète and the two walked in, no longer alone, but together.

On the ride back to the school, Brown unsettles her and Jak. He blathers on his cell phone, discussing vacation plans to Puerto Rico, shaking with asthmatic laughter over a joke told by whoever was on the other end of the line. *As though there isn't a dead girl in the hospital.*

— Where's Stephanie Martinette? Libète interrupted. Our guardian.

— She's been contacted, he said brusquely. He returned to his conversation. Libète's hand found Jak's. The boy squeezed back.

The sky turned mackerel-colored as the Sun dropped from view. Brown turned off Route 9 and idled at the campus gate as Véus slid it back. As they drove through, Véus could not meet Libète's eyes. *The poor man. He blames himself.*

— Secure them, Charles, Mr. Brown ordered. Charles cocked his head and gestured toward the children. Come along. Please. Won't you?

The children slid from the backseat and followed him.

— Where are you taking us? Jak asked Charles.

— I am . . . we're going . . . ah.

85

He marched them to a block of rooms on the school's second floor. Libète couldn't rouse herself to demand more of an answer; her thoughts were still lingering on the memories of Didi laid out, the sound of her parents' grieving, the hospital's antiseptic scent. Charles deposited Jak in one room and slid a chain through the door's external handle and a padlock through the chain. He took her to another down the hall.

Before entering, she saw Brown ascend the stairs. A renewed fierceness cut through her languor. *Why are we being separated?* she asked.

— *Safety*, Brown replied. Charles pushed her in and closed the door. She heard the chain slip into place and a lock click shut.

— *Bah!* she spat, and banged on the door. Though the room was an unused teacher's apartment, it felt like a jail cell.

They could have at least let Jak and me stay together. To commiserate. To mourn. To shake and tremble. She saw it so vividly: Jak in a quiet panic as he was shut in his room, as if being locked alive in a tomb.

— *Oh, God! Libète* cried out. *Didi. Poor, poor Didi.* She prayed for her friend.

Hours passed.

She moved from the rigid chair in which she had been sitting and praying and laid on the room's bed and cried into its pillow. Suddenly, the lock clicked and the chain fell and the door opened.

— *Manje,* Charles said, entering. *Eat.* He deposited a steaming bowl of porridge on the floor and left. The bowl would remain there long after its dancing wisps of steam had vanished.

• • •

A knock. It came from nowhere. Another rap.

— *Just leave me alone, you idiot!* Libète shouted at Charles.

Another knock. *Charles I am not,* a voice replied. *You don't know me.*

Libète recoiled. The voice was feminine.

Rushing to the door, Libète pressed her ear against it. Who's there? What do you want?

— To talk. To you. I have questions.

— About?

— Lots of things. Didi. Notes. Poison. The voice paused. *And numbers.*

Libète trembled.

— I heard about the radio show, the voice said. I think I can help you. The words were smooth yet earnest; they compelled trust.

— Who *are* you?

There was another pause, a long one. A friend. Most assuredly a friend, she said. My name is Maxine.

— Even if I wanted to open up, you can see the door is locked.

— Ah. But I have the key.

— Then why knock?

— Respect, my friend. Respect. May I enter?

Libète ran her hand over her plaits. Y-yes. Libète stood up straight. *Yes*, she repeated, with more certainty. The lock came undone, and Libète stepped back. Low light from the hallway limned the woman's form as she slid in and closed the door.

— The lights, Maxine asked. Must they be out? The dark is so uninviting.

— No, Libète murmured. She slipped back to the bed, leaned against the wall, and pulled her legs to her chest.

The woman glided over to a desk lamp and flicked it on. With a quick turn of the chair, she sat down. Woman and girl each took in the other.

Face: Round, pretty, gold hoop earrings

Skin: Mahogany

Hair: Straight, cropped to shoulders

Age: Middle

Fashion: Impeccable

Libète could not bring herself to look and assess the woman's eyes.

— So you're the *petit prophète*, eh?

The girl nodded. Maxine smiled, showing a beautiful set of teeth framed by lovely, wide lips. She wore a strapless dress that was patterned and smooth. She reached out her hand, and thin silver bangles sashayed around her wrist. Libète met the hand with her own, and shook it.

— Now that we're acquainted, you can call me Max. Friends do that.

— I don't understand what you want.

— I know Brown. He asked me to come.

Libète straightened, disdain on her face. You're *friends* with him?

Maxine's cheek puffed as she thought. Let's just say . . . he calls me 'Madanm Maxine.'

— What's your game, then?

— Game? I don't play games. I'm a truth-seeker. A professional one. A question-asker. A *digger*.

— A journalist? I'm not talking to the press. Not now.

— I don't deal in the written word, no.

— What then?

— *Mwen se yon ankètè.* I'm an investigator. Of a type. She leaned forward. I find hidden things. Dig up truth.

Libète's brow arched.

— I don't usually disclose my clients. But I know I can trust you. Remember the Bellerive family's kidnapped daughter?

— Who was taken and tortured?

Maxine nodded. Remember how she was mysteriously reclaimed and restored to the family?

Libète nodded. Maxine smiled. Many cases are less dramatic. Unfaithful husbands. Unfaithful wives. My business runs on all types of unfaithfulness.

— There's no lack of faith in my situation.

— But this is not business, my dear. I'm here talking to you for another reason.

— Oh?

— For justice.

— And that means trying to find out who did this to Didi?

Maxine nodded again. Libète's eyes were hollow. Maxine clasped Libète's wrist. I want to *help*. I've followed you. Your work.

Libète pulled away.

— The story behind your uncovering of Benoit's crimes. Your skills at detection. Fine eyes for clues and reasoning to match. Your persistence is exemplary; a model for all in my field. Myself included. But more than this, you're a voice worth listening to in a world of *blah blah blah*. Maxine smiled, reaching into a leather purse to withdraw a notepad and pen. She crossed her legs. The tension in Libète's shoulders eased.

This is a special woman.

— I've spoken with Jak already. But I need more details. Everything you can give me to help me get started. The police, as you well know, are worthless creatures. Dogs chasing their own tails. No, I'm here to find out who did this to your friend, she paused. Who wanted to kill you and Jak. She scribbled on her pad, her face darkening. And to make sure they pay.

Libète liked the sound of this. She moved to the edge of the bed. It's obvious who it was, Libète whispered. Benoit.

— Supposition is proof of nothing. Even if you're right–which, I agree, is a very real possibility–supposition cannot stand in court. That's partly why Benoit has skirted the law so far. Well, that and the bribes he's paid. We need incontrovertible *evidence*.

— There were two deliveries last night: a card in a nice envelope, and the sweets, dous makous.

— Jak's told me as much. You have them?

— The card is in my bag. The dous, I don't know what happened to them. At the football pitches, probably.

Maxine patted her purse. I've already recovered them. They'll be studied. Why do these 'gifts' get left for you?

— People like me, I suppose. What I say. What I – she looked upward for some ephemeral word – represent. Ever since Benoit was arrested, since I started going on the radio and getting interviewed, similar gifts have flowed. Probably a few times a month. Mostly by *ti machann*, street vendors, from Cité Soleil. The occasional admiring boy. Véus, the guard, said two women dropped them off. But I'm sure now they were doing it for someone else.

— Surely. Maxine scribbled furiously. Have you done anything recently that could make you a target?

— Nothing out of the ordinary. Planning the rally, I suppose? Our community organizing? But there's no obvious difference between this time a year ago and today. I've thought Benoit might take aim at us, but he's under close watch by the press, many of whom are my friends. It would be too obvious if something happened to me. We always assumed that was my shield.

— And the card? Maxine read its message aloud. *Stay away from the rally. Enemies are close.* Odd.

— It could have been a threat as easily as a warning. From friend or enemy, I don't know.

— Do you know anyone else who might target you?

Libète shrugged. The former headmaster and teacher we got dismissed? Loan sharks we've outwitted in Bwa Nèf? René, the man who kidnapped me who went to prison? Different gangsters? She sighed. It's a long list. But there's no one I've been a threat to as much as Benoit.

Maxine's eyebrow peaked. And what of this radio program?

— I don't see how these things are related. The items came during the show, maybe even beforehand, from what Véus said.

— I wasn't able to listen to the program. But it sounded like some-*interesting*-things happened.

Libète shook her head. I'd almost forgotten. There was a man. Who called in. He... he was killed. At least it sounded like it over the air. And he told us these... Numbers. Some men broke into the station

afterward, roughed up the host, ruined the equipment while looking for a recording.
— Jak mentioned the Numbers too. Any idea what they could be?
— I don't.
— Do you know the digits?
— No.
— None at all?
— I didn't care last night. I had a lot on my mind. Jak knew – she stopped herself, not entirely sure why – *some*. Said he couldn't remember them all. Maxine looked at her pad as she wrote. Libète shifted on her mattress, locking her arms in place.
— You're sure? Maxine asked.
— *I'm sure*, Libète snapped.
— Libète, I'm just trying to help. Maxine laid her pad down. You haven't heard, then?
Libète looked at her warily.
— I ... don't think you understand exactly what's happening here. Your story–and I believe every word you've said–is one version. But there's another. One that's already been picked up by some of the press. Maxine took a deep breath. Libète–you're being ... *accused* ... of killing Didi.
— But ... how could *anyone* ... She could not summon words.
Maxine remained composed, her professional steeliness keeping her from comforting the girl. You have friends in the press, but so does Benoit. They say that the sweets were yours, given to Didi.
— But why?
— That she had taken too much of the limelight. Was starting to overshadow you. That you wanted to make yourself look vulnerable and frame Benoit. These are the sorts of things they're saying. Maxine overcame her inhibitions and laid a hand upon Libète's shoulder. I'll do everything I can to discredit the story. It doesn't seem like it will be too difficult once your side gets out. That's why I'm here. But as you know,

tar sticks in Haiti. Empty accusations can travel far before there's time to rebut them. For now, this is the safest place. If police come tomorrow to question you, ask them to at least hide you and keep you safe. I'm going to make some calls.

Libète didn't acknowledge a single one of Maxine's words. She buried her head in her hands.

— I'll be back in touch tomorrow. Get some rest. There's nothing to be done now, and there are difficult things in store.

When Libète still didn't respond, Maxine grimaced, rose, lowered the light, and closed the door, locking it behind her.

NEW LIFE, NEW DEATH

Vòlè pa wont, men lafanmi wont.
The thief has no shame, but the family is ashamed.

Pitit se richès malere.
Children are the riches of the poor.

There is an economy of light in the church where all of Foche assembles. It is as if the light peers ahead to the grim proceedings to follow and knows to retreat.

Libète and Magdala enter, their eyes trading the deep brown earth and brilliant blue skies of the outdoors for the glum little building's brick and shadow. The hum and murmur of low conversation drops out.

— Sit, Magdala whispers. I sit at the front.

Libète searches furtively for a vacant spot on the benches made from boards nailed into amputated tree trunk bases.

— Over here! Dorsinus says, breaking the quiet. He signals to Libète with a wave.

Against the crowd's curious stares, Libète floats toward the man. His presence is a surprising comfort. Magdala moves intently and seats herself on the left side of a table that doubles as the church's altar. A man dressed in slacks and a pink button-down shirt is opposite her. He jots and scribbles in the notebook before him.

Libète glances at Prosper, seated among other young men: some strong, some weak, some handsome, some plain. He stands out, and her eyes linger on him a second longer than she intends. Their eyes hook. She reels hers away with a bashful turn of the head and they land on the tin roof trussed with limbs of kayimet, and then on a sad, slanted chalkboard dusted with white fingerprints and a solitary, ghostly *w*.

— Where have you been? Dorsinus says, shielding his mouth with his hand.

— I could ask you the same.

He tumbles his hand through the air. His eyes do a dance. About, he says, before clearing his throat. Libète's nostrils curl. She knows the scent of breath laced with *kleren* from days gone by; her Uncle, his drinking, the dark days of living with him in Camp Capvaa after the earthquake. She shifts in her seat, away from the man.

Conversations resume, but they are hushed, more reserved than before.

— What is this meeting? Libète whispers. Is it the one-who-is-lost's sentencing? Magdala told me nothing.

— Yes, but first a gathering of Kè Ini Gwoupman Peyizan La.

Libète nodded, taking in the name. The Hearts United Peasant Group. Her brow lifted. Some kind of solidarity group?

Dorsinus nods with his whole body. Yes, and a notable one! Hearts United is known today all through these hills. A real model for development. The words are an echo of Prosper's, and she shrinks. She looks to the boy again, ashamed for dismissing his account earlier.

— You're a member?

— When my wandering brings me here, I'm a member.

And suddenly, she walked in.

— All rise! shouted the man with the notebook and the busy pen.

— Ah, the *animatris*! Dorsinus whispered. The one behind all of this– Madanm Janel!

Prosper's mother. Libète recognized her right away.

Elders filling the pews and youth lining the walls jolted. All who were not standing rose. A polite but strong applause broke out, and Janel looked genuinely embarrassed. She signaled for it to stop with a modest flick of her head as she sat at the center of the altar. She brought a pair of ill-fitting reading glasses to her face. Shall we begin? she asked, full of solemn intent.

Libète measured this "animatris." She skewed closer to pretty than ugly; mother and son shared the same intense eyes, subtle nose, and muscular build. Dressed humbly, the leader's head was covered in a light red wrap, her body in a breezy patterned dress, and her feet adorned with orange sandals.

Libète cupped her hand and leaned toward the old man's ear. She's really the head of all this? They let a woman lead? In Libète's experience, community groups were often dominated by men, usually the loudest, sometimes the most dense. Dorsinus winked.

— I must thank everyone for coming out today, Janel said. I know some of you have traveled from far, and I want to say that we appreciate your presence here. Her gaze seemed to settle on Libète. Madanm Magdala, will you open our time?

Magdala had particular trouble looking into Janel's eyes. Yes, Madanm Prezidan. She stood. My friends–her voice faltered. Magdala clenched her eyes shut and began to sing.

I must give the good Lord thanks; thank you . . .

The assembly joined in, though Libète did not know the lyrics.

. . . For all that He has done for me

Many uncovered their heads, closed their eyes, lifted their hands, or covered their hearts. Libète snuck a glance around the room as the melody lifted high, bringing a new and unexpected brightness to the place.

She glimpsed many hunched forms, bare feet, and gnarled joints–the toll of a hard life in a desperate place.

It's in the way that I live
That I daily thank Him

Dorsinus was looking straight up with his eyes wide and mouth stretching into a smile that crossed his face. The "blind" man apparently saw a marvel where Libète saw the church's roof.

I had gotten discouraged with life
Because of the hardships I was going through
But when I called out to God
He listened to me, He took my needs to heart

The words, sung passionately by Magdala, bounced off Libète like pebbles against a wall. Tears ran down both Magdala's cheeks. She finished the song and breathed deep again. She returned to her seat, refusing to wipe her face.

The song had lightened the air but tinged it with melancholy and relief, if such things had scents.

— The agenda for our gathering is very simple, Janel declared. The first item is the land. Namely what is to be done with the community plot.

Grumbling broke out among all the members. Libète gave a questioning glance to Dorsinus, who merely shrugged.

— The second item is to determine our response to the grand larceny by Félix Dieudonné.

— Madanm Prezidan, said a man with peppercorn hair who stood from his seat, his index finger pointing up, a hat held in his other hand. A word on the subject?

Libète recognized him immediately–the older man with the sugar cane, who had spoken when she had slid her hand into the crevice. Janel bobbed an assent.

— With respect to the offender, I have reflected much on the situation.

— And what are the results of your reflection, Mesye Jeune?

— He should hang.

Clapping broke out among the row of young men, followed by cheers and jeers in the rest of the audience.

— Jeune, Jeune, Jeune. Janel clicked her tongue. We've been through this. A violent reaction to a nonviolent crime is an affront to God.

— Then bring in the police!

— If we involve them, he will be taken and beaten and tortured.

— So be it! shouted a woman from the front row. She turned to Magdala. He *should* be locked away!

Magdala shook with small, silent sobs. Janel put a bracing hand to her thigh. Libète felt indignity well up inside her. *Magdala's hurt no one. They shouldn't treat her like this!*

— We're all fingers of the same hand here! protested a man from across the room. Surely a noose is the wrong response.

— He should work till he pays off the debt! offered another.

— Sell those goats of his! They'd pay for our losses!

— Those goats are his mother's property.

— The mother is responsible for the child! shouted the woman from the front again. Raising a son that steals from his community! This theft is like reaching into our bellies and pulling out the food we've already eaten. From our *children's* bellies! Bah!

Janel stood, raising her hands. The room immediately quieted.

— Félix has done wrong. There must be a consequence. But he *is* one of our own. If a child of ours wrongs us, we don't abandon the child. We don't turn our back on him. Why turn to the law when the law has failed us time and again? She nodded to herself. Mesye Secretary, was Félix summoned here?

— He was summoned.

Janel frowned. I had hoped he would come to answer for himself. Madanm Magdala, will you approach your son and invite him once more? Before a final decision is taken?

Magdala nodded.

— He is apart from us, Janel added. He is alone. That is a type of punishment already.

— This is nonsense! Jeune cried.

Many in the church-cum-courtroom seemed to share the sentiment. Libète saw Prosper sitting low in his chair, his whole body a scowl.

— And to all of you who would try to become the law yourself – Libète thought Janel's eyes flicked to her son – remember that God judges you by the standard you use to judge another! If Félix does what he can to make restitution, he should be invited back into the fold. That is my view of things. He is a good boy, a good young man. And I love him, as if he were my own. As you all should.

The room was silenced, but for the sound of the secretary's pen scratching. Magdala stood and excused herself, finally wiping away the tears. Janel returned to her seat and replaced her glasses. Now, let us turn our attention to the question of the land.

Libète sat in awe of the woman.

— We have a guest with us. Mesye Rodriguez, you may address the assembly. All turned to take in a group of four men standing, backlit, in the entrance to the church. Two stepped forward: one black, the other fair-skinned, maybe Dominican or Cuban. Libète's gaze lingered on the other two men in dark uniforms who remained at the back, dressed like the guard she had glimpsed at the mountain gate earlier. A huge dog sat obediently, panting just outside the church door.

The delegate, Rodriguez, wore a light linen suit that had browned a bit with dust. He wiped his brow and smiled. He was young, handsome even.

— Hello, he said. In English. The man at his side, dressed in a collared shirt and slacks interpreted. I greet you from the University of Jackson.

The crowd muttered a greeting in return.

— It's good to see you all again. I've not been with you since we first reached the agreement for our archeological team to excavate the other side of the ridge. I've missed your hospitality. He smiled while the interpreter finished his greeting.

— Well – he cleared his throat – this has proven a fruitful partnership. A model of academic and community collaboration. We have been happy to provide you with new water sources, seed, fertilizer for the common plot and your farms, and new tools in exchange for that care and hospitality and patience. We see Foche is thriving, and we are pleased.

The town watched him, not betraying their feelings.

He continued, dabbing his brow. We're coming today with another proposal. An offer for further collaboration. We would like to expand our excavation–temporarily–into what you call the common plot. Evidence shows that on that land we will likely find artifacts of much greater historical significance.

A hand rose, and Rodriguez acknowledged him. Jeune stood again.

— Sir, this is a different situation. Those are our fields. The other side of the ridge was terrible soil, little-used. Those crops on the common plot are thriving.

— We understand the cost involved. We're willing to give every member of Foche a generous farm grant.

— How much are we talking about? asked another man.

— Fifteen hundred US per head of household, lump sum. As the interpreter finished, gasps broke out.

— That much!

— Think of all of the livestock that could be purchased!

Rodriguez smiled. We would need to begin our dig in the next several months, after the harvest, to keep within our project funding.

— And how long would this dig last?

— Up to one year.

— Only a year? a woman said. This, this is a miracle! I can pay for my son's medicines.

— I can pay off my debts to that grandon down the mountain who squishes us tenants under his heel!

— I could repair my house–build a *new* house!

Rodriguez was getting excited now. After one year, the plot would be returned to the community's control. Foche is fortunate Madanm Janel had the foresight to bring you together in sharing the land. Reaching separate agreements with each landowner would have made this opportunity impossible.

There was applause and Janel gave a humble nod.

Dorsinus stood. I have held my tongue, he roared.

— You ought to keep it that way! someone called out.

— This is *madness*. Dorsinus slurred the final word.

— Aw, shut your mouth! What right do you have to speak?

— How *dare* you! Am I not a child of these hills? I go and come. But I have the privilege to speak. I will speak!

— Let him. Janel said this, her words rising above the competing voices. This is a chance to debate. Agreeing to this proposal, or rejecting it, is a democratic matter and worthy of serious deliberation.

— Thank you, Madanm Prezidan. Dorsinus staggered down and out of his row. You cede control of the land to these crooks, these outsiders, you give away yourself. If you turn over the land, even for a thousand *billion* goud, you sacrifice your souls! Your very souls!

Libète felt her heart thumping anew. *Dorsinus is right!* This was nothing to rush. That plot producing as it was–it was an undeniable achievement, a real marvel.

Jeune called after him. Listen to yourself, Dorsinus. Sober up and then we might tolerate you.

Now Libète's blood boiled. *Just because he's voicing dissent.*

Dorsinus gave a wave of his hand. Shut up, Jeune.

— You're disgracing yourself.

— I am a man. I have a voice. I will use it!

— Maybe, Rodriguez said, we can have a subsequent meeting soon, maybe in a week? After you all can reflect on this offer and ask further questions?

— Yes.

— That sounds good.

— *Absoliman.*

Dorsinus swore. You are fools if you listen to this one. They want the *land*. The land!

Janel stood. Maybe, Mesye Dorsinus, you might save your further remarks for the following meeting?

Dorsinus ran his tongue over his front teeth, bit his lip. He harrumphed and left the church, bumping shoulders with one of the uniformed men standing at the entrance.

Libète felt possessed: all her thought proceeded down a single channel, compelling her to stand. *What am I doing! Stop it! Stop it!*

— Madanm Prezidan, may I speak? All of the assembly's eyes snapped to Libète.

— And who are you?

Libète's eyes bounced from face to face. I'm called . . . Sophia. And I'm Magdala's niece.

— Ah! More Dieudonné stock? I should have known! Get her out!

— Silence, Jeune! Janel's eyes flashed. Go on, Sophia.

— It seems to me–as an outsider–that the crops there are a miracle. Her heart pounded as blood thumped in her ears. Any sharing of the land, even to God himself, would have to come with the certainty the future is ensured. That you all are protected.

— Who are you two to speak? Jeune said. These two know nothing of our suffering! Others agreed with Jeune's sentiment.

— We are merely discussing the situation, Janel said. I know feelings run deep, but I also know that a conclusion can be reached. Just as the decision to bring the land together was shared, the decision to lease the land must be. She turned to Libète. But for the time being, maybe it would be best if the discussion was left to members of the community?

Libète felt like her legs would give way. She lowered her eyes, patted down her capris, and walked out the door. *Stupid, stupid, stupid . . .*

— Are there others who wish to share? Janel asked. Clamoring broke out. Prosper leaped from his seat after Libète. She walked at a furious pace, tensing as she slipped out the door and past the waiting dog.

— Sophia! Prosper called as he reached the doorway. He held out his hand, inviting her back.

Libète looked over her shoulder, then looked away, continuing in the same direction as the old, drunk, blind man.

• • •

The Dieudonné household was not a happy place.

Dorsinus finished his whittling and his rooster figurine sat there on a stone. Like an assembled puzzle, there was no wonder left in the completed thing. Finality, he muttered, the ultimate bore. He cast the shavings into the fire Libète built in preparation for cooking the evening meal, cornmeal porridge and bean sauce. The two watched the grated slivers of wood char and turn to ash. Dorsinus took a conspicuous drag on an opaque plastic bottle. Medication, he slurred. For my gout. Libète turned away and noticed Magdala coming close, returning from the direction of the fort.

— Ah, Magdala! Dorsinus said. You've returned!

She nodded, sadly.

— What of the boy? Did he relent?

She turned her face away and pushed through the knotted lavender sheet to enter her shack. When she did not emerge, Dorsinus rose to inquire further.

— Leave her be, Libète said bluntly. Her pain is a kind that doesn't desire comfort.

Dorsinus scrunched his face, sniffed deeply, took another sip. What is this place becoming? he asked the open air. He lifted up his figurine, admiring his work.

— Very good, Libète commented. For a blind man.

— It's nothing. A travesty. My worst work. He cast it into the flames.

— Ay! What are you thinking? She grabbed a stick to salvage it. Dorsinus walked away.

— Get back here! Libète called.

But he was gone. Though he staggered, he had a set direction, as if possessed. To part with the land, the wealth of us all! he hollered. What a thing! *Yon peche*, he shouted for all, and for no one. *A sin!*

None listened but Libète.

He went up, down, walked footpaths among the golden weeds till the Sun abandoned the land. The few people he saw along the way he cursed. His mind was addled, weighted, his fingers frantically rubbing what hung around his neck.

He emptied his bottle and dropped it to the ground. Reaching for his chest, his hand clutched something beneath his shirt, a talisman, his source of security.

Darkness reigned.

An hour or hours later–he did not know–he came down the mountain. What had been around his neck was there no longer. He stumbled to the community plot and was reduced to tears. The Moon was hollow, as if embarrassed by his show. He cursed, he pissed, he sank to the ground, he wept.

And then one was upon him, an arm around Dorsinus' neck, a hand over his mouth. The old man's eyes were wide with fear–terrible and uncomprehending–and with a flash of strength he was able to tear the hand away and let his voice cry out in wonder: *My eyes! I can see!*

Libète stirs.

Not because of the subtle slide of a note under the door, but because the door–the one to her cell, the one formerly locked–is cracked open. A band of light sweeps into the room and rests on the wall, easing her out of her dreaming.

She rubs at her eyes, squinting. Now she sees the note, white paper leaping out against the polished concrete floor. She stretches and moves toward the door. Wary at first, she tests to see if it is truly ajar. The door's hinges creak as she rocks it back and forth. The paper now in hand, she unfolds it and holds it up to the light. The scribbled cursive is rushed and ugly.

Ou bezwen soti. Kounye a.
Moun ki touye Didi ap vini pou ou.

— *You need to get out*, she reads aloud. *Now. Didi's killer is coming for you.*

Hand shooting to her mouth, she nearly drops the paper, but notices a final appended sentence. *Go to the back wall.*

Could she trust the message? The card the night before was too obscure a warning to do her, Didi, and Jak any good.

Jak. He'll know what to do. She retrieved her shoes and book bag from the foot of the bed. In another moment, she was down the hall. She knocked on the door where Jak had been deposited. The lock was gone.

No answer came. She tried the door and, surprisingly, it opened. No one was inside.

She cursed, worry scaling her stomach's walls. *What is going on?* Her mind revisited the note. *The back wall.*

Viewed from above, the school's layout was U-shaped. Her room was at its left peak on the second story. The entry gate crossed the divide between the two peaks, and Brown's office was at its trough. There was roof access where she could reach the school's back wall–she and Jak regularly snuck up to look out over Cité Soleil–but this was crazy. She would have no way to get to the ground, no way but hanging off and letting go. She'd certainly break her leg if she dropped from that height...

She needed to try. Maybe Maxine had left the note? Or Véus? How many could even be on the school grounds at this hour?

She slipped to the end of the open-air corridor, running fast and keeping low. Though it was late, the light in Brown's office remained on. Holding her breath, she spied through his window, its slats cranked wide open. Brown sat at his computer, clicking away as he typed. Charles stood at his side, and the interpreter's head kept drifting to the left, as if he were about to fall asleep. She ducked and slipped under the windows, pausing when she heard Brown speak.

— This is shaping up poorly. Max left a while ago. She didn't come up with anything.

A moment later, Charles spoke. Maybe there wasn't much to share. He paused. Or maybe Madanm Maxine didn't want to tell you. You say she's a–what's the word–confidante? But is she really worthy of trust?

— Her fee–her *exorbitant* fee, if you ask me–makes her trustworthy. The boy is still sitting tight?

Charles said nothing, and Libète couldn't see him.

— Good, Brown said.

Libète was perplexed. Jak wasn't in his room. *Why would Charles lie?*

— Get ready to move him first thing tomorrow. If she's alone it will keep her off-kilter when the police come around.
— Off what?
— Dammit, you'd better learn your English if you're going to stay my interpreter.

Libète wanted to scream at them both but kept quiet and slinked away from the office. When she reached the wall she and Jak used to reach the roof, a conspicuous chair sat at its foot. *Left for me . . .*

She hopped atop it and pulled herself up and onto the cinder-block wall. She stood and walked across the short span as if it was a balance beam. She reached the classroom roofs and scaled them. *Where could they have moved Jak?* The question still dogged her. She wondered if she should abandon this plan and instead seek out Véus. He could surely help. Maybe he had delivered the note but didn't want to indicate his involvement in her escape? Adrenaline forced her forward.

She sprinted along the roof's margins, looking for anything else that might have been left for her. There were huge black cylinders to one side, used for storing water, and the tips of naked rebar poking from the edge of the wall. She flipped an upturned bucket at one corner, but there was nothing there that would let her safely rappel down the wall.

Reaching the back end of the roof, she looked down.

Bondye! What is that?

There was a cart down below, adjacent to the wall. It wasn't abandoned–it was strapped to a mule.

— *Psst!* A person, a man on closer inspection, stepped out from an awning on the opposite side of Route 9, the long road bisecting Cité Soleil. She squinted. He used hand gestures to direct her to jump down.

She paused. This was a dangerous game. Why would she jump? Why not climb off this roof, head back down the wall, close the door to her room, and return to bed? This was surely the more sensible course–but much at the school was not right. She trusted Maxine, felt sure she was playing Brown, but then what was motivating Brown? And where was Stephanie in all this? Had something befallen her?

She thought back to the note. The one left for her last night had been benevolent, a warning. She wasn't perfectly settled about this new one, but the handwriting seemed the same. Or was this a trick of her memory, borne from her desire to have them match? If she had heeded the original warning and been more cautious, Didi might still be fine and life unchanged.

Libète wanted to shout at the man across the street to show himself, but knew she couldn't without likely alerting others. He kept repeating his pantomime for her to jump.

She looked down again and realized the cart was stacked with mattresses.

A prayer escaped her lips, along with a curse. She lowered herself and hanged from the lip of the wall.

She let go.

She landed with a thud on the mattresses, and her legs broke her fall.

The man slinked across the road with his face still obscured.

— *Eske ou byen*? Came the worried question. Are you all right?

She gasped. *Uncle?*

— Wake up, Sophia. Please. I need your help.

Magdala stands over Libète, holding a lit kerosene lamp. In the twilight between slumber and waking, she strikes Libète as menacing.

— Wha–what's the matter?

— A baby is on the way. The mother-to-be's father, he came to tell me, then left.

— What?

— I need an assistant. The hour is late.

— To deliver a child? You're a *matwon*?

Magdala lifted Libète up by the arm, a show of surprising strength. Get up.

Libète rubbed her eyes and tried to suppress a yawn. It's not that–I'm willing. It's just . . . I've never helped bring a child into the world. Her wakening mind traveled back to her time at the hospital. She had *seen* a number of deliveries, but never aided Sister Françoise. *M pa kalifye,* she sputtered. I'm unqualified.

Magdala didn't slow to listen. She sped around the room, collecting towels and sheets, a bedpan, all while holding her lamp high.

— She's already far along–grab that kettle, Sophia–but there are *konplikasyon yo.*

— Complications?

Magdala gave a grave nod.

They stepped out of the shack to greet the still air and crickets' songs. The stars here still marveled Libète; they were so very bright, unlike in Port-au-Prince, where city lights and smog drowned out their distant dancing. She thought her heart's anxious thumping was audible, but stopped, listened close. There they were again–the drums, signaling something.

— What's that beating out over there?

Magdala's face tightened. Nothing. Just a dance.

— At this hour?

— We must go. Can you run?

— I think. My toes . . .

Magdala looked vexed.

— I can try my best.

They jogged in an entirely undignified manner, but birth was a time of seeming indignity.

— There will be much blood, Magdala warned her, huffing.

— I'm used to blood.

Magdala eyed her warily. They continued down the main road to a solitary shack. Magdala's bobbing light made their shadows buck and strain.

As they approached the home, a cry shattered the quiet. A man– ostensibly the anxious soon-to-be grandfather who had called Magdala– tended a fire over which a pot of water bubbled to a boil. His whole body was a hollow arc stooped over the edge of the flame. Libète saw the prying eyes of weary children peeking from a nearby lakou. Whether from the cool or a creeping sense of wrongness in the air, Libète's skin prickled.

— Are there no women to help? Libète asked.

— *Mon dieu!* A curdling scream came from inside, trailed by an agonized moan.

— There is a neighbor inside with the girl, yes.

— Isn't this woman better suited to help than me?

— I'll need you both. Few are willing to help this one.

Libète couldn't understand the why of this, but followed Magdala anyway.

They entered to a distressing scene. Weak candles laid about the room cast a macabre light. The woman helper sat, stunned, in the middle of the small square space on a *ti chez ba*, her hands covered in dark blood. The mother-to-be sat on the family's upturned *chodyè*, their cooking pot. She was gaunt and pasty, and slumped feebly against the wall. Libète gasped upon realizing it was the pregnant girl she had seen just yesterday on the road.

Magdala handed the lamp to Libète and pushed the helper aside. Thank you, Philomene. Sophia, hold the light over my shoulder. Délira, Magdala said, taking the mother-to-be's hand and holding it tight.

— Help us, said Délira, help – another curdling cry and moan. The girl's eyes fluttered and the helper gasped.

— Pran kouraj! Courage is what is needed now, Magdala said. Libète looked down. The bleeding was indeed profuse. Too much, Magdala remarked. Towels? Soap? Water? Magdala posed the questions to the open air. Philomene, still staring at her hands, merely turned her head toward the boiled water the girl's father now let cool on the *recho* outside. Sophia, she said, spread the towels on the bed. We need to move her.

Libète did not respond. Her minor surgical help had included handing tools to doctors and nurses in a pinch, but that was gun wounds, split knees, cut feet. A delivery, a new life, this was something else, this was...

— Sophia!

Snapped back into the moment, Libète remembered her alter ego.

— Wi, Magdala. Sorry. Libète jumped toward the towels and spread them before returning to Magdala's side. They pulled Délira up and did their best to shift her to the bed. More wails poured from her, and already the blood had spread down Libète's clothes. Philomene, Magdala called, brace her from behind!

Philomene floated over as if in a daze and threaded her arms under Délira's armpits.

As they washed their hands, Magdala leaned close to Libète's ear, and spoke low and urgently. The blood, it's more than I have seen before. Délira *ap emoraji*, hemorrhaging, to be sure. I need you here, and I need you now.

Libète nodded. Hemorraghing, she had seen it before, when–

— She is here too soon! She is early! Délira whimpered. I'm cursed, I know it–I'm certain!

— When the baby comes we do what we can to make it on time, Magdala said. We take her as we find her.

Magdala inspected the young woman, felt her abdomen. Magdala broke into a sweat, but her face and body were stern and resolved.

— My dear, we are in an urgent time. Your child must come now, and you must help it.

Another moan, and Délira's eyes flitted and sank.

— How are you here? Libète hisses. The new shock at finding her Uncle is too much.

— In time, in time, he replies. Get under cover now. I'll explain as we go. Libète pulled the offered sheet over her head and peeked out from beneath, expecting a quick getaway. Uncle gave a click and snapped the sisal reins tied to the mule. The animal refused to move.

— Come on you dumb *bèt*! Uncle growled.

— When did you get a *milèt*? Libète asked.

— He's new. Uncle hopped down from the lip of the cart and tried to slap the animal's backside. *Come on, come on,* he entreated. *No reason to hold things up!*

Libète laughed, and it felt palliative. Far too many times she had seen similar scenes play out, but Uncle was the insufferable beast and Libète the exasperated one. The dissonance between past and present experience with the man was jarring. In the wake of her Aunt's death in the quake and their shared displacement in a tent encampment, she and her Uncle had been at perpetual odds. The aching, brutal hunger that set in when his profligacy took hold and he drank their money away. His endless threats culminating in capricious beatings. Darkest of all, was the night of her abduction and near kidnapping from their shared tent. It happened while her Uncle had slunk off to indulge his vices. When she was recovered, he had sworn to change his ways. She had given his word little weight–it was like a bucket with a hole, good intentions always seeped out and away.

The mule finally budged, and Uncle gave a victory shout before biting his fist and looking around to see if anyone heard. He leaped back up on his cart and gave the girl a toothy grin.

— Where are we going, *Tonton*? Libète asks from under the sheet.
— Home, he says. You're going home.
She had been wrong about his promises this time. After the dark events that catapulted Libète into the middle of Benoit's plot for office, Stephanie had soon arrived like a guardian angel, pulling Libète out of the camp and placing her in the boarding school. Uncle's friendships based on shared drink and drugs vanished when he had none to offer. Unable to rely upon his wife's business or Libète's free labor, he had to scrape by on his own. A friend took pity and let him serve as a *bouret* man, lugging goods around Cité Soleil on his borrowed cart.

After a time, Libète climbs up from the mattress to sit beside her Uncle, wearing the sheet like a shroud. Each time one of the wagon's uneven rubber tires makes a full rotation, it results in a large bump.

— To safety, he continues. I'm getting you away.
— From what?
— That's for another to share.
She huffed. How did you get the note to me?
— Get a note to you?
— Under my door.
— I left no such thing. His face drew back. I only have the note you passed to me.

Alarm stretched across her face. She exhaled deeply. I left no such thing.
— But of course you did.

She punched his shoulder. I'd know if I did! Give it here! He reached into the breast pocket of his worn polyester sport coat, pulling out the paper. She devoured the contents: *Bring your cart to the school's back wall ... midnight ... something soft to land on ... I need you ... Libète.*

— These aren't my words! she protested. She found her old self claiming her with each new breath. Where did you get this?

He turned dark, his face not like she'd seen since the days in the camp.

— Ah, Uncle, I'm sorry. She rubbed the back of her hand against her cheek, remembering he was illiterate.

— A woman from the market brought it to me. Said it was passed to her. I had another read it to me, he mumbled. I thought it was from you. Because it said it was.

— You're right, Uncle. Of course.

— If a note says it's from a person, why wouldn't it be from that person?

— I understand completely, Uncle.

— The thing, it makes no sense.

— We'll figure it out. Her mind raced. She compared her crinkled note with his carefully folded one. *The same writing.* Someone had infiltrated the school, or maybe co-opted someone from within to guide her out of her cell, to the roof, onto the cart. Maxine, perhaps? But this conclusion disagreed with her advice to stay put.

— What should we do? he asked. Hide?

She looked him hard in the eye. Whoever was behind setting her free would surely have been watching his plan unfold. No, she said. We wait.

And so they did.

They retreated to a corner of Bwa Nèf, as safe a haven as there could be in times like these. Libète sat beside her Uncle on a log, a small fire crackling in the bottom of a sawed-open oil drum. He held a knife in his hand and cut an orange in pieces. He smiled as he handed her a slice, and she smiled back, but weakly.

— Thank you, Uncle. He gave a meek nod.

They faced the nearby lane so that they could at least see someone approach. Their conversation was mostly perfunctory: about weather, new violence in the slums, marriages and deaths, business, and a host of unchallenging things that fill one's thoughts and permit a retreat from the dull pains of life.

Partway through a recounting of his day's hauls through Bwa Nèf, her Uncle stopped midsentence.

— Do you think–the one behind this all–could it be . . . *him*?

She knew at once he spoke of his son, Davidson. The young man had fled the night of Benoit's arrest, recruited by the villain along with other youths to catapult themselves into a pitched battle with the local contingent of UN peacekeepers. It was believed all over that the troops had been kidnapping and prostituting local girls.

— Maybe, she told him. It was appealing: in all of the intrigue in which she found herself embroiled, perhaps her cousin was a watchful presence and protector after all. It's a comforting thought, no?

His face was laden with sadness or regret, Libète couldn't tell which. A very comforting one, he said. He reached for the orange, shared another piece, and retreated into himself. *A good man beneath it all*, she mused. Mèsi, Tonton. For everything.

— The least I could–

— *Psst! Psst!*

Libète shot up. The soft, vulnerable version of herself was engulfed in an instant. Who are you? she barked. What do you want? She dropped her orange into the flames and picked up a rock. She stood, arm cocked, her body again tense and mean.

Uncle, quick to remember her past furies, was clearly more afraid of this girl possessed than whoever lurked in the shadows. He stumbled back against the outside wall of his shack and cowered, bottom lip bobbing.

— Peace! the voice called. Peace!

It was familiar, but vague, somewhat distant, and impossible for Libète to place. She loosed a feral growl. *Show yourself!*

And he did.

And she smiled.

Libète hears music: beautiful, majestic even, keeping time with her heart's mad rhythm. It sounds like old symphony recordings she'd listen to with Elize in his shack on the edge of Cité Soleil, or with Stephanie when they cooked meals together. Her subconscious mind toggles through these associations gingerly while her body and being are engaged by a strong grip that forces her fingers together.

Délira screams. Lucid now, the girl giving birth forces herself up against Philomene's backstop and writhes, and the blood, it pours. Still, the girl's efforts are weakening.

— *Pouse*, Magdala hollers, *you must!* The head is out and you must push!

Libète wishes she knew how to help. Délira strains and breathes, and in the briefest of moments their eyes latch and Libète squeezes the hand back, hard, as if to say, I am here, we are here, you are not alone. All the while the beautiful music swells inside Libète's head.

— Bondye, protect these lives, Magdala mutters, keep them safe, bring them through, you are good, you are good–pouse!

The child–the living, breathing child–is out, and it is a miracle.

Magdala cradles the child and Libète nearly lets loose a whoop and Philomene sighs and Délira lets her head slip to the side, a small smile on her face as she pants and pants.

The music quiets, slipping away as unexpectedly as it came.

— Sophia, dip the knife in the boiling water and bring it.

Within a minute the cord is cut and placed in a nearby bowl. The babe–a boy, it turns out–is passed to Philomene to wash and swaddle. Libète takes the woman's place holding Délira up.

But Délira, she is faded. Magdala is worried. It must be the *madichon*, the spell that lingers over this family, she mutters.

— What is it? Libète asks, bewildered.

— The blood, Magdala says. It does not stop!

Magdala brings the lamp close. It is true. The puddle on the bed was sopping and spreading. Délira is limp, again on the verge of unconsciousness.

— We need to boil my herbs, put her over the steam! Magdala shouts. That will purify her, help stop the bleeding!

Libète's mouth dropped. She knew little, but enough to see this was a preposterous idea. Délira was still hemorrhaging and the rising steam would burn her while having no medicinal effect at all, Libète was sure. She knew from a similar case what might be done. The music swelled again with her fears.

— Madanm, she is slipping away. The bleeding has to be stopped. What if we keep the water aside and massage her uterus–

— What are you talking about?

— It will help stop the bleeding. I promise. It must be done.

— How would you–

— *Please.* Trade places with me. And bring the baby back.

— What? But Philomene is cleaning him. That's–

— *Listen* to me. *Trust* me.

— But how–

— *Take her!* Libète shouted, her worry impossible to conceal.

Magdala did, this slight tempered only by shock. Libète rushed to the child and pulled him from Philomene's arms.

— Délira, you must hold your baby to your breast. You must.

But Délira couldn't lift her arms. Libète cursed. Philomene! Hold the child to Délira's chest so that he might feed. Now! Libète pulled at Délira's shirt until it ripped.

— Why? Magdala asked.

Libète didn't know how much to say. It releases a chemical–in the body–that helps stop the bleeding. Libète's hands had already flown down to Délira's pelvis, massaging the outside of the uterus.

— What are you doing? How do you know these things? Magdala cried out. She needs to be steamed!

Libète shot Magdala a murderous look. Please! I beg you–just–*silence*.

By coming closer Libète saw the blood still flowed. Terrified, she kept pressing but eased off, knowing that too much pressure would go beyond making the uterus contract and actually invert it, creating all manner of new complications. The child had taken the breast, and Libète was grateful for this. She kept at the uterus, pressing, pressing, pressing.

In time, the bleeding slowed. And then, it stopped.

One never forgets those they save.

Lolo!

In that moment, thoughts collide in Libète's mind.

So thin. Her arms slip around his gaunt frame.

So nervous. Her touch shocks him.

So tortured. His eyes speak fear.

It was a long embrace. She grasped him desperately, as if he might otherwise slip from her life again.

She finally pulled back. Her smile was wide, and unexpected warmth shot from her core to the tips of her toes and fingers. You've returned! she said. You've returned!

Lolo's smile strained his face, and he threw a nod to her Uncle, who floated off to the side.

— I wasn't sure you'd be happy to see me.

Libète feigned slapping him. How could I not be?

She had been his salvation. When Lolo was arrested for Claire and Gaspar's murders, it had been Libète who had exonerated him, freed him from his cell, let him reenter a world that had accused him, condemned him without trial, forgotten him. No matter what may happen later, such a person is a token to be touched and kept close, remembered on those long, sad days when fear creeps in and casts doubt on who we might believe we are.

Yon jou tankou jodi a. A day like today.

She wrapped one arm around him to usher him to the fire.

— So you're the one? The one who brought me here?

He gave a sheepish grin. The smile came easier now, like the muscles in his face had warmed up. The fear etching his features vanished.

— Uncle? Some space, please?

— The mule, he muttered, I'll go . . .

The man was hurt by her dismissal, she could tell. She turned back to Lolo anyway. So you left the notes?

— That's right.

— You snuck inside the school?

He shook his head. The interpreter delivered it.

— Charles?

He gave a nod. He slipped it under your door and let you out, as I asked. I gave the note for your Uncle to the machann, and she passed it to him.

— Ah. Ah ha. And what of the third note? The same woman?

— The third?

— The third. The two for my Uncle and I, and the warning yesterday.

He nodded, slowly at first. Of course. Yesterday's warning note. The same woman. She passed the two.

Libète picked at a scab, the remnant from a day-old mosquito bite. I wish your warning had been more of a warning.

He was uneasy again, his eyes flicking between her gaze and the flame.

— My friend, Libète added. The death meant for me came to her.

Lolo swallowed. That's . . . why I had to get you out of the school. Why I'm here this very moment. Benoit, the beast, he's coming for you. He killed your friend.

— I knew it! But . . . why now? After so long?

Lolo reached into his pocket and registered the time from the face of his cell phone. Libète, we must go.

— What do you mean? Wait. I don't... don't *understand*. Where did you go, Lolo? How do you know what Benoit has done?

— There's time to explain, but we have to leave.

She tried to form a sentence, a second, a third, but none took. Finally: Where? *Why?*

— Libète, he meant to kill you. But he's done even better.

She clenched her eyes, trying to comprehend. Lolo, mark my words. I will *never* flee Cité Soleil. Nothing could make me abandon it.

— But Libète, you're–. He slid at an angle, his sallow cheeks puffing. You've fallen into a trap. I've pulled you out, but only for a moment. He's bribed the police before, and he's doing it again. They weren't going to question you first thing in the morning. They were going to disappear you. Make it seem like you were running.

— But I *am* running.

— He's decided discrediting you, turning you into a criminal before he kills you, is even better.

Libète fell into a vertiginous haze. She took Lolo's arm to brace herself.

— Libète, we must go. *Now.*

One never forgets those they save.

They left the shack elated, even though their clothes were stained with blood and sweat. The child was alive. The mother was alive. *Delivrans* was the new boy's name. Deliverance.

Magdala had hugged Libète. It was not a polite and reserved embrace, but a joyous, abandoned one. The kind touch felt good to Libète, indescribably so.

Philomene tended to Délira as Libète watched Magdala clean and swaddle the boy, massage his misshapen head with castor oil till it was rounded, and then stuff the umbilical cord with herbs before burying it and the placenta under a nearby sapling. They walked the child around the home three times to ward off spirits. Libète was pleased that the piqued tension between her and Magdala had disappeared. They bid Délira farewell and left her in Philomene's care. Délira's hovering father had strangely vanished.

It is a perfect morning, crisp but not too cool. The Sun creeps over the peaks to reach out and stroke their skin, making them radiant. Exhaustion is nothing, not in a world as pure and merciful and hopeful as this one.

They walk hand in hand, recounting the night: their fears, each crisis, every prayer. After a time of sudden silence, Magdala speaks.

— Where did you learn such things, Sophia?

Libète shrugs demurely, looking away. As I said, I saw such things done once before. That is all.

When Libète looks back, there was such *pride* in Magdala's eyes; it feels as good as a second embrace.

The pair approach Magdala's lone shack. Saint-Pierre is there, and the beast's form is as reassuring as a solid marble column.

But then there is also a cluster of men on the road. Maybe a *konbit*, a work team? Breaking from early labor in the fields?

No, Libète realizes. They have another purpose. Their tools are laid down. Their arms are crossed, brows knit, and legs straddling earth. She sees that a terrible thing has been deposited at their feet.

— What do you suppose that is? Magdala asks.

All joy the pair share gives way. A familiar hat had been dropped by its owner. His empty bottle is beside it on the ground. Magdala claps her mouth and lets loose a cry. Libète trembles.

New life and new death.

Always the two come together.
That is our world.
Always.

THE OPEN QUESTION

Lanmò toujou gen koz.
Death always has a reason.

Libète's soul aches. Lolo has her by the hand.

Her mind sputters. She thinks of Didi's parents. Their faces broken by emotions too deep for words. Their sadness would turn to hatred–not aimed at some unknown murderer, but Libète herself.

Lolo led her through dark corridors and passages, each turn making her lose her bearings. He whispered: . . . *Such a blow . . . I was too slow to come . . . Benoit will pay . . . I'm sorry . . . I'm sorry . . . I'm sorry . . .*

I didn't thank him. Her ncle. Another reason to hate herself. He didn't utter a word as she was led away in a daze. *Maybe he has changed for the better and I for the worse.* She hoped he wouldn't hold it against her, if she saw him again.

Her feet were cinder blocks and her churning mind was barely able to make her body move. She couldn't reconcile this new reality. Slander of all types could be tolerated, but Benoit's plan to make her face the charge of murder from the grave? With no chance to speak out?

— What of Jak? The thought parted her haze.

She thought she saw Lolo bristle. *Surely a trick of shadow and light.* Is Jak all right? He wasn't in his room.

Lolo paused. I made arrangements for him too. He'll be joining us.

This relieved Libète tremendously. Her hand wanted her friend's reassuring touch.

Lolo led her along before stopping abruptly in a wide, brick road in front of a squat building. She heard the dull hum of current passing through power lines overhead and realized she knew the place, and well: Bwa Nèf's old, green-painted cinema, set on Impasse Chavannes. A chain was wrapped around its entrance, padlocked. It snapped open as Lolo inserted a key. She'd not been inside the place since the day Claire and Gaspar had been murdered and she barged in, voicing that unthinkable reality to a room full of Claire's friends.

— Why now, Lolo? she blurted. Why is this coming now?

He shushed her, looking this way then that, and herded her inside. I'm not sure.

The cinema was black as pitch, its windows covered to keep out the light. Lolo withdrew his phone, hit some buttons, and the screen stayed lit, casting a blue glow over them.

— We missed you, you know. I missed you. Leaving us so quickly, without a word!

Lolo looked away before turning back, locking eyes with Libète. His face was hollowed.

— After my release from prison, I was targeted by Benoit. Blamed along with you for what happened in the election. Forced to hide. But I was a nobody while you became a somebody. I've been hiding all over Port-au-Prince. Struggling to survive.

— Have you been in touch with Davidson? Yves and Wadner?

He wiped away the memory of his childhood friends with a dismissive wave. I don't know where they are or what they're doing. They abandoned me when I was in jail. I want nothing to do with them.

Libète found this unsurprising. But you've been all on your own? What of your family? Other friends?

He arranged some chairs into a row.

— You look . . . terrible, she murmured.

His eyes flashed before he stifled the flame. I'm sick still, wi.

— The *tibèkiloz*?

Lolo coughed as if in reflex to the word. Still TB, he said. But in treatment. Always in treatment.

He walked around the room, testing the metal sheets covering the windows. I may be gone for a while, but I'm coming back. It may be a few hours, maybe not till morning. No one will disturb you here. He reached into his pocket and fished out a bag of peanuts and a square sachet of water. Take this.

— I'm not hungry.

— Good. That's good. But you'll need to eat. He forced them into her hand. I'm sorry that's all I have. There will be more. Later.

— Why are you leaving me?

He bit his lip. I need to get Jak. And I'll be back before long to collect you. I've been in touch with Stephanie Martinette. We'll all be together soon. He picked up his phone and stowed it away. In a moment, the door slid to a close, the chain was replaced, the lock clamped shut.

Collect me?

Plunged into new darkness, Libète shook. She was unable to shake the sense of being laid within a coffin before its lid is nailed into place.

Death. Libète shakes her head. It is ever-present these days.

She looks on Dorsinus's face. His eyes are closed. His clothes are mud-streaked, more so than usual. A long rope is tied around his ankles, its excess coiled near his heels. Four men are there. Jeune, his adult son, and another familiar-looking young man Libète hadn't yet met. The final one is Prosper. Libète cannot look at him, and so studies the dead body lying among the rocks, dirt, and weeds.

— Ladies, no need to come close, Jeune says. Junior, grab the old drunk's ankles, will you? We'll carry him.

Junior, the other man Libète had encountered carrying sugar cane the day before, gestures. He mimes what looks like the unravelling of a knot in midair.

Jeune nods in acknowledgement. Right, he says. Prosper, undo that knot at Dorsinus's feet. Libète cocks her head and looks at Junior, at the others, but they avoid her eyes. Junior's tight-drawn lips and gesturing seem to surprise only her.

— We found him this morning, down there, Jeune proffers, pointing to the nearby ravine. Prosper climbed down with the rope. We dragged him up.

— But how? Magdala chokes out, looking at each of the men in turn, disbelieving.

The mime holds out the bottle. The sweet scent of evaporating kleren fills the air.

— Done in by his drink? she says.

— It looks that way, says the unknown one. Prosper remains quiet.

Libète crosses her arms, holds herself, begins to cry. She knew him but a few days, and yet!

— Cover him then, Magdala says, turning away and shaking her head. Prosper lays the old man's straw hat over his face. She wraps Libète in her arm while her own tears fall. *The stupid old fool*, she spits under her breath. There will have to be a funeral, Magdala says, this time so all can hear. It will be modest, but we will not let him go without. I'll take care of the preparations.

— Who'll pay for that? says the unknown man. Not the funeral society! That's for members only.

Magdala glares at the young man, who shrinks back. If you had a few more years, you *might* actually know what you're talking about! You'd know that when he was here, Mesye Dorsinus gave freely whenever others passed away. And *generously*.

Junior mimes again, this time summoning an invisible string about his neck.

— Ah! Jeune says, patting his son's arm. Of course! What about the old man's fabled gold, huh? We tolerated his boasting for years. The pouch! He reaches for the collar of Dorsinus' shirt and begins feeling underneath it. Where is it?

— Don't disrespect the dead! Magdala snaps. Her eyes burn with new fire, and she swats Jeune hard: he is the one who would see her son hang, who desecrates her old friend's body.

— Even in death the fool robs us, Jeune mutters while holding Magdala at bay. Check his pockets, he orders. Prosper swallows, his eyes bouncing between Magdala and Jeune. He does as Jeune says.

— Don't disrespect the-

— Ay! A *mabouya*! Jeune shouts. There, at your feet!

Libète looks down and lets out a yelp. All leap back, her included. What is that thing? she cries.

Slinking from beneath the corpse was a lizard striped in yellow and black over its brown scales. It moved tentatively, like it too was intoxicated by night and was now forced to confront the astringent day.

— That's a bad sign, Prosper says. A bad, bad sign! Jeune grabs Dorsinus's hat.

— Hey, leave that there! Libète shouts.

Jeune glowers and grabs the lizard with the hat held in his hand. The creature thrashes in his grip, but he takes it and rushes down the hill without another word.

The mime, with sunken, scared eyes, points a trembling finger at the girl. All of them turned to look at Libète, and she shrinks under the weight of their stares. She doesn't understand.

She stormed off.

She had almost blurted *"Fools, all of you!"* but managed to keep the lid on the jar. *This is what I get. I open up, I suffer.*

Libète detected Magdala following her at a distance, but she refused to look over her shoulder. *At least I won't be trapped in this forsaken place much longer.* The thought was little consolation as she trudged on alone.

Libète reached Magdala's home first. She busied herself in the yard feeding the chickens, and Magdala walked past Libète. I must prepare for the service, the woman said sideways, not able to look at the girl. Magdala set to preparing a fire, laying out charcoal beneath her old iron pot.

Libète wanted to cry. What just happened there?

Silence.

— Madanm Magdala, *please*. Tell me.

— It's nothing. Nothing. She said the word a third time. She opened her mouth again, but closed it. Magdala reached for a bundle of dry grasses and laid them alongside the charcoal, lit a match, and let the tinder catch and crinkle and blacken.

— The men believe it is a *baka*.

— A baka?

— A baka.

— Well, what the hell is that?

Magdala looked over her shoulder before speaking in a low voice. It's a dark creature. Used by someone to enrich herself. At the expense of another. In the night, the creature sucks wealth away, stealing it for the owner. Jeune went to kill the lizard properly. To cast it into the dark for good.

Libète rubbed her tired eyes. How?

— Cut it. Send it down a latrine, probably. Magdala stared at her and after a beat, spoke. Was that your baka?

— You really think... you think that I...

— Is it yours?

— No. No!

— Well, we'll know soon enough. Once it's dead, the owner will die too.

— It was a mabouya, Madanm Magdala, a *lizard*. I don't know anything about such business.

— You swear?

— How can you even ask me this?

— How can I not? I've known you two days, Sophia. You show up with Dorsinus. You don't say a word about who you are, where you're from, where you're going. Like some, some *vagabond*. A criminal! And then speaking up in that meeting, like you know what's best for Foche! I heard tell! And now Dorsinus ends up dead, his gold stolen...

Libète stretched out her arms. Search me! Tears fell down her cheeks. Search me, then! I've nothing to hide!

— Then tell me who you are.

— I can't! *I can't!* Please, I beg you, don't ask me that.

— My life is hard here. I've all but lost my only son. All of Foche blames me for what Félix has done. And now my 'niece' has caused Dorsinus's death by witchcraft! I tell you, word has already spread through Foche. Everyone–*everyone*–is wondering whether that creature was yours.

— Then let them think it.

— You are making things difficult for me. Imposib.

Libète went inside to collect her few things. She was still covered in blood from the delivery but had only dirty items to change into. She came back outside. I'll head right back down the mountain, then.

Magdala watched the girl limp off, alone and bedraggled.

The woman's heart cracked.

It ached.

For she *had* searched Libète. She had seen her fullness, her depth, in unguarded moments of both peace and crisis. She knew that the girl couldn't be behind such a dark thing, but the doubt remained. Magdala placed water above the flames. But could she bear to take on the added disfavor from keeping Sophia? After Félix and his stubborn, thieving ways had already taxed her so much?

— Don't go, Sophia, she called. Please don't!

But Libète trudged on. The girl knew the absolute importance of velocity in such departures–direction *and* force–but in truth, in the moment, she knew not where to go.

There is no sense of time in the dark.

Cast into a perpetual twilight in the old cinema in Bwa Nèf, she tries to lie across three chairs pushed together. Deep sleep proves impossible.

Numbness is what she longs for now. The state her ncle existed in for so many years. Floating through the brutal world in a fog. She had snuck beer and kleren before, just tastes, and now longed for the temporary forgetfulness she had not experienced but knew they could bring.

Though hunger grips her, she cannot bring herself to eat. Lolo's food sits before her, just beside her book bag. She feels she doesn't deserve it. *Not a bite.* Is this denial out of penance? Or maybe solidarity with the dead, those who hunger no more? She does not know, for she feels she does not know herself anymore.

There are so many questions she wished Lolo had answered. Where specifically had he been? After the reunion with Jak and Stephanie, where would they all hide? And of course, lurking under it all was the most important question: how did he have insight into Benoit's plotting?

Her mind is so exhausted it cannot do the labor necessary to piece the different fragments together.

The answers matter little to her now, anyway.

Didi is a soul-hollowed husk. Her life and her kindness, vanished.

Since the death of Libète's mother–a memory distant in both time and place–Libète had not felt a hurt like this, that so grasps her insides and registers a dull pain that lingers behind her breastbone. Her tears flow. And they flow. And they flow.

Motes of light showed around the edges of the door. Libète rubbed her eyes, wanting to claw them out to get at the tiredness that seemed to linger just behind. She got up and floated about the room. The light was meager enough that her eyes could adjust to the dark, and she could see hollow shapes, lines, support pillars, and chairs lying around the room. Her mind nearly untethered from her action. There was a hint of madness to her thoughts, and she tugged and stroked her braids as she made the rounds.

She rubbed her eyes, harder now. There was a curious new source of golden light that rose from the center of the floor and poked through the bars her fingers made.

Before her was a new creature made of leaves and bark and branch.

Libète recoiled with such a start that she tumbled backward, falling to the ground. This trick of her mind, this Visitor, lurched toward Libète with the grace of a palm blowing in the wind. Libète saw it had arms and legs affixed to a solid oaken body, with articulated fingers made from twigs, and roots for toes. The light bathing the room bloomed from a hole in the Visitor's chest like a knot in a tree, and the Visitor reached out its hand toward Libète. Everything the light touched turned to flora, and within moments the room resembled a dense rainforest.

Eyes fixed in terror on the Visitor, Libète could see the creature had a shorter body, round, with bold braids made of plaited vines atop her head. It was a startling likeness–she resembled Didi.

Didi. Libète swiped at the air in front of her, an attempt to ward off the approaching Visitor, and she repeated the gesture time and again. Suddenly, holes within the concrete floor formed. The Visitor's face contorted in fearful surprise. Thorned tendrils shot through the crumbling ground and snapped around the Visitor's limbs, bringing her to her hands and knees. Libète tried to back farther away, into the new brush that had claimed the room, but the distance she imposed between them only seemed to give the vines more strength as they wrapped around the Visitor's limbs and crept farther, moving toward the light in the Visitor's chest. When they reached it, they extinguished whatever lay within. The Visitor became immobilized, her ruddied bark frozen in pain even as the tips of her branches reached out to prick Libète's skin, as if to offer a caressing, understanding touch.

Libète screamed.

She was off the ground, rushing to the metal door. Pounding, shouting, *Ed m!* until her voice settled into quiet sobs. *Help me, help me, help me...*

She turned around and the light was gone, the new vegetation vanished as quickly as it had spread. She breathed heavily. The emptiness had returned. She noticed the edges of the door let in faint light.

She screamed and pounded again with a series of futile slaps. At the instant her last slap landed, the door gave a furious shake. She stepped back, marveling at the power in her hands before another pull came, and another. The door was straining against the lock, and Libète wondered if she should hide. Had the police found her? Were they ripping the door off its hinges so they could take her and cast her into more darkness?

She heard muffled voices, and cursing. The door lurched again and she saw there was a hook fixed near one of its hinges. The nearby cement turned to dust that danced in the widening band of light.

And then it happened. With a furious crash, the door shot outward and down but was held hovering at an odd angle by the still-intact lock and chain.

And there, among it all, were Stephanie and Jak, each poking their faces into the open doorway that out led to Impasse Chavannes, Bwa Nèf, and the unknown.

She had walked until she knew she was safely out of Magdala's view–and Foche's. She pushed down thoughts of what would come next like plugging holes in a sinking ship–pills nearly gone, new accusations of theft *and* murder, not a friend in the world, no store of food. The ship already seemed to be taking on water too fast to save it. If she could get away, she'd have to again rely on strangers' hospitality. But would any in this place, on this mountain, on other mountains, give her anything? And if she went elsewhere, might she ever be found again by the friends who she hoped sought her?

She had stowed her few possessions in the crevice before climbing up the sloped rock face to take her current place on a boulder. She slipped her hand in warily at first, and then sneered. A hand caught in here, Jeune had said. Needing severing? She huffed. *Nonsense.* The odds of rock shifting were close to nothing. She extracted her notebook and pen from the crack where she'd hidden them the day prior and pushed her nearly empty bag in deep, so that they were hardly visible.

Atop the boulder half-buried in earth, she looked out on the sprawling land. The dried and distorted pages of the notebook sat in her lap. The pen in her hand began to scrawl furious words. Creating an account. Recording her experiences, all of the secrets, all of the revelations. Capturing it in writing made it finite and somehow validated the pain and loss.

Seeing her experience reduced to a set of letters put in a particular order on a physical page gave her pause. What a difference between the endless sheet of white and those few, blue strokes of her pen! The vastness of her hopes and likes and vanities and hardship reduced to a serif here, a loop there, another capital letter starting another chain of meaning of which she was master.

She couldn't help but look to the last page, to see if it was still there. A set of digits, laid down months before, plucked from Jak's memory. She had reversed their true order–a last-ditch effort in case they were discovered. If only she had never encountered the Numbers at all. Would everything she had suffered these past months have been prevented? She could never know.

Her pen gave out while crossing a *T*, and she cursed. She spun its point on the page until a blue spiral appeared and she could continue committing her thoughts to writing.

— What are you doing?

The sound–like a man's voice, but not quite–made her jump. She snapped the notebook to a close and nearly flung the pen away, like she was caught in an unseemly act. The figure was set against the Sun, so it took Libète a moment to register who stood before her. He was young, maybe her own age, and wore an orange tank top that was tattered and dirty.

Félix.

He slid down the hill from behind to look at her squarely. You can write?

She said nothing.

— Read?

Still nothing. She glared at him, not letting a single gap in her armor show.

— You're from elsewhere. It was not a question, but a declaration. His hair was overgrown, and was smattered with twigs and other bits of plant detritus. He had a smell too–the scent of labor that hovered over everything here.

— Leave me be.

— What's your name?

— What's *your* name? she asked, even though she knew it.

He shifted his weight. I saw you. From far away. You looked like you might be crying.

— I was not.

— I know that now. *Ou bezwen yon bagay?* You need something? he asked.

— Non.

— But you look like you need something.

— You look like *you* need a bath.

— You're the one coated, in, what? Is that blood? Are you hurt? His eyes widened. Did *you* hurt someone?

This was the wrong thing to say. She stood up, wiped her pants of dirt, and started down the hill, clasping her notebook to her chest. Leave me alone.

— I'm sorry.

— I don't care.

— My name's Félix.

— I know who you are.

— You look like you need something, he repeated.

— Why would I want anything from a thief?

His jaw clenched. He looked down in shame, but up in anger. Fine! He spun, and stomped off and away.

She felt a tremendous frustration claim her, seethe out of her. *Stupid ... idiotic ... bah!* He had made it a hundred yards when her stomach gurgled its discontent. She *did* need something. Many things. She returned to the crevice and stuffed her notebook in safely, her pen stowed in its wire spirals. She swapped it for her bag and began to follow Félix.

He didn't notice at first, or didn't seem to. She trailed behind much of the path while he moved at a steady clip back toward the decrepit fortress. He was already up many of the trail's switchbacks and the faint incline to its first terrace and collapsed wall when she was certain he realized she was there. She wanted to flee, but instead kept her head to the ground until she stood about twenty feet away. He stared blankly.

— Because, she murmured, a bit woozy from the exertion. I do . . .

The last bit was unintelligible, whispered under her breath.

— What's that?

— I do need something, she said.

— So you insult the giver, eh? Is that your way? Repaying kindness with rudeness?

She looked him in the eye. Her shame had limits, and she would have none of this. What does someone who steals from his people deserve but disdain?

— Not all thefts are the same.

— Says the thief.

— Look, I don't need some blan lecturing me.

— *You're calling* me *a blan?*

— You're not from here. Your accent is different. He crossed his arms. I hardly know anyone from Foche who can read.

— It's nothing special.

He rolled his eyes.

— You want to read? A thought sparked.

— Of course.

— How badly?

He shrugged. Badly.

— A trade then. You give me some food, a place to stay. Just for a few days. I'll be leaving soon. I can teach you until then.

He spit. I have some food–*not stolen*, he snapped, prematurely answering her questioning thought. And there is a spring, not far, for drinking. Washing. A small one I found. I couldn't steal from that.

She lifted her chin. And what about a place to lay my head? Or have you claimed the whole fort?

He held out his hand with a grand sweep. Many rooms, he said. No roofs. Take your pick, as long as it's far away from mine.

— I told you I won't be staying long.
— Good. Because I wouldn't let you.
— Dakò.
— Dakò, then.
She moved in the direction of the spring and they glared at each other all the while. Let me get some of this blood off, she said. And lay my head down. But make no mistake. We are not friends. We are not acquaintances. We are *nothing*. You watch yourself. Touch my things, touch me, and *mwen pral gen san* ou *sou rad mwen an*. I'll be wearing *your* blood.

The door falls to the ground.
Attached to it is a hook, and to that a rope, and to that a car.
— *Vini*, Stephanie says, worry making her voice shake. She grabs Libète's forearm. We need to go.
Jak has his arm around Libète as they move down the road toward Tòti, the idling green Land Rover. Uncle sits at its wheel. Neighbors disturbed by the commotion pry.
Libète is at the vehicle now. Wait, she says. Wait! *It is all too much, simply too, too much.* Her mind stalls as it tries to shift to a higher gear. Uncle, what's happening?
He is downcast. I let you be stolen again, he said, each word weighted with shame.
— Stolen? But, by whom? Benoit? Hold on, let go of me. She rips her arms from Jak and Stephanie. My things! They're still inside!
— Jak, go grab them! Steffi gave a flick of her neck and Jak rushed to the cinema and came back with her book bag.

— Where's Lolo? We can't leave him! What's happening? Libète is screaming now. Stolen by who? *By who?*

Jak pulls himself around, grabs her by the sides of her face, locks eyes with her. Things are no good right now. No good at all. But they will be.

— But Lolo–

There is something in his look, the shape of his mouth, his face turned cold. It is something she does not understand. He can say no more, not now, not yet. He grabs her hand, fingers locking with hers, and he is dragging her into the vehicle, but she cannot go with him. Not like this.

Uncle lifts her against her will, puts her inside. She resists these tides beyond her control. By whom? *By whom?* None will fill her question's gaping space with the answer she knows yet refuses to believe.

Thrown in the seat. Buckled tight. Jak's head in hands. Steffi in the driver's seat. Her eyes in the rearview mirror. So very terrified.

There is someone there.

Libète turned, and at first noticed nothing. The machin's burst of speed made the neighbors pouring into the street appear as a blur. But then she saw. There was Uncle, who stayed behind, but another person who rounded a corner, running madly after them, arm outstretched, fingers grasping for her.

Lolo!

He was yelling and shouting and screaming until her ncle caught him and threw him to the ground and the people encircled him.

She cried out, for it was all too much, simply too, too much.

She awakes, looking up into the wide blue sky.

Félix did not lie-the old fort did not have any roofs. A bird cuts through the open air. She envies its speed, its grace, its freedom.

She lies on a bed of gravel and weeds, her head rested on her bag of meager possessions. Stones stacked on stones, the fort's walls reach high. There is a bowl next to her head, full of desiccating rice. Her stomach shouts. She scoops it up barehanded, devouring the stuff. Exhaling deeply, her most acute pangs subside. The insufferable gloom returns. *How foolish to think it might end. That suffering might not cloud every little thing, every single moment . . .*

Her mind travels to innocent days. *Not innocent days*, she decides–that would be too early, before she could think and remember. More like ignorant days. Of not knowing the darkness of human hearts and the hopelessness that permeates everything.

The ignorant days were those at the St. Francis school. Of visits to art galleries. Dinners with poets and artists. Holidays spent with Stephanie and Jak in Cap-Haïtien, Jacmel, Les Cayes. Days of leisure and learning. To read a book by Jacques Roumain or Marie Vieux Chauvet! To listen to music, Martha Jean-Claude, Boukman Eksperyans, even Sweet Micky! She hated being cut off from culture. From knowledge. Memories of such pleasures caused dull and persistent pain, like that of a missing limb.

How were Jak and Stephanie these days? She hadn't the slightest idea. Had their plans too been so easily cast aside by Fate? She longed to see them, to laugh with them, to dream of a brighter future for her and her poor countrymen.

She saddened at the thought. Libète had believed she'd moved beyond recurring hunger pangs, dirty water, needless sickness. Not that she had become better than to suffer those things; she had been rescued from them, as all those who were in misery ought to be. No, Libète was still a product of where she grew up: birthed in the backwater La Gonâve and forged in the crucible of Cité Soleil. Foche's poverty was still a world she could understand and pass through. But it was no longer *her* world. It was foreign, as were its customs and its people.

People like Magdala. Like Dorsinus.

Magdala was a kindred spirit. Libète knew that. There was something achingly familiar in her way, an essence that drew them together. Did she remind Libète of her own mother? Of Stephanie? Not quite. Magdala had a gravity that was foreign to her mother's soul, and a grating edge that Stephanie lacked. Though Libète did not know Magdala's past, that there was no husband, no immediate family besides Félix, spoke much.

She thought of poor Dorsinus. Ridiculous as he was, there was kindness there, and admirable conviction. Indeed, if not for him she might have withered away on the river's banks, or been found by those dogs and their masters. She shuddered at the thought, and shuddered again. To be suspected for Dorsinus's death was another blow coming just months after her name had been smeared with the loss of poor Didi.

Libète sat up, wiping sleep from her eyes. Based on the Sun's progress, she had slept for hours.

She poked her head out of her staked claim, a small room on the fort's eastern side. Félix was nowhere. She decided to explore the ruins.

She felt like an infiltrator, stepping back two hundred years to the French outpost in its heyday, and then in its demise. She pictured Frenchmen trembling as Maroons–self-freed slaves–overcame their defenses. The rumbling cannonade, the smell of spent gunpowder and smoke making the oppressors cough and hack even as they were cut down by machetes and pikes. She found Félix's blade leaning against a wall and picked it up, feeling its heft in her hand. Clenching her jaw, she imagined plunging her own cutlass into an enemy as he begged for mercy in a foreign tongue, gurgling as blood filled his mouth, as his body slumped to the ground. She imagined what it was to experience killing someone hated and how good it might feel...

— You're up.

She jumped, blinked twice. Sucked out of her imaginary world of death and revenge and back into waking life. She laid the blade down and said nothing while straightening her shirt's creases.

— You were staying at my mother's, no? With Dorsinus?

She looked him straight in the eye.

— Why did she take you in?

Her eyes did not waver.

— Why did she put you out?

— What did you spend the money on? she asked.

— Excuse me?

— There's not much to show for it. Not much at all.

It was his turn to be quiet.

— Let's make another deal, she said. How about you don't ask me about anything from before today, and I do the same. We can keep things simple.

— I see why she kicked you out, he grumbled.

— *What was that?*

— Whatever. He scratched his head then massaged the bridge of his nose. Can we start the lessons? I want to see the benefit of my bargain. Before you disappear, having eaten all my food.

Inertia kept her still. She finally moved to grab a stick from the ground–one firm and small–to scratch the earth. Have any water?

— A bucket, filled from the spring. He pointed to it in a corner. She picked it up and threw it on a patch of loose dirt.

— Hey! That's where I sleep!

— Oh. She knelt down and began stirring the new, soupy mud. This is where we'll write.

— Why not your notebook?

She didn't answer. She shaped the first letters of the alphabet in the ground.

Félix inhaled deeply. Dorsinus told me you were a *kesyon*. A big, open question.

She cringed at the man's name. He spoke with you?
— He spoke. And unlike some, listened. He said he'd come again today.
— You don't... you haven't heard?
He shook his head.
— Dorsinus–he–*died*. Last night.
Félix twitched. Shock at the news was writ large across his face. That's not possible. I saw him yesterday evening. He told me all about the sentenci–the meeting, and about the plan to take our land. It's not possible.
— All I know is what I saw, Libète replied. This morning, early on, I helped your mother deliver a baby for a woman in the lakou down the road, the one called Délira, and–
— Is the baby okay?
— *Yes.* She let the word stretch and Félix's body loosened. Libète was disturbed by how quickly Dorsinus seemed forgotten. The baby–Delivrans, she named him–is all right, Mesye *Concerned-for-His-Dead-Friend*. You'll need more focus to learn to read, she grumbled.
He tucked away his relief and gave a violent wave, becoming sullen. You're an outsider. You don't understand. He sat uncomfortably, unsure how to handle the disparate feelings brought by news of Delivrans and Dorsinus, life and death.
— Dorsinus fell. Libète blinked away new tears. He was drunk–his bottle was emptied out, and he tumbled down the slope, down into the crops. *Kou kase.* Broken neck.
— Jezi.
— Don't take the Lord's name in vain. He looked at her blankly. She was surprised she said it, a reflex from another time. Félix stood and walked one direction before stopping, like he forgot why he got up. He walked behind a nearby wall.
— Where are you going? Huh? I've got to teach you, remember? 'Benefit of your bargain?'

No reply came. She tapped the ground impatiently, letting the beat slow. She looked over her shoulder and bit her lip.

She crept toward the wall, not making a sound, and inclined her head to listen. She heard sniffling. Crying. The two were sitting on opposite sides of the wall, facing opposite directions. She was letting her insides show again, letting them seep out on display for the world to see. This scared her tremendously.

— They're blaming me, Libète said into the open air. The people who found him. They think I did it. They saw some stupid bèt, a big lizard, crawling by Dorsinus, and said it's a baka or some such thing. Stupid superstition. Everyone thinks I planted it, that I was behind his death . . .

She waited for him to ask the natural question, the one she surely would have asked him if their roles reversed. The question did not come.

— Let's go.

— What?

— There will be a funeral. I need to go. We need to go.

She huffed. The pair we are? You think a thief and a murderer will be welcome down there?

— Let them think what they will. It's time, he said.

And that is all he said.

IN MEMORIAM

Mò pa jije.
The dead aren't judged.

— Tell me what's going on.
Life along Carrefour streams past. Vendors hawk wares. Hundreds of oblivious passersby go about their lives, unaware of what Libète and Jak and Stephanie have escaped. Stephanie pulls over after a motorcycle seems to linger behind their vehicle a bit too long. She watches it pass, only to resume her course along the road a moment later.
— Answer me! Libète shouts.
Neither Stephanie nor Jak will speak.
Unbelievable. She punches Jak. What are you not telling me?
But he is nearly catatonic. His eyes are hollow and his expression void, like he's lost the ability to detect shapes and faces and see things for what they are.
— Libète. You must calm down, Stephanie says.
— *Tell me what's happened, then!*
— Libète, Stephanie said definitively. Shut up.
She crossed her arms. I . . . will . . . *not!* Why did we run from Lolo? Stephanie glared at Jak, but the boy remained distant.
— Tell her, Jak.

But he couldn't. He gave Libète a pleading look, which only maddened the girl further. She unbuckled her belt and slid her hand along the door's release. She punched it open, nearly clipping a dirt bike trying to pass. I'll jump out of this damn machin if you don't start talking! I'm not staying with you two if you keep secrets from me like everybody else! Her voice was tremulous, and her whole body shook.

— Calm down!

— Lolo is no friend, Jak blurted. No friend of mine, no friend of yours.

She let the door hover open and the road streaked past below. What?

— I never told you, Libète. I never told . . .

— Told me *what?*

— *It brings back too much* . . . Jak grabbed his head and dug his fingers into his temples.

— Jak, if you don't tell me what you mean, I will kill you. I mean it. I will take my fist and put it straight through your chest.

— Let him talk, Libète. Give him space.

— Claire and Gaspar, Jak choked. Lolo knew. Lolo helped.

— Helped what?

— Kill them.

— What the hell are you saying? He was–*is*–innocent!

Jak was crying. That's an untruth. One I let you, *wanted you*, to believe. To keep you *safe*.

Libète's teeth were digging into each other, top row against bottom. Pain shot from her gums. You're lying.

— He didn't put the knife into Claire, didn't strangle Gaspar. But he led them to the knife, and strangling hands. So another could do the job.

— You're lying, she repeated.

— Lolo tripped up. In the hospital. The last time you or I saw him. He told two versions of his story. Two versions. And I caught him in the lie. He led them there for money, and revenge. Maybe not knowing all that would happen, but still knowing harm would come. I told him to leave, to never come back, or I would turn him in. And he threatened me.

A string of curses burst from Libète's lips. No. No, no, *no*.
— It's the truth. I promise. I swear. I promise . . .
— He lied to me. *You* lied to me?
— To keep you safe, Libète. To protect you.
— Oh God! With the door slammed closed, she laid her head against the window's hot glass and wept.

Dorsinus's body lays there, clad in white.

Magdala's hospitality was without end. Though drained from the delivery of Délira's child, she had accepted the responsibility of dressing her friend's corpse, bathing him, perfuming him. Her one-room home is lit with candles, and linens hang from roof to wall. Magdala stands within the doorway, greeting those who come and blessing those who leave.

When a member of the Kè Ini Gwoupman Peyizan dies, there is a funeral. This is the way it has been, and will be. When life strips one of dignity, in death there should be no humiliation. The community makes sure of that.

But was Dorsinus a member of the Gwoupman? Technically, no. But Magdala had convinced everyone. Dorsinus had drifted through Foche enough, sweat alongside enough people in the fields, offered a bottle of rum here and there, shared his take from his meager mining on extravagant celebrations. The majority of people in Foche would not disrespect him in his passing.

Dorsinus's circumstances made the arrangements as easy as they could be. He had no kin in the area, so there would be no traveling mourners to prolong the ceremonies. The customary burden of washing all of his linens and clothes to prevent his spirit from lingering was mitigated by the fact he had just two sets of clothes and no bed to call his own. But what of the burial? He can be laid down in my family's plot, Madanm Janel had offered. The itinerant preacher and undertaker, Reginald Honorat, had traveled up with his own donkeys from down the mountain, dragging a coffin behind him on his wagon. He happened to have a coffin ready that would accommodate the old man—with only the slightest bit of bodily manipulation, he said.

Members of Foche brought firewood, rice, and rum, and helped tend to the cooking that greeted the body under the watch of the late-afternoon Sun. Reginald lingered in the room in his frayed suit, his skin sallow, leading the ceremony known as *nevenn*. He sat on a stool with the open pages of a yellowed prayer book. Memorized scripture and hymns slid out of his mouth. The only openly nonplussed members of the community were a trio of professional mourners; Magdala had refused to pay for their tears and chorus of wails. Dorsinus wouldn't have cared one bit, she said. He would have called it a waste.

By the time Libète and Félix came down the hill, the crowd had grown. The Gwoupman's music brigade was present and accounted for. They chose more sedate selections than their usual boisterous drumming and trumpeting, meant to spur on members' toil in the fields.

When eyes first fell on Félix, there was pointing. He ignored it. Two broke off from the throng as if to intercept him and Libète. One was Prosper, and the other the young man who had found Dorsinus.

Félix raised his fists. Let me pass.

— You don't deserve to be here, said the young man.

— It's for your own good, Prosper added. He cocked his head and took note of Libète, who stood crossly a few paces back. Félix turned toward Libète, appearing to relent. With their guards down, Félix crashed through the pair and proceeded down the hill. Both youths' tempers flared, but Libète stepped between them, a hand for each of their shoulders.

— Not now, Prosper. Take it up with him later.

— You shouldn't be seen with him, he muttered. It's not helping your reputation. He said this earnestly.

— Why, Prosper, do you even care about my reputation? She left them and proceeded down among the assembly. The drummers stopped. Félix didn't.

— Manmam, he said, as he entered his old home. Magdala looked down. Libète nodded to her, and in return got a furtive glance. The others in her house slid along the walls and out. Only the preacher, the boy, the girl, and the dead remained.

— Here to pay your respects? Reginald asked.

Félix nodded, and wiped his eyes with his forearm. He took in the scene: a lit lamp beneath the bed to guide Dorsinus's spirit on his journey; a cup of holy water residing beside alcohol offered for the Vodou spirits; a wooden crucifix; and as an emblem of Dorsinus's work, his worn pick axe. Normally the ceremony followed the burial, but they seemed to be compressing the schedule for convenience. Libète took a deep breath, and a mélange of smells filled her nostrils–lavender, vetiver, soap, and rot. She coughed, fist-to-mouth, followed by more coughing, uncontrollable coughing. She looked from person to person, losing so much air she felt she might suffocate.

— Are you all right?

— Need some water?

She held up her other hand. And then, by sheer resolve, stopped.

Doing so made her throat rough. Her reddened eyes stung. Félix watched her warily before turning to kneel at Dorsinus's feet. He murmured a few words, maybe a prayer. And with that, he was back up, ready to rush out the doorway and retreat. But he couldn't so easily.

Outside he was met by a wall made of people, built high with crossed arms and hard stares. Even the children scorned him.

Félix stepped forward, expecting the wall to part, but it was not to be so easily breached. Libète held her breath. *This won't end well.*

— Please. Félix's voice was almost inaudible. I came to say good-bye. That's all.

A man spoke. You're not supposed to be here.

— Wi. Not during the day, said a woman.

— How about you finally tell us where the money is while you're here? said another.

— I have nothing to say, he replied.

Gasps. The wall could breathe as well as watch.

Jeune stepped forward. You little prick. He had a small cup in his hand, its contents sloshing about. In a flash, it was in Félix's face–rum, the smell unmistakable–and the older man slunk back. Prosper reached for a stone near the open stove and hefted it, ready to throw.

Libète felt a sudden pull at her torso, like an invisible rope looped around her, yanking her forward. She found herself between the boy and the stone and the wall, her mouth agape.

— This is not the way, she blurted.

— Who's this girl again?

— Who does she think she is?

— Someone get her out of the way.

— You can take care of her! I've got another rock ready for him.

— All I wanted was to help carry him, Félix hollered. To help bury him. I owed him that.

Prosper cocked his arm. Libète cringed, waiting for the inevitable *thud* to knock her down, or out.

— The girl is right. A form stepped in front of her, eclipsing the Sun.

Janel!

— The boy's debt has been paid.

— What are you talking about? Jeune slurred.

— The stolen money has been repaid. In full.

— By who? Prosper said, bewildered.

Janel inclined her head toward the home. The one inside.

The wall began to buckle.

— Between our meeting and his dying, Dorsinus came to me. 'To correct Félix's mistake,' he said.

— He ransomed the boy?

— He did.

— Félix still owes us. The boy has to pay us back himself!

Janel shook her head. He doesn't, she said. Dorsinus wanted to provide a way to heal the community, and he did.

A yelp erupted. Without looking, Libète knew it was Magdala.

— Félix, you may again walk among us during the day, Janel said. Félix rocked; pivoted one way, and then the other. He began trembling, overcome, and took off in a run back toward the fort.

— But that's not how it works! shouted another.

— It was Dorsinus's wish, Janel said. His last wish, it turns out. We'll not go back on it.

— It's that girl's fault, Jeune shouted, spittle spraying from his lips.

Libète was horrified. It's not true . . .

— I'm not afraid to say it! She cast a spell over Dorsinus, took his other money, and his life. Made him do it. You can see it–

— I don't know anything about anything! Libète cried out. Please, believe me!

— The lizard, the lizard, I told you all about the baka! She's in league with the boy, abetting his thieving!

Libète shook her head. Walking away was all she could do.

The wall, though it had buckled, still stood strong.

Stephanie hates secrets.

She hates keeping them and hates having them kept from her. They are her avowed enemy.

Their drive continues. Before long, Port-au-Prince gives way to verdant Gressier, Léogâne, and the winding mountain pass that takes them through trees and crops and rock before reaching the downward slope of the bluff's opposite side.

At least we're getting closer, she thinks.

Checking her mirrors again–she hadn't been able to stop since key met ignition–she saw Jak's long-faced reflection in the window and that Libète was still asleep. His eyes were dull, ignoring the strength of the Sun as it reached its zenith.

Memory returns her to the day she first met the girl.

Live radio was a thrill, one of the most ecstatic things Stephanie had experienced. Every visit was drenched in adrenaline. She had just turned off the microphone that day, removed her headphones, and let her heart return to its regular patter before stepping outside to find the bony girl in her ratty clothes, hiding in the wall's shade. This girl, whispered a guard, she asked for the poet.

If I only knew then what she brought with her . . .

It was a horrible thought. Stephanie chastises herself for her invisible crime. Libète was a herald of profound good–and ill. Coming on the scene to forever burst any sense of comfort and order and regularity. *Like a child,* Stephanie supposed. *Like a daughter.*

Flattered, intrigued, and basking in the radio show's afterglow, Stephanie stepped forward. I am the poet, she said.

Poetry. Her chosen trade was taking what was naught and turning it into what was. Lines of unexpected beauty, lightness, and depth, conjured from the nothingness of an empty page. She could make ink dance into any form: a caressing feather or a deadly bullet. She wrote. She wrote.

With her upbringing, it was impossible for the poetic not to become the prophetic. Gerry, an old school friend and current host of one of

Haiti's most prominent talk shows, had given her some of her most-treasured gifts: a platform and a megaphone. She summoned lines of verse for his show like she never had before. Such lofty ideas passed from her head, transmuted in her heart, before escaping through her fingertips or mouth.

The girl. That bony girl was a paradox. Timid, but with hard eyes. Named Libète–*liberty*–but so clearly enslaved by some idea or obligation.

At first the girl spoke only in questions:

Do you have a father?
Do you know your true father?
Do you want to know him?
And Stephanie answered.
— Yes, I have a father.

After her mother was killed and her father Elize fled, she had been taken in by Moïse and Cecilia Martinette. In Moïse's home, no societal ill escaped labeling, registration, or cataloging. He had seen too much speech stifled, too many generations wiped away by poverty, too many friends killed. Privilege has to be spent, Moïse would say, a favorite aphorism. He was a beloved professor, a public intellectual. When the military junta had finally laid down its power in the late 1980s–really just scattering for a bit before a quick return, like vultures around roadkill as a car approaches–Moïse was quick to speak out. After the wave of democratic revolution ridden by President Aristide, Moïse had considered entering into politics–many encouraged him–but Aristide's first ouster, only a year after, spoiled any appetite to become a cog in *le système*, as he derisively dismissed the powers that be.

Cecilia died in a car accident when Steffi was ten, twenty-one years ago. Her second mother was warm and loving and far too young to perish.

Stephanie's relationships with her adoptive siblings were hardly conventional. Laurent was always an enigma to her. When she was taken in and adopted at age five, he was already fifteen. He was a recluse even then, and spoke to her very little. Moïse had another daughter, Ingrid, even older than the boy. She had traveled to the US for university and become an entrenched member of the *dyaspora*. As far as Ingrid was concerned, planes traveled one direction only: Port-au-Prince to Brooklyn. Stephanie and Ingrid had never even met face to face, as she was at university in New York when Stephanie entered the Martinette home. There remained only enmity between them. No one enjoyed being replaced by a prettier orphan–a do-over for her parents to raise. Only when Stephanie was a graduate herself, little-known but already well regarded by Haitian society, particularly the progressive segment, did Laurent begin to interact with her. Laurent traveled to the US, to the University of Wisconsin, to obtain his doctorate in sociology. Despite an offered teaching fellowship in the US, he returned to Haiti. A spot at the university opened up, as Moïse always explained it, and so Laurent filled it. Moïse would never admit to nepotism in the arrangement. When asked why he returned from the US, Laurent always answered the same way: too cold.

As in public, Moïse loomed large at home. Too large, maybe. His convictions about every facet of life came with a temper: the same one that could righteously rage against social ills could not be bottled and capped so easily. Attempts to do so saw him retreat into hardness and depression. Cecilia had learned to leave him be, until some coup at work or in national politics could rouse him. It was a terrible cycle, only worsened after Cecilia's premature death. And so he took much pleasure in Stephanie, at her growth, her keen mind, and her inquisitive spirit. He called her his *Ti Bon Anj*, his good little angel. She lived to lift his spirits, probably the reason why she had chosen a life of letters herself. Moïse's support–financial and parental–sustained Steffi and made that life of abstraction possible. In his advancing years, he needed further care too. How could the daughter–with all of her needs assumed through adoption–not take on the responsibility of caring for the adopted father?

The bony girl asked her second question, and Stephanie answered: I do not know my true father.

It was fact. She hardly remembered his name; this may have been willful. Moïse at first had spoken of Elize and his wife, Fleur, often, always with great affection. That was when Moïse believed Elize, reeling from the murder of his wife, would soon return from his travels.

After one week away: "Your father needs some time."

After one month: "He says he'll return once it's safe for him."

After one year:

Nothing. A gap. The man called Elize and all he represented became a fiction. He hovered in streaks of memory, like a character encountered in a novel read in one's youth: a musk here, the glint of his cufflinks, a brow furrowed as he labored over his words. Her mother was the same way. Memories of her touch and a few salvaged photographs kept her more than just a wisp of a name.

— Do I *want* to know him? Stephanie echoed back the young girl's third question. Categorically, definitively, unequivocally–*no*. She thought her answer was clearly stated.

And yet, the girl pleaded. It's not what you think, Libète had said. Elize regretted it all. He wanted to be good, but bad dwelt in his body. He wanted to find her, but guilt kept him away. And now, his body was failing. He was dying.

And yet, Stephanie ignored the pleas. Despite an invitation to visit Elize in a hospital bed in Cité Soleil, Stephanie left the radio station under the girl-named-Liberty's watchful eyes, never expecting to see her again.

It took her a night and a day and a night to decide. She did not tell Moïse about Libète, nor asked him about whether to abandon the father who abandoned her. Meanwhile, news broke in the run-up to national elections about the arrest of senatorial candidate and man of industry Jean-Pierre Benoit. The dramatic video from the arrest ran on a loop over those few days, and there, on the margins of the scene, was the bony girl who accused him. The same girl who had met her at the radio station two days before. It then came as a throwaway line in the news coverage: the small girl was in the hospital, cut down by a bullet after intervening in a shoot-out. Such stories of injured innocents poured out of Cité Soleil all the time. But this one had a face and a name that stuck.

Libète.

Stephanie followed the rainwater's paths down, down, down. She drove to the hospital in her Land Rover the next day, leaving her paradisiacal home in the green hills of Boutilier. She slid down the winding roads, leaving safety and peace and security to enter the dusty, Sun-drenched buzzing of Cité Soleil.

She had passed through Cité Soleil before, but always with four tires and a foot and a half of air between her and it, never putting sole to earth. The hypocrisy of her words–Solidarity! Justice!–so publicly broadcast while she lived a relatively sheltered life made her cringe.

Her true father. And the girl named Liberty.

Her mind about God was never settled. But Fate? Fate was something she was certain of, found incontrovertible. Original sin chipped away at some sense of justice of hers, like she and all of the human family were set up to fail from the start. She was more comfortable with the small *g* type, or with no deity at all. Life's drama unfolding as a narrative, however, made sense to her writer's mind, and her encounter with Elize changed her. Reconciliation did that. He passed away two days later.

He was gone, but with his passing she was left with not one, but two new relationships.

Two abandoned children. Two adrift children. Two remarkable children.

And now Stephanie, with the example of Moïse and Cecilia and the monumental burden Fate had placed on her, had to take a gamble of her own. To leap from a life of letters to one of flesh and blood.

Guardianship. At age thirty-two. Of two near-teenagers. She could almost see Fate's cosmic pen as it inked the bonds meant to tie them together.

Over three years had passed since that day.

She looks again on the girl in her backseat, held in the safety of slumber.

If I could go back and do things differently...

If I could prevent what is coming to you and Jak, what has already arrived, I would.

I hope you can see this. What I'm giving–willing to give–for you both.

I hope you can see.

— Is that the ocean? the girl asks. Libète is awake.

— It is, my dear. It is.

• • •

Libète sat in quiet the rest of the way.

The others did not trespass against the silence. There was no need. Libète now knew where they were going. She held her tongue as an act of protest. Answers could come later.

When Tòti went off the main road through a seaside city, it passed down a small lane lined with private residences perched along the water. Libète took in its lazy airs, its color, and sunny disposition. They had entered Jacmel, and its beauty made Libète feel sick.

Every other retreat to the Martinettes' home here had been joyous. Time to wade in the water, play table tennis, watch films, enjoy fast Internet access, sip sodas, slip out in the evenings to eat griot and fried plantains and ice cream at the restaurant just down the road. She already had memories from the place to fill stacks of photo albums.

As they idled outside the home's compound, Jak hopped out with a key given by Stephanie and drew back the entry gate. He walked up to the villa's front door as Stephanie pulled Tòti inside. It rocked to a stop on the chunky white gravel laid in a loop in front of the home. Stephanie and Jak unpacked the vehicle as Libète stayed in her seat, belt still buckled, as if nothing had changed. They went inside.

That's it. She finally relented after a few minutes. Without air conditioning, the SUV was an oven.

She rubbed her eyes and wiped her brow. What would her approach be?

Stay silent? She sighed. That wasn't sustainable. Besides, there was too much she wanted to know. Remonstrations couldn't be made and apologies accepted if she bit her tongue.

Start talking again? But that would be too premature; simply too soon.

Only speak in single words? That was good. A happy medium.

She cast off her sandals in the cavernous entryway by habit, rounding the corner into the main living room.

— Shit! she shouted. What's *he* doing here?

It helped nothing that at the dining table sat Stephanie, Jak, and the object of her new dismay, Laurent.

Félix and Libète watch from far off as Dorsinus is sealed away and the last nails driven in his coffin. The Sun chooses to bathe the funeral in orange. Six young men hoist the coffin and carry it at a near-jog to the funerary plot. The people of Foche make a serpentine column that slithers along the mountain trails. Libète and Félix make up its flagging tail.

She noticed Félix's hands open and close unconsciously, as if he itched to take part in bearing Dorsinus's body. The coffin moved forward, back, dipped, and spun around as the young men sang and chanted.

— What are they doing? Libète asked.

He looked at her as if she should know. Shaking him up, he said. Confusing his spirit. So he won't return.

She nodded, feigning understanding. Of course, she said.

The body was laid in the ground and the preacher Reginald said a few more words. There were some tears, though they were few.

The pair still gave a wide berth to the mourners who were now a coiled snake. Félix shook silently. Libète thought of giving him a comforting pat, but decided against it.

A string of people spoke, and the two were just close enough to hear their words. They shared remembrances about the man: his stories, his "blindness," his kindness, his scheming and dealing, his living and dying. Magdala went last.

— Much has been said of this person we all know, but I see now – she exhaled – we did not *know* him. Say what you will, we did not *understand* him. But his time is done. She turned to address the corpse. Dorsinus, you are dead. You gave much to many. But we owe you nothing more. Not a thing! So don't you stick around. Don't you settle here. You were always happier wandering these mountains. Seeking your fortune. Chasing love and not finding it. Preaching in between. So go. Maybe now, with new eyes, you can go and do whatever you want. We thank you, but we don't want you.

Those assembled each took a handful of dirt and, in turn, tossed it on the coffin buried just deep enough in the ground to satisfy custom. And then the snake of people unwound itself and slipped back toward Foche as orange light gave way to purple.

— Let's do our part, Libète said.

She headed down alone as the two diggers began undoing their earlier labor. Toes at the precipice, she stooped and picked up a handful of dirt. She hesitated. She thought of bodies of friends laid bare on the ground, to whom she'd never been able to say good-bye. She let the coarse dirt slip from her palm and fall through her fingers' sieve.

Félix still stood off. She beckoned, wiping her hands off. The diggers looked at him. He shook his head.

— You make no sense, she said.

She walked past him. Félix stared at the hole for a minute longer before turning to follow her back over the hills, back to Foche, back toward his fortress, and into falling night.

— I'm not staying in the same house as *him*. I don't care who's chasing us.

Stephanie spoke. Libète, that's a foolish thing to say. The girl's eyes flashed. Please, Stephanie said. Do this for me.

— Do *what*, Steffi? You've not explained a single thing!

— I don't blame you, Libète, Laurent said. If it helps, I'm just as unhappy to see you.

Libète rolled her eyes. Why are we even here?

— You're in danger, if it wasn't obvious. On all sides. We looked the other way for too long.

— Who? Who? Phantoms? *Lougawou yo*? It's bad enough you don't even know from whom we're running!

— It's still not clear. Benoit is the obvious threat. But there may be others.

Libète sneered.

— We only know what we know: harm comes to everyone around you. *Everyone.* So shut your mouth.

Stephanie had never spoken to her like this before. *And I've never spoken to her like this.*

Libète kicked a chair out from under the table, plopped down, and crossed her arms.

— The studio was broken into.

— You told me that.

— But Gerry...

Stephanie dabbed at her eyes. He was killed yesterday, she said softly. In his home. Beaten and left to die.

— I'm... sorry.

— The knife attack at the station. Didi's poisoning.

— And your kidnapping by Lolo, Jak added. We can't forget that.

— Lolo was trying to *protect* me, she snapped. He left the note warning me.

— Lolo was trying to trap and kill you, Stephanie said.

— How do you know?

— I know.

— So tell me, then!

Stephanie shook her head. I can't. Not yet.

— Jak, you then. Tell me what she knows.

— I don't know either. *Mwen gen konfyans nan li.* I'm trusting what she says.

— You too, Jak?

He looked hurt as he sat at the wooden table. He slumped as he traced the tabletop's grain with his fingertip.

Stephanie spoke. You can be dead, wanted for murder, or both. It seems they are content every which way.

— So Lolo was trying to kill me, huh? With what? She reached into her bag. Poisoned peanuts?

She held a handful up to her mouth. You tell me what you know, or I'll eat. I'll show you this is ridiculous.

Jak touched her shoulder. Please. Stop.

Laurent lunged at Libète and ripped the food from her hands. He threw it out an open window.

— You stupid, stupid girl!

Libète shrieked. How *dare* you!

He looked at Stephanie dumbstruck. You bring an imbecile like this into my house? I didn't know I was signing up for a suicide watch!

Libète was aghast. Watch? What's he talking about? We're staying here?

— I'm being followed, Stephanie said. I need to leave before–

Libète ran outside.

She walks through the dark ahead of Félix, down slopes, up slopes, on-road and off. He tries to cover the ground between them, to catch up, before slowing, stalling, and dropping back again.

— Sophia, he calls feebly.

But Libète moves faster, the day's events proving too much for her. *I am alone... I am alone... I am alone,* she mutters the words like a mantra.

The road is quiet. Foche is weary. Minds are worn from work, rum, and pushing through the heavy motions of mourning. All know tomorrow will come, so they lay down to prepare for more planting, more cultivating, more cooking, more hunger.

She follows the fork in the road, heads toward the imposing iron gate.

— Why are you going off that way?

— Leave me alone, will you?

She moved to the steep incline and the start of the rock that sat atop the mountain like the regal arch of a crown. She found the crevice.

She would leave. Tonight. She was done with this place. More death. Narrow peasant minds. Endless superstition. This was not the safe haven she was promised, not by a long stretch. She endangered herself every minute she remained and she would *not* let...

It wasn't there.

She reached in till her arm was consumed, scraping her hands as her desperate fingers ran over every crack.

Her notebook. Her notebook was gone.

A band of light passed over her, the sound of engines' rumbling following shortly behind. She ducked, breathing hard, breathing fast. *If anyone reads that–if anyone sees–*

The thought immobilized her for a minute. She then took off toward the fortress.

So preoccupied, she did not give a second thought as to why, with the Sun at rest, a line of three heavy trucks, more than anyone had yet seen come to Foche, would line up at a locked gate at the top of a remote mountain, filing through one by one by one, until all were swallowed, and the barrier slid shut once more.

She dashes into the villa's courtyard, her tears pouring, the light blinding.

Too, too much. It's just too much.

She sits in the white gravel against Tòti, burying her face in her hands. There is a timid *crunch crunch crunch* from behind, but she doesn't look up, she doesn't care.

— Can I join you?

Jak.

Another step toward her.

— Can I sit?

She says nothing.

— I thought he wouldn't return. Jak sat. When we were moved to the separate rooms last night, I was numb. My mind . . . it just stopped working. I couldn't–can't–believe Didi's gone.

Libète let out a rueful moan.

— And then Madanm Maxine came. With her questions. She asked me about the Numbers, what I knew of the note, if I had seen him.

— Who?

— Lolo. She knew about Lolo. Said that she had seen him.

— She said nothing about him to me.

— She warned me that if I didn't tell her all I knew, she couldn't protect me from him, from Benoit. That Brown would boot me out. That the police would take you away.

— She's just after the truth. Investigating. Like we should be doing instead of hiding away like . . . like . . . *criminals*. Did you tell her about the Numbers?

— I told her I knew nothing. And she left. *Orevwa*. I waited. Thought things over. I eventually banged on the door. Yelled for Charles to let me get to a phone, to call Stephanie. When he didn't come, I did what I had to.

Libète looked at Jak with anticipation.

— It took me a while, but I took the sheet, tied it to the window bars, climbed out.

She clicked her tongue. I missed that in my hurry, she said.

— The drop hurt. She noticed his knee was swollen and a bit bruised. I saw her leave in a car, out the front gate, Jak said. And I went as fast as I could for Véus. Told him we had to check on you. That we were being held prisoner. We rushed up to your room, but you were already gone.

She shook her head. The pieces weren't falling into place. Then how–how did you find me?

— Besides Véus, Brown and Charles had keys to our rooms. Véus nearly woke up all of Cité Soleil shouting for Charles–shouting, shouting, shouting. We found Charles trembling in the kitchen, in the walk-in freezer. Chattering, saying he was sorry, he was sorry. Jak was wide-eyed, recounting it all into the open air. Véus started to hit Charles with the butt of his shotgun. It wasn't pretty.

— A good man, that Véus.

— Charles had been paid to unlock the door and leave the note. Paid off. By a 'hollow man,' he said. Someone thin, someone young. That's all he knew. Véus cursed him, spat on him, and jammed a broom in the door's handle, locking him in the freezer. Libète–Charles was paid a thousand dollars.

— A thousand Haitian?

— American.

— To leave a note?

— And open a door.

— Bondye! And you knew it was Lolo?

— I feared it then. Had a vague idea. But it didn't make sense.

— What then?

— We called Steffi. We were so, so scared. Thought you were gone for good.

She braced his shoulder. Thanks, Jak. He nodded sadly.

— Over the wall, the note said. So I went looking for clues, for anything really. Véus was raising a storm inside still, shouting at Brown, cursing the whole school. I noticed the grass and reeds at the back of the school. No one goes back there, no one at all. But even in the moonlight, I could see they'd been trampled on. Some broken. It was clear a set of wheels had passed through, too narrow for a car. But a cart? It could be a cart. I wanted to run after the trail then and there, but I finally reached Steffi. When she arrived, we drove straight through the fields, bounding and getting mud on Tòti, hitting a rock so hard I thought our axle would break. The trail led right back to–

— Bwa Nèf, Libète said.

He nodded. We drove the streets looking for anyone awake. It was all dead. Quiet. We drove until we saw a fire. A flame.

— I can see the rest. See it clearly. You found Uncle. He told you about Lolo. Knowing–what you kept from me about Lolo–you went searching. But how did you find me in the cinema?

— Your ncle grew suspicious. He didn't like something about the way Lolo was acting. He followed you and Lolo. Saw where he put you.

Libète punched the car tire from where she sat. Could I really have been so blind–so stupid–not to see the truth about Lolo?

— You believed that he was good. You had faith in him. Those are good traits.

She leaned into her friend, staring straight ahead.

— I think Steffi is right, Jak said. Someone tried to kill you–likely Lolo. If he was moving that much money around it had to be from someone with a lot, likely Benoit. But Didi died instead. Brown had some agenda of his own, but Lolo got to Charles and lured you out. It makes sense. Even better than your public murder, which surely would have reflected back at Benoit, they could tarnish your name with Didi's death and then kill you behind closed doors.

— If you had just told me about Lolo, Jak–if you'd let me know instead of trying to hide me from reality...

— You'd hurt enough just then. Jak said this with an edge to his voice. Your kidnapping. Those bloody bandages on your arms. Elize nearly gone. In that moment, sitting there in the hospital... No matter what, I couldn't see you weighed down the slightest bit more. So I took it on myself. To lighten your load.

She hugged him and he tensed. The embrace had her looking over Jak's shoulder, and she saw Stephanie and Laurent on the porch, watching over them.

Arms still around him, she whispered. *Tout bagay... kraze.* It's all... broken. Every little thing...

He pulled himself away, and dug his teeth into his bottom lip. We're here, he said. You and I, we're still here.

Libète limps to a finish.

She is tired and the fortress mount is steep. She berates her body for its weakness, lets her panting and aches subside. After collecting her things at the fort, escape is the only option. As she enters under the stone archway, she knows crossing Félix is inevitable. She hears his voice, but there is the sound of another there too. She claps her mouth and tries to cap her breath as she listens around the stone corner. Her prying eyes soon follow.

Magdala.

Félix stood before her, rigid. His mother embraced him, held him, wept over him.

Even Libète, so set on a swift departure, paused. She longed again for the maternal touch that death had stolen from her. She had thoughts of Stephanie's affection, but that was an imitation with which Libète had been too easily satisfied.

— Please come back to me, Magdala said.

— I asked you. I begged you not to ask me to.

— But the debt, it's forgiven! You're a part of Foche again!

His head turned from left to right. My decisions are mine to own.

— But why? her voice faltered. Why live as a villain, to be gossiped about–bringing more shame on a mother who cares for you?

His lips were stitched shut, and his eyes closed to trap his tears.

Libète stepped out quietly, hoping to sneak past, retrieve her things, and be off. *Vanishing will be best. They'll soon forget about me.* She made it to her room and stowed her things in her tired bag. She slipped it on and pulled its straps tight.

— Sophia. Magdala spoke the name.

Libète stood up straight. Wi? she said nonchalantly, as if she wasn't a voyeur, as if she wasn't about to disappear.

— You're going? Félix came alongside Magdala and gave one of his inscrutable looks.

— I'm ... exploring. The mountain.
— At night? But it's dangerous.
— That's right.

Félix walked away abruptly.

— You, too? Magdala sounded frayed. My son entrusted to me by God, and you, entrusted to me by God-knows-who? Leaving in the dark? Without a word?

Libète felt an unexpected shame.

— You may think I'm a know-nothing, Magdala said. But I do know things, even when I don't. And I know you're running.

Libète's cheeks burned.

— You're someone special. I can tell. I can see such things. The woman sighed. If you run to keep your life, then run. But if you run because you are afraid of the unknown, then stay. I will keep you, Sophia. Just know that.

Libète took a wavering step away. Magdala's glare was unbearable, and she could feel her heart bonding further to this woman's. This frightened her. Still, Libète stepped toward Magdala and, with clear eyes, searched Magdala's own.

— You are a good woman.

Magdala closed her eyes, held her hands up, shook her head. Only God is good. If someone gave you to me, you are mine. It is that simple. I need know nothing else. And I won't leave you. Just as I won't leave my son.

Libète's hand stretched out involuntarily, wanting to feel Magdala, and the woman's own hand connected with her.
— I will stay. Until I can't.
— No running off in the night?
— No running off in the night.
— You promise?
— I promise.
Libète folded into Magdala's arms.

Libète leaves the ground floor and ascends the villa's stairs to claim one of the empty rooms. It has a queen-size bed, a desk with a closed laptop, a print of one of Jacques-Richard Chery's paintings, and its own tiled bathroom. She looks out the slatted windows and becomes entranced by the ocean, its undulating waves, its boundless energy. She sighs.

The sound of footsteps on the stairs stirs her. Libète plops on the edge of the bed. She takes stock of herself. Her cheeks are chapped by her drying tears and she uses wrists in an attempt to rub them away. Her hair is matted with sweat. A fine dusting of dirt reaches up to her knees. She smells terrible.

A knock at the door. Another, weaker.

— Aren't you leaving? Libète asks without looking.

Stephanie hovers in the doorway, unsure whether the question is an invitation. Not yet, she says. Libète walks to the bathroom and begins to wash her face and arms. Where were you yesterday?

— I received more news early in the morning. They followed Gerry home, and... A few of us gathered at his house to comfort his wife.

They killed him there, with his wife in the other room. Remi and I went together and–
— You were with Remi?
— Is that a problem?
Libète stepped into the bathroom's doorway. Her look was fierce.
— I *needed* you.
Stephanie looked out at the same sea. *A never-ending give and take,* she muttered. She faced Libète and spoke. I'm not strong. Not intrepid. Not who I want to be. Libète could barely hear her words.
— Don't give me excuses.
— I'm not you, Libète.
— I thought you loved us.
Stephanie sat down on the bed. You can be cruel. Saying something like that.
— And you can be selfish.
Stephanie rose. I am going away. For a few weeks.
— Running away? While my world falls apart? Back into Remi's arms?
Stephanie slapped Libète. She let the offending hand hover in the air, and looked at it in shock.
Libète was stunned too. She stepped back and into the bathroom. She slammed the door.
— I'm sorry, Libète. I shouldn't have–I don't know what came over–
— Just go.
— Let's not part this way, Libète. Let's not. Please, come out. Stephanie put her flat palm against the door. I don't know what's happening, and . . . She started to cry.
Libète turned on the shower and drowned out her pleas.
"I needed you."
"I'm not you."
To each hearer, the judgment in the words echoed like gavel strikes. Stephanie left.

Libète and Magdala head down the slope toward home with their arms linked. Magdala speaks.

— If you are staying, Sophia, if you're really here, there is one thing.
— Yes?
— You cannot be so apart.
— What do you mean?
— The tongues will stop their wagging in time. But you mustn't give these gossips more fodder.
— I never tried, Libète said glumly.

Magdala nodded, rolling the thought around in her head. You... you need to be a performer. You need to be who you aren't. Can you do that? Can you slow down and play a part, Sophia?

The question's irony made Libète cringe. I think I can, she said.

— Be as one of us. Magdala rubbed the words into Libète's back like a salve. Be one of us. Set yourself apart, and you'll be so. Come into the fold, and you'll be safe.

Libète thinks on what this means. An acceptance. A defeat. A loss. She pushes the thoughts aside. For now, it is a relief to take herself off, fold up the old skin, make sure the creases are smoothed out, and put herself safely into storage.

Until they come for me. Just until they come.

PART II

Good, as it ripens, becomes continually more different not only from evil but from other good.

—**C.S. Lewis,** *The Great Divorce*

*There was a Land.
And in that Land was a Boy.
And in that Boy was a Seed.*

*Long before the Boy was the Land.
Full of crafted spires and flowing rivers.
The Land was blessed, and planted with Goodness.
This Good, it grew out of the ground in budding green.
The people tended it, knowing their lives depended on the Good.
And then the Good was harvested, plucked from the trees.
They took it and beat it and crushed it and cooked it.
And the Good entered them, passed through them.
It gave them life.
And all that came with living.
No one told the people how to live.
No one took what was not theirs.
And this is how they lived in that Land.*

*Years and years passed.
And with them came more blessing and more heartache than can be known.
It was in this same Land the Seed was planted in the Boy.
And He grew.
Into a strong tree.
A tragedy befell Him and his family.
And the Good was no longer enough for Him.
With great effort, He pulled up his roots.
He left the Land and all that it was.
He sought the opposite of the Good.
And He withered.*

THERE IS A LAND

On his long journey He found darkened places.
Places that seemed to have never known the Good.
He passed from such place to such place.
Never to lay down roots.
His branches became gnarled and His body warped.
And He thought this was His destiny.

One day in such a place, He came upon a Girl, curiously on fire.
She laid on the ground, and Her burning never ceased.
Her fingers of flame kept Her from ever planting herself in the ground.
All others of good sense had fled far from Her.
Because to approach was to risk catching her Fire.
Please, She cried out to Him.
Help me quit this flame!
For I am tired of it.
So very tired.
And there is no one who will help!
Like the others, He passed her by.
He knew what fire would mean to Him.
And His wooden limbs.
But Her cries moved Him.
They stirred something He had lost long ago.
And He returned.
He came close.
He touched the flame.
He took the flame.
And He burned till he was consumed.

In Her new freedom, She rose.
And She wept.

His burned trunk and limbs lay before Her.
She found the air was filled, but not with ash.
The Fire had done a wonder!
Long-absent fruit on his boughs flourished and opened.
More Seeds were freed!
And the Girl-Who-Had-Burned gathered them up.

The Girl knew what She should do with the Seeds.
She should plant one.
She should plant many.
In thanks for what He had done.
And what He had given.

But the Girl stood there, looking into the Land She did not know.
She saw Her life stretch out before Her.
And a heavy question rested on Her lips.
She knew that which She should do.
But could She?

THE PEASANT

Tan ale, li pa tounen.
Times goes, it doesn't return.

Four months later

Come join us, come on, you'll see where we are

Hoe meets earth, and the motion feels good.

Come join us, come on, you'll see where we're heading

Strike! in turn, Strike! in time, Strike! goes the dance.

Come join us, come on, you'll see what we need to do

Time in the field empties Libète. In the row of corn that climbs above her eyes, she disappears: a straight path behind her, a long line of clear purpose before her. She sings along:

When we look at the country, we see division
When we search for hope, we find the blows of batons
When we gather to talk, we discover togetherness

Let's put our shoulders together and see if we can arrive

They reach the finish of their gold-green rows.
It is the end of the trance. The end of the dance.
Libète crouches, lays her hoe down. Her torso heaves to catch and hold breath. She takes stock of her body and its hard, aching muscles. She has a small puncture wound in her heel from a sharp rock. It bleeds. She hadn't noticed.

— Are you well? Magdala's head pokes through the line of corn. Libète looks up, blinded by the hanging Sun but comforted by the voice, and lifts her hands. She smiles, biting her cheek, inhaling. *Mwen byen*, she says. I'm well. She holds her palms up and to the light. They've blistered again.

— Ay! Sophia! Magdala takes the hands in her own and inspects them closely. You must protect yourself! Magdala removes rags from her hands and gives them to Libète. Your hands still aren't yet ours, she whispers.

She does not tell Magdala that this very difference is why she lets her hands rip, mend, and callus. Magdala means nothing by the remark, but Libète resents it. This passes. She can harbor no ill will toward the woman. Soon, maybe, they will be, Libète says.

Magdala wipes her brow with the back of her hand, catching the beads of sweat that escape her headscarf. They have been in the fields since before the Sun deigned to show itself.

— Ay, it's a dry day, Magdala says. Too, too dry. Why does the rain just decide to stop when we need it? The little drops, they just stay at home instead of making the leap. They should do their part!

— God must be busy elsewhere, Libète says. Too busy to make them jump.

Magdala bends to stretch her back. I suppose so.

There were fifteen others working alongside them to cultivate the common plot, and the woman and girl rejoined the rest. They circled around a deep bucket of water, taking turns scooping out a drink with a small, cut gourd floating on top.

— You're getting good, Sophia! said Agustin. He was the elder *sanba* there, calling out the song and setting the konbit's tempo.

— And fast, said Klesyis. I checked your work. I wanted to find fault – he cracked a smile – but found none!

Libète blushed. Mèsi, she said quietly. Magdala beamed, patted Libète on the back, and took a draught of the water. She passed the gourd to Libète.

— Maybe she can do all our rows. Prosper said this, walking up from his own line while rubbing his coarse hands together. Whether he was praising her or ridiculing her seemed lost in his flat tone. Her smile slipped away. He took a drink of his own before adding, Klesyis is right. She did do a good job. Her eyes met his before leaping back to the ground.

Through his spare teeth, Klesyis let out a laugh. Like you're one to judge, Prosper! Maybe she can help you out! Your rows look like you needed to take a leak and had to hold it. He zigged his hand through the air. Remember–straight, son! Straight!

Libète lifted the gourd and opened her throat, taking in the water in one gulp.

— All right. Everyone good? Everyone ready? Agustin asked.

The group panted a combined "Wi."

— Well then–*line up!* Agustin started pounding out a beat, a familiar rhythm, and it animated them anew despite their empty stomachs, aches, and weary limbs. They grabbed tools that had been laid on the ground.

— Sophia–since you were last to drink, you can refill the water, eh? Klesyis asked. It'll give us old hands a head start too. He winked.

— Of course, she said, offering a meek nod. She lifted the bucket. The scraps of cloth in her hand dulled the blisters' pain.

She headed up the steep slope toward the top of the plot where women queued up at the cistern filled by the university's capped spring. With their own buckets and jerry cans, their laughter and gossiping could be heard from all over.

— *Eskize m*, Libète said. I was asked to get water for the konbit and want to get back before they leave me behind.

— Of course, of course, Sophia! said Ketteline, a large and boisterous woman who stood halfway down the line of ten women. You work for us in the common plot, we work for you!

Libète gave a grateful nod and put her bucket on the ground. She tied the line to the bucket's handle and sent it down into the cistern's dark. She braced her legs at the cistern mouth, clenched her teeth, and tugged the bucket back up.

— I remember when you first came–you could only lift a thimble at a time!

— Yeah, made us wait all day! Ketteline shouted. They burst into a fit of cackles. Libète couldn't help smiling too, nearly losing her grip on the rope.

— Look at you now!

Libète's muscles flexed as the bucket climbed in smooth, fluid motions. When she got it up, she gave a small bow. With Ketteline's help Libète hoisted the bucket high on her head and carried it back down the slope. She felt light despite the load.

Agustin's fist was bouncing fast against the taught drumhead now, forming a low rumble. Libète put the bucket down in its original spot. The others had just begun, having defied Agustin's orders and stretched their rest to the limit.

— You're over here, Sophia, Prosper called. He signaled to the row next to his own.

— *M ap vini!* She let the bucket touch earth and was careful not to spill. Taking up her hoe, she walked toward Prosper. He stared as she approached, and she tried to ignore him, biting her bottom lip.

— Hey–where's my pick axe? Klesyis called out from several rows over. I left it over here.

— Take mine, you ass, Agustin called. You'll have to look for yours while you work! We're starting. No more delays!

She took up her place and looked down the row. She breathed long and deep, as if she stood poised at a race's starting line. Her mind soon slipped into gear, parts churning, thoughts accelerating until they were lost in the whir of it all.

Can you play a part, Sophia?

Her memory flitted to Magdala's question posed several months before. Unsure how to answer then, she was no longer. It had changed her in an instant, flipping Foche from a foreign place to her own.

— What's on your mind? Prosper asked.

— Hmm? she said, pulled from there to here. Not a thing, Prosper. My mind, it's empty. Like an open field.

Come join us, come on, you'll see where we are . . .

Libète dreams in shadows.

Surreal from the beginning, the dreams' meanings are lost in vague imagery. Each is drenched in water and shrouded in black. Full of falling, and running, and worry. She awakens.

It is only a few hours since Stephanie left. Libète moves to the bathroom, lets the water run over her hands, cups it and brings it to her face to wash away the thick layer of age that has accumulated in the course of the last day.

Darkness covers all. She fumbles down the stairs, hoping Laurent will be absent. He sits at the dining room table with Jak. Jak shoots up on noticing her, and his chair flies back.

— The ogre stirs, Laurent mutters.

Libète squints, running her hand down the bannister. She pauses at the bottom step.

— Food.

Laurent purses his lips. I cooked, he says.

She sniffs and scrunches her nose, taking in the wafting scent of char from the kitchen.

— It didn't go so well, he says. The cleaner will be back by tomorrow.

— Food, she says again.

— Fortunately the restaurant around the corner was still open. I went out.

She sneers.

— I'll get you a plate, Jak says. He moves toward the kitchen.

She slinks to the table and sits, shielding her eyes from the nagging fluorescent light overhead.

— We don't need you, Laurent. Jak and I are mature. You can leave.

— Steffi said you needed to hide. Something else about adult supervision? I protested–I have a book to write, I said. I can't handle the distraction, I said. He huffed. Steffi didn't seem to care.

Libète noticed a cocktail glass drained of its spirits, leaving two melting ice cubes. I'd have preferred Steffi, she said.

— I'd have preferred Steffi, Laurent said.

Libète sighed.

— She took my car, something I'm none too pleased about. She left that green rust bucket in the drive.

Jak returned with a heap of rice bedecked in steaming *sos pwa*, chicken, and fried plantains. He had given her extra sauce–her favorite.

— The computer. In my room, she said. Can it get on the Internet?

— It can, Laurent said. But I think we need to have a talk about what you do online while here. It's hardly a secure–

She took the plate to her room and left them.

— Sophia–you can't leave without a farewell. Magdala stands with hands on hips. You owe me as much, she says.

Libète rolls her eyes. Back at their shared home, she has just rinsed off and is halfway out the doorway. She moves toward Magdala, whose forced frown turns to a smile. Libète hugs her, kisses her on each cheek.

— Orevwa, auntie, orevwa.

She stepped out and saw Saint-Pierre standing in the wide shadows of the old mapou. She went to greet his sad, long face. A dull day for you, Pierre, no? She stroked him and caught her small, distorted reflection in his unblinking eye. We'll put you to work soon, she said, checking the strength of the knot tying him to the tree.

Libète's limbs felt deadened. Loose and wobbly, she finished each day in the fields having pushed herself harder than the day before. No one else cared that she progress in such a way, but the discipline was important to her. Their acceptance of her was important.

In her other hand, she carried a large square of crinkled brown paper, carefully folded. It was the soft kind that wore easily along its creases and threatened to fall to pieces if not shown proper respect. Libète had asked a vendor for it at the market; it had cushioned a glass pitcher up from down the mountain, and was otherwise fated to kindle a fire. The vendor handed it over. Inside the pocket of Libète's sundress was an even more valuable possession: a pencil, carefully sharpened.

The road was peaceful. Libète greeted several residents coming in from tending their own *carreaux* and hectares spread throughout the mountain. Peering out, she couldn't spot any trucks or jeeps crawling up the mountain. Their rumble and the strain of low gears were familiar sounds these days. Moto taxis had proliferated too, with the improved road; return-trips from Foche down the mountain had become a brisk business. Riding the bikes used to mean you had money or were sick, but not anymore. The oldest member of the community, a spry ninety-four-year-old woman, had made the trip down the other day to visit a younger brother down in St. Marc who was ninety-two. They hadn't seen one another in at least sixty-five years.

The peace along the road was broken before long. She heard shouting from among the corn, and saw Ossaint, Vernard, and Jezula.

— You're harvesting my crop! Taking my work for your own! Jezula shouted.

— Shut your mouth. My land starts there, between that rock – Ossaint pointed to a larger stone along the roadside – and that stump. Always has!

The woman flew in front of him and jabbed a finger into the man's chest. If that stone happens to move by your own hand it doesn't let you claim the earth! You're acting like . . . like an . . . *American!*

His nostrils flared. He did not appreciate the insult.

Land ownership made for a complicated patchwork of parcels. Large plots had been divided and inherited and sold and subdivided and traded. Written titles meant little; often neither party in a dispute could read the frayed papers produced to bolster a claim. Blurred lines between plots were dangerous, Libète had learned. They led to flared tempers and thrown fists.

— You have no right!

— We're out here all the time! Ossaint said. We never see you at work. So you want to redraw the lines and claim our crop. Getting fat off *our* sweat!

Libète walked past the marker stone often. She knew its location well, and also knew it had not moved. It was deep in the ground, and if it had shifted it would have left a noticeable indentation in its former place, or the ground would show evidence of tampering.

She felt the impulse to intervene turn over in her stomach.

She took one step toward them, but then returned to the center of the road. *Best not to get involved*, she whispered under her breath. She let their shouting drift and fade away as she continued her climb.

When the road's two tines forked, she took the trail toward the fort. Partway up, she came upon Junior, Jeune's mute son.

— Bonswa, Mesye Junior. His barrow had been covered, but overturned. He was frantically trying to return the items–rope, a pan, some long-handled tool–under its protective canvas. Libète's voice made him stand erect. He forced a nervous smile.

— Where are you heading?

He made a pointed roof with his hands.

— Isn't your home that way?

His smile twitched at its edge; a tick. He nodded, pointed over the hill and then made his hand a half circle. The smile took too much effort, and his face slid into a neutral mask.

She scratched her elbow.

— Do you . . . need help? She went to lay her things down.

No, no, no, he said with his hands, and held his heart in gratitude.

— Dakò, she said. *Bondye beni ou*, God bless you. She proceeded up the trail, feeling his eyes prying into her back before he returned to the loose supplies.

The fort stood as it had. When she came close to it, she hollered, Come out you French bastards! I've come to kick you from our land!

Félix emerged with a half smile. Libète waved. She had yet to actually make him laugh.

He stood with arms crossed, his head pivoting to track her as she walked past. He followed behind slowly, respectfully.

— Are you well? he said.
— I am. A bit sore. You?
— *M fatigue tou.* I'm tired too.

She went straight to a spot on the floor that was shaded. She imagined it must have been a dining hall in days of old. She sat, careful to protect her modesty. His eyes slipped mechanically to her bare legs before returning to her face. He reprimanded himself for the lack of discipline. His lips tightened.

— You sleeping better? she asked.
— My dreams are ... still dark.

Libète nodded knowingly. Her mind slipped to her most recent nightmare, one she remembered too well. Jak was bound on an operating table and was being tortured by masked surgeons. It was terrible.

— But it's not that. I'm sleeping okay, he said. Anton had me fix his house's wall. He rubbed his head. Loads of brick involved. Took all morning.

— Ah! Good! She looked him in the eye. Another inviting you back into the fold!

— Only because I'm good with a trowel and they can pay me less kòb than anyone else. How's my mom?

— We were at the common plot all morning, doing our share. Libète played with a tall weed. She's well. Misses you.

— I'll come by soon. Tell her so.

Libète frowned. He said this nearly every day. I will, she said.

She looked down from her vantage and saw another truck pulling up to the gate hewn into the cliff.

— Seeing those trucks come and go. I don't know. It makes me uneasy, Félix said. He shifted his weight from one leg to the other. Didn't Rodriguez say the university was slowing down its work until the common plot was harvested?

— They already started in. Pulling up more bits of ground from all over it. 'Samples.'

— And no one's saying anything?

— They keep showing up with more goats, more chickens, more seed, more trees to plant. Holding up their end of the bargain.

He spit. I don't like it, Félix said. They're up to something.

— I could care less what they're doing, she said, taking the pencil from her pocket. She unfolded the paper, busying herself. Félix squinted, looking at the back of her head. He didn't believe a word she said.

She smoothed the paper out, revealing lines of microscopic type: repeating vowels, consonants, three-letter words, the simplest of sentences. Enough talk, she said. Ready for today's lesson?

The second day at the Martinette villa was much like the first. With her internal clock busted from the odd hours kept since Didi's poisoning, she stayed up late online, combing news sites, checking her e-mail and Facebook profile. Jak had joined her, but fell asleep in the wicker chair he had dragged in from another room. The laptop screen cast an eerie glow of changing color across her face.

She had searched for her name. There were the old articles and editorials that touched on her–she was familiar with all of them–and photographs–she had viewed every one–but they were pushed aside by a number of new news pieces, as if her past had been overwritten.

She was disgusted. Her enemies had indeed moved beyond attempts on her life to attacking her reputation.

Stories condemned her. They spoke of the sinister poisoning of a friend, an escape from imminent arrest, and a bizarre scene of damage as accomplices tore off a property's door in Cité Soleil. Steffi, Jak, Didi–all were there, named and pictured.

It didn't matter that the authors were most certainly paid off–this was how news so often worked in Haiti–but even some of the smaller presses and independent papers were picking up the story fragments and judging her without so much as a basic inquiry. All she needed was a phone and she could be in touch with the whole of Haiti. Clearing her name was her first imperative. She jumped into her e-mail and began drafting a statement. She'd have Jak look it over in the morning–he was good at honing her arguments and moderating her excesses.

She looked at the boy. Even in sleep he couldn't quit his nervousness. He could try to mask it, but it was a gossamer veil. Her guilt crept in again. *Again, I drag him into this. I dragged everybody into it.*

Stirring, she turned the computer off and prepared for sleep. It was five o'clock, and new light was breaking out across the sky.

She sighed. Jacmel's cooling sea breeze was nothing like the heavy air of Cité Soleil. She looked out the villa's window at the sleeping sea town's roofs.

There came a sound from down the hall: speech, loud and angry. It made her jump before realizing it could only be Laurent.

His chamber was a few rooms down. With feline steps she glided across the gleaming tile floor to peek in his room.

He sat perched over a desk. His words–those not clipped–were slurred, guttural mutterings she couldn't make out. He was writing freehand on a thick pad of paper. A glass sat beside his left, writing hand and next to it a bottle of imported whiskey at its quarter mark. There was something else appointing the desk, blocked by his hunched form. *A framed picture.*

Libète meant to simply lean farther into the room but brushed against the door. It gave a terse creak; she gave a curse. Laurent jumped in his seat. With his alcoholic fog sucked away, he slammed the photograph to the table. He breathed unevenly and stood. Libète shrank back as he strode toward her and lifted his hand as if he was preparing to strike her. She cringed and braced herself.

The door slammed shut.

— Good progress, Félix. Libète stands up. You've been practicing.

He lays the pencil down. I've written the alphabet into the earth so many times the dirt could recite it.

— I wish we had more paper.

— Me too.

Libète bites her lip, as if there was something more to say. Well–I'll be going. She begins folding the paper gingerly.

— Why don't you teach others to read? Félix blurts.

— We've been through this.

— But I was thinking. You could do it in the church. Be a teacher. For everyone. So few of us can, and not many can teach so well.

She blushes at the compliment. I've said–

— I know, you've said, but . . . it's selfish. You want to become part of Foche, no? What better way? Why are you still hiding out when–

Libète darkens, and Félix knows he has transgressed. She forces the paper together hastily and rips it before moving across the uneven stones, under the half-fallen archway, and out.

Félix sighs, flexing his fingers as he watches her go, and wishes he had something to occupy his hands. He retreats farther back into the cracked walls and curses himself.

— No questions! she shouts over her shoulder. We promised!

...

The path home was empty; daylight flagged. She muttered the entire way.

Didn't he know she wanted to teach? Her pride clamored for it! To proclaim from the mountaintop that she was the most educated person on it! She was sick of feigned ignorance, her infantilization in all things, biting her tongue at stupidity when it reared its face, turning a blind eye toward small injustices, swallowing her thoughts and convictions on every subject from science to religion to national politics to–

Stop. She breathed deep to regain her composure and slow her barreling train of thought. *This is wrong. I am wrong.*

Without Magdala and Félix she had no release at all. The pressure of her lie built with nowhere to escape but their ears. Without them, honesty would become a fictive thing for her, like politicians' truth, the International Community's benevolence, like . . . she huffed. *God's goodness.*

When she arrived home, the shack was empty. She was grateful for it.

She slid the brown paper into a cavity in the wall and slipped back into the yard. She patted the goat's budding horns, tended their new piglet, and settled back down in the small rectangular plot that lay behind the house.

Magdala had let the small garden go around the time of Libète's arrival, while still feeling the heaviness of Félix's theft and shunning. Weeds had choked the beans and beets and cabbages. Libète may have never worked in fields before, but maintaining a family plot? That was at least familiar.

Back on La Gonâve, her first home, she passed hours with her mother tending to their own small supply of plants. In her memory, her manman stood tall, healthy and strong, with a perpetual smile–brilliant, like the Sun, but at a more bearable strength. All colors were vibrant and alive, and their bellies were always full. They were perfect days.

In fact, the Sun had been blistering hot. Green life mingled with brown decay. Hunger lingered like an unwelcome guest. Her mother's face blurred now–there was never a photograph taken of her to refocus the memory. Even though Libète knew her glamorized remembrances were faulty, she had good reason to indulge in a bit of misremembering when life had treated her so harshly.

Her fingers reached into the loam and pinched the weedy roots that fought to remain and choke out other life. An hour passed.

— If you do that in the dark, you'll pull up the good with the bad.

Libète jumped, but didn't look over her shoulder. I hadn't noticed how dark it had become, Libète said. She continued pulling at the weeds; she was close to finishing. I thought you'd have rested, Libète said. You sounded spent after our time in the fields.

— New life called, Magdala said, laying her bag down. Over the hill. The family hired a moto to carry me most of the way there and back.

Libète looked alarmed. Did you need help?

— The baby came easily. She was small–very, very small.

— And well?

— We can hope. I'll check back tomorrow. Any food ready?

Libète's dirt-tipped hand flew toward her forehead. I'm so sorry–I would have, I just . . . just wasn't hungry.

— You must wear a tight belt! Magdala laughed. It's no matter. I'll start some water if you can still cook.

— Of course. Of course. Mèsi. Libète yanked another obstinate weed up. She took the small pile of dead weeds she'd collected and stepped toward the fire pit where Magdala had coaxed the flame into life. She dropped them in and watched them take light as they curled and writhed. She felt a wave of satisfaction.

— How was Félix?

— He had work today. With Anton. And he's coming along with his reading. He's smart. A good student.

Magdala beamed as she dumped a bucket of water into the pot. I am glad to hear it. Magdala leaned over and planted an unexpected kiss upon Libète's head. You're doing well here. Foche's people are warming

to you. Good things come from their lips. That baka business is old news, *gras a Dieu*-everyone seems to have forgotten.
I'm old news. Libète cringed inwardly. *Forgotten.*
— That's wonderful, Libète said, evenly. She went back to her weeding.
Magdala's gaze trailed after her. I know it's hard for you, being here, with us. I know! But you are safe, and that's all I meant. I'm sure there's a good reason your friends haven't come for you.
Old fears crept in. Libète's hand quickened at its work. She began retreating into herself, and the fear became anger. She tried hard to keep herself from turning sullen, from turning on Magdala–
— Oh God! Libète shouted, flinging something into the air. Magdala let her spoon clatter into the pot.
— What? What is it?
Libète clapped her left hand over her mouth as her eyes jumped between her right hand and what she had thrown.
— A lizard, Libète said, forcing it out of her mouth.
Magdala sighed. Just a fright then! No matter, at–
— *No,* Libète said. It's dead. Left there. For me.
— That's a silly thought. How could you know?
— Its head – she swallowed – it was cut off.

Libète wakes to a green gecko on her pillow.
He–or she–lays staring at the wall, its eyes narrow slits. Its body inflates with the same speed it deflates, quick and sharp, as if it just crossed a finish line.

Libète lays there, numb and unthinking. The bed's white linens still look pristine. Choosing not to pry the top sheet back is a quiet rebellion.

The Sun is high already, and the shadow of a hanging lacquered charm in the window sways and twists, casting flecks of light throughout the room. She rubs her eyes and yawns before brushing the creature away. It moves with indifference.

— Are you awake?
Jak's voice came from the other side of her door.
— What?
— Are you up? Dressed and all that?
— Yes.
— Can I come in?
Her brow furrowed. As you wish.
He entered, looking sheepish.
— Were you just sitting there? she said. Listening?
— Laurent is still asleep. You two seem made for the night.
— Me for good reason.
— Did you dream?
— Not after the last nightmare that woke me. It was a mercy. Like my mind flipped a switch. I'd still be out if not for Mesye *Zandolit* on my pillow. Jak lit up at the sight of the creature. He collected him from the bed and cradled him in his hand.
— I'll keep him! Some company when you sleep all day.

She smiled, struggling to hide that she thought the sentiment was very childish. He felt her disapproval and quietly slipped the lizard into his shirt pocket for safekeeping as he sat on the edge of the bed. This place is no good, Jak muttered. Everyone sleeps till the middle of the day. It's like ghosts speak in the silence, in the sounds of the ocean outside. Libète rubbed her face. She didn't say anything. Jak touched her knee.

— Ah! His eyes lit up and his index finger stood erect. He went out into the hall and brought in a plate covered with a plastic mesh dome. I made you breakfast.

• • •

They went outside, to the back of the property. There was the villa itself, which was white and clean. Its classic architecture was reminiscent of the old wooden gingerbread homes in Port-au-Prince they'd seen when they strolled downtown near the Champs de Mars. Either its interior had been rehabilitated, as it was all stuccoed white, or the exterior was faux, made to match the neighborhood.

The house was set into an open yard of smoothed white gravel. Palm trees were carefully planted along the property, and a high, barbed wall made it feel lonely–except along the shore, where a concrete lip had been poured and a short ladder extended into the water. There were other trees too, peppered throughout, and one could walk among them and pick bananas, mandarins, and almonds still in their hard, hard shells.

They sat on the lip and dipped their bare feet into the water that calmly lapped against the wall. They saw a woman, surely the maid Laurent had mentioned, keeping a wary distance from the two as she swept out the entryway.

Libète stared out over the placid ocean. The sea could care less about all that's going on, she said. Very self-centered, Nature is.

Jak didn't know what to say. He dipped his baguette into his mug of coffee – black and with sugar, lots of it – and took another bite. It was an excuse to keep quiet. He had snuck out the front gate to the bakery, a subsidiary of the corner restaurant, and used his little pocket money to get the bread and some wedges of Bongú. Libète spread the cheese on her own bread and chewed slowly.

He swallowed with a gulp. I always forget how beautiful it is here. Strange, huh?

There was a lone, small boat floating in the water about a hundred yards off. It was late in the day for a fisherman to be out–they usually started early in the morning. *Maybe it's a diver*, Jak thought before reeling in his curiosity. These have been hard days. I'm grateful for this escape.

Libète darkened. Our world is all one piece. We can't pretend it's separated into nice little sections. She picked up a long, smooth rock and threw it as far as she could. Evil in one place can't just be imagined away by looking the other direction.

He bit his bread again, speaking with his mouth full. I'm mourning too, he snapped. Mourning Didi. His voice cracked. And I'm here with you, Libète. My world's as broken as yours.

— Sorry, she said, and meant it. He looked away and itched at his scrawny forearm. He placed his arm on Libète's back and patted her–it was an awkward gesture. She looked him in the eye, her features softening. She leaned into Jak. With her arm wrapped around him, the two cried softly.

RITES

Se pa tout moun ki ale legliz pou priye.
Not everyone goes to church to pray.

Se pa lè yon moun ap neye pou ou montre l naje.
When a person is drowning is not the time to teach him how to swim.

— Christ! she shouts. She flails, trying to rid herself of the upward-drag of the man's grip.

All had seemed so very quiet and beautiful under the water just a moment before...

Neither she nor Jak could swim, at least not before coming to the villa with Stephanie. Though they grew up on the edge of the sea, the water was something to be feared. Dipping their toes in had been as far as their courage extended. In Cité Soleil they had a friend, Girard, who in great courage ventured out to show his arms' and legs' strength. He was dragged back to the shore with empty eyes and water-filled lungs. With Stephanie's encouragement–she had bought them swimsuits–they descended into the water, at first with hands in reach of the ladder. Over time, they waded, but never ventured far from the concrete lip.

Today, she and Jak compete to see who can hold their breath the longest, but Jak has stopped the game. He never wins.

This round, Libète hovers just beneath the surface of the water. She clasps her nostrils just below where a pair of goggles digs into her face.

Though she doubted the existence of mermaids, she nevertheless hoped she might spy one under the water. They supposedly dragged the drowned—including her ancestors cast over the bows of slave ships—down to new life in the underworld beneath the sea. Fishermen swore they saw them all the time, and to Libète it seemed the sight of the supernatural might make all of this mess of a world actually make sense. Until recently she had believed there was a certain teleology to everything. Despite the past's massive heartaches, she believed all things were progressing toward a more peaceful and more just future for Haiti, and for herself. If there was no shadow realm, no existence or rest after death, no God, the flagrant injustice of the world would simply be too much to bear. It would lead one to despair . . .

A thought occurs and it is mad.

It would be a test. A small one. Maybe if she let herself go just a *bit*, let a little air escape her lungs, a little water come in, she could fool one of the sea maidens into showing herself. *Just a little . . .*

She lets her lips slip open, just barely.

A gargantuan splash broke the water's surface, followed by thick arms wrapping around her and a tug upward. She burst through the barrier between the world below and the world above.

She cursed and thrashed.

— Calm down, calm down! Laurent shouted.

— What the *hell* were you thinking? She extricated herself and spun before battering his chest. *Are* you thinking?

— I thought you were drowning! he hollered. Jak ran out of the house. The juices he had gone inside to retrieve splashed all over as he coursed toward their shouting. I thought you needed help! Laurent said.

She shrieked, ripping off the goggles and throwing them at him. She climbed out of the water and walked toward the house, vitriol dripping from her lips. Laurent muttered too as he left the sea and held out his

arms to let the water sop off. He next sat and peeled off his penny loafers before looking at his watch closely to see if it was waterlogged. He swore.
— Is she okay? Jak asked.
— She's an ingrate is what she is. Laurent trudged off.

Délira stands before Libète in the gray-block church as Reginald Honorat speaks the liturgy into the air, lifting scriptures from their tattered pages so that the words flutter up to roost in the hearts of their hearers.

Délira holds her child. Delivrans's eyes peer over the edge of his mother's shoulder. His round and pleasant face is shadowed by a low brow that makes him appear as if he is skeptical of everything the preacher recites. Libète smiles. His face reflects her heart.

The decapitated lizard, of the same family as the baka found under Dorsinus, had been a cruel warning. Magdala tried to dismiss it as an accident: its head was surely severed by the chop of a hoe.

Libète disagreed.

She had tended to the small garden the day before, and hadn't used a hoe on it for a long while. The body was placed there. Why? To tell her she was being watched? That she was a stranger? That accusations against her weren't forgotten? To Libète's dismay, word swept through Foche about the headless creature–gossip surely spread by the culprit.

Libète watched the old lay priest as his book seemed to weigh down his hands. He gave a speech on the rite of baptism without even looking at the words. *Can he even read them?* The audience's tightly drawn faces and absent stares made it clear the speech had been repeated many times over at many similar gatherings over many years. Only Délira stood entranced, and she hosted a wide smile and light in her eyes. She gently rocked her increasingly fussy baby.

Reginald produced a glass chalice from his satchel, and an assistant filled it with water boiled to such an extent as to confer holiness.

— Délira, what name do you give your child?

— Delivrans.

— And what do you ask for your child?

— Baptism.

— You're going to bring this one up Catholic?

She nodded.

— And where's his father?

— There is . . . none.

An anonymous cough rose up from the back of the church, followed by another's disapproving grunt. Délira looked so very sad standing there alone, Libète thought. She moved a step closer to her friend.

With a sigh and a tightening of his lips, Reginald reached for the chalice after anointing Delivrans's head. You're going to renounce Satan from here on out? He signaled down low, to her pelvis. Keep things closed tight? he whispered.

She nodded bashfully.

— Say it aloud, for everyone.

— I will.

Reginald closed his eyes and began a recitation:

Powerful Bondye, Jezi's Papa,
by water flowing and the Sentespri
you made free from sin all sons and daughters
and handed them all new life to put on.
Put your Holy Spirit over them
to lead them.
Give this one smarts and wisdom,
level thinking and a brave heart,

a spirit of know-how and big, big respect for You.
Give them open eyes to see what You made.
We ask this in the name of Jezi.

Libète watched, but did not listen.

She still struggled to understand *why* the dead lizard had been left. She had been so careful to not stand out these past months. It's that you stay, Magdala had said. That's the 'why.'

When she was unable to rattle off the Catholic prayers there were murmurs that only fueled suspicions about the baka. It was Magdala who recommended Libète go through this bit of ceremony in the hope it might convince Foche that Sophia was a good Catholic who wouldn't dabble in bakas and other dark arts. Libète at first balked–though generally ambivalent toward all things religious these days, her Protestant roots ran deep. Please, Magdala had asked. Convince them. For me.

Libète acquiesced.

She looked up from her musing just in time to witness Reginald say, Then I baptize your child in the name of the Father. Of the Son. And of the Holy Spirit. He poured the water three times, anointing and then wiping the child with a white cloth. Amen, he said. Finished.

Delivrans had given a cry at the water's touch. Délira's tears mingled with the holy water in the basin on the floor. Délira smiled, kissed Delivrans, and her joy spread through the congregation's members. She whispered sweet words into the child's ears and cupped his head. My jewel, my gem, my prize, she said quietly. Libète, standing close to her now, could overhear. She smiled herself.

— Sophia, you may come.

Libète nodded and stepped forward.

— My child, are you ready to proceed with your confirmation?

— I am.

— Very good. Reginald again let his eyes slip closed. He reached far back in his mind to pull out the required words.

— Can I say something first? Libète said.

The preacher, pulled from his trance, was caught by surprise. It's, uh, *unusual*. But you may. If you must.

— Right. She turned to face the assembly, and made a point to silently lock eyes with every person, every soul. It took a full minute.

— I thank you for welcoming me into the fold. Foche is my new home, and I am grateful for it, and for you all. Libète felt confusion set in; these words she had prepared somehow felt . . . *sincere*. Not forced at all! An impossibility!

There was little time to let the thought linger. She scanned the audience again, wondering if she had missed the one for whom she looked. Her face stiffened on noticing two of the private security guards who hovered at the door to the church with shotguns slung over their shoulders. She kept looking. No, she was certain now. Félix had not come.

She turned back to the priest, and he began to speak:

> *Remember you have been given a spiritual seal,*
> *the spirit of wisdom and understanding,*
> *the spirit of good judgment and courage,*
> *the spirit of knowledge and reverence,*
> *the spirit of holy fear in Bondye's presence.*
> *Guard what you have received.*
> *Bondye has marked you with his sign;*
> *Jezi has confirmed you*
> *and has placed his pledge, the Sentespri, in your heart.*

And with that he anointed her forehead with oil in the shape of a cross.

Reginald smiled. You are welcomed, Sophia, into this church, into this community, and into Bondye's open arms.

Her lips parted, and she raised her hand to them in shock. Despite her knowledge, her doubts, and the fact this act was empty, in the moment, she felt an impossible wash of peace that had been absent for so very long.

Another week passes.

Libète spends only an hour or two out of her room each day. It is a sort of vague protest against being in Jacmel, in this house, and under Laurent's supervision. She sleeps. She writes in her notebook. She reads. She cries.

Jak and she play card games, dominoes, chess, but these diversions are fleeting. Libète is always distracted. All of her moves are defensive, and Jak routs her easily. She has always been a sore loser, but something is changed. There's new fear wrapped up in each and every match, and each mounting loss seems to chip away at some greater sense of identity. Jak lost on purpose once, but it ended poorly when, after a moment of pleasure, Libète realized what he'd done and cast the board and game pieces across the room, only to then slam the door behind her on a dumbfounded, cowering Jak.

Stephanie was supposed to have returned by now. Libète had written a catalog of the harsh things she would say to the woman, but superstition made her feel like this act might be behind her delayed return. One day Libète pulled Stephanie's first collection of verse from a bookcase downstairs. Published while Stephanie was still at university, the poems are beautiful and return time and again to themes of the world's stupid brokenness and the impossible hope that manages to break through its cracks. Libète hated them.

And then there is Laurent.

He and Libète rarely talk. He moves mostly from his bedroom to a locked hallway chamber that he enters and exits discreetly, often in an alcoholic fog. Libète notices him swim in the ocean early every morning for a half hour as she is going to sleep, and this timing is unfortunate. Laurent is most sober when he exits the water, and yet they never cross at these times.

Few requests are made of Libète-the maid tends to most matters of cleaning, though Laurent insists that he, Jak, and Libète eat dinner together. Libète assumes this is some vestigial habit from his own troubled upbringing in the Martinette home, and after protesting at first, she now suffers through it night after night. The meal is inevitably takeout from the corner restaurant, and their menu was already growing stale. At first the three would sit in silence around the table, the tension thick, but this unnerved Jak. Often he begins repeating trivia he's learned from haphazard explorations of Wikipedia or his reading of the day's news.

— Martelly got a new law passed. And there's word overdue elections will finally be scheduled.

Tines pierced food.

Jak sighed, trying again. I found out how gold is pulled from mining tailings. Small operations use mercury, but big operations use cyanide to attract metallic molecules . . .

Knives scraped against plates.

Jak looked at chunks of *tassot* on his plate, searching for a topic that might inspire these two to talk. How is your writing going, Mèt Martinette?

— His name is Laurent. He's not your professor.

Laurent eyed Libète. She's right. I've told you. No need for honorifics here.

Jak nodded twice, beaming inwardly at the meager success of getting them both to speak.

— My writing. It's... slow. Words flow, but they're not particularly good. They invariably end up in the wastebasket. He tapped his finger and his knife bobbed in his hand. She looked him in the eye.

— That's something new.

— What?

She spun her fork in the air, looking for the right word. Humility. He raised his bottled soda in a salute.

— What are you writing about, anyway? She asked.

— My volume is entitled *The Impossibility of Democracy in Haiti*.

She couldn't help but snort. Really?

He took another bite. Really. It's a survey of the politics since Duvalier left, and a forecast for the future.

— You make it sound like it's a story with an ending. Democracy, true democracy in Haiti, hasn't had a chance. Coups, outside interference. Haiti is moving forward whether you like it or not.

Laurent balked. Why? Because you say so? Because of your pretend legislature that trots out the same empty rhetoric I've heard since before Duvalier fell? The political game is set and rigged in favor of the powerful. They will never let the masses govern Haiti, not ever.

— So it should be allowed to remain that way? You're resigned to it? You sound just like the elite you accuse. Obtuse, paternalistic, pessimistic–

— I write from a bottom-up perspective, my dear. Though I applaud your vocabulary's reach.

— How can you purport to speak with such a voice?

He slapped his forehead. If only I'd asked you before writing three hundred pages on the subject! You could have saved me some grief! He took a swig of Coke. The system is fundamentally unjust. I'm merely calling it as it is, not peering out through rose-colored glasses. Hope is gone–nothing can be created from nothing.

They sat in silence.

— I'd like to read it, Jak said. It sounds... challenging.

— Why, thank you, Jak.
— I wouldn't touch it.
— Thank you, Liberté. He always used the French pronunciation of her name.
— Eskize m. She pushed her chair out and left, ascending the stairs.
— They're your dishes to do this evening, Laurent called, a hint of frustration creeping into his voice.
A door slammed.
— I can do them, Mèt Martinette, Jak said.
Laurent looked at the boy, lips scrunched. I seem to have forgotten that Coca-Cola, in its essential state, does not contain a drop of alcohol. He slid away from the table, on toward the bar in the kitchen.
Jak gnawed his meat in silence. It was tough, and a bit of fat stuck in his teeth that no amount of his tongue's prodding could remove.

Libète comes upon the fortress as the Sun slides down and the day pales.
Magdala had prepared a special meal following the Sunday morning baptismal service, featuring tassot. The beef tasted delicious going down and brought to mind the past. Remembering was the opposite of what she'd longed for today.
— You there? Libète called to the old stones.
— I am, came the feeble call back.
— You didn't come.
— I didn't.
She grumbled but climbed the small mount anyway. She passed under the main arch and saw Félix reclining. She didn't look at him. In fact,

she looked everywhere besides at him and withdrew an old, loose-leaf page.
— What is that?
— A page.
— From what? He held the paper up close to his eyes, reading the header. *Bib La*, he said. The Bible? Where did you find this? Her mind flitted to the priest and the heavy, aged book in his hands. When she first met Jak in Cité Soleil, all those years before, he had some similarly plucked pages.
— The owner wasn't using it, she said. So I borrowed it. For practice.
Félix began to read slowly where the page was marked:

> Then I saw "a new heaven and a new earth," for the first heaven and the first earth had passed away, and there was no longer any sea. I saw the Holy City, the new Jerusalem, coming down out of heaven from God, prepared as a bride beautifully dressed for her husband. And I heard a loud voice from the throne saying, "Look! God's dwelling place is now among the people, and he will dwell with them. They will be his people, and God himself will be with them and be their God. He will wipe every tear from their eyes. There will be no more death or mourning or crying or pain, for the old order of things has passed away."

They sat with the words, and she wondered if they might be true, and if true, trustworthy.
— I thought you said you and God are done with each other.
She coughed. Folded the page. Sat up.
— I did.
She had taken this scripture on purpose. In the past it had been a comfort. She thought the words might spark some fleeting sense of faith, as had the confirmation, but it was as if the black text was engulfed by the page's yellow. Like an incantation that had lost its magic.

— I did, she repeated. She reached for his wrist to place the page into his hand, but instead gave a shout.

— Bondye! What happened? She noticed his palm was wrapped in a strip of cloth darkened by drying blood. She began to unwrap it, and he let her.

— An accident. In the fields. With my *machet*.

It was a nasty cut, wide and deep. She noticed the remains of a shirt on the ground, streaked with mud and blood. I stumbled and rolled down the slope. I tried to grab for something and caught my blade.

Her upper lip curled. Maybe punishment for working on the Sabbath?

— Maybe.

— You know, if you had come to my confirmation, maybe this wouldn't have–

He tensed. Why would I go to an empty ceremony? You playing some part for all the world when you don't even believe the words? You don't mess with that stuff. God doesn't.

She dropped his hand. Her face soured. Machete, eh? You slipped. You fell. I bet you were there again. On the other side of the ridge. Weren't you? Watching them and their silly little dig and dreaming up all manner of evils!

— They have more machines there. They have big buckets with teeth, tearing at the earth. And they're hiding it all with their tarps. They've even built some kind of shed.

— You and this land. It's an obsession!

He bristled.

— Look at you, Félix! Wasting your life in this forsaken place. Why haven't you gone the same way as the others your age who left Foche long ago? You're smart. You could go anywhere and *chache lavi*. Cap-Haïtien. Port-au-Prince. You have a keen mind. A strong body. You could make something of yourself. Instead you lurk about with ideas of conspiracy bouncing around the insides of your hollow head.

— Why do you care what I do?

— If you have gifts you should use them! For others! To make a difference!

— We disagree. About what a difference is. When I work in the fields, when I coax and strain and struggle–and there is food I can eat, from my own hand, that gives me life, gives others life–

— You're such a peyizan, a peasant. She said it like a slur. A world, out there, where you're free to walk and you just let its good go unexperienced and its bad unrighted! Instead you hold onto Foche when it wants nothing to do with you.

— You don't know what it is to be committed to a place. To a piece of the earth. You've never fought for a place.

If he only knew the foolishness of what he says. She felt anger prickle behind her eyes, followed by her heart's rising beat that muddled her thinking.

He continued. I say yet again: if you feel so strongly about insulting my home, then maybe you should go.

— But you know *I can't!*

— With you, all I know is how much I *don't* know. Confirmed for a lie? Who you are, the real you? That's the question I keep asking.

• • •

When she returned to the Dieudonné home the sky was purple with pillared clouds rising across the land. Libète could see a low light inside the house.

Why do I even bother with him?

Libète knew she could tell Magdala and Félix at least some of the truth. But when she had lost control of nearly every aspect of her life, holding tight to her secrets was her only consolation.

She and Félix had tried to calm down from their heated words but their tempers simmered too close to a boil. She left the ripped, worthless page with him and promised to bring back a balm from his mother. Infection was an inevitability with a cut like his.

— Madmwazel! Sophia! The voice came from the side, near the sentry tree. She squinted and saw that there, behind Saint-Pierre, stood a man. It was Jeune. He smoked a cob pipe.

She instantly transformed, hiding behind a smile.

— Ah! Bonswa, mesye. You're here? Gracing our home?

His smile was wide and too practiced.

— I am. I came to congratulate you. You're one with us now.

Magdala poked her head out of the house. Do you need food, Jeune?

No, no, just a few words of congratulation for the one set aside for God. Magdala nodded and went back inside.

He turned to Libète. Will you walk with me?

She wanted to scream, "No!" Of course, she said.

They began to stroll away from the house. Out of Magdala's earshot, Libète was sure.

— So you're a woman of letters, eh?

Libète inclined her head. I've never learned to read, mesye. Not even letters. I can only sign my name.

— Is that why you stole pages from Reginald's Bible?

— You're mistaken. I merely looked at the written word. It's unbelievable to me that such beauty as what the preacher says can be in such strange shapes and lines. I took nothing.

He bit his lip, sucked his teeth, and looked at the vast mountain range before them. *I know you are all lies,* he whispered, still facing the sky. *And I will know who you are and why you're really here.*

Blood shot to her cheeks. She turned to walk away, and he grabbed her wrist.

Libète bristled. Take your hand off me or you'll find a stump in its place, she said sweetly.

He smiled, tight and wide. He loosed his grip, and let her go.

— Madanm? Madanm Manno?

Three times a week the maid comes to the villa. She is old and heavyset, her hair hidden in a wrap. Libète always greets the woman with a smile, though Madanm Manno never smiles back.

Is she mute? Clearly not. She spoke when she wanted to, just not around Libète.

Is she embarrassed? But of what? She was old and wizened.

Is she ashamed? It made no sense. She carried on with Jak in conversation, but never Libète. She was at ease around Laurent, and the two joked. The humor was often ribald, and she would cackle and cackle and cackle. But with Libète, there was no hint of kindness or comradery.

Madanm Manno washes dishes now, standing at the kitchen sink, humming the climbing melody of a folk song while Libète listens from behind a corner, holding a stack of dishes collected from upstairs in her arms.

Laurent must have told her something about me. Something vicious.

Libète wears her best smile and glides into the kitchen. Bonswa, Madanm Manno. How are you today?

She gives a nervous acknowledgement, and her eyes dart back and forth as she scrubs.

— May I help you? Can I dry? Or possibly rinse?

— Non. That's all right.

— But most of these are my own plates! It's only right. I'd very much like to help you–

The woman plunged the plate in her hands back into the basin. Please, madmwazel. Please! Let me just do my job!

Libète recoiled at the words' cutting tone. She dropped the plates on the counter, likely cracking the bottom one. What did Mesye Martinette tell you? What lies has he spread about me?
— About you? He's said nothing!
— What's so wrong with me, then? Why can't you treat me like a human being?

Madanm Manno cocked her head, like the question made no sense. I . . . I'm sorry–but we're from different places. You and me, different places. Her embarrassed eyes shot down to the bin of clean water, and she scrubbed even harder.

Libète went up to her room's full-length mirror, looking at what lay before her. All she saw at first were her uncomprehending tears. But then she saw the surface. She wore new denim jeans, an attractive top, all bought on the Martinette's tab. Her hair extensions and pristine nails. And she saw it. What the woman perceived her to be.

Madanm Manno did not see beneath the surface of things. She missed the scar marking her shoulder, earned by stepping between the bullets flying between her people and UN troops. The vanished welts from her Aunt's blows, borne and absorbed deep into Libète's body. The years of hunger pangs, first on La Gonâve, and then again in the tent city after the earthquake.

This woman saw none of these things. Instead she misinterpreted the girl's aloofness and depression for the arrogance of the rich, the pampered, the apathetic. She mistook Libète's attempts at solidarity for paternalism.

The woman thought that Libète–of all people–was *privileged!*

Tearing up, the girl grabbed a pair of scissors and began cutting her braids, one by one by one, until not a single strand of the artificial hair remained on her head.

A FAILURE OF THE HEART

Rete twò lontan nan mache fè ou fè dèt.
Staying too long in the market puts you in debt.

A week or two, Stephanie had said she'd be away. It has become seven.

The days slip past. They are long and monotonous. Libète spins herself into a digital cocoon.

Log on, check inbox, assassinate Benoit's character.

Early on she had created fake profiles to defend herself on the presses' websites, but the articles about her had dried up. She became upset about the paucity of stories rather than slanderous ones. The world had moved on. She was forgotten. And so she turned from defense to offense, and before long, to hate. At any positive mention of Benoit or his businesses she left a string of comments attacking him, pouring the invective into her keyboard.

Research, wade through tweets, scan the news.

Jak tried to engage with her at first. He tried to lead her out of the anxiety of seeing herself forgotten. He knew she needed to heal, but that would be impossible if she mired herself in the past. Instead, he encouraged her toward more positive pursuits.

Engaging with the news: Today, despite the accord, President Martelly was still dragging his feet when it came to scheduling new legislative elections, ostensibly to keep his grip on the reins of government. A moratorium on foreign companies' mining was enacted in retaliation.

Researching the Numbers: Twenty-one-digits long. They thought they might be a code, or maybe GPS coordinates. Jak tried inputting them every which way and they came up mostly in the Indian Ocean. They still had no idea what made them worth killing for.

Getting off the computer completely: Jak tried to pull her outside into the Sun, but her preference was to haunt the Internet late into the night. She still slept through much of the day, mostly to avoid Laurent. Jak saw her take her pills, but she did so surreptitiously. He asked her what her medical condition was, but as always she was cagey. It's nothing, she'd say.

He didn't like this one bit. She had no reason to keep the truth from him. He wanted to help her, to cure all that tore at the Libète he knew. The Libète he loved.

Bouncing between Laurent and Libète's grimness drained him. Exhaustion and apathy became his other friends.

Reading material around the house was too niche. Jak tried plunging into Laurent's collection of academic texts. These were mostly in English and littered with jargon that was beyond him. He was fourteen years old, after all. Other diversions were few.

He took to sketching. He had never taken time to indulge the hobby before, but now discovered he had an astute eye and a measured hand. His favorite subject was Libète. He could content himself for hours capturing her features–the perfect spacing of her eyes, the slope of her nose, and her lovely cheekbones. He drew her as she was a few months ago, brave and at ease with herself–not slouched before a computer screen.

— What are you sketching now, Jak? Libète looked over from the computer. She often didn't show interest.

He subtly slipped a prior page down to show her.

— Just another one of a rock.

It was a beautifully rendered picture of a stone near the water outside. Libète shook her head. All that time drawing a *rock*? You're so *odd* sometimes...

It was a close call. He made sure to hide the notebook to avoid anyone from accidentally coming across his stippled renderings of her.

He had kept the lizard in an emptied fish tank. The Martinettes had let its prior occupants go belly up long ago. Jak had scavenged through the compound's debris for materials to build a more authentic habitat for the creature. His favorite touch was a coconut, hollowed and halved; it made for a lovely little hut for the green fellow.

Every day Jak carried the tank out in the Sun so that the rocks in its bottom would warm. The lizard would creep out of the shell and linger on the stones for hours. *Even in captivity you can find pleasure,* Jak thought. *If you can, I can.*

He had bonded with Laurent, much to Libète's dismay. He had no problem sitting with the man and asking an endless string of questions. Absent from his students, Laurent was eager to offer full seminars for the boy. They could talk for hours. And yet, the closer he grew to the teacher, the more Libète drifted from Jak. He found himself keeping a careful balance between the two, for in the balance was peace.

Early on, after Jak had taken in the lizard and as he was just beginning to draw, Laurent pulled Jak aside. I see you have a way with animals, he said. What is your opinion of birds?

— You have a bird here? Of your own?

Laurent smiled and escorted him to a door in the upper-floor corridor. Jak always assumed it was some kind of closet.

— When do you take care of it?

— It's the last thing I do before I go to sleep. They ascended the stairs. No matter what has happened in the day, Laurent said, it feels good to know you're responsible for something.

— And when you're away? Who takes care of the bird?

— Birds, Jak. When the family is away, Madanm Manno keeps them.

They opened a hatch onto a level surface covered in linoleum in the midst of the roof's sloping red tiles. There was a cage of pigeons, gray and white with black-flecked wings. Jak gaped. Why so many?

— When I was a kid–a little younger than you, I think–this is how my friends and I communicated. Before cell phones and e-mail, before phone lines were affordable.

— They can find their way back here?

— They can find their way between homes. One of which happens to be here. Laurent smirked. It's how I best communicate with my father. Little messages here and there. Let's send the old man a message. He reached for a wooden box mounted on the side of the cage, pulling open the hinged lid to extract a pen and a strip of paper. He scrawled and let Jak glimpse the paper.

All is well with the ti pwofesè. *The ti pwofet is the same as always.*

— I'm the professor? Jak asked, marveling at the association.

Laurent smiled and rolled the paper narrowly so it resembled a cigarette. Father asks after you often. In fact it seems you two children are all we discuss these days. He's deeply troubled by these developments.

— And Steffi? Have you heard from her?

Laurent seemed unsure how to answer. Not really. She checks in with Father. But I'm sure she's well.

— Why don't you text her? Or e-mail?

— Fear of being monitored, I'm afraid. He opened the cage. When the phones and Internet are run by only a few companies and the government can access such information, people like Benoit, the monied – he reached for a bird – can sort through our messages as easily as their own. He withdrew a dark gray one and it cooed at the touch. How about you, Hermès? Have you eaten well, my friend? Yes? Ready for another trip?

— How often do they travel?

— From here to Boutilier, they can be back and forth in a day. But they sadly outpace our desire to communicate. And anyway, it's not good to trouble the old man, and *everything* seems to trouble him these days. Even if our dear Libète were on the ground, bleeding out, I'd simply tell the old man tout byen! Everything's fine! Just to keep him from worrying out of his head.

Jak didn't appreciate the conjecture.

— Sorry. But you take my point. When we retreat from the world after shaping it, we realize our powerlessness. It can frighten. He wrapped the message about Hermès's ankle and clasped it secure with a small metal band.

— Could we send Steffi a message? Maybe?

— I'd... like to. He stroked his chin and exhaled, turning glum. Where I think she is right now? No, I don't think so. But soon, it may be possible. I'll let you know.

Jak became very quiet.

— How are you doing with all this, Jak?

— I'm scared. I think.

— That's understandable.

— Not for myself! Jak blurted, as if fear for oneself was a sin. For her. I'm afraid. She's not well.

— You care for her much. I see it.

The boy touched the wire mesh of the cage, looked away. He was going to protest, but couldn't. He sighed.

Laurent's lips curled into a small, sad smile. With a grand flourish, he tossed the bird into the air. It shot to the north, and the two watched it go until it was lost in the turning sky.

— You're a good friend, Jak. If you weren't here, who knows which of us might have killed the other first.

Jak smiled. Thank you for sharing your flock with me.

— I should have sooner. I'm very protective. They're like my children.

The thought was very nice, but also very sad. Jak forced a smile and stepped back down the stairs.

He knocked on Libète's door. She absently bid him come. Her eyes were locked on the screen as she tapped away furiously.

— Where were you?

— I'll tell you later. When you're done. She gave a distant nod.

Jak positioned the terrarium on a chair sitting between him and the girl and pulled out his pad and pen. He started a new sketch, yet again of Libète, and he mused over Laurent, a man of wealth and status and position who was most content while tending to a cage full of birds.

— Is sketching another stone really that satisfying? Libète said.

He hastily flipped the page to an older sketch.

— Just another one of my lizard, he said with a smile, showing her his work.

— You've got that?

Libète grunts, hefting a basket brimming with mangoes. I do. She lets it spill over into one of Saint-Pierre's saddlebags. Magdala does the same, draining a full sack of beans pulled up from the fields.

— Well, let's go then.

They started down the mountain path with the old donkey clomping along, greeting the Sun and the sky and the others who come up and over the earthen banks to meet on the road.

— The more I think on it, we must beware of Jeune, Magdala murmurs between well-wishing. You already saw what he wanted to do to Félix over the stolen money. String him up in a tree! She spit. He's had it in for our family for a long, *long* time. Since I was your age he–why, good morning, Madanm Brizard! she hollers. Libète gives a wave to the woman just cresting a nearby hill. They let Madanm Brizard walk in front of them.

— Why's that? Libète whispers, turning back to Magdala.

— Who can know? He knew my father, knew him well. They worked the fields together. I remember when I was young, around your age–before my parents died. Jeune started acting strange toward us.

This piques the girl's curiosity. How did they die? Libète asks.

— Killed. Murdered. In a way that no one should be. No one *ever* should be.

— Do you–do you think Jeune was involved?

— No, no. Not a chance. He's not really a killer, I don't think. They exchanged greetings and smiles with a trio of women. A boy followed them, leading ten piglets with the help of a switch.

Magdala patted Saint-Pierre carefully. I think it was guilt. A heavy, heavy guilt, Magdala said. That his friend suffered, and he did not. At least that's what I told myself. But this treatment of Félix and you! Well! She grunted. It makes one ask questions, no? We'll keep our eyes on him. He's made other enemies in the village. Back when times were so, so bad. If he tries something, we'll have friends in high places to stand beside us. She pointed to the sky, intimating God. Libète gave a patronizing nod.

They tipped the last hill, and the flattened ground came into view, like an open palm with beckoning fingers: *the market.*

Many had already set up their stalls. Most stalls were carefully balanced poles, and some were covered with tarps. There were already a few hundred who had come to dicker, and the din of it all was powerful.

They reached their spot, familiar now to Libète after these past months. There were so many outsiders at each market, she still wondered from where in the hills they could possibly spring. Thanks to the road, there were even men and women with a small fleet of trucks who would buy here and sell down the mountain.

— Look! Magdala said, signaling with her chin. The devil himself, tearing through town.

Jeune was barking orders at Junior, who seemed utterly bewildered. The son had apparently bumped a plastic egg crate and let it fall. Some of the contents spilled out. They looked like artisanal handcrafts or painted masks of some sort. Others watched furtively, knowing better than to gawk. Jeune stormed off as his son covered the crate and secreted away whatever was inside.

— *Psst.* Both Libète and Magdala jumped, turning to a woman who popped up between them. What have you got? Mirlande asked quietly, eyes hooded. She was young, a few years older than Libète.

— Mangoes and black beans, Magdala replied.

— Mangoes are fifteen apiece, and a *ti mamit* of black beans is forty-five, Mirlande whispered. And then she was off, approaching the next trickle of sellers.

The market was all about alliances, Libète had learned. There were two prices for everything: the *andedan* and the *deyò*, the inside and the outside. Sellers from Foche colluded to fix their prices. It was their only line of defense against the outside speculators who abused their ability to reach other markets and pay the farmers who did all the hard work for practically nothing. If a seller did cave in order to make a big sale–something not unheard of–they would earn the aspersion of all of the other sellers. If they had few friends in the community, they might even lose their spot at market. The speculators knew the collusion happened, always complained about it, and said they'd go elsewhere, but the new road and its easy access made it too much of a chore to do so.

Before the last few abundant harvests, during the Bad Times, the market was a shadow of itself. They'd seen prices dwindle for decades against the onslaught of cheap foreign food and impenetrable urban markets, and this quiet act of rebellion gave them power.

Libète untied one of the saddlebags, and Magdala did the same.

— I'm going to go back for the last basket of grains, Magdala said. Can you tend to things here?

— Of course!

— And no eating the mangoes! Magdala's grimace faltered, a smile breaking through.

— I would never! Libète said as she tucked a mango playfully in her skirt. Both cackled.

Market was a respite for Libète. She loved the energy of it all, the friendliness of distant neighbors reconnecting, the gossip that even she was invited to participate in. Weekly, on Mondays, it also meant postponing a morning's labor in the fields. Besides church, this was her best opportunity to watch and learn how to speak like Foche, stand like Foche, look like Foche. She pried with the eyes and ears of an anthropologist while she began stacking mangoes in a small pile on a rectangle of frayed plastic tarp.

— That's a good job. She looked up. It was Délira, cradling Delivrans. Libète offered a broad grin.

— What are you selling? Libète asked.

— Not selling. Just browsing.

Libète frowned. Do you . . . need food?

— No, no! Délira laughed, the edges of her smile giving way. We're well, thanks.

Libète looked into her eyes, and the young mother pulled away from the stare. I know you've been struggling, Libète said. Not being able to work. I heard your father's gone aga–

— My health has always been bad. And it's a good thing when he's gone. Neighbors help me–*us*–when there is nothing. *Youn ede lòt.* One helping another. That's what we say around here.

Libète looked around and nestled an already ripened mango into the baby's swaddling. *Magdala and I are some of those neighbors,* Libète whispered. *Magdala won't mind.* She smiled. *And Delivrans will appreciate your sweeter milk.*

Délira was bashful at the show; such charity normally came at home, the giver looking the opposite way. Délira took the offering. I didn't come looking.

— There's no shame here. As you said, youn ede lòt. Your hunger is my hunger. That's all.

— I'll take one of those too. The heavy words came from behind Libète. Happily, sir–that'll be . . .

Libète sputtered as she turned and took in the man, his eyes veiled by sunglasses. She glimpsed her reflection in the silver lenses; she appeared wavy and distorted. Her eyes slid to the shotgun hanging from a strap over his shoulder. He wore fatigues that were a weave of black, tan, and green camouflage.

One of the guards. From the dig.

— That'll be fifteen goud.

— Not free? Wilnor, the man called out, this pretty little one is charging a bundle over here for her fruit! Giving me the *outside* price! Another guard turned in response. Wilnor walked toward them, pulling a large black dog whose panting unsheathed his sharp teeth. Libète immediately looked down and away, wanting to hide. The first guard leaned in close, and his breath violated her. My dear, but the two of us, my brother and me, *we're insiders*. Here to help. Help the university. The guard laughed, reaching up to stroke Délira's baby's cheek. Surely that deserves a discount?

— Leave her be, Cinéus, Wilnor said. You're troubling her.

— What's your name? Cinéus said.

She said nothing.

— What's your name, girl? he repeated.

Libète let herself float away, escaping this moment. He grabbed her chin and looked into her eyes. *I asked you–*

Suddenly another appeared behind the men with genial arms to wrap around each. Friends! Cinéus! Wilnor! How are you today? Making the rounds, eh?

It was Prosper, all smiles. He patted the one called Wilnor on the back and reached to give the dog a rub behind the ears. Let me show you around. This is only one of Foche's fine sellers. I can introduce you to others. Cinéus looked to Wilnor and let Libète's chin drop. Maybe they'll drive an easier bargain, Prosper said, winking.

As he led the pair away he shot Libète a concerned glance over his shoulder. He turned back to the two and continued his lively tour.

— Are you all right? Délira asked.

Libète's chin quivered, and she inhaled deeply. She held her eyes tight, and breathed out through her nose. The fear, what she had believed she left behind those months before, had claimed her. When she opened her eyes again, she was Sophia. Of course I'm all right. She forced a smile.

— Bastards, Délira said. At least you have a protector on your side.

— Excuse me?

— Prosper, Délira said with a sigh. He's mad for you. He doesn't even look at other girls now. Libète looked at the boy as he touted some plantains from the opposite side of the market. *The consummate salesman.* It was not lost on Libète that he had been kind enough to lure the thugs as far away from her as possible.

— What's that to me?

— Nothing. Nothing! Délira grinned, still trying to ease the sting of what had just passed. Libète saw her look after the boy herself. Sadness clouded her face. You can have him, Libète said. He's yours. I don't want anything to do with boys. Her thoughts drifted for an instant to Jak before she reeled them back. No good can come of them.

Now Délira looked adrift. Prosper would never be interested in me. Sick and all. With a bastard.

Libète reached out to her while stroking the child's fuzzy head. Delivrans is precious. He has a father. If someone touched you, whether you wanted it or not, they need to take responsibility. You both shouldn't suffer. You just need to name him.

— No, she doesn't.

Libète jumped at the voice. Don't sneak up, Félix! She batted at him, though he didn't flinch.

— She doesn't have to tell anyone anything, he said.

Libète lifted her hands, looking back and forth between the two. Fine. Fine! We all can keep to ourselves, everything to ourselves, we don't need to tell anyone, anything, ever! And suddenly, a thought sprouted, like a germinating seed just breaking soil.

Could they–could he be–

Libète almost gave voice to the notion just as Magdala rejoined them. She stifled the thought, and the three youths stood looking at their toes.

— What's the matter? Magdala asked. All of you look like your only goat's been stolen.

— It's those men, Félix said. One of them touched Sophia.

Magdala's eyes widened. They *touched* you?

Libète shook her head. No, no, it was nothing, just a–

— I'm going to Janel with this, Magdala said. None of us agreed to this when we said the university could come. Armed guards walking about! In our town! When they stayed behind the gates it was something else. She looked around for Janel, who was visiting with other sellers around the market's perimeter. Félix, you stay with Sophia. He gave a dutiful nod, and Magdala went straight for the leader.

— If they touch you again, let me know, Félix said.

Libète cracked a smile. Oh? And what will *you* do about it? Félix just stared with the same impassive look. She stood up straight and gave a short military salute. Fine. As you order, sir.

— The same goes for you, Délira. You and Delivrans, Félix said. The girl gave a nod, still looking down. Libète looked at the two and raised her eyebrows, swallowing her smile. She saw Wilnor and Cinéus were starting to circle back.

— Félix, can you watch the produce? Libète asked. He nodded. Let's go browse for a bit, Délira. Can I hold Delivrans? Délira handed the baby over like she was sharing a favorite gift. He was robust and healthy at four months now, but judging by Délira's appearance he seemed to be suckling his mother's weight away. Her sickliness was even more pronounced without the baby in her arms.

Libète rubbed her nose with his. He gave a look of wonderment, as if discovering something revolutionary. Libète couldn't help but reflect his expression.

— How about – Félix coughed – how about I watch him for a moment? While you two walk? Libète thought of denying Félix's request but saw his earnestness. She knew better than to poke fun. Libète looked to Délira, who gave a quick, bashful nod. *He must be the father.*

— All right–I'll take my turn later. Libète passed him the child, and Félix's own face transformed. The two young women began to stroll, walking counterclockwise around the market, keeping the guards and their dog opposite to them.

— You know, you shouldn't mock him so, Sophia.

— Ah, it's nothing. Félix is a good sport. Knows it's all just joking. He's too serious for his own good, she said.

— Still, he's good.

Libète let the simple declaration stand. Her mind raced back through every other exchange she'd ever seen the two share. They walked in silence, taking in the outsiders haggling, their assistants loading up bushels of produce into their waiting pickups, old women exchanging gossip. Do you . . . do you like him? Libète asked out of nowhere.

— Félix? She acted as if it was an accusation. Like him? No. No! Félix is too . . . too young. He's a year younger than me.

Libète shrugged. It's just that there seems to be something there.

— No, there's nothing.

Délira paused suddenly, as if she expected Libète should too.

— What?

— Are you deaf? Janel is calling you!

Libète cursed. She hadn't responded to "Sophia" being called out. This happened, but less these days.

— Yes, madanm? she called.

— A word?

Libète nodded and peeled off. Magdala stood next to Janel with disapproval heavy on her brow.

— Let us walk, Janel said. Magdala began to follow. Ah, just the two of us. Janel smiled. Magdala gave a reluctant but acquiescing nod.

Libète stayed half a step behind the woman out of deference. Janel moved as if she transcended the place; not as one above it, but one with authority. Libète had exchanged only a few words with her since the town meeting to discuss Félix and his fate. Truthfully, Libète was intimidated by her. Everything she saw and heard about the leader continued to inspire admiration.

— How are you finding Foche? Janel asked. It's been–what–five months?

— Just four. It's a good home for me. The people, they're very kind. Very open to me, after the, uh, misunderstandings, when I arrived. I appreciate everyone.

— And we appreciate you. We lose too many to the lure of the cities. They think there is hope there – Janel shook her head – so they abandon their homes. Who they are. It's good to see a young person arrive rather than leave.

— Foche has much that I've not experienced. In the city . . . Libète hesitated; this was a foolish slip. Where I come from–in St. Marc–we struggled to eat. To find food. Here we can grow it. People actually *own* the land–they don't all pass their lives paying rent. Libète couldn't believe her own words. She felt like Félix's echo. This place . . . it speaks to me.

Janel nodded her approval, glancing over her shoulder at the two interlopers and their dog a number of stalls away.

— Then you understand why we fight for what we have; why we have to accept these fools treading our earth for a time? The dog was barking now, competing with the two men as they raised their voices over some disagreement with Jeune.

Libète hesitated, wanting to speak her dissatisfaction, her disgust, but bit her tongue. I . . . can understand.

— It won't be for much longer. They tell me their survey is coming to an end. After they search the common plot – she rubbed her hands against one another – finished business, she said.

— Ah, byen.

— Truly. Janel's face darkened. I'll speak to these pigs about them touching you. It won't happen again.

Libète gave a small bow. Mèsi. *Mèsi anpil.*

— Get away from my stand or I'll slit your throats!

The activity all around the market stilled and quieted. Every eye turned, every ear inclined.

It was Jeune who shouted. He was livid, shaking, his eyes enflamed, rage seething from his every pore. The dog barked madly, yanking at its leash. Jeune seemed shaken by its bared fangs.

Janel immediately began toward the conflict, leaving Libète alone. Libète felt a keen vulnerability, even though all eyes were drawn away from her.

— Stop this at once! Janel roared. How dare you break the peace!

— Quiet, woman! Cinéus roared, his eyes tethered to Jeune's. She interposed herself between the two and gave the brute a withering stare. They had a whole conversation with their looks. His lip twitched and jaw clenched. He backed off an inch, and then stormed off.

Libète's mouth dropped. *What power she has!*

Wilnor, surprised and unsure, relaxed the dog's leash. It was a mistake. The dog leaped on Jeune and the man crumpled to the ground. He tried to shield his face against the guttural barks and snarls. Wilnor immediately reclaimed the dog, slapped him across the snout, and tugged the beast away. A bird's call encroached on the utter quiet.

But all was not well with Jeune. Though teeth had not sunk into his flesh, the old man still laid on the ground, clenching at his chest. Breath escaped him.

His son was back, and he was the first one to Jeune's side. His voiceless worry shook Libète. The two guards watched in stunned silence. Others ran to Jeune. Janel laid her hands on his ankles as desperate prayers leaped from her lips.

— They put some spell on him! one shouted.

— Those *sanmanmans* are killing him!

It was a heart attack, Libète knew. She had seen it before, at the hospital. The constricting chest. Shortness of breath. A possible failure of the heart. And she knew the elements of cardiopulmonary resuscitation. She could recite them: chest compressions, a hundred in a minute, breath passed through the mouth. She had practiced them. She thought of running to Jeune, her muscles almost reflexively springing her to action.

The thought seized her: *At what cost?*

Sophia would not know CPR.

Sophia would not leap into the crowd.

Sophia would not be able to save this man.

As Libète stood equivocating, the old man's heart failed.

Libète awakens in a terror.

Her dream was steeped in dread. People spun about, grim masks hiding their faces, and she seemed to recall San Figi there among the macabre masquerade. The other faces were those of foul creatures. Didi in tree form may have been there among the group, hovering at the edges of the grand chamber; it was impossible to know.

Hours pass before she can slip back into the black escape of sleep. Her waking hours have been worse than the momentary terrors of her dreams. In those gaps are where her fears are given conscious life. She wonders if others close to her will bleed and die. She fears for herself, wondering if after death her memory would fade from even those closest to her. She had been so reckless before! So fearless! But now the fight in her has faded, and Libète desires *rest*.

She wakes again fully at the sound of glass breaking. She shoots up in bed.

An intruder?

She's up, creeping toward her door. The sound had come from Laurent's room. She slips into a pair of pants and steps down, down the dark hallway, toward a feeble light.

She remembers the last time she'd come upon him in the night–and his drunken anger.

Jak pokes his head out of his room, squinting. Is everything okay?

— Let's check, she whispers. He joins her and they stand at the threshold to Laurent's room side by side. She leans toward Jak's ear. You go first. He likes you.

Jak swallows, and knocks. Mèt Martinette? Is all well? Jak pries the door open, steps inside. He is surprised–and then sad. Libète pushes the door open to see for herself.

She sighs.

Laurent was on his hands and knees. He wore a tank top undershirt, and his feet were bare. His hands bled as he marshalled broken glass into a pile on the floor. Papers were strewn about.

— Oh, Laurent, Libète said.

He looked up at the kids. His mouth was parted and cheeks puffing. His eyes were clouded by a rummy glaucoma.

— *Lage m*, he slurred. Kreyòl rather than his usual French. *Leave me alone.*

— Your hands, Mèt Martinette! Jak said. The blood dripped on the floor, on him, everywhere. The pages of his manuscript were dotted red.

— Help me, Jak, she said under her breath. She went to take one of Laurent's arms. He recoiled from her touch, but she persisted. Jak took his other arm and they lifted him.

— Do you think *only* of yourself? He said this to Libète.

She thought of scorning him, but she couldn't. She felt only pity.

— Don't *help* me. Don't help *me*.

— Be at peace, Jak said. They led him to his bed, sat him down.

— Jak, can you get a towel for his hand?

He answered by going into the bathroom. She sighed and looked at the man. He couldn't meet her eyes.

— I asked–I didn't ask for you.

She went to collect his papers. They were sopped brown from the rum. Her face scrunched as she held them up and looked for a place to hang them so they might dry. Jak reentered with a hand towel he placed into Laurent's palm.

— Hold that tight, Mèt Martinette. The title Jak used before his name, meant in all sincerity, only seemed to anger Laurent. He thrashed his arm away.

— You kids did–

But he stopped, as if he'd forgotten why he opened his mouth. His head slumped against the wall. His eyes watered. His lips tightened.

Libète shook her head back and forth. With thumb and index finger she picked up the larger pieces of the broken glass, depositing them in a wastebasket. Madanm Manno can take care of the rest, she said. She set the basket on his cluttered desk. A cell phone laid flipped open amid the papers.

— I thought you said he was staying off all phones.

— That's what I thought, Jak replied. Maybe he got another?

There was a text message open. She read it aloud for Jak's benefit: *My love to all of you in case–*

Her hand shot to her mouth.

— What? What's it say, Libète?

— *In case this is farewell.*
— Who's it fro–
Jak knew as soon as he asked.
— Bondye. He started to breathe in staccato. Are there... are there... other messages... from Steffi?
Libète pressed through. Nothing. Looks like there aren't, or maybe everything else has been deleted. He tried to send something but it just says it couldn't be delivered. No credit.
— When was her note sent?
— An hour ago.
Libète dropped the phone. Laurent made a subtle, plaintive sound, like a moan. He seemed to be dallying between the conscious and unconscious.
— I need... need to go, Libète said. Go pray–no, not pray. Think.
Jak nodded soberly. I can keep watch over him, he said, pulling a chair up to the bedside. Just to make sure he's all right.
It was only on leaving the room that Libète saw the picture erect on the desk, the one Laurent had slammed down all those weeks before.
It was a portrait of Stephanie.

• • •

— She texted again.
Libète stirred. It seemed sleep only came when she tried to stay awake.
Jak was close to her face, seated on the bed next to her and nudging her. She's safe, he said. For now.
Libète took a deep, long breath. Exhaling felt like expelling a heavy spirit. Thank God.
— The prayers. It seems they worked, he said with a meager smile.
Libète rubbed her eyes. And the drunk?
— He's doing okay, I think. Sleeping it off. His hand stopped bleeding.
She rolled over in the bed and hugged her pillow.

— Jak, I can't handle this much longer. This place. I can't–
— I know, he said. I know.

A failure of the heart.
A failure of my heart.
Her mind is made up. She banishes hesitation–there can be none. Only action.
She threads through the crowd, pushing her way toward Old Jeune. The mute kneels to his left, breathing quiet fear as he coaxes his father back. Libète goes to his other side. Jeune's eyes are emptied as death slips across them. She pulls his shirt apart with a furious rip and listens for a heartbeat.
— What's this girl doing? she hears muttered. Who's she think she is? Libète puts the voices from her mind. There is no space for them, not with what she has to do.
Her fingertips kiss on his chest. She begins the compressions, quick and continuous, pushing, pushing, pushing.

There is the music

She kneads the life back into him, until it is time. Hands to his head, she pulls his chin up, puts his head back.

It swells, the orchestra's sound; glorious

She pinches his nose, breathes in, and blows into his mouth the holiest of kisses, the kind that can restore life. She fears. Failed hearts, truly stopped, need more than futile pushes and borrowed air to hold death back. They need a shock to start again. A shock.

Violins cry in pain, cellos weep

More compressions. His empty eyes stare at her while his mouth, pursed and curious, frames the question, Will I live? With each push, she forces down her fear, fear of what will happen to this one–this created, living *man*–who minutes ago stood but then tripped the line between here and there, life and death.

The percussion sounds as brass blares

He does not respond. He will not respond. This is not enough. Her actions can only preserve, not save. More gifted breath. There seems no change. No change! She checks his pulse; nothing. He's already slipped, already gone.

From where does this music come? What place within her does this improvisation erupt? It is nothing she has heard before. There is no hook to past memory. The staccato rhythm gives way to plaintive dirge, free of form yet so utterly true.

There is truth in the melody

Compressions. More breaths. The people are murmuring, and she casts out any recognition of them, letting the rhythms drown out their noise. It is her. It is him. It is the music.

A crescendo

She breathes. She breathes.
He breathes.

He breathes! Like a crack, the air seeps into his lungs without her aid. She still coaxes the heart on, but lightens her touch. You can do it, she says so low that only Jeune's son, Junior, can hear. His tears slip and soak into Jeune's shirt.

She slumps back on her knees, dazed.

The music slips and falls and fades.

— Back up! Janel finally shouts. Give them space! The son picks up his father's hat to shield the ailing man's face from the Sun. Libète sees Junior weeps in great, tremendous sobs as he grasps his father's hand.

Joy erupts in shouts, and praise, and weeping, so that you could not contain it if you tried! Mèsi Bondye! is cried, Mèsi Bondye! Alleluia!

Libète is lifted from the ground and met by congratulating hugs and slaps on the back. Someone lays a woven basket at Libète's feet and things are placed inside, a yam, a mango, two ears of corn, gifts for the girl who has wrought a miracle. She sees Magdala and Félix, radiating joy she is unable to reflect. Libète offers humble thanks to each who gives out of kindness, but her smile is false. She knows what this miracle really means.

Separate from this scene, tucked away behind matchstick stalls and tarps, stand Cinéus and Wilnor, watching with slit eyes. Even before neighbors carry Jeune away to his home to recuperate, before Libète is allowed to leave the market, the pair have slipped away. They whisper as they recall wisps of something once heard.

— Who is this one? Cinéus asks his brother.

— That could know to do such a thing! Wilnor replies. A peasant girl!

— Unbelievable.

— Do you think–

— Could she be–

— But here? Of all places–

— The one we've heard about?

— The one they're looking for?

The fireworks exploding in the sky herald change. They are beautiful and brilliant and defy the darkness that surrounds.

— Hard to believe it's already here. When the days feel like forever.

— Kanaval, Jak sighs. What a thing.

— And we're stuck in here, Libète says.

Carnival's arrival felt like a perfectly timed diversion. The prior nights' events with Laurent cast a pall over the arriving day. Though they longed for rest, the Sun peered over the ocean and made its unwavering demand that they live and move and hurt. Laurent remained in his room much of the day. Madanm Manno had checked in on him, and Jak had spoken with him a little, but Libète had stayed away.

— I don't think he remembers much. Enough to be ashamed.

Libète was wary to mention the picture on his desk, but it had been on her mind the whole day.

— Did you see the portrait?

He stroked his chin. You mean of Steffi?

She gave a long and expectant nod, full of gravity. Jak missed any meaning.

— He swatted it down when I walked in on him our first night here. A day later I went snooping through his room – Jak glared, but Libète didn't care – it was nowhere to be seen. I thought it was surely kept in his desk's top drawer. The one that's locked.

— *Libète*. Jak didn't like where she was leading him.

— Steffi's message. Laurent has been lying all along. Saying that he hadn't heard from her, that she couldn't be in touch!

— Still, Laurent was pretty torn up over the message.

— Jak, do you think Laurent is . . .

— What?

He was going to make her say it. Her mouth pressed in a tight line.

— In love ... with ... his sister.

— No. No, no, no. There must be something else there. How could that be?

She shrugged. Steffi is adopted. And they're different ages–separated by, what? Ten, twelve years?

— Steffi said he went to college at eighteen. She was just a little girl when she was adopted. It's not like he grew up with her.

— Still. It's gross. She snapped her fingers. Maybe that's why he acted like an ass back at Moïse's house on New Year's Eve. Because Remi was there! He was jealous!

— Hmmm. I could *understand* being in love with her–

Libète laughed, the first time in a long while. Jak, I didn't know!

— Wha–no! No! I don't mean I *do* love her, just that if I were, if I was older . . . ah, leave me alone!

She cackled. Woo! I won't tell, Jak, I won't tell. Don't you worry!

— Let's not talk about it anymore.

— Suits me just fine.

A new round of explosions filled the sky, and Libète turned toward them, watching streaks of ruby fade to nothing. Her smile faded. *That's all life is. Bursts of happiness, soon gone.*

She rubbed her hand against the spackled balcony wall. The world's passing us by, Jak. Out on those streets is the biggest party in all of Haiti. Carnival in Jacmel. She clicked her tongue, shook her head. And we're under house arrest.

The fireworks were just the formal start of festivities that would have been set in motion for weeks prior. Carnival in Cité Soleil was as crude and alive and joyful as Carnival ought to be, but paled next to Jacmel's. Here, it became its own religion. It was legendary throughout the Caribbean and Stephanie, the connoisseur of Haitian art and culture, had strangely wanted to keep them from it. Instead they embarked on week-end trips around Jacmel; she would take them to the waterfalls and blue-green pools of Bassin Bleu, the pine forests of La Visite, or even farther afield. Stephanie was not particularly religious, but it seemed like the revelry awakened a penitent spirit pounded into her by the Catholic sisters who had taught her in school.

We'll go when you're older, was her refrain whenever they begged. She was a surprising prude, treating them like they were innocent and to be sheltered from bawdy humor and sex.

All that when they came from Cité Soleil? Ha!

Just walking down the street, the things you'd hear! They were packed so tight in the slums you couldn't help but catch the telltale sounds of people in the act. And Jak and Libète's peers in school were already deep into experimenting with sex–not on the campus grounds, at least not that they were aware.

Libète assured Stephanie in plain terms that she was well acquainted with such things, but utterly immune to temptation. Revolutionaries have no time for such business, Libète had said dismissively at the sight of kissing on screen or handholding in public. Love–romantic love–it's a distraction from the things that really matter, Libète would say. And besides, Jak can hardly bring himself to say that little three-letter word.

Such conversations discomfited Stephanie greatly.

Libète thought of herself uttering such sentences with conviction just a few months ago. Her self-righteousness now made her queasy.

Another firework exploded, lighting up her eyes and Jacmel's bay. The street near their home was clotted with cars full of pilgrims who had come to celebrate from all over Haiti and abroad.

— I'd give anything to be down there. To see the parade tomorrow, the costumes, the papier-mâché, Jak mused. What a thing! To just sit and watch. Maybe even sketch as they go by . . .

Libète looked at her friend, held rapt by the sparkling streams of gold and red and blue. Her brow dipped and her lips curled into a smile, forming a familiar but long-absent look, one, that if seen by Jak, would have made him profoundly worried.

MASKS

Malè yon nonm ki mete konfyans li nan yon nonm.
Woe to the man who puts his trust in another man.

Sunday sees Libète renewed.
 The hour is early. She knocks on Jak's door.
 — Jak.
 No reply.
 — *Jak!*
 Still no answer. She knew telling Jak her plan in advance would have seen him rebel against it, so she didn't. *There's no time for this.* She barges in the room, and Jak leaps out of bed.
 — Libète! He jerks a sheet over his lower half. I'm in my underwear!
 — Aw, big deal. She walks to his trousers folded carefully over the back of a chair, picks them up, and throws them to him. Get those on.
 — Is it an emergency? He pulls the sheet over his head and, stumbling ghostlike, tries to pull on the pair of pants.
 Libète smirks. Wi. A *gran* one. And we've got to go! Quick!
 He races for his shirt, and his fingers nimbly feed the buttons through their holes. She is already down the stairs and out the door. He catches up with her. Here, she says, handing him a piece of bread, the cheese already spread inside.

— Why, thank yo-wait a minute. What's going on here?
She tightens the straps on her red pack. Kanaval, she says, a smile lighting her face.

Libète looks to the pitted road as she walks behind Saint-Pierre, Magdala, and Félix, worrying, worrying, worrying. Félix and Magdala glance at her over their shoulders, unable to understand her quiet. It was as if leaving the market a hero was the worst that could happen.

Nearly everything they had carried to market had been snapped up post-*resureksyon*-what Jeune's revival was being called-and now, they have a fistful of notes and coins while Saint-Pierre ports the weight of Foche's kind thanks back up the mountain.

— Wait, Libète says. Félix tugs at Saint-Pierre's bridle to slow his ascent.

They are passing Délira's home.

— She's not home yet. No one's there, Félix says.

Libète struggled to lift off the saddlebag full of gifted food. Magdala's lips pursed and she reached for Libète but said nothing. Libète carried the bag into Délira's home and emptied the produce in a heap on her friend's table. Libète toted the empty saddlebag and walked ahead and alone. I didn't deserve this, she said over her shoulder.

Félix stood dumbstruck. But you saved him!

— *Him* no less! Magdala added. You worked a miracle, Sophia. Did a good thing. I didn't even know you had that in you!

Libète spun. I *hesitated*. To protect myself. And now everyone is wondering who I really am again, how I could know to do such a thing.

— That's just ridiculous, Félix said. This will make you loved by everyone! It's the best thing that could have–

— Just leave me alone.

Magdala rushed to her, embraced her, held her tight even as Libète struggled against the restraining hold. It's true. There will be more questions now. But what you did, she whispered, was *right*. It was *good*. Such good acts, the ones that cost us, are lights in the dark.

Libète finally succumbed and leaned into Magdala's arms.

— We'll face whatever may come, my dear. You are not alone. Whatever happens, you are *not* alone.

• • •

The rest of the day slipped away.

Magdala went to check on the new mother and her infant on the other side of the mountain, an obligation she couldn't forget. She asked Libète if she wanted to join her.

— I still need to think, Libète answered absently.

Magdala gave a wary nod. She left the girl with her heavy mind.

After Libète swept out the house, wiped dust from every surface, did the wash, fed the pig and goat, and prepared an early dinner of *bouyon*, she had run out of chores. She bathed in the midafternoon to cool her head and, as the last effects of adrenaline receded, found herself utterly exhausted. She descended into sleep.

Hours passed. She woke to a dim house. Numbed, Libète rose from her mat to sit in the doorway and watch the world as light faded from it. The breeze blew and caressed her like a consoling touch. She closed her eyes for a long while and controlled her breathing. She heard the melody again, the same phantom music from Delivrans's birth, and now from Jeune's resurrection. It was like a call emanating from deep within herself.

She opened her eyes and flicked the lingering flecks of sleep from them. She cocked her head. There was something curious there, resting on the roots of the mapou tree.

Can it be?

She got up and walked suspiciously to the spot, looking down the road, into the fields, up the mountain. No one was near.

It was. *My notebook!*

She slid her hand over its cover, felt the spiral ring, opened its pages. It was intact!

All of her memories laid down, a fixed and definite record, a tether to everything she'd been through and everything she'd faced! She fell to the ground and began revisiting the past.

She skimmed through Jak's small sketches stuffed inside with her poetry and thoughts. But they were still there too. The Numbers. She had woven the digits through past entries so that only she knew how to recollect them. She considered burning the notebook on the spot but knew she never could. There remained an irresistible power in the knowing.

She revisited her compositions, enjoying a Libète who seemed so self-assured and content, until all her joy turned to sadness. She came upon her final and most recent piece, a tribute she had been working on when the notebook was stolen. Seeing the words snapped her back through time, bringing to mind all of the pain that had carried her to Jacmel, and all of the pain that carried her from it.

It was still incomplete. Hope had stilled her hand then, and it did so again now. She reread the opening stanzas:

There was a Land.
And in that Land, there was a Boy.
And in that Boy, there was a Seed.

Long before the Boy came the Land.
Full of crafted spires and flowing rivers.

It was blessed and planted with Goodness.

The words brought such pain, and yet, peace. She turned the dog-eared page, her eye leaping to its end to notice something previously missed. New words, written in a bold and unfamiliar hand:

Follow the drums when they sound again.

And following it, appended to her own verse in the same handwriting, were words that stopped her heart:

*There is a Land.
And in that Land, there is a Girl.
And that Girl, she is on Fire.*

With the help of a ladder they are up and over the gate–Laurent and Madanm Manno have the only keys–and on the street, running, running, running.

It is exhilarating, like those days of weightless ignorance in Cité Soleil when the Sun beat down and their spirits could not care less, days altogether pleasant and altogether wonderful. Jak still protests, but half-heartedly, out of habit. As they know too well, life can be short, and this, *this*, he does not want to miss.

Most who walked Jacmel's streets at this hour were heading to early Mass. Some looked to resist or condemn the carousing the day would hold. Others prepared to scrub their souls clean before they blackened them again by late morning.

The children knew these streets from past days spent with Stephanie in lazy cafés and age-old restaurants. She introduced them to the history of the place as she had experienced it growing up there.

They passed the town hall and square, moving down the Rue de L'eglise, past unmanned stalls and closed stores. The streets were immaculate, as if the slanted sunlight sliding across the streets had purged them of all refuse. Anticipation ran through the roads like a current, passing through all who put foot to earth.

— Just a few hours and it's all going to be packed.

— Look, Jak! There's your cathedral!

They took in the decrepit church–the Cathédrale de Saint Philippe et Saint Jacques–and listened as choral hymns wafted out into the streets like a perfume.

— Saint Jacques. Has a nice ring, no?

Jak smiled, before turning to look down the road, saying nothing. His face soon soured.

— What's the matter? she asked.

He bit his lip.

Libète's skin prickled.

— Nothing, he finally spoke. A trick of light. I don't like how empty the streets are.

— Let's . . . keep moving.

Instead of promenading down the middle of the road, they took a different path, walking under hotels' and stores' covered sidewalks. They looked over their shoulders at turns.

— Laurent will be worrying, Jak said.

— I left a note.

— I doubt that will help.

The churches began letting out, and the penitent streamed into the streets. Everything was coming alive. The crowd gave them their anonymity again, and they breathed more easily. They reached Avenue de la

Liberté. She ribbed Jak. You've got a church, but I've got a whole *avenue*. She flashed a smile, so rare these days, and it made Jak light up.

Though they'd never seen it, the two knew the parade would begin here and would flow around the perimeter of the city, along Avenue Barranquilla. They watched from the side of the street in wonder as trucks with floats began lining up and people converged from all corners: band members with their instruments in hand, dancers in flowing dresses, costumed figures. Music began clamoring as laughter rose higher and higher.

Watching was not enough. In they plunged.

They strode through a troupe of youth costumed as Taíno Indians, members' skin lightened with paint and their hair bedecked by cords of sisal and elaborate feathered headdresses. A young man aimed his mock bow and arrow at Libète as if to fire, and she put up her fists, daring him—they both cracked smiles.

Also weaving through the assembly were ghouls, blood spilling from their eyes, their faces turned into bone masks. Jak was unnerved, but tried to not let it show. A mule was also there, wearing tennis shoes. And behind him, political figures: all of the recent presidents of Haiti in papier-mâché standing in a line: Martelly and Préval and Aristide and Baby Doc, joining hands and dancing in a circle.

The children turned from this and looked upon the massive form of a float, the *Nèg Mawon*. The symbolic depiction of the former slave had a machete in one hand and a conch shell in the other, ready to call others to take to the hills and rebel. At the level of the truck bed were three young men wearing scandalous dresses and wigs.

— Where's your dress, Jak? Libète asked.

He grinned.

The bottles were being knocked back too, as important a preparation for many as applying face paint and becoming someone else. Libète pointed. There, coming down in a pack were the costumed *chaloska*, ghoulish military men inspired by a police chief notorious for killing political opponents. Decked in dark uniforms, their faces were obscured by dark sunglasses and massive red lips that reigned in jagged teeth. Their prey was small children.

Their leader wore a tricorner cap and had a fat belly. He was the first to lunge at a group of unwatchful children. These uninitiated ones bolted behind mothers' skirts and fathers' thighs, trembling while onlookers laughed, just as onlookers had laughed at them generations before when *they* had been the horrified little ones.

But one small girl stood her ground, a who-do-you-think-*you*-are sneer on her face. She pointed to the lead chaloska:

Chaloska m pa pè w
Se moun ou ye!

"Chaloska, I'm not afraid of you! You're just a human being!" she screamed.

The leader fell into a fit of shakes and tremors and fled. She yelled it again and again as she pointed a finger at monster after monster until they had all been made to cower and run. She turned back to her awestruck friends and revealed to them that with the same incantation they too could protect themselves. Libète smiled. *A girl after my own heart.*

Jak tugged at the back of her shirt, pulling her out of the way of a shirtless man with snakes draped over his head and shoulders. The man laughed at Jak, who could only stare back at him.

A fight broke out between two floats' crews after one truck driver slipped into a neutral gear and slid back into the front of the other float, nearly unsettling the massive Nèg Mawon.

— Calm down! someone shouted.

— It's Kanaval! It's Kanaval! said another.

— Let it go! Save it for another day!

A police pickup, summoned by the shouting, drove through, and a tense officer barked through a megaphone, threatening to arrest anyone who ruined the day and marred Jacmel's reputation. The world is watching, he intoned. The world is watching!

Libète hid her face at the sight of the police and withdrew behind a column. The easygoing spell cast over her by growing crowds and increasingly bold costumes was broken.

— Don't be afraid. No one will recognize us here, Jak said.

— I know, she said, a bit too harshly. She didn't like being made to fear or feeling the need to hide. In its way, the apprehension was yet another victory for Benoit.

— We can go back, Jak said. If you need. There was disappointment in his voice, faint and feebly hidden.

The walls of the Martinette Villa had kept fear of discovery at bay these past months. Though Benoit of course had no idea of moments like this, when he inflicted paranoia on her, she resolved not to feed her fear.

She wrapped her arm around her friend's slumped shoulders.

— I need nothing! Today, Jak, we live!

The distant drumming is underway. A call.

Follow it, the notebook says.

She reads and rereads the scrawled message until the land has been overtaken by darkness.

Whoever stole her writings was literate, as evidenced by the note. He or she knew things about her she had told no one else, not even Magdala. But why was the notebook suddenly returned?

She had been advised by Stephanie and Laurent not to commit too much to the page, and her scribblings were mostly fragmented: lonely stanzas, pieces of speeches, blog posts she'd yet to enflesh. Life in Cité Soleil was a common subject throughout, yet the references were often veiled. Didi was mentioned by name. As was Jak. She couldn't imagine a soul on this mountaintop who could take in these ramblings and extract fact. But the observant reader might still trap hints.

With fears of discovery allayed, she poured over her words dispassionately and with new eyes. She was struck by the fire in the author's pen: her beating heart, her passion, her resoluteness.

It saddened her. What had she become these past months, as she let herself live out a fiction? Sophia was not an ideal. She was safe. Weak. Fearful, even. Satisfied with obscurity, others' ignorance, the status quo, injustice...

— Sophia? You there?

Libète jumped. She turned to find Félix standing at the garden gate.

— What do you want? she asked quietly.

He walked toward her, but hesitated. I wanted to ask... I wanted to see how you were. If you were feeling better.

She shrugged.

— Where did you learn to breathe life like that?

Libète debated how much to share, but she knew she could trust Félix with this bit of truth. A hospital where I volunteered, she said. The same as where I learned about delivering babies.

He nodded.

— Is that all you came to say, Félix?

He shook his head. Something is happening here, Sophia. There's a strangeness in the air. I feel it. He clenched something in his hand. Whatever it was made him uneasy.

— Please. I-I have a lot on my mind. He noticed the notebook in her hand.

— Is that... yours? She nodded. You found it then?

— Whoever stole it returned it. That's all I can figure.

— Bondye. What a thing. I wonder why now?

— Must be the 'strangeness.' She rolled her eyes. That drumming doesn't help. What is that anyway? Why isn't anyone willing to tell me?

— No one knows. His words were instant, unfeeling.

He's lying. She rose, stepped toward him, a sharp anger pushing her forward. She searched his face and his eyes and poked his chest. I don't need shit like this right now, not from you.

He looked like he wanted to tell her everything. She softened. I'm sorry, Félix. I'm sorry. What's that in your hand?

He nodded twice, opening his hand to reveal a small figurine. It was a rooster.

— That's–that's Dorsinus's work, no? Where'd you get it? From inside the house?

— It's not yours. I was down at the cemetery today.

— Just hanging around graves?

— Of course not. I was visiting, and this was left on – he paused for dramatic effect – *Dorsinus's marker.*

Libète's snorted a laugh. These hills–it's–it's *insane!* The nèg is dead. *Dead,* dead.

The drumming grew louder and she inclined her ear. What the hell is that beating? she muttered under her breath.

— I'm telling you, Félix said. Things are going on here. They're coming. Big things. Bigger than Foche has ever seen.

— I couldn't care less, Libète said.

— That's a lie.

Libète waved him off. The dull rhythms accelerated now, growing in volume, impossible to ignore. *Follow it.*

She slipped back inside to don her worn sandals and sought out a match and a tallow candle. She forced herself between Félix and the gate. Her candle was now aflame.

— Where are you g-going? Félix stammered.

— The drums.
— Sophia, *ou pa ka fè sa*. They aren't for you!
— If you know something, tell me.
— I can't.
She pushed on.
— I can't follow you there! he shouted, the timbre of his low voice cracking. There will be consequences!
He clasped the wooden bird in his hand and watched a long while, until the light of her candle disappeared behind the mountain's hard, ominous lines.

The colors swirl and the bodies move, an impenetrable mass of life.

The spectators–those who stand at the sides taking in the bands and demons and slaves and beasts and Indians and dancers and statues–can no longer deny themselves a place. They become the Parade.

And Jak and Libète are there. In the middle of the jubilation, caught up themselves, distant from all the pain that paralyzes them, the accusations that exile them, the fears that bind them.

The Parade is thick. Clammy bodies press up against each other, jumping, laughing, sometimes grinding. Strangers alienated by the challenges of daily life come together to protest against death.

When it was on the very cusp of beginning, Libète had thought she would like to wear a mask and become something altogether different. But now she has banished the thought. Today, she does not want to hide and cower and pretend. She wants to once again *be*–Libète Limye, her very own selfsame self.

Jak is free too, maybe for his own reasons, but maybe because seeing Libète at ease makes him at ease. *Rara* horns blare staccato rhythms that animate the Parade to step and dance. Jak and Libète's hands grip each other's tightly, for losing the other in the crowd might mean losing them for good. But their hands are sweaty and slip; they are quick to grasp again to bond them together.

But the bond breaks.

The crowd engorges as it winds around a corner and pushes through a bottleneck. Libète figures Jak will step back into reach, but he's pulled away.

The fiction falls. The fear, imperfectly tucked away, bursts its top. Her breathing, already fast, becomes hyperventilation. Jak! she chokes out, her voice unable to climb above the horns. *Jak!* she cries.

But she cannot stop. To do so means fighting a surging wave of people.

— Please! Let me pass, please!

Libète pushes toward the side, fighting revelers who treat her fear with dismay as she prays Jak might be spotted and found.

She is nearly out and her eyes are fixed on one post along the colonnaded road. *He'll do the same. He'll be there. He'll be waiting.*

She reaches for it, her hands clinging desperately as if to a ship's strong mast in a storm. She holds tightly–*so tight!*–fighting the winds and water until she–

A hand. It grabs her shoulder from behind and squeezes. Libète spins, her eyes watering with hope.

She is greeted by a mask that–once pulled away–unveils a face she never expected to see.

The drumbeat pulls Libète forward through the night like an invisible lead around her neck. Up, over the peak, down, into the brush and sparse woods. The Moon is out, the stars are out, but they offer no comfort.

She nears the source of the sound. She extinguishes her candle.

Stepping from tree to tree to keep her cover, she takes in the scene.

The colors swirl and the bodies move, masks hiding faces.

Firelight springs from the center of a circle as dancing forms stop and start. Their robes of red and black both glint in the firelight and swallow the light whole. Their masks look like malformed skulls. A ten-foot timber pole stands erect near the flames.

She watches, unblinking, searching for hints of the familiar in the twirling movements, but finds all is transformed by the song, the drum, their beckon. She tries to make out their words, but they're indistinct.

But it is *familiar*. This very spot. She's come here to retrieve wood to smoke and render into charcoal. But the clearing in the trees had been so unassuming by day.

There are at least twelve caught up in the dancing, a pair of drummers, and a hunched figure off to the side. These men and women were surely from these hills, some most certainly her neighbors. She thought she had begun to know this place. But that there was some hidden, Vodou-infused secret society here in Foche, *Chanpwel*, as similar groups were known across Haiti, turns her blood to ice.

Félix knew about this. As did Magdala. Their reluctance to speak about the source of the drums told it all. But why not explain? How could this group inspire so much fear?

She slips behind a tree and moves nearer toward the flames. An incense's sweet aroma mingles with the smoke's char, and the scents climb high, high, high.

The figures are otherworldly, some moving as if possessed—*maybe because they are*, Libète thinks. The hidden faces bring to mind Carnival in

Cité Soleil, in Jacmel, but these are not for adornment or for scaring children. They are practical, meant to be worn again and again.

Her eyes latch onto the stooped man who sits to the side on a rock. A brimmed hat disguises his features. He holds an ornamental cane and taps it obediently to the dull rhythm. Libète does not know the Vodou pantheon well, but this god she knows. *Papa Legba. The Keeper of the Crossroads.* At his feet and undisturbed are intricate *vèvè*, designs drawn on the ground with powdered cornmeal to summon the spirits.

The drummers' hands fly. The leader pounds the *tanbou* in his hands, speaking an enticing and dangerous language she cannot understand.

He hands the drum over to a woman who takes it dutifully. As the beat resumes, he steps forward. His dancing is a marvel. Unlike anything Libète has seen. The dancer is caught up in a thrall, and the others pause to pay him respect.

Papa Legba raises his hands.

The rhythm stops. The dancing stops.

The master dancer rushes to Legba's side and gives him a bracing arm. He inclines his ear to capture Legba's whispered words and acts as a megaphone, shouting them out to all.

— I call you to order!

The voice is unfamiliar.

— You've all heard by now. About the malefactors trespassing in our community.

— What can we do? answered one of the masked.

— We wait. Not because we support them, but because we must. Because these fools have been granted license to be here by one higher.

— We can't defer forever to some secret *houngan* elsewhere, said another of the assembled. No one in this zone should have more authority than you, Legba. We've let these fools stay long enough. Any good they've done for us isn't worth the insult of their presence.

There is a silence; the crackling of twigs rising from the fire can be heard.

Legba whispered, and was amplified. This balance of authority has served us well for a long, long while. We will let it carry us further. But I agree. Our waiting will not be idle.

The old man stood despite the apparent exertion it posed. The dancer tried to help but saw his hand batted away. Legba whispered further. We'll prepare by night, in case we're needed by day.

There is more said, but the words, Libète does not hear them. Her attention is pulled to her left as a wisp of a breath plays across her bare shoulder.

Félix, she is certain, *finally caught up with me*. She turns to scold him with a silent finger.

She instead faces a demon.

She cannot think of her name!

The crowd pushes her, and they pull apart before they're swept back together.

What was it?

The digger! The investigator! The truth-seeker!

Her mind's tumblers spin until they *click click click*. The lock pops open.

Maxine!

The woman smiles broadly, and her expression radiates joy. She hugs Libète, kisses her, once, twice, three times. I've found you, my dear! I've found you! Maxine's eyes are wet, and Libète can't help but reflect back the woman's relief. She hugs her back, not understanding why she does so.

— Come with me, my dear. I can get you out of here before Benoit's thugs close in. They've been on the prowl, scouring Jacmel the past few days. I'm just glad I found you in time!

Libète is confused: the noise, the movement, the smells, her fear. Each pushes her beyond herself.

Maxine pulls her arm as they thread through observers still reluctant to join the Parade. They reach a narrow alleyway between two buildings.

— Where... where are we going? Libète asks.

— To safety. You're staying at the Martinettes', I assume?

Libète nodded.

— I'm surprised they didn't steal you already! It's all so very obvious. Just shows you the quality of Benoit's hired help. I'd have come to the Martinettes' right away if I wasn't so tied up with other clients. This timing–

Jak! The thought pops like a bubble. Libète tugs hard. He's here, Max! Jak's with me. I just lost him, in the crowd. We can't go anywhere! Not yet! Not without him!

Maxine looked back down the long alley, into the crowd. She sighed through gritted teeth.

— Walk down this alley and take a left, she said. You'll see a blue jeep. You know what a jeep looks like? Libète nodded. Max reached into her pocket and removed a key and what looked like a biscuit in the shape of a bone. She put both into Libète's open hand.

— Give this to Remus and you'll be fine, Maxine said. She pointed to the bone.

— Remus?

— My jeep's security system.

— Where–where are you going?

— Up, I think. This café's balcony. I'll see if I can spot Jak. She handed Libète her mask, a narrow purple one that one would wear to a masquerade party. Put it on, she ordered. Libète did. And take this. Maxine reached again into her bag to withdraw a small knife in a black sheath. I'll be along as soon as I've got him.

Libète, having regained some of her senses, suddenly glared at Maxine. The woman's tight expression broke like a cracked facade.

— Libète. They have been trying to catch you, and kill you, and if you do not do everything I tell you, *every single thing*, they will succeed. Now *go*! It was a feral command, that of a protective lioness for her cub.

— I'll do it, Max.

Libète ran, down the alley until reaching a street that was nearly deserted. See scanned the cars and trucks and motorcycles. *There it is.* Parked at an angle to the curb, the jeep looked like it was left in a hurry. Its window was cracked. Libète looked in warily. Re-Remus? She held the sheathed knife in one hand and the biscuit in the other.

The dog's bark was powerful. In an instant he leaped from the back of the cab to its front, rearing his teeth. Libète yelped and took two stumbling steps back, landing hard on the cobblestone ground.

— Dumb mutt! She unsheathed the knife and held it in her right hand, popping the biscuit–now broken in two–between the window's lip and frame's edge. The black dog devoured the morsels and wagged his nub of a tail with abandon. After finishing, he righted himself and looked at her contentedly. His jowls sagged and tongue bobbed, panting in what had to be a sweltering box.

— Are you gonna be good? She waved the knife in the dog's face and he looked pleased, as if it was a bauble with which to play. He sat before opening and closing his heavy chops.

She took this as a "yes."

With the key turned in the door, her left hand reached out and tugged at the door handle. She kept the knife drawn. The door opened a crack. Remus simply cocked his head.

She opened it farther, and he shifted seats to sit in front of the steering column. Libète had never seen a breed quite like him: ugly, and yet entirely at ease with his looks. She took a seat of her own, letting the door stay open and her feet dangle out the machin's side. She hazarded scratching Remus on the back of his neck. He let out a pleased *grumpf.*

She looked up and down the road, but traffic-foot and otherwise-was nearly nonexistent. A song ended and cheers shot up from the Barranquilla.

— With you, Remus, I think I'll be safe.

He didn't answer back.

She smiled faintly.

Bondye

We've not spoken much lately. For good reason.

But if you're there-if you're love-if you're capable, protect me.

Protect us all. No more of this death. No more.

I can't promise you anything. Can't promise I'll be better. That I'll be able to serve you better.

But deliver us. If you can.

Am-

Pop. Remus's ears perked up. The back left side of the jeep dropped, quickly. The dog shot to the back window. Libète gasped.

Pop. The same sound, but on the other side of the jeep. Libète's side. The dog barked madly, until a gun exploded and a bullet tore through the black canvas canopy, silencing the animal.

Libète screamed. While she was scrambling to draw the knife and flip the lock, a dark presence swooped forward and ripped the door open. The knife shook in her grasp as her wide, trembling eyes filled with the face of a beast of an entirely different kind.

CROSSROADS

Fòk ou bat tanbou a pou tande son li.
You must beat the drum to hear its sound.

She is tugged from shadow into firelight by a tense hand. Escorted to the flames at the heart of the circle, she wonders if she'll be cast inside. The fear climbs her throat and makes her choke. She channels the feelings, swallows them, forces them down into the pit of her clenched stomach. The memory of the small girl casting away the chaloskas comes to her:

I'm not afraid of you! You're just human beings!

She breathes deep, feels the folded page in her skirt's waistband, and breathes again. *The invitation. I was summoned*, she reminds herself.
She takes the fear, makes it do her bidding. *You all have the benefit of masks. I might as well take mine off.*
Libète pulls off Sophia's timidity–her brow tightens. She unfastens Sophia's suffocating deference–her fingers become fists. Libète is Libète: all gristle, all coiled rage, and fury.
She rips her escort's hand from her shoulder, and he raises it as if to hit her. She sneers, daring him. Those assembled gasp. The hand stalls.

Legba, the bent old man, lifts his cane. He whispers again in the drummer's ear.

— You came, the drummer says boldly, still serving as a mouthpiece.

— I did, she answers. She withdraws the paper, forcing it in the escort's hidden eyes. I was told to. I don't know by whom, but I was told.

The old man whispers again:

There is a Land.
And in that Land, there is a Girl.
And that Girl, she is on Fire.

Libète spoke. Are you . . . are you the one who wrote those words? You took my notebook?

The old man neither nodded nor shook his head. His slit eyes simply bore into her, pass through her.

— I see what others do not, the drummer echoed. I see all things. For I'm the Lord of the Crossroads. All coming, all going, it all passes before my eyes. No one stays who I say goes, and no one goes whom I order to stay. And you have been placed under my jurisdiction.

— Under your jurisdiction? Ha!

Her derision sent a shock through those gathered. You stole from me, Libète said. You took my secrets. And I'm supposed to thank you for returning what's mine? I don't know what this little club is, but–

The captor cuffed her, hard, and she fell to the ground. She rose, possessed anew.

— You have no authority over me! I won't cower before fools who hide behind masks!

— Who are you to speak of masks, 'Sophia?'

— Sophia! *Sophia!* Félix rushes in, breaking past a band of men. He leaps between Libète and the old man.

— You! Legba trembles, speaking for himself. You were told not to come again! *You were told!*

Félix dropped to his knee and bowed, raising his hands. I mean no disrespect! I didn't want her to intrude on the *Sosyete*'s meeting. I knew she had no place here, but if I spoke of the Sosyete, if I stopped her, I would have broken its code.

— You're the only one unwelcome here, said the escort. His eyes flashed from behind his mask. Félix strained to check his anger.

— Quiet! Legba commanded. Sophia, you've been brought here for a reason. There is no need for further delay. By order of the Sosyete, you are to leave Foche.

Libète buckled. Her eyes bounced between all of the empty stares. Her teeth began rattling, and her heart descended low inside her.

— Leave? she murmured.

— We've sheltered you from whatever you escaped. Foche will bear your presence no longer. You are a threat.

Her mind reeled. Are you–do you mean–what happened today? With those fools Cinéus and Wilnor?

The mask bobbed.

— Why would I be cast out when I helped save one of you? She turned to the others. Why, when all I've done is work the fields, eat with you, share life with you, would I be–

— You were granted a license from on high. It has been revoked. That is all that will be said.

— But, I–I have nowhere. No one!

Félix looked up at her from the ground. Their eyes connected before hers again swept the circle's unsympathetic faces.

— You have taken more than you have given. You will leave tomorrow.

— So soon?

— Please, Félix spoke, give her more time. Just a little. It's a cruelty, an unnecessary–

— *How dare the thief ask for a special dispensation!* You were told if you ever returned you would not live.

— I've abided by your other rules. I have done everything in accordance with the Sosyete's laws. Everything! I stayed in that fortress all by myself each day, I–

— You are on a precipice, Félix. Soon to be forced from Foche for good. If not for your mother, not for the old drunk, you would already be on the path down the mountain, or worse. Tread lightly, son of Foche, or you will be no more.

The cruelty of the thought convulsed Félix, and he fell facedown to the ground. I would choose death over leaving! Please, I take it back. Please.

Legba looked at Libète. She had shrunk. She fixed her eyes on the flames. We needn't be too harsh, Legba said. After what you did today, tomorrow would be a cruelty. You have one week. Simply . . . disappear. If you breathe a word of this to others, you won't even be permitted that much time.

The escort took her arm and leaned in. He whispered, *It will be all right.*

She saw his eyes up close, heard his voice, but with her mind afloat could not connect them to a known person. Félix pulled the unknown speaker from Libète's side and led Libète away.

As they crossed the circle's threshold into the wood, the drummer gave his strength to Legba's words once more.

— Papa Legba has a final question for you.

She turned to look at him as a profound heaviness made her person sag.

— Who is your fable about?

Libète inclined her head, unsure.

— Who is the boy you wrote of in your journal? Legba clarified. The one who had within him a seed?

She looked into the field of masked faces, one by one by one. No one, she replied to them all. A ghost. She turned away. No one at all, she murmured.

Libète screams again, until the hand of this masked man, this beast, clamps over her mouth. She jabs reflexively with her knife and inflicts a cut on his forearm. He bellows, slamming her wrist into the dashboard. She yelps and drops the blade, but is quick to bite his hand, kick at his groin. He is a determined blur, and before she knows it she is pulled out of the jeep and onto the street.

He tries to say something. She is wild, a beast herself.

— *Motherf–*

— *Take your–*

— *I'll kill–*

She spews venom, each sentence aborted by a new effort to fight him. His own curses are muffled and alien, lost behind his mask.

Pressed facedown into the stones, her arms pinned behind her back, there's the ratcheted clicking of something clasping onto her wrists. Cuffs, she realizes. Her foot catches a seatbelt and she tugs with all her strength as he drags her off, but her attempt is futile. He's yelling as he grabs at her headscarf and jams it in her mouth to shut her up. He pulls his elbow back as if he might hit her. She winces. He stays his punch.

In this pause, she takes in the beast anew.

His mask has loosened, falls, but the face is drowned by the Sun that drenches him in brightness. There are only hints of the face. A large beard, hard-edged cheekbones, and a broad, shaved head. Finally, the curvature of the head eclipses the light.

Dimanche!

In such moments, the mind seizes.

Dimanche? Here? But why does he lift me? And his talking? Words? What can they mean?

He huffs. Her head splits into sharp-edged thoughts. *Too little air. Fire at my wrists. The light! The light. The light . . .*

She lands gently, her body wedged *V*-like into a strange pod.

Her eyes don't blink. They can't. They lock on him and the remorse on his face as he sits down on–what?–a motorcycle?

— Where is Jak? he says with blunt urgency. He kicks down, bringing the machine to life.

Libète watches him with fixed eyes. He curses and pulls the scarf from her mouth and looks anxiously over his shoulder.

— It's you. It's you, oh God, it's been you all along! she says in an accusing refrain.

— There is no time! Where is he?

— But why?

— *Tell me where he is!*

He pleads, does not demand.

— I'm here for you.

People are coming out to see what were first believed to be fireworks, not bullets.

— To save you! he adds.

— Who?

— Who what?

— From who?

It dawns on him: all her fierce resistance finally adding up to something fathomable.

— From that, that – he pauses, trying to find a word – that *monster!* Maxine!

Libète watches him.

—How could you do this to me?

His mouth gapes. With the words he is pierced.

— You're taking me, she says. You're taking me . . .

He grabs her head in his hands, and she winces, waiting for the mountain of a man to press his hands together and for her head to give way

and collapse. Tears bud in his eyes, and he touches his forehead to hers. Father, forgive me–
She comprehends nothing.
— Libète. I swear to you, what I do, I do for you. Jak is in danger, incomprehensible danger.
— I ... don't ...
— Where is *she* then? Where is Maxine?
Libète wants to believe, wants to hope this apparition can be good. Mustering faith, she says, In the crowd. Searching for Jak.
— Dear God, he says. He reattaches his mask. The bike speeds forward with Libète inert in the sidecar.
Words, curious words, spring to her lips:

Even when I walk through the darkest valley, I fear no danger because you are with me.
Your rod and your staff–they protect me ...

Dimanche pulls up to a small alley and eyes its width. Libète takes him in again, his taught muscles, new scarring on his forearms, a simple green T-shirt, denim jeans, boots. Formidable. Strong. *And desperate.*
— You said he was lost in the crowd?
She simply looks at him. He flicks his wrist, and the bike shoots down the lane. He throws on the brake and skids to a halt before a gush of people stomping past in rapturous rhythm. He jumps up on the seat for a better view and tries to spot the woman or the boy.
— Uncuff me, she says. He looks at her, his face again expressionless. Please, she says louder. She turns and rattles her wrists. Uncuff me.
He reaches for the keys in the ignition and undoes the bonds.
— I need your help, he shouts over bamboo horns' blaring.
She nods. For Jak, she says.
— Wear the scarf around your face. She ties it and resembles a bandit. Good. Now go and keep watch back at the mouth of the street. Keep an

eye on the jeep. If they come out, honk the bike's horn. Right here. You see?

She nods.

— Do you know how to ride one of these?

She nods again. Her cousin had taught her long ago.

He mutters something and plunges into the crowd. She sees he reaches for something in his waistband: a gun.

Libète's mind raced as various possibilities collided, demolishing one another.

She pulled the bike slowly into position to maintain a vantage over the abandoned jeep, summoning everything within her not to drive off.

After some minutes–five, ten, fifteen, she couldn't tell–Maxine and Jak came. Darting across the street as fast as they could shuffle. Maxine had a natural athleticism and struggled to pull Jak along with his defective leg. He looked terrified. Libète watched Maxine's reaction. On her approach, the woman noticed the first burst tire and then the other. And next the bullet hole through the canopy.

Her calm veneer vanished. She threw down Jak's hand and reached for her ankle, pulling up her pant leg and removing something that looked like–no, was certainly–a gun. Libète's breathing quickened as Jak shrank back from Maxine. Maxine thudded her back against the jeep and sidled along, gun drawn as she reached for the door's handle. She tugged it open and gasped at the sight of Remus. Jak wanted to peek in, but she held him back. Her face contorted with anger, she pulled out her phone and began speaking in a flurry of French.

Libète hovered her thumb over the horn's button, readied to press it, but stopped herself. She instead pulled the bike out from the alley, slowly at first, testing the steering, then sped up, taking the turn too quickly and scraping the sidecar's finish. She proceeded toward Maxine and Jak.

— Max! Max! she yelled, waving madly. The woman spun, gun out, ready to fire. Libète ducked. It's me! she shouted. Don't shoot! The bike crept up slowly. Maxine lowered her phone.

— What happened?
— A man, he came at me. But . . . I got away, took his keys.
— A man? Maxine was incredulous.
— Yes, a man.
— Did you know him?
— Non. The lie came to her instantly, without deliberation. He had on a mask, Libète said. I couldn't see who he was.

She cursed. We need to get away from here. Let me get my bag. We'll take the bike.

Libète nodded. Okay. Whatever you say.

— Jak, get in the side. He hesitated. Jak! Maxine roared. His head bobbed and he got in. Maxine leaned back into her jeep for something else when they heard the shout.

— Hey! *Hey!*

She pulled herself out of the jeep, her gun already pointing at the source of the bellow. *Dimanche!* He ducked behind a corner as she fired, the bullet's collision making a spray of stone erupt near his torso.

Jak was in.

— Libète, slide back! Let me on! Maxine shouted. Libète looked at Maxine and sneered.

Jak and Libète sped off.

Félix walks ahead, speaking at Libète, not to her. I told you not to go, he says, I told you . . .

Libète says nothing in return. She cannot fathom what the order to leave means, not at all.

The safety of Foche was being stripped away like a carpet pulled from beneath her feet. All she would have to leave behind flashed before her: the garden's produce she would not foster and protect. Delivrans's first steps, his first words. The common plot's harvest. Magdala's maternal care. She would drift unlike ever before. Curiously, she thought of Elize, her mentor, who had for so long floated across the Haitian countryside, unable to find a place to settle his troubled soul. She found herself wanting to embrace Félix in that moment, this on its own an incomprehensible thought.

Words finally percolated to her mind's surface. A matter of time, she blurted.

Félix was still midrant. What? What's that?

— This was coming. I can see it now. It was just a matter of time. Whether tonight or tomorrow, a week, a month; it wouldn't have made a difference. I was never welcome here.

Félix looked as if he wanted to speak.

— But why the show? she asked. Why go to all the effort?

— The Sosyete is the Sosyete. They do as they will.

— You know *them*.

— I do . . . I mean . . . I can't talk about it.

— You've kept this from me? Why?

— It is the code. Members can't speak of it—

— You're *one* of them?

Félix held his hands in front of himself, his outstretched fingers absorbing all his frustration, forcing his mind to wrap itself around his next words carefully. I was. I was being initiated.

— So the masks are nothing to you? You know the faces behind them?

His nod was heavy.

— Well, tell me then.

Silence.

— You won't? I can keep a secret! Obviously, I can! I've done it for months.

268

— Not knowing is for your own good.

— How *dare* you! You're just as silly as the rest of them, dancing behind false faces. How can I trust you? Huh?

— But I told you: I'm not one of them. It's all *konplike*.

— Complicated? Bah!

— They might kill you, he blurted. If you knew. They'd likely kill me. Just as they did to Dorsinus.

— Dorsin–what are you saying?

— They were behind it. I'm almost certain.

Libète put her hand to her forehead. If you can't tell me who they are, then *what* are they?

— The Sosyete goes back years, generations. To slave days. The mawons, the slaves who took to the hills, formed this. It was them who fought the French in that fort and claimed it for their own.

— They dance around at night and wear costumes. Hardly greatness.

— Everyone here knows what they are. The drums, they remind everyone. By day you follow the laws and rules of your people. But night, that's governed by them. The Sosyete only accepts those who will die for it. Do whatever Papa Legba, and the ones above him, order.

— I've heard of Chanpwel before, Libète said.

— Hearing is not understanding. This is just one body, you see. Of many. All throughout these mountains. Our country. The *gouvèneman*, it's divided up all of Haiti into *sections*, *arrondisements*, but the sosyetes, they've got their own divisions. When you cross from one to the next, you better do what they say. Or they come in the night and you end up like Dorsinus.

— Why do the people accept this nonsense?

— Because the Sosyete, they *are* the people. They do what's needed for the people. Fight battles. Protect one another. Look after the interests of the community. It's a good thing. Can be a good thing. I swear.

— Members living double lives, one by day, one by night? It's not democratic. It's rule by fear. By the powerful.

— I was nearly one of them, he said, pride smattering the words.

— Then you're a fool too. She left him standing there, though a thought soon dawned on her. If you still think they're so good, why didn't you become one of them?

— I crossed them. And paid for it. They nearly forced me to leave the land, just as they threatened tonight. But that, that would end me, Sophia. I begged. I cried, like some pitiful kid. They showed me mercy. By day I had to stay at the fortress. I couldn't leave it or they'd order me killed.

— But you're walking with me now.

— Dorsinus. He paid the debt.

— The debt from the stolen money?

Félix nodded. The *banbòch* that happens each year. The big celebration. I was the Sosyete's temporary treasurer, entrusted with the money. And I spent it.

— On what?

He searched her eyes, looking deeply into them, like he'd never permitted himself before. You-you can't ever tell. Not a soul. She'd pay for it. They'd hurt her somehow, I'm sure.

— Who?

— Délira. Her baby.

Libète took this in, trying to weigh the words' meaning.

— Délira, she has a sickness. Her baby, in her belly, was making her sick. The first time she was pregnant, she almost died.

— What are you saying?

His words came fast now, like one wanting a confession to be over.

— She saw a doctor. Down the mountain. Who told her she needed medicine. A very expensive medicine. And that she, and the baby, might die without it. The Sosyete refused to help. It was a bad decision. Délira's father is an evil man and they weren't going to help him, even if she and her baby were the victims. There was nothing, nothing that anyone would do, besides pray, maybe pay the local houngan to make some remedies. She was just waiting, getting so very sick. All while I sat on that pile of money. So I used it.

Libète gasped. You did that, for them? On your own?

— I was nearly inducted into the Sosyete. Because of her father, I knew they wouldn't go for the idea, even if it was a cruelty. I just couldn't let them make a decision like that. So I went down the mountain, and I bought that medicine...

— Is... the child yours? Is that why?

He gave her a scolding look. Does it even matter? His look softened. No. Her father is the father, at least that's what we all think. He looked away into the rustling trees and breathed slowly, in and out, like a porter whose burden had finally slipped off his shoulders. Libète looked at him, differently than she had ever before. His sacrifice spoke to her.

He gritted his teeth, forcing air out in a huff. Even they take their orders from one higher, he said. One is over all this land. One with even more authority than Legba. The Sosyete is accountable. Word is that the one higher is a great man, a powerful sorcerer. The Sosyete was ready to kill me. But this one, whoever he is, ordered a different punishment. 'House arrest,' it was said. I was worried I would be snuffed out in my sleep, but just as they can murder, they can protect. Their strictness saved me.

— This is... this is unbelievable.

— But true.

— Why not tell everyone? Tell everyone what took place? That you did a good thing, and not evil? Wouldn't that change things? Restore you?

— As I said, I fear they would take it out on her. On the child. So it's a secret between me and her. And now you.

— They are cruel. Dangerous.

Félix didn't attempt to refute this.

Libète and Félix approached Magdala's shack. Light emanated from inside through the gaps in the walls, only to be swallowed up whole by the dark.

— She's waiting up for you.

Libète nodded. Your mother is good to me. He took his turn to nod.

— What will you tell her? he asked.

— Not a thing. Her voice cracked. I can't tell her I have to leave. I can't believe this is happening . . .

Her words failed.

— It was worth it, Sophia. Even with all that's happened, I would help Délira again.

She turned and smiled sadly. My name isn't Sophia. It's Libète.

And she strode from darkness into light.

They pull away in a blur, threading up the street, swerving to avoid late-coming revelers and oncoming traffic. Libète pushes the bike hard but fears losing control, and it is this alone that moderates her speed.

— Was that Dimanche? Jak shouts. Well, was it?

— It was! she shouts back.

Jak's color drains. What did he want?

She tries to piece together an understanding of the last half hour, but the competing versions were irreconcilable.

— I don't know! Us? The same as her!

— But I don't unders–

— Just be quiet and let me think!

The sounds of partying, horns, and booming music died down. They were on the edge of downtown Jacmel and approaching the villa.

Bondye, please...

But the prayer, it did not flow. She and Jak were alone. She felt it. Completely and utterly so.

— Why are we going back to the villa? Jak asked. These villains, they could be waiting!

— We have to warn Laurent and Madanm Manno! Besides, all of our clothes and things are still there.

Jak sighed, shifting uncomfortably in the sidecar. He nodded gravely.

They turned onto the lane at the corner restaurant, rattling down the road and coming to a halt in front of the familiar wrought-iron gate. It was quiet, thankfully, but then Libète noticed the twin gates–which should have been locked shut–were ajar.

Libète killed the bike's engine and jumped off, rushing to poke her head through the iron. There was no movement, no sign of trouble. She noticed a pair of deep ruts recently worn in the gravel, certainly from vehicles peeling out. The Land Rover was still sitting there inside, close to the front door.

Jak was behind her now. We need to go in, she mouthed. He buried his disagreement and slipped a stone he had scooped up from the ground into her hand. Her fingers tightened, accepting the meager weapon.

They slipped inside, and she dashed toward the front door as Jak lagged behind. The door was splintered around the handle–a sign of a forced entry. They tested it, and its hinges gave a mournful croak.

Libète inclined her ear. There was sound inside, a person. She drew up her rock.

She pushed the door harder, and a shrill scream let out, a woman's.

— They're gone! He's gone, you dogs, you sons of bitches! Just leave us be!

It was Madanm Manno, whimpering from where she sat on a living room chair. On seeing the children, she grasped her chest and collapsed to the ground with a yelp.

Jak moved to her and patted the woman's back, whispering comfort.

Libète had other concerns. Is anyone else here? Libète barked. Madanm Manno shook her head with a cry.

Libète began walking through the different rooms, inspecting the damage. Paintings ripped, chair cushions slashed, tables upended. Everything was in disarray. Where's Laurent? she asked.

Eyes clenched, Madanm Manno opened her mouth, but nothing could escape. She sobbed instead of spoke.

— Where is he? Jak said softly. Do you know what happened to him?

— He ra-*an*, she slurred. Ran. Into the water. They tried, they tried to get him. The three men, those who came, and they shot at him, but he swam out, swam away, swam off. I don't know if . . . I think that he's . . .

— What?

— Dead! she sobbed.

— You saw it all?

— I did. *I did!*

Libète clouded. And how did 'they' get inside?

The mere asking of the question made the woman burst into new plaintive sobs. She let her hands open, and a few thousand gourdes notes fell from them.

Jak stood up, repulsed. Libète shook her head, a sneer on her face. We get our things, she said to him, and we go.

They rushed up the stairs. More damage: vases shattered, cabinets ajar, drawers pulled out. What were they looking for? She entered her room, seeing her clothes littering the floor. The computer was gone.

— They ripped up my notebook, Jak hollered. Most of my pictures! And Mesye Lizard's home is broken!

A minute later they reentered the hallway at the same time.

— Do you have your pack? Jak nodded. The open door to Laurent's room caught Libète's eye, and she went down the hall to inspect it.

It was the most lived in, and the most upended. The desk lock was busted, and Stephanie's portrait was just a broken frame in a mess of glass. His manuscript papered the floor again. His phone was gone, but who knew if it was stolen or was with him when he dove into the sea? All other trinkets and knickknacks, everything of value, had been taken as well. *What were you after?*

She stepped back into the hall. Jak stepped out from the stairwell that led to the roof. His shoulders slumped.

— What did you see up there?

He just shook his head, eyes watering. It's not good. I found this among all the bread crumbs and feathers. A small note. I think they missed it.

I'll meet you where the old Martinettes rest best.

The penmanship was chaotic, scattered. The last letter's tail left a grim trail across the scrap. Still, it was unmistakably by Stephanie's hand.

— I think he was trying to get a return message off. But had to run.

She read it again. *Where the old Martinettes rest best . . .*

The two looked at each other, searching the annals of their memory, puzzling over the seeming riddle. They thought of all of the places they had been with Stephanie, with Laurent, the Martinettes. Was it too obscure of a clue, something only the siblings would know? Finally, Jak's eyes sparked, and the mere suggestion of knowledge tripped a line in Libète's mind.

The cemetery!

CITY OF THE DEAD

W ap mande simityè si l pa bezwen mò.
You're asking the cemetery if it doesn't need the dead.

They leave Madanm Manno among the wreckage she had wrought.

Jak says farewell, despite everything. Libète does not.

Libète mounts the bike, brings it to life, and the two pull away, fast and foolhardy and reckless.

— Slow down! Jak cries.

She takes a wild, skidding turn.

— You wanna miss Steffi? She'll leave us behind!

They speed along the southern edges of town, their horn causing all in the street to part. She has Jak wear the headscarf, anything to disguise themselves as they cut across town. Her pack is tucked deep in the sidecar with the boy and his things. He bows his head and holds his hands to his eyes. Libète thinks something is caught in his eye, but then he doesn't remove them.

Reality, dogged as it was, had caught up with them. It took hold of her friend and dragged him down. She gave herself over to hot hatred rather than fear.

The shoreline was visible, spied in the gaps between blurring trees and homes, appearing animated, like a flipbook. They passed the old customs house, edged around the green grounds of École Frere Clemente, and wove in and out of a series of tight, emptied-out lanes between buildings and shops before reaching the city of the dead.

They went around to the side, avoiding the main gate as Stephanie always did, and deposited the bike near a gap in the block wall on its southern side. The wall was covered with advertisements, political graffiti, and the remnants of posters. They stepped through the entryway.

There were few souls about.

Stephanie had brought the children here. She took a perverse pleasure, it had always seemed, in walking through the colorful landscape of crypts that looked like miniature churches, gravel crunching beneath her feet. Libète edged among the low and decrepit tombs with her arms inevitably crossed and top lip in a bunch. Jak was more circumspect, trailing behind both, and he could be heard whispering prayers.

The last time they had come, Stephanie had walked very slowly. She cleared away a bit of weed that had invaded a tombstone's lettering or removed an encroaching hibiscus plant and plucked the red flower gingerly.

— What are you doing? Libète had asked.

She smiled. Tending the dead, I suppose.

Stephanie led them to a columned mausoleum, its marble polished and facade well kept. FAMILLE MARTINETTE was chiseled above. She laid one of her collected blooms on the shaded stone ground. She sat and smiled. Can we stay? For a bit? While I write?

Libète rolled her eyes.

— But it's not even your family, Libète said. You're like a branch, just . . . grafted onto the Martinette tree.

Jak slapped Libète's arm.

— What? It's the truth. We haven't visited Elize's marker in months. He was your real father.

Stephanie forced a sad smile. She took out her pen and laid her feelings down on her note pad. Jak went and sat close to the woman, in the shade and out of her view. He mouthed something to Libète, but she couldn't follow. He formed the silent words again: *Di 'desole.'* Say *'sorry.'*

Libète had rolled her eyes and walked off, picking up a fallen stick to poke and prod tombs.

— She's being foolish, Steffi.

Stephanie continued her writing without looking up. She's being Libète, Stephanie replied.

Libète heard the words; they made her broil. She knew Elize so well, and yet Stephanie rarely asked her about him. To have one right before you who could help illuminate where you came from, to fill in deep holes in your memory, wouldn't that be a gift? To Libète, it was silly for a writer who committed so much to paper, memorializing the most trivial of details, to choose the holes.

Days like those with Stephanie, full of endless time together, seemed so innocent to Libète now. They had nearly driven Libète mad, but now, it was what she longed for most.

The other people in the cemetery today were sedate. Some were carrying out their duty to the dead, clad in black mourning garb. Two middle-aged men were despondent, or maybe just world-weary, laying under the few sickly trees and seeking solitude. The only noise came from those using the cemetery as a shortcut, either returning from the Carnival festivities or moving toward them.

She spun around, her Sun-drenched and fear-racked mind making her so very tired.

— Jak, I'm confused. Which way–which way was it to the Martinettes'?

He pointed resolutely, as a compass does north. They wound through more grave markers.

Dimanche's villainy was a blow. When he disappeared, forced into hiding years before, she had imputed nobility to him. Now he was just another person trying to use her for her own ends. Just as Stephanie did. Just as her Aunt Estelle had. She was like a well-worn prop, trotted out to say the precocious *bon mot* or spout justice and peace to those who hoped oh-so-fervently that hope was not lost.

She was tired of this adult world she was inheriting. Tired of the deadly games, the rank injustice of all they had built. She felt like lying down under one of the cemetery's bowed trees, closing her eyes, and never having to pry them open again . . .

Steffi. Libète thought of her immaculate clothes. Her styled hair. Her lavender scent. Her careful ways. Her practiced perfection in speaking, writing, and caring.

Libète thought of what she would tell Stephanie if she saw her. She would vent all: that Laurent was probably dead and it was Stephanie's doing. That leaving Libète and Jak in Jacmel had been an unforgivable offense. Libète sighed. That facing this terrible world would have been all right if Stephanie had just kept her close, so that love–or whatever fiction of love they shared–could sustain her.

Each step toward that damned mausoleum made her blood boil, so that when Stephanie revealed herself, Libète could only stop.

The two children, for that was what they were, stared at their guardian.

She was hollowed. Sallow cheeks, new lines under her eyes, hair in knots.

Jak stepped forward. Libète could not.

Libète watched him move toward her, his arms out, until he reached Stephanie and gave an embrace that was desperate and relieved and whole. And her eyes filled with tears. His arms wrapping around her validated the burden she chose to carry.

Libète stood there, numb. Stephanie wore the hurt on her face and extended a begging hand, beckoning her to come close too. But Libète still could not.

Stephanie parted from Jak. He was reluctant to let go. She sat him down on the mausoleum steps tenderly. She started toward Libète.

This is your fault.

Stephanie's eyes still watered.
Your brother is dead.
Their eyes connected again before words could be spoken, before touch could be exchanged. Libète's lips parted.

— You abandoned me to the–

Stephanie took her and hugged her fiercely. Libète tried to accuse, but Stephanie's arms closed tightly. The words, they could not form, and hatred, it could not stand.

Libète fell limp, letting Stephanie keep hold of her till they both collapsed to their knees.

— *Cheri, cheri, cheri,* Stephanie said. My dear girl. How I've *missed* you!

Libète simply shook in Stephanie's arms, her tears dripping down the woman's back.

— Libète, Jak shouted suddenly. *Run!*

Libète's heart leaped before her legs could follow. From within the shadows of the mausoleum stepped Dimanche.

The corn stalks rise above her head. She is grateful for the chance to hide among the rows before knocking them down.

Less than a week. The flames, the masks, the command to go spring to her mind.

She slashes, cutting stalk from root. Again, and again, till the sweat drips down into her clothes. She channels everything into those cuts. She begins to cough, and she cannot stop.

Her body shakes as if in a fit, and her throat is on fire. She wonders, could it be? Her pills had given out long ago, but she thought the gathering storm of disease had passed without making landfall. Suddenly, the heaving subsides. *No, surely not.* Surely she was fine. She resumes her slashing.

— Sophia? Where are you? Libète hears the words but doesn't stop her cutting. Sophia? *Sophia!*

Libète finally lowers her blade.

— Wi, Magdala?

— Are you well?

— I am.

— You seem ... burdened. Not even a word for me this morning.

— It's nothing.

— Why don't you join us, over there? She pointed. With the other women? There's no need to be alone.

Libète wiped her brow, shielded her eyes. I'm fine over here. She swung her blade again.

Magdala's hand grasped Libète's wrist at the apex of her swing. What is *happening*, Sophia? Their faces were close, noses nearly touching. Libète could not meet the woman's pleading eyes. You've not acted this way since, well, since you arrived.

— Please, just ... just leave me be. She sniffed back tears.

— You act as one who isn't loved.

— You don't know what I'm fleeing from, Magdala. Or where I'm going.

— So put down your blade, your sharp words, and tell me.

Libète finally let her body slacken and the machete dropped from her grasp to slip into the ground.

— My dear, dear girl, she cooed. I'm here. I'm here. The Good Lord, he's here.

— He's put me–putting me–through hell. This – she shuddered – *suffering*, it has no purpose. No matter where I go, what I do, every path leads me back to pain.

Magdala took this in quietly.

— We all suffer. If you saw each person's path, from start to finish, you'd see such anguish and hurt. I'm just a woman, never having left the mountain, but I know things. You can't outrun the Lord and his plans, the joys they hold, and the pains. You can only learn how to handle the pain. Me, myself, I've learned how to *use* it.

Libète looked up through tears. Magdala continued. When my parents were ripped from me, and I saw their dead bodies, and touched them, I was destroyed. The sadness, it tore me to pieces. Magdala looked to the sky. And I knew I was beyond repair. And yet, a neighbor came along to comfort me. When I was hungry and couldn't provide for myself, another came along to feed me. When my husband left, there was another friend who lived on with me. Even you, arriving to be with me when Félix was hated by all. It was all one helping the other. Now I store up comfort and hope to pass it along to the next one who is hurting.

Magdala sighed. Pain is a question I have no answer for. The why of it. And I'll take it up with God and the Virgin Mary when I see them. But I can often see a purpose, and opportunity, no matter what has been taken. I just don't see them right away.

— I have to leave, Magdala. I've been ordered to leave, and I'm scared, I'm so very scared. Her voice was tiny. The woman held her at arm's length and searched Libète's face.

— Who? Who would make you go? Those brutes with the dog?

— The... the Sosyete. Though Libète's eyes were closed, she felt Magdala's hands stiffen around her own.

— They summoned you?

Libète answered with a moan. Magdala stroked Libète's head, time and again, and leaned in to whisper. Sophia, whatever you are, whoever you are, *you're mine*. God's given you to me, and I won't let them make you go. They would have to kill me.

— You're wonderful, Libète whispered.

Magdala patted Libète's head once more. Now, please, you must stand up. Libète rose. I don't want the others to see and ask questions. Anything involving the Sosyete is dangerous. But we'll think of...

Libète looked up into her face, a thought sparking. Magdala clapped. We'll appeal to a higher power!

Libète did not follow. God?

— Ha! Ha ha! No. I mean *Janel*. That woman–she has authority! She'll have an idea, some way to get them to let you stay. Come now. She lifted the erect machete and restored it to Libète's palm. The end of hope is the end of us all. Don't you forget it.

— The end of hope... Libète let the words trail off into the air, the phrase familiar even though its provenance was vague. She couldn't place who had said it, but nodded anyway, allowing Magdala to hold her wrist and lead her out of the corn and onto the road to Janel's.

Libète reaches for a weapon while Stephanie reaches for the girl. Libète finds none.

— You bastard! she shouts, springing into action anyway. Jak had fallen backward from his place on the mausoleum steps, scurrying along the ground like a crab.

— Stop! Stephanie shouts.

With her running start, Libète jumps onto a tomb and into the air, sailing toward Dimanche. He catches her, barely budging in the process, and subdues her. He grips her arms tight so that she can't pummel him and pins her against the crypt's wall.

— Your mask is off now, is it? She spits at him, and the spray hits his shoulder. He looks down, then back at her, meeting her withering stare with empty eyes.

— *Libète!* Stephanie blares as she loosens Dimanche's tight grip on Libète and pushes herself between the two. Control yourself! He's a *friend*, as he's always been.

The few people haunting the cemetery watch.

— That's a – Libète bucks – *lie!* Her mind struggles with the claim. He tried to steal me!

— To rescue you! Stephanie retorted.

Dimanche demonstrated no particular need to vindicate himself. He stepped back into the slanted shadow and reached for a handkerchief, first wiping his sweaty, bald head and then the spittle on his shirt.

Stephanie grabbed Libète's head and looked her in the eye. If you only knew the foolish things you're saying . . .

Libète resisted her hold again.

— We need to go, Dimanche said, inclining his head toward the onlookers.

— But Laurent! We have to wait, wait and see if he comes, Stephanie said weakly.

— He's dead, Jak said. His renewed presence nearly made them jump.

Stephanie gasped. No . . . no. That's not–how did you know to come here? The message I sent by bird–

— We found it in the villa, Jak said, on our return. On the ground, near all the dead ones. Madanm Manno, she informed. She said Laurent ran into the water as those who broke in fired at him. He didn't run back out.

Stephanie held her hand to her mouth. Just like the old days, just like the old days, she said. No one is safe . . .

— We need to go, Dimanche said again.

— I'm not going anywhere with *him*, Libète said.

— Where's the motorcycle? Dimanche asked. Jak pointed. Dimanche started toward the cemetery's breached wall. Back to my place, he said. We'll decide where to go from there.
— But can't we wait a little more, Stephanie asked, just in case–
— No.
She nodded, and stood. Jak, Libète. Come with me.
— I need an *explanation*, Libète said, stomping the ground. *Now*.
— You will have it, Dimanche growled. Just shut your mouth and do as Ms. Stephanie says, or else you'll find you won't be able to speak.

• • •

They heard the motorcycle's kick and rumble before they piled into Laurent's car, the one Stephanie had held in her custody these months. The black BMW was scratched in many places and had a crunched back fender. It had been pristine when they last saw it.

They rode along the shoreline in an impenetrable silence. It was easier not to talk. Stephanie needed to process news of Laurent's death, while Libète mulled over the possibility that Dimanche was somehow a friend rather than foe. She ran her hand over the supple black leather of the backseat, feeling its soft ridges and seams. Jak's hand met hers there, and she let him hold it tight.

The tinted windows made ebullient Jacmel a world of shadows. To Libète, the city now seemed alien and profane, for it and its people did not yield to the weighty things that lay behind and before her.

— Where have you been, Steffi? These past months?

It takes half a minute for her to answer. That's a long story.

— Please, Jak said. Please tell us.

She sighed. I've been trying to secure your protection. I called upon my father, his connections, political and otherwise. You saw the news online I take it? New assassination attempts in Port-au-Prince. Lax, lazy law enforcement. Hardly an investigation into the radio station and

Gerry's murder. 'No political will,' the chief of police said to my face. 'Benoit is insulated,' another high-up officer said to me. I tried to feed the press stories about you, Libète, tried to get them to print the truth about why you'd disappeared. Not because you were guilty of Didi's death, but because of fear of persecution, because you had so obviously been targeted. But my 'friends' in the press, after what happened to Gerry, didn't want to step in front of that oncoming train. Stephanie looked at the children in the rearview mirror. So at long last, I went straight to the devil himself.

— You mean?

— Jean-Pierre Benoit. I went to his home. There was no other way I could see to make it stop.

— *Se vre?* But why? Jak said. Right into the lion's den!

— I saw no other way. He welcomed me, all smiles. Treated me like an old friend. 'Out of respect for the name Martinette,' he said. I was in no mood for pleasantries. I asked him what it would take to leave you both alone.

— And?

— He denied everything. As he always has. I told him that we knew Lolo was from him, baiting you, trapping you, attempting to poison you after his first attempt did Didi in. 'Lolo? Who is this Lolo?' he said. He assured me he only has your best interest at heart, that he wishes you no ill, even after you tarnished his name. That he understands you're a delusional girl who cooked up an impossible story and that he, though victimized, could still look past everything since the legal proceedings were thrown out.

— The villain!

— He said that if something happened to you, his enemies would bring it home to him, parroting our own belief. 'Their well-being is my own,' he said. He credited you with much intelligence for realizing this.

— You believed this stuff?

— I almost shot him. Then and there. I had a gun in my purse.

— But you didn't. Libète's words rang with disappointment.

— I left. She sighed. To the world, I continued pretending everything was all right. My phone, it was being monitored. The technology they use, you hear the clicks on the line. It's almost like they want you to know they're listening. I had to be exceedingly careful.

— So you and Laurent used the birds?

— We did.

— Two nights ago. Laurent was drunk. You texted. He thought you might have died.

Steffi pulled the car over. She rubbed her lips, and Libète saw her hands tremble on the steering wheel.

— That night, just after meeting with Benoit, our home in Boutilier was firebombed. Father and I barely got out alive.

— My *God*. Libète undid her belt and climbed to the front seat. She took Stephanie's hand. Will it ever stop? She reached her arms around the woman, who now seemed very much like a girl herself.

— I'm just so happy - tears began pouring out - so happy to see you both. It's thanks to him, for sure.

Libète was confused. Laurent?

— No-yes, him too, but no. Inspector Dimanche. His story, ever since that night he first opposed Benoit, has remained your story.

Libète walks intently, her machete at her side. The tin slope of Janel's roof comes into view, spied over a hill's subtle crest. She breathes deeply. The stakes of this conversation were as high as the mountain was tall.

Magdala believed it would be better to have Libète speak with her alone. If others knew Magdala and the girl had been discussing the Sosyete's inner workings, it would only create more trouble.

Libète rounds the hill's edge and takes in the house. The home sits in a hollow and is wedged into a natural indentation in the rock, looking out on an enclosed yard. It is modest, like the other homes in the area, and that is telling. With Janel's relationships to outside groups, she could have benefitted personally over the years, but she still lived as the rest of Foche. Her lack of airs and commitment to solidarity made Libète's admiration for the woman swell.

Libète jumps. Prosper is in the yard, sharpening his own machete with a stone. He too is surprised to see her and lowers the stone and blade to his sides. Wha . . . why are you here?

— Your mother. Is she in?

He swallows. His eyes are saucers. He nods, like he's expecting her to say something else. Her brow tenses. What's the matter with you? she says, her words hushed and severe.

— She's inside. Excuse me. Prosper drops his things and leaves the enclosure, almost as if afraid.

This was not the entrance she had expected to make. She stood straight, smoothing the pleats in her sweat-stiffened skirt, and refastened her demure mask to again become Sophia. She knocked twice on the worn, wood doorframe. Honor, Libète called.

With a beat, the response came called back. Respect! You may enter!

Libète pried the door open. Janel sat at a desk with a pen in her hand and a ledger laid out before her. The uneven slats let the west-slumping Sun illuminate her desk.

— Ah, Sophia! She removed her oversize glasses, perched on the tip of her flat nose. One of the glasses' temples was substituted with a pen. What brings you to my home? You're welcome, of course.

Libète lowered her head but couldn't help taking in the space, searching its corners out of the sides of her eyes. *Crucifix, pots, beds, table, a single framed picture, scattered books*–
— I have a request, she finally said.
— A request?
— A request.
— Yes?
— It's a heavy thing.
— Heavy, you say?
— Very heavy. The heaviest.
— Oh? The animatris shifted in her chair and leaned forward. Feel free to speak. This space, it's safe. As safe as you'll find.

Libète felt the tension slip from her shoulders. I've run into – she whispered, her hand lifted to shield the words – *the Sosyete*.

Janel tensed. Without hesitating, she stood to close the front door and curtain the windows. The room plunged into low light and shadow. She went to Libète and took her hands. Tell me, she said. What has happened.

They sat on a bed. Libète couldn't meet her intense stare. I was summoned. Last night. Called to one of their gatherings.

— You... saw them, then? The membership?

Libète nodded, but then shook her head. I saw them, but their faces were covered. I–I didn't recognize them.

Janel stared into open space. They are a force to be reckoned with, she said. I've had my dealings with them. And have my suspicions about its membership. They keep secrets well, and hurt those who violate those secrets. Janel's words seemed a recitation. You must tell me why they called you. This is not ordinary.

Libète crossed her feet, scratched her knee. The leader, Papa Legba, said that I must go.

— Ordered you to leave?

— In one week. Because I'm a risk. Because of what happened with those two guards.
— A heavy thing, indeed. You'll go?
— I don't want to.
— But you must. The Sosyete stands on the edge of a blade, between good and evil. Those who cross them suffer. You're fortunate they summoned you and didn't steal you in the night. This, this is a blessing.
— But I have nowhere to go. No one to go to. Foche, it's become my home.

Janel's expression was steely yet compassionate. She gave the girl a bracing hand.
— This is an injustice, to be sure. You've been accepted here. A risk, they said? What risk could you possibly pose, Sophia?

Libète cringed at this particular use of the fake name, knowing very well the risks she posed. Madanm Janel, I come to you with hope. I was thinking about something else Legba said. Foche is theirs to control, I understand that, but he said the order to go came from one even higher.
— What are you asking of me?
— To intervene. To save my life here.

Janel stood up and paced. Now this, *this* is a heavy thing. To make such a request . . . it can be dangerous! She looked at Libète, who looked emptied.
— I'm sorry I came. The girl rose, looking downward. Of course I couldn't ask this of you. Threatening your place here, when you do such good, to protect myself–it's a selfish thing.

Janel stopped Libète halfway toward the door. But an understandable one. And I will do what I can.

Libète swelled with new hope. She took the woman's hands. Thank you, thank you, *thank you*.

— It's all right. Sophia, I don't know you well, but when I see you, I see *strength* buried down deep. You remind me of myself, just about to discover how much power you have.

— Mèsi. Mèsi anpil.

— If I can keep you here, I will. But prepare yourself for the worst, while hoping for the best.

Libète nodded, wicking away tears.

— And thank you for coming to me with this, Janel said. For trusting me with it. I want you to know–

Three knocks on the door made her pause. Mother?

— I'm still with Sophia, Prosper.

— I think you need to see this.

They can hear the dull rumbling before feeling the ground shake with small tremors.

The two walk toward the door together. Janel was restored to her regal bearing. What is it?

Prosper looked at Libète warily. The guards – he signaled with a slant of his head to the large truck that was parked nearby – they have someone for you.

— Some*one*? Not some*thing*?

Janel stepped out toward Cinéus and Wilnor. They stood in the truck's bed, hands on their weapons.

— Madanm, Cinéus called out with a deferential nod. We've caught a thief on the road. He was trying to make off with a car, and it turned out to be the local houngan's down the mountain. We took him at the mayor's request for fear a group might rise up and kill him. We thought you'd protect him here.

— How... helpful of you. Janel was genuinely surprised.

— You can come close, but be careful. He has some sort of sickness. He's in and out.

— Out right now, Wilnor called. He's all over the place.

— Delusional, Cinéus said.

— Right. Delusional.

Janel walked up and inspected him. Well, what do you want me to do with him?

— Lock him up. Foche has a shack for such people near the market, no? When the police come through in a few days you can hand him over.

— That's a big responsibility. Why don't you keep him locked up at your camp?

— The bosses wouldn't have that, Cinéus said.

— Not at all, Wilnor added.

— Take pity on him, won't you? He's in a bad way, even if he's a thief, Cinéus said.

Janel looked askance at the ailing man and sighed. Her body shielded him from Libète's view. Something in the man's state seemed to prick Janel's conscience. We can handle him for a few days. Prosper, go with them. Get the key from Jeune and unlock the shed. We haven't had to use it for some time. She said this quietly, just loud enough for Libète and Prosper to hear.

— Not since Félix, Prosper whispered.

— Sophia, please go with them. Maybe your healing hands can do some good to keep this one alive for the next few days?

Libète looked at the guards: Cinéus with his lascivious eyes and Wilnor with his dull ones. Libète gave a nod. Of course. I'll do what I can.

Prosper climbed over the lip of the truck bed and extended a hand to Libète. She took the help and joined him.

She sat down and crossed her legs. She took in the accused's gnarled form, his scarecrow limbs. His feet faced her, and she could not see his face. *Whatever he has is a bad disease.*

The man mumbled something and shifted to his other side.

She convulsed at the sight, her heart's palpitations as loud in her ears as the truck's revving engine.

Before her, laid low by his illness, was Lolo.

THE END OF HOPE

Se pa bon pou yon moun konnen twòp.
It's not good for a person to know too much.

Dimanche hides his motorcycle under a ratty tarp while Stephanie parks nearby. He is already sitting on a crate and tending to a ripped net when the other three walk up.

Libète takes in the surroundings. The stately palms and pebble-laden beach and lone, leaning shack set back from the water and a boat that was Dimanche's own–it all smelled of dead fish. *This is his exile?*

Dimanche threads nylon through nylon. He took a large knife and cut a new strand of filament.

— Dimanche, we need to talk. Stephanie says. Alone.

He grunts, finishes tying a knot, lays his work down. As you wish. He brushes his hands off and follows her into the shack.

— Look, Libète! Jak says. One of the caged traps is propped up in the shadow of the shack, and within it are three pigeons. Libète nods and then paces, her arms crossed.

She watches the water as it slides in and seeps out. *A never-ending give and take.* Jak prods, analyzing the stack of traps and equipment Dimanche had accumulated. Dimanche's boat was all white, bland compared to others down shore awash in primary colors. A rope hangs from a cleat at its back, and paddles lean against the boat. Its only flourish is the name MARCEL printed on its side. It gives Jak pause.

Shouting erupts from inside the hovel: 'We have no choice!' They are Stephanie's words. Jak and Libète look at each other.

Dimanche sweeps the curtain hanging in the entrance aside. His face says nothing, and he's back to his nets without a glance or word. The children step toward the shack. There is sobbing within.

— Don't, Dimanche orders. He recommences his careful threading. She needs some time, he says.

Libète's eyes are slits. So you're a fisherman? She realizes how little she knows about the man when his uniform is stripped away.

— I wait. And I catch. Yes.

— Your boat, Jak says. I've seen it. Libète looks at Jak in surprise.

— Have you now?

— You're the one who sits out there on the water near the villa. Late in the day. The only boat, Jak says.

Dimanche gives a tight smile. Keeping watch, he says. You're still observant, Jak.

— You have birds too?

— Ms. Martinette brought them to me. We kept in touch that way, and with the Monsieurs Martinette. The 'Pigeon Post.' He chuckles.

— Why are you messing with those stupid nets at a time like this? Libète blurts.

Dimanche reflects for a moment, looks at her through tired, red-webbed eyes. I understand them.

— Jak and I need protection. I get that. But from the truth? Not from the truth. What's going on here?

He searches the children's eyes in turn. These troubles... He sighs, laying down the broken net and choosing his words with care. What we know: Benoit wants you dead. Indisputable fact. And he has tried numerous times to effectuate that will. Also fact: despite an initial belief to the contrary, this woman Maxine is not with Benoit. She remains an open question, as is who directs her. Whoever these people are, they want you alive. Very much so. So much that she and her people thwarted Benoit's attempts to find you after you left Cité Soleil. I have seen them even go so far as to kill Benoit's thugs.

Libète cannot make sense of it. But if they're helping us, then why–

— They do nothing for your benefit. Whatever happened on that radio show, the call, the Numbers uttered by the murdered man on the other end of the line: this spurred them to action. Dimanche darkens. This information, these Numbers entrusted to you, are of great value to someone.

Libète balks. This is all... just because of... they can have the damned things! If it will make it stop, the world can know! 2563–

— Silence! he shouts. Not another soul can know! Not me! No one! Forget them if you can, any mention. Benoit is a monster, but he is forced to occupy a public spotlight. This limits him. But these others, I have observed them carefully. They are not constrained by light. Dimanche stares off toward the vast, vast sea. He winces. They are cruel, through and through. Shadows of men.

— But we never *saw* you these past years. Not once!

— The fatal car accident that missed you on the road to Jacmel? Two years ago? You remember?

— Yes.

— It was an attempt to collide with Ms. Martinette's vehicle. To kill you all. And remember Jak's spelling bee, at Hotel Karibe? How you were locked in a room and the door mysteriously opened?

— Yes.

— And the eviction protests at the Sylvio Cantor camp? When you were almost crushed by the bulldozer?

— Yes.

— And the night of the Numbers, at the radio station. The *malfektè*'s knife that slipped through your window?

— Of course.

— I made sure it went no further. And then my card—
— Your card?
— 'Enemies are at your door.' I had it passed to that doorman.
— That... was you?

He gave a short, sad nod. It's the one time I wish I hadn't stayed in the dark. I knew something foul was up. My informants in Cité Soleil told me as much. But I didn't want to reveal myself to you or anyone else, not yet. I was too cryptic. Your little friend paid the price for that mistake.

The memory of Didi writhing felt like a poke at a healing wound. How long did you know... he... was there? Plotting. She couldn't say Lolo's name.

— I didn't know, not then. I just knew someone was making a move. Like you, I had always believed he was innocent. Jak kept Lolo's involvement in Claire and Gaspar's deaths a secret from everyone. I didn't pay attention to Lolo until it was too late and you'd tripped his trap. Those hours you were missing in Cité Soleil were... unsettling.

Libète was seized by new disbelief. By God! We're talking about *years*, Dimanche!

— You didn't have eyes for anything but the surface of things. Where everything seemed safe and under control. I kept that illusion up for you.

— How did you survive, then? Libète said. Steffi knew you were there all along? Looking after us?

— She did, after a time. I let her know. But you two children, we decided, should not live in fear if you didn't have to.

— But that means she didn't bring you into this. Who would pay for you to ensure our safety if not Steffi?

His lips stayed tight. It's a condition of the job that I cannot reveal your benefactor.

— Is that so? Her brow furrowed. Who. Else. Would. *Pay*... Ah! Ah ha! It's Moïse! Moïse Martinette. Isn't it? She laughed smugly. Of course it is. There's no one else who could afford to do so. She looked at Jak, who shrugged. It sounds possible, he said.

— He's a good one, that Moïse, Libète said. Dimanche let her revel in her conclusion and the momentary bit of satisfaction it brought.

Libète felt a set of eyes on her. She turned to see Stephanie waiting in the doorway to the shack. With her composure regained, Stephanie walked out toward them.

— Libète. Jak. The decision has been made. We are going to separate. Jak with me, Libète with Dimanche. Get your things. It's time to go.

Cinéus and Wilnor carry Lolo into the shack like he's a dead man. Libète does all she can not to run far and fast.

They lay him on the ground. There's a dirty bucket thick with calm flies, and the men's careless shuffling sees the flies rise and then return to the bucket's filth. Libète hovers behind the guards, outside. She palms at her throat, and then her chest. She feels another bout of coughs coming on.

— I'll go and get him some water, Prosper says.

Libète's face tightens. She does not hear the words.

Lolo. Here.

It is incomprehensible. The intersection of her parallel lives makes the world seem like it might implode. *I can never get away. No matter where I go. Nothing I can do–*

— He looks like death, Cinéus says to himself. Don't you catch what this one has, girl! We wouldn't want to see you in such state.

— Are you all right being left with him? Wilnor asks.

Libète sniffs and nods without speaking. The odds were impossible. How could this be? A cruel coincidence? God's judgment for running, hiding, and spurning him?

The two men left her as she stared at Lolo, a husk of a man. Prosper returned with a lidded plastic bucket full of water. He laid it down.

— What a disease. What do you think he has?

— Tuberculosis. She spoke the word as a reflex.

— Yeah? How do you know?

She didn't respond; only knelt before the sick man. Lolo's breath was shallow, rasped. Her thoughts flew again before returning, like the flies.

— What can you do for him?

— I'll... need to try to wake him before long. Give him water. Try to get him to eat some food. He needs rest. His body is shutting down because of the illness. She suddenly realized that the stains on Lolo's shirt were dried blood.

— Sophia. I... I just want to say that... I can't imagine what you're going through.

She spun. How could Prosper know who this man was? What his presence here meant to her?

— I know you've been told to leave Foche. And I just want to say, I think it's wrong.

Libète snapped to attention. She rose. You listened to my conversation with your mother? But you couldn't have. You left when I arrived...

It dawned on her. *You were there*, she whispered. She looked at his eyes; registered them. They were the same ones she had seen behind her escort's mask. You're one of the Sosyete!

— I'm an initiate. I have no power. If I did, I would speak up for you. It's wrong what they're doing.

— Who? Who are they? Others from Foche?

— I... can't say. The words pained him. You know I can't. But I hope you know that I want to.

Thoughts of remaining now almost made her laugh. With Lolo here, everything was changed. Flight was a necessity. Unless...

A new, terrible thought came to her.

— Wash your hands when you get home, she ordered.

— What?

— I'll stay with him.

— I can't leave you alone with this one.

— *I'll* stay with him.

— He's a thief! What happens when he wakes?

She felt flames rise inside her chest. So many repressed feelings; they were the air to give this fire life.

— I don't *need* you, Prosper. She rose up. I don't need someone as weak as you. As pathetic as you. Creeping in where you're not wanted, living in the shadow of a great mother. You need to *go*, and you need to go *now*.

Prosper's jaw clenched. Each sentence was a new slash and cut, ending his hopes that she might want him, might care for him. He deflated. She could see her words had her desired effect.

He left, simply floated away.

The coughs arrived again, making her heave, bringing her to her knees. She wiped at her mouth with her wrist, pulling it away in horror. *San*. Blood.

She too had Lolo's disease. Contracted when and how she did not know. All of these months since arriving, she had been without medication. She had finished most of the treatment cycle, thought it might have been enough to keep her latent form of tuberculosis from becoming full-blown. She had felt no real change in her health, only a tugging at the back of her throat these past months. There had been mild fear of infecting others, but she was close to none but Magdala and had willed herself, despite the evidence, into believing she was well. And now, Lolo's arrival seemed to aggravate the condition. His presence tore down every bit of fictive protection and health she had built around herself these months.

There was nowhere she could have peace unless his threat was stamped out.

She undid her headscarf and balled it in her fist. Her mind was blank, her face empty, raw impulse motivating her as her conscience's influence was rendered null.

She took the mass in her hand and guided it to cover the subtle slit of Lolo's mouth and end him.

She runs, runs fast down the shore.

She runs, runs till her lungs cry out.

She runs, runs till her sides scream.

She collapses, falls to the ground, fingers snagging the earth like anchor flukes. She would have sobbed if only she could breathe.

The prayers–long percolating, ready to bubble out of her–she caps.

Non.

This is not the time to call on some aloof Deity, the uncaring Thing of reputed power, the knowing Author of all this misery.

Non.

She hears the motorcycle coming along a parallel road, the bike's grumbling cadence now familiar. Her tears wet the pebbles below, mingling till they dry and disappear. Soon a shadow hovers over her, and she can look only to its owner's familiar feet.

He kneels beside her, bends over her, pauses before he wraps his arm around her. All will be well, he promises. All will be well, Jak whispers.

How can you say such a thing? How can you know? she wants to scream at him.

But she doesn't. She can't.

He pries her hands from the earth, dries her eyes with the backs of his wrists. And seemingly possessed, he kisses her forehead, softly.

Libète, my friend, he whispers. *There is more.*

Despite everything, she believes.

• • •

Her mind lingers in the fog of what followed her flight: the beach, the kiss, the walking back hand in hand. Stephanie and Dimanche setting to packing, planning in hushed voices, animated by new purpose and fear.

Questions were finally posed.

Why are we separating? *Too dangerous to stay together.*

Where am I going? *The north.*

With Dimanche? *Yes.*

Where is Jak going? *The east.*

For how long?

Silence. Empty air.

Jak and Libète sat side by side in the beached boat, given the gift of a final, quiet moment together.

He reached into his things and withdrew his salvaged notepad. He opened to a page, flipping through notes and sketches to a beautifully rendered portrait of her. Though torn into fragments, it was her, the restored her, smiling, eyes alight.

— You did that? She gave a sad smile, seeing herself as she longed to be.

— Will you take it? To remember me?

Her head bobbed.

Dimanche had a green canvas duffel he threw in the sidecar, a sack half-full. They saw him turn and pause to take in the boat, the peaceful water and dull, descending Sun. He turned his back on his nets and traps and solicitude to look at Libète. We'll get you more things, he said quietly. On the road. To wear. Stephanie was fussing with the BMW's trunk, its lid reluctant to clasp shut after its unmentioned collision.

A bird, a final messenger, was placed in Libète's red book bag. To carry word once we've made it to where we're going, Dimanche said. There's no phone coverage there.

And then it was time. Dimanche, stiff and tall, shook hands with Jak and Stephanie. The tension between girl and woman had settled again, and they kissed the other's cheeks coldly. Libète was reluctant to catch her eyes. Go safely, Stephanie said. You too, Libète said reflexively.

When Libète reached Jak, she could not look at him. These new, strange feelings stirring within her both frightened and consoled. The one held the other for a time, knowing they faced a future where the only certainty was that they would not enter it together.

— Now, Dimanche uttered.

Libète whispered to Jak and Jak whispered back, words none but the two of them could hear.

They separated.

As Dimanche kick-started the bike and Stephanie turned the car's key, Stephanie spoke for them all:

— *N a we talè,* she said, her eyes wet. We'll see you soon.

Libète holds the cloth an inch from Lolo's mouth.

She sees his brow is crumpled. The corner of his mouth tugs, as if what plays out in the depths of his subconscious is torturous. She breathes, and deep. Her fingers are inflexible talons, grasping the scarf.

There is more.

The words resurface, inexplicably so, spoken to her in what feels like another age. Her eyelids flit. Her mind toggles from past to present to past.

Jak.

Wha-what am I doing?

She reels back, repulsed by what has claimed her. And yet, unable to resist, she finds herself returned to her perch over Lolo, her cloth again at the ready. A battle rages inside.

— *I'm so tired*, she sobs.

The door to the shack opens, and Libète leaps backward.

— Sophia? Magdala stands there, mouth agape. What are you doing?

Libète stammered something. Shame was writ large across her face.

Magdala laid down a bowl of piping hot cassava. Janel asked me to bring this one food, Magdala said. She shifted her stance and looked at what the girl grasped. Again she asked: Sophia–why were you so close to the sick man?

Libète skirted against the ground and into the corner. I'm a wretch! she cried. A wretch!

— Sophia! Magdala shouted. What's come over you?

— I'm not Sophia, I'm not Sophia, that's not my name. Please, please don't call me that.

— You don't look well, Magdala said. She touched Libète's forehead. You're ill! You're feverish! And what's this blood on you?

— The fever's nothing! My name is Libète. And I was going to kill that man.

Magdala recoiled. How could you consider–

— *Paske m fini!* I'm finished, I'm finished, I'm finished.

Magdala tolerated none of this. She grabbed Libète's shoulders and shook her. Calm yourself! The strength behind the words gave Libète pause.

— Sophi–I mean, Libète–tell me more. *Please,* so I can *help* you.

Libète couldn't decide which place to start. I, I'm from Port-au-Prince. I was pursued, chased far from home when I came to you. I was accused, falsely, of the murder of a friend. I fled those who would take my life. And I know something, a secret, information that if learned makes my life–the lives of everyone I care about–worthless.

— What is this secret? What could it be?

Libète's lips pursed and eyes watered. I don't even *know* its meaning. But I don't dare share it. I don't dare place this burden on another's shoulders. She moaned. I've thought about it for all of these months and I can't understand it. I have many enemies. I ran afoul of a certain businessman. I ruined his name by making known his secret crimes. He wants me dead, I know. But there are others who want this secret. It's the only thing that kept me from harm before I arrived here. So one hand shielded me while the other hand tried to end me.

Magdala shook her head. But who is this one here, then? The one who would end you or the one who would shield you? To find you all the way on the other side of Haiti! Ay!

— He is–*was*–a friend. I saved him a long time ago, and he betrayed me. Tried to poison me but poisoned my friend instead, the one whose death I'm blamed for. But how he has come to be here–I have no idea!

— He mustn't see you then! You must hide! He's a thief, I hear? No one will believe a word he says anyway. I'll tell Janel! She'll see you protected.

— No. I have to go. Now. It's certain.

Magdala gripped the nearby wall for support. Then tonight, if it must be! Get down off the mountain! This will pass! Yes, yes. It all will pass. Magdala's face betrayed the confidence of her words. Libète buried her face in her hands.

— Li-bè-te. Magdala said the name like it was difficult to pronounce– Foche will not let these vagabonds take you. Go away, just for a time. Félix can go with you. The Sosyete, they'll change their mind if Janel is on your side. She'll find a way!

Libète looked up with glistening eyes. You think?
Magdala nodded. I do. After all, the end of hope–
— Is the end of us all, Libète said, finishing the sentence.
— Go, Libète. Collect your things. I'll keep watch over this one and make sure you have time to get away.
Libète hugged the woman fiercely. You are too good to me. I'm just a visitor who overstayed her welcome.
— A visitor? Please! Magdala poked Libète's chest. You're my daughter, through and through.
Libète kissed her cheek. Mèsi, Magdala. For your hope.
Libète took up her abandoned scarf near Lolo's head. She turned back to see Magdala leaning against the wall, wide-eyed and gripped by fear.
— What is it? Libète turned back to Lolo. He faced them with open eyes and loosed a shout that defied his shriveled form: *It's her! I see her! The murderer is here! Libète is here!*

FLIGHT

Fòk ou konn chemen anvan ou pran wout.
You must learn the way before you take the road.

They speed up into mountains bathed in cloud, a great haze of unknowing. North, north, north, until the light is spent, and they are spent.

A bump sends her bouncing an inch. Dull pain jumps from her battered muscles. Libète's body aches from the day's exertion: fighting off Dimanche, in whose custody she now found herself, and sprinting on the beach, an attempt to escape the very life she found herself careening toward. She shifts in the sidecar. Her knees are tucked into her chest and her chin tucked into her knees, to fit their bags, hide her face, and permit her to drift in and out of deep sadness and into sleep.

Another bump, and slowing. Dimanche pulls off the road into an ominous grove of trees.

— Why are we stopping here?
— You need rest.

She extracts herself from the sidecar. Her legs prick as her blood circulates again. It is cold, and a breeze heavy with unease twirls about in the mists. Uncurling makes her shiver. He sees this and takes off his loose, billowy jacket. Put it on, he orders. She does ungrudgingly.

The bike's headlamp stays on, and he sets his sack before it to rifle through its contents. He hands her a blanket, then a half-full water bottle and peanuts, all without instruction. We'll start again in a few hours, he finally says. There it is again, the pistol, pulled from his waistband as his gaze sweeps the rows of trees. He kills the light when the stillness satisfies him.

Moonlight struggles to pierce the canopy. She stumbles over the uneven clods of earth as her eyes adjust to the dark. She turns, questions the dark: You going to sleep?

— No.

— Aren't you tired?

— No.

She lays the blanket down on a patch of level ground and wraps herself. Sleep descends after a time, but a final thought arrives before its fall. *What are you, Dimanche?*

Lolo shouts, and he shouts, and he roars.

Libète cannot move, she cannot. Magdala throws the bucket of water over him, and he gasps and chokes. She next butts Libète to the side and straddles Lolo, the skeleton he is, and pins him with her strong arms. Her hand soon locks his mouth tight.

— Go! Get away! Magdala shouts.

Libète trips over the doorjamb and makes a mad sprint. Neighbors poke heads out of homes, but Libète is gone, slipping into darkness behind outcrops and cornstalks. Worrying about Magdala, she spins. Cinéus and Wilnor rush up to the shack, their dog lunging ahead of them.

She sighed. *Finally they'll do some good.* Shouting spilled from inside, and then a scream. Magdala was there, in the entrance, and Wilnor yanked her by the wrist. She fought the grip and pummeled him. He retaliated. The blow, a hard one, sent her to the ground.

Libète ran toward Magdala reflexively, then stopped. Whether because of fear or selfishness or reason, she paused.

Cinéus next brought out Lolo, who was sopping and genuinely weak. He was bent double over the ground and coughed into it as his lungs denied him breath. All she heard was shouting, incomprehensible words, but still Libète knew. *They're in league!* And yet again, Lolo was a lie.

She tried to fit the pieces into place. *Benoit sent Lolo here?* As far as she knew, Benoit wasn't still pursuing her.

Neighbors began streaming to Magdala's aid. *Foche won't let this stand.* Weapons were drawn, and the shouting became cacophony.

It was a race. Libète didn't know how long she had before Cinéus and Wilnor had dealt with the growing crowd and began prowling the hills to find her.

Her lungs burned as she tore along the mountain trails, speeding up inclines and treacherous drops to reach Magdala's home. Her bag in hand, she stuffed everything she would need to hide: clothes, her recovered notebook and pen, a cup, toothbrush, matches, her roll-up sleeping mat, and three unripe avocados. She would head down the mountainside where she wasn't so known, glean from crops, live in shadows, and let the truth gradually untie the knotted plot in which she found herself entangled.

She sprinted out the door and shot up the path toward the fort. It was past sundown. Félix would most certainly be there.

— Félix! she called in a rasped roar. Félix! She continued to work her way up the darkened rock path. The boy appeared, modesty seeing him don a collared shirt.

— Sophia? He finished buttoning it up. I mean, Libète?

— It's me.

— *Sa k ap fèt?* Did Janel say she could help?

— She said she'd try-but that's nothing now, absolutely nothing. I have to leave. Your mother . . . Libète struggled, her sick lungs rebelling against all of the exertion. Needs your help, she gasped.

— Leave? My moth-are you all right? Unsure what to do, he steadied her with his hand.

She shook her head. I'm not. The dig's guards. The one called Wilnor, he hit your mother.

Félix's eyes stretched wide, and he grabbed his machete. He's dead. Félix began to head down the mountain path.

— But Félix, Libète called out, desperate notes ringing in her voice. She sent me to you. Entrusted me to you.

Félix paused.

— A man, from my past. He's here. With those guards. I don't know what it means, but it's bad. I need to get away and hide. Your mother helped me escape. And with the Sosyete about, I just, I just don't know whom I can trust.

— You're asking a lot of me. You know that.

She opened her hands, closed her eyes, and whispered. I know.

He came close again, his top lip trembling. I'll make sure you're safe, he said, but then I have to return for her.

— Of course, Félix. Of course. She reached for his hand and tugged it. You're a real friend.

The softness of the words, the touch: they undid him. He could only turn away from her. He looked over the path from Foche to the fortress and beyond, like he could see through the ridge's curtain of tall rock and into the small plateau behind.

— Go and hide inside the fort. I'll keep watch. We'll go later, he said under his breath. Once people are settled. Once everyone will be asleep.

— But - she finally breathed deep - why wait?

— All but one path takes us down the mountain by the way you came.

— So?

— The path we need, the safest one, the one I know will take you to a small forest in which you could find food and hide... it's a different way.

She followed his line of sight, straight to the dig site.

— To get there, we have to pass through there.

Dimanche struggles to wake his charge. Not with the decision to do so, but the way in which to carry it out.

Is it best to shake her shoulder? Or say something to make her stir? He didn't want to frighten her with an unfamiliar voice in an unknown setting. Heaven knew he'd scared her enough already.

He stared up into the nightscape unpolluted by electric light. He awed at the same constellations he had charted as a boy, when he had been so sad to hear tell that the Americans had already laid claim to everything in the sky. He chuckled. His aspiration to be the first Haitian in space died young, as with too many of his other impossible hopes.

Dimanche knew their intended route north. He'd studied a map by flashlight while she slept. They would stay to the east as best they could and then cut across to reach Cap-Haïtien. Libète would soon ask as much, though their ultimate destination he would withhold–that could wait. He knew she'd never agree to it, and he didn't look forward to the moment when she discovered the truth. He had already been mulling over what he'd say to get her to accept what she never could on her own.

He looked at a watch he kept in his pocket–23:47. Still kept on a twenty-four hour clock, a lingering habit from his days in the police. Assuming they passed without trouble, Stephanie and Jak would be poised to enter the Dominican Republic at first light. He hoped they would find the anonymity they sought there.

Libète gave a sad moan and turned over on her mat. He thought of himself at her age. *More similar than she knows.* So full of bluster, so set in his ways, so vulnerable. But he had had no one to hold the dark at bay once it descended. *No one to defend me.*

But he *is* here for the girl. He *will* be.

Wisps of memory arise:

Father's hand on shoulder
Callused fingers on wood cracked
Smiles ever widening

They made him feel an unexpected gratitude.

We're so very, very similar.

He settled on a branch ripped from a tree. Standing a yard away, he poked her foot, and she woke with a gasp, like coming up from deep water.

— It's time to go.

The hour is late. That is all she knows.

Libète had hated losing track of time here in Foche. She could have cared less in her younger years on La Gonâve, or in Cité Soleil. The Sun and shadows were the only necessary arms on the clock. Of course she could not sleep tonight, not with so many competing fears crashing about inside her like waves. So instead of sleep she lays on the stone, under the stars, with Félix's blanket over her.

Félix had retreated somewhere deep inside himself and would not resurface. He kept watch over the path, letting his knife blade rise and fall on the earth in dull, quiet taps. She would have liked to speak to him and think things through as she might have done with Jak.

She closed her eyes again.

The guards and Lolo were working together to some end. The brothers brought him here. But how did they find him? Why would they do so?

What had Lolo cried out?

"It's her! The murderer!"

A false accusation, but not so far off. His words were prescient. She had nearly done him in.

She remembered Cinéus's eyes hovering on her after she had resuscitated Jeune. She had read a perverted intent into them, but maybe it was something else. Recognition of some fact. After all, who were these guards, these men who cast long shadows over the earth? They were no university employees. Ha! Private security more like it, of the type Benoit would hire. Maybe word traveled up and down their organization's sinister lines of communication and this recognition somehow saw Lolo dispatched all this way to identify her. To speak conclusively to whether this peasant girl with a healing touch was who they had been seeking.

Memories descended: of the dark night of the dogs, the red flare, the water cold and fast. The recollection of them made her mind stall.

A hand clasped her mouth, and her eyes shot open.

Félix stood over her, his finger crossing his lips. He signaled to a trio of men moving up the trail. She nodded, keeping the outward silence while her heartbeat grew in volume, filling her ears. They collected their things.

— *Follow me,* Félix whispered. Libète did.

He took her down into an indentation in the ground, past what would have been the fort's great hall. They positioned themselves beyond a column, a vantage where they could see Félix's space, his bed, cookware, and beyond that his goat pen. He pushed Libète back like a protective hen would with her chick, but she would not have it. She peered out too.

Cinéus and Wilnor came into view. Their dog's lead strained as the creature pulled ahead. There was a third man with them, unknown, indistinguishable by his darkened outline. Too hale to be Lolo, but not a hulk like the other guards. It suddenly clicked as his gait gave him away.

Prosper.

She palmed her aching, fevered forehead. Why was he with them? *Helping* them? She cursed herself for her spiteful words spoken earlier. But could that outburst really cause him to now side with this lot?

The three men poked and prodded a bit, discussing the situation at a volume that lacked discretion. They let the dog pull them around in circles, but he seemed a shiftless sort of creature, much like his owners. Libète hooked onto the tail end of Cinéus's shout, delivered after upbraiding his brother for forgetting a flashlight: If we don't find her, then the reward vanishes!

So it was about money. Her face twitched with new worry. Some in Foche might easily turn against her for the right sum. Even those she thought friends. Even Prosper.

Félix pulled her without a word, and they slipped off and through a twist of old chambers till they entered a depressed room that led to what they had always figured was a dungeon. They heard the men fumble about in the dark–Cinéus cursed Wilnor again when he hit his head on the archway–and pass from Félix's room and into the Great Hall. Libète tensed at the sight of the dungeon, a narrow, black passage just wide enough for a person to sidle into and stand flattened. Félix tried to push Libète inside, but she fought him. The darkness within repelled her. Dull steps signaled one of their pursuers' approaches, and Félix, taut with alarm, slid inside himself and was swallowed. The footsteps grew closer. Libète breathed deep and forced herself in too.

The space was cramped. Libète had never known herself to be claustrophobic, but the stale air and forced immobility claimed her. Rapid thoughts of captured rogue slaves cast into this man-made fissure and made to stand for aching hours made the walls feel like part of a closing vice.

Félix grasped for her hand, and a modicum of peace transferred through the touch. Her breathing finally slowed and became faint. She thought about praying but resisted. Yet again, where was God? He had thrown her into this place. Like the French oppressors, ready to torture for any disobedience.

A form, edged in moonlight, slid into the fissure's opening. Exploring the dark. The outline, its size and smoothness, was Prosper's.

Libète stifled her breath. Félix squeezed her hand harder.

Prosper stood, peering. Libète was sure he saw them hiding. She could see the whites of his eyes reflecting the Moon. The passage of a few moments stretched into the eternal. The dog barked again. There was more indistinct chatter.

Prosper turned his face away. Nothing's here either, he called. He left.

Libète nearly collapsed.

Dimanche and Libète approach Thomonde. The bike's appetite for petrol and their appetite for food prove too much.

They had spoken little, as Libète still keeps to herself. As they reach the edge of town, they slow to roll up and over a speedbump. Libète speaks. Where are you from, anyway?

He doesn't answer.

— Did you grow up on the water?
— Wi.
— In Jacmel?

— Wi.
— In that shack?
— Wi.
— Is that how you know how to fish?
— Wi.
Libète thought this over. Are you telling me the truth?
— Non.
She grimaced. What's your game, Dimanche?
— My game? My *game* is to keep you alive, and free. I've been many different people these past few years since arresting Benoit. Mainly learning to live as a shadow.
— That's melodramatic.
— That's truth.
— Then it seems I've ruined your life.

He stays quiet, and his silence speaks. She slouches, bouncing as they push over another bump in the road.

At least the morning was beautiful. The Sun was still so small and so bright, it lit up an enormous, open sky bereft of clouds. They puttered past homes lined by cacti fences and goats and dogs and chickens and bustling children. Libète noticed Dimanche tense as a grandfather yelled at his small grandson. *He's nervous. Alert. Afraid.* Where she saw a small break in domestic tranquility, Dimanche sensed lurking threats. Libète wondered if she too was traveling down a road where paranoia could claim her so easily.

They pulled into the gas station and, on stopping, leaped off the bike. He was quick to summon the sleeping attendant, and the man sauntered over with a shotgun in hand. The station itself was simple, like those in Cité Soleil. An elevated cylindrical tank, fenced in, so that gravity forced the gas down and into the bike's tank under the seat.

— Go to the toilet. Do what you need to do, and quickly. Then come back. His eyes darted back and forth as he spoke, sizing up their surroundings.

— You forgot to tell me to first unbutton my pants.

The attendant's eyes bounced between them, groggy and confused. Your daughter – he yawned – will need the key.

Libète let slip a peal of laughter. Dimanche's scowl made her realize her mistake.

— Yes, father, Libète said. I'll do as you say.

She went to relieve herself, unzipping her bag to check on the pigeon inside while walking to the toilet. After finishing her business, she noticed a bucket of water and soap. The water was tinged with murk, but her whole body was covered with a layer of dirt; she at least wanted her hands and face cleaned.

— Lourdmia, Dimanche called as she stepped out and back toward the bike. Libète looked around, confused. It took a moment to realize he had assigned her a new name. Those women – he pointed to a pair on the side of the road – go see if they have any clothes for sale. He cupped his hand and mouthed, *I don't trust this one*, pointing to the attendant. The young man was back in his chair, picking inside his nose and examining the results with an empirical curiosity. Libète rolled her eyes. *So, so paranoid.*

— Yes, Papa. She held out her hand, and when he did nothing, rubbed her thumb against her index finger. He reached into his duffel and withdrew two thousand-goud notes from a wad an inch thick. He was careful to hide this from the attendant.

— Shit, Dimanche! Where's that cash from?

He held a straightened finger to his lips. Get something simple, he said, that won't draw attention.

She took the money, without thanks, and moved off to the two women who were still arranging their clothes for sale on a patchwork of tarps.

— Bonjou, medam, Libète offered robotically.

— Why, hello, *machè*! What are you looking for?

She looked at her and blinked twice. Clothes.

The seller's kindness withered. Libète sorted through the small piles, quick to choose essentials. Pants that looked like they'd fit. Some T-shirts. A hooded sweatshirt in case more cold nights were to come. With her hair and her fraying knit cap, she could pass for a boy. She told herself the desire to appear as such had nothing to do with the swell of feelings she had experienced back on the beach with Jak.

— How much? Libète asked.

— For those? Well, those, those are some premium items. Basically new, I'd say. Straight from Europe. If you read the magazines you'd see that those couldn't be parted with for less than . . .

Libète rolled her eyes. She had no time for games. She dropped the notes on the ground, far more than enough, and walked away with her clothes.

— *Monnen*? Change? the seller asked.

— None, she said, shrugging. Premium items.

Dimanche was repacking his jacket into his bag. Got what you needed?

She gave a nod and stuffed the clothes into his duffel.

— We still need food, he said.

She called to the attendant. Hey, Mesye Miner! Found what you're digging for up there?

The attendant shot up straight, wiping his finger. His nostrils flared. Where can we get some *pate* for the road? she asked. He pointed down the road with his digging implement.

The attendant, much offended, watched the pair as they rode off and paused at the food vendor. With a frown, he took out his flip phone and a card tucked inside. Alo? Wi? It's me. Who? Guy Saingelus. The gas superintendent. Which one? In Thomonde. Yes. I know. I know. Yes. Well, your man and girl, I think they just left. About that reward . . .

Minutes pass. Libète tries to leave the dungeon, but Félix won't let her go.

— *Wait*, he whispers. *They might be hiding out there.*

She rips her hand away. *Not a moment more in here.*

The evening air is like a tonic, and she gulps it in even as she doubles over. Félix emerges next and looks around.

— You need to do what I say, Libète. You don't know this place, our mountain, like I do.

— Whatever, she wheezes.

— I won't take you farther if you don't agree to do what I say.

— I'll take whatever you offer under advisement.

He slapped his machete against a stone column. *Promise me.* You're not alone in this! Don't act like you are.

She took another deep breath. I promise, she said, her voice small.

— Let's go then. He handed Libète her pack, and they finally left the fortress behind, starting the climb up the steep rock wall. When they reached its summit, they saw the small basin that had otherwise been blocked off to Foche. All of the dig's lights were off and generators put to sleep.

— If Cinéus and Wilnor are looking for you outside, Félix said, it probably means there aren't other guards left. Let's stay toward the edge of the basin. The old trail is on the other side, the one that leads to the forest. It's steep. A mother and child fell to their deaths a few years ago. He offered a hand to help her descend. So now, he continued, people take the longer road out of Foche and connect with another.

Libète rubbed her eyes, hoping it would sweep away the weariness that lingered there. How will I get food and water out here?

There was a long pause. What you can't scavenge, I'll bring to you, he said. By night. I'll make this same trip.

— Thank you, she said, a mere whisper.

They continued on till they neared the tents where the diggers slept. Libète didn't like what she saw.

The excavation had swelled over time. There were more tents up here, more vehicles, and the gash in the ground had clearly grown. It was covered by sections of opaque plastic elevated on a network of poles.

As they stepped closer, they got a better look at some of the equipment laid off to the sides. It was odd; large and mechanical, made for moving huge amounts of earth. It defied notions of the archeologist's subtle, careful work. *It's all so strange . . .*

Everything seemed arrayed to keep the activity away from prying eyes. She was just grateful that all of the workers' tents were darkened and situated in a cluster.

Félix's hand leaped out, holding her back. They froze. He pointed to his ear, and Libète inclined her own.

A voice trespassed against the quiet. It was a man's. But it didn't *speak* so much as *sing*. It came from inside the central work area, over the main dig.

Félix was possessed by the voice. Its call pulled him from the relative safety of the perimeter, and he moved step by step toward the camp's center.

— *What are you–*

But Libète could not risk another word. She paused, dallying on the outside, furious at Félix for taking such a foolish risk. She saw him, his machete drawn up while he dug around in his pocket. Libète rushed to catch up, watching what he withdrew.

It was a small wooden figurine. The rooster.

She followed and drew nearer to the tarps. The low, rasped singing grew in clarity.

Félix pulled aside the hanging plastic.

Before them sat Dorsinus, sitting upon a crate, whittling away, singing his song, defying death.

PASSED THROUGH THE GROUND

Kote zonbi konnen ou, li pa fè ou pè.
Where the zombie knows you, he won't frighten you.

The wind whips their faces, the bike growls, but Libète shouts anyway. Curiosity pries her from her silence.
— Where'd that money come from?
— I told you. He bellows to be heard. I can't tell.
Her eyebrow arches. Well, what's it for then? What are you saving it for?
— You think I was hiding out in a shack for months for my own good?
She scratches her cheek. It was clear "yes" was the wrong answer. Your family?
He sneers.
— All just for Jak and I? But . . . why?
He looks at the open road. I chose shadows so you could be in light.
— Nonsense, she says.

He releases the gas and pulls hard on the brake till the bike skids into the shoulder, kicking up a spray of thick dust.

— Look, Libète says. I appreciate your help, but I *never* asked you for this. Not then, not now.

He spoke in quiet, quiet words. I lost everything for you. My career. My rank. My home. His eyes seared her. My good name. So I changed. Everything. All because you pushed me to act that night.

She felt sympathy, but this cauterized into something like indignity. Justice *demanded* Benoit be arrested, she said. Dimanche–the one you say is gone–cared something about that. That little girl tugging at his sleeve only reminded him. Libète picked at a bit of foam liner on the sidecar.

— It makes the consequences no less severe. His breathing was hard, and she wondered if he might hit her. All I had, over all of my years of work, was my *authority*. And that's gone.

There was nothing more to say, and he started the bike again. They rode in silence for a time before he squinted. He saw a line of distant forms that looked like a shifting mirage. His jaw tightened. Get ready, he said. He slowed the bike, but did not stop it.

— For what? Libète moved her hand, unshielding her eyes.

— Police inspection. A checkpoint.

— What if it's them?

— I know.

— Can we turn around?

He shook his head. Whether police or our pursuers, they'd know we're trying to avoid them. We turn, and they'll be after us. Dimanche reached into a side bag and handed her something heavy, wrapped in a chamois cloth.

— Is this – she slipped her fingers along its burnished metal – is this your gun?

— Just in case.

— Keep it yourself. I don't touch these things. I'm nonviolent! she said, puffed up.

He forced it into her left hand. Hide it! Hide it!

She wanted to debate further, but there was no time. They'd meet the roadblock in less than a minute. Her heart thumped madly. She put her right hand over her chest in a futile effort to calm it.

There were three men in police uniform at the checkpoint. All wore camouflage in various shades of swirling tan. Kneepads, heavy vests, black helmets, guns slung about. They looked like the UN troops in Cité Soleil, but were clearly Haitian. The policeman in the middle of the road finished searching the back of a walk-in truck bed that had lost one of its two doors. With the bike's approach, two officers who had been leaning on a beat-up white sedan had been brought to attention. They reached for weapons–a shotgun and a machine gun–and stood a few feet behind the middle officer.

— Give me your ID and registration.

Dimanche reached into his bag and rifled around. When he took more than a moment, the two policemen raised their weapons. He withdrew a small ID card, surely falsified, and a paper copy of the motorcycle's title. They lowered the guns.

— Everyone's jumpy today. Who're you after? Dimanche asked the policeman. The man answered with a grunt. Libète held the gun in between her legs and grasped it for some sense of security. She looked ahead, her eyes fixed on the road that would soon leave level ground and climb upward, into the mountains.

The policeman looked at the card closely. Another vehicle, a *taptap* full of passengers, had pulled into line.

— Can I have my ID back?

— No. Drive over there and kill the engine.

— Ah, is that really necessary? My daughter and I are just on a drive home from Mirebalais, and there's no need to point your guns at us. This is nonsense. We're going.

The first officer raised his gun.

— Get off! Now!

Two vehicles now waited in the checkpoint queue. All their passengers' eyes were curious and watching.

— All right, all right, Dimanche said, reaching for the keys. Ah, I forgot! The starter isn't working. This thing, if it turns off, it won't go again. I've got to keep it on or . . .

The officer, in a flash, rammed the butt of his rifle into Dimanche's head and sent him spilling to the ground. He rose, staggering to find the three armed men arrayed about him, ready to shoot.

Libète takes a step closer to the living dead.

Dorsinus. In the flesh.

Brik kolon brik, the man sings, *Brik kolon brik*. The lyrics are nasal, caught up high in his nose.

She had seen Dorsinus lying dead on the road.

His empty eyes, his neck twisted, his face distressed.

They had buried him!

Félix circled the old man. Dorsinus continued his whittling, taking no notice of the youths. His singing skipped from verse to verse:

> *Little bird where are you going?*
> *I am going to Lalo's house*
> *Lalo eats little kids*
> *If you go she'll eat you too*

Brik kolon brik, he sings again, *Brik kolon brik*. Libète knows this song, etched into the minds of Haitian children. She joins him, harmonizing softly.

> *Nightingale eats breadfruit*
> *Rolling, rolling I come from the village*
> *All birds fall in water*

Dorsinus looks up at her from his whittling. His eyes see but do not see. A smile curls at the corner of his mouth.
Lady, please dance with me, he sings to Libète.
Sir, I am too tired, he sings to Félix.
Sir, I am too tired, he repeats.
— A *zonbi*, Félix whispers.
Libète nods.
She has never seen a zombie before, not in person. Rumors of them swirled in Cité Soleil, but they were often stories whipped up to scare children.
— I should have known, Félix says. He curses.
Libète's lips purse. What do you mean?
— He paid my ransom. Spoke against all that's going on here.
— You think the Sosyete would do this?
— I don't know. I just know they *can*.
They took in the pathetic man. His clothes were tattered and caked in mud. His hair and beard were clumped with thick clay. He smelled terrible.
— His *ti bon anj* has been stolen, Félix added. He has no reason left.
People had bifurcated souls, as everyone knew: the *gwo bon anj*, and the *ti bon anj*. Félix and Libète saw proof before them that with the latter gone, only the last flickers of the divine spark that all people have remained.

Félix bristled. The Sosyete threatened me with this. If I broke their order. Being made a zombie, that's their greatest punishment. Worse than death.

Libète had her doubts about zombification. She had heard different, less spiritual explanations. Carefully measured toxins administered to make the victim appear dead. Once raised–dug up– another drug makes him docile and dulls his mental faculties. In effect, making a perfect slave.

— What if it wasn't a punishment? Libète offered. It could be, but... what if there's another purpose? Look at him. His hands. They've had him here for months. He's been digging, Félix. He's been *digging*.

Félix wasn't following. He wasn't able to move past the state of the man who had exchanged fates with him.

Libète looked past Dorsinus to the grounds that the university had been so careful to conceal from prying eyes. Look at how deep they've gone, she murmured. It was a pit of profound darkness. Just look!

Félix did. The gash had long, long ladders going down, and there was tall machinery that looked powerful. Pumps. Cranes to raise and lower materials. Under the constructed shed structure she could see what looked like some sort of large pool.

— Félix, we're so foolish. If we had thought about it, if we had considered all they were taking away...

— What do you mean?

— They aren't recovering the past. Of course not. They started by searching. Surveying. Sampling. This... is the beginning.

Félix was trembling. What are they doing to our ground, Libète? What do you mean?

She raised her hand to her forehead. It's so *obvious*. This, this is no university. Félix looked terrified. These men, whoever they are, have come to loot. They have come to plunder. They have come to steal.

Libète cannot breathe. The air, it does not come.

Dimanche staggers with his hands raised. Blood runs from a gash on the side of his head.

The one in the road keeps his gun trained on them. The first driver in line honks, but the trailing policeman holds up a hand that tells him to wait. The bike sits rattling, and Dimanche is tight with anger. Next to his size, these men, whoever they are, look like teenage boys dressed in costume.

— Turn the bike off, one says.

Dimanche doesn't move.

— Turn it *off*.

Dimanche does, hooking eyes with Libète. Libète shrinks to nothing. The officer thrusts his gun's barrel into the back of Dimanche's head.

— Get against the car!

Dimanche moves slowly and plants his hands on the unmarked vehicle. Libète squirms, drenched in her own sweat. One of the officers looks at her through his balaclava's eye slit. There is more honking.

— Let us go! shouts a taptap passenger. Don't keep us here! We don't care for any of this! We're just trying to–

The policeman aims his gun at the vehicle, and all complaining stops.

The thought of falling into these men's hands dredges memories most unpleasant:

Stolen by night most black
Bullet's sharpness slipping through flesh
Death, in my hand, pointed at another

One of the men patted down Dimanche while the one with the shotgun held it to Dimanche's back. The third turned and stood watching it all, the barrel of his gun pointing downward.

— Search the bike, one said. And the girl. Libète clenched the pistol grip.

They will not take me.

Libète pulled the nickel-plated thing from its cloth, taking it in. Death, in her hand . . .

. . . *They will not* . . .

. . . pointed at another.

She stood in the sidecar, unnoticed. She raised the gun, unnoticed. She roared.

— *Get down on the ground, you bastards! I'll blow your heads off! I'll blow them off!* She fired the gun with a wince and shattered the car's back window. The pistol's recoil nearly unbalanced her.

The men's faces showed flashes of reflexive thought, wondering if she had meant to hit them. Truthfully, she didn't know whether she had.

Two dropped to the ground as ordered. The one who pointed the shotgun at Dimanche did not. She fired toward the ground near his feet. He gave a yelp and slid against the truck. She had hit his ankle. Dimanche grabbed the man's shotgun in an instant and aimed it at him.

— No! Libète shouted with a shock of repentance. Dimanche looked at her. He was utterly claimed by rage. The one Libète shot gave a fearful screech. His blood was starting to flow.

Dimanche kicked the others' guns away and moved to the side of the car. He fired into one of the truck's tires with a deafening sound of shot flooding rubber and denting the hubcap. The car slumped. Pump. He walked to the other side and burst the other tire.

— Get their guns.

Libète tensed, coming back to her senses. She hopped down and grabbed the pistol and rifle and returned them to the sidecar. Dimanche moved to the truck's hood and fired again into the car's engine for good measure.

— You bitch! the shot one yelled.

She bristled. She wanted to walk over to him. She wanted to look into his eyes. She wanted to end him. Her shoulders slumped, and she shuddered.

Dimanche ran back to the bike, adding the shotgun to their cache. Within moments they were off.

Her adrenaline pumped. She could not look away from her guardian and the fury that hovered over him.

Again, the question rose: *What are you, Dimanche?*

But with it came a new question too: *And what am I?*

They have come to loot. They have come to plunder. They have come to steal.

The thoughts fall into place. How had she not seen it? How had Foche not? A benevolent university. Men coming and going. Working day after day for months. Armed guards in their midst. Ha!

— From the beginning, they've lied to Foche, she said. They're here for gold!

— Gold?

Libète's thoughts kept coming to her. The realizations flow.

She remembered the news stories, gleaned over the months hiding away in Jacmel. Gold was found in the north of Haiti, she told Félix. People always thought that it was here, but it wasn't confirmed till recently. When companies started *exploring*.

— How . . . do you know all this?

— The whole country knows it. At least the parts connected to the rest of the world! It was on the radio. Online. In the news! I remember now, I remember! President Martelly had the government passing out permits to foreign companies who paid up. It all happened behind closed doors, and the senate finally put a stop to it. A halt on all permitting until the process was opened up. Until they had an idea who was getting what. Companies could prepare to extract, but not actually take.

She held her hand to her head, dumbstruck. Twenty billion, Félix! They think there's that much gold in the ground here in the north! Who knows how much they might have found here!

— But if it was stopped, how could this be?

Libète chuckled at his naïveté. This is *illegal*. Whoever is behind it, they're trying to get a head start on the gold rush. Hide what they're doing and then slip out of here. She was getting louder as her realizations rolled on, dangerously so. Exploration before exploitation! These bastards!

— Maybe they're good? Félix said, hoping. These people, they've given us good things.

— They hand out some seed, cap some springs. They're just giving Foche breadcrumbs to keep us in our place. Keep us from asking questions. While they strip our wealth from beneath us!

— Strip?

— You don't know? Of course you don't. How would you?

— What are you saying?

— Gold mining. They're starting here, keeping it small to keep from getting noticed. But when this really starts, when it's too late, they'll have torn up these fields and disappeared. Already they want the Common Plot. Our water will become ruined. I've seen pictures, Félix. Pictures! Everyone will have to leave. Foche won't exist.

— But Janel wouldn't let something like this happen. She wouldn't agree to this. Neither would the Sosyete!

Libète couldn't piece it together either. Janel must not know the truth. The Sosyete must not... no, no, they do! They must have handed Dorsinus over to them! Put him in the ground, then dug him up. He's a slave doing this work! Look at him. He's only able to do the things he's done his entire life. Mining. Whittling. I'm sure they have him working down there, or up above. Maybe letting him become poisoned by the mercury used to separate rock from gold.

Félix was bewildered. *The land... not the land... not Foche.* He grabbed Dorsinus's face and looked into the man's empty, empty eyes. Now he really *can't* see. Can't understand a thing. Poor, poor man.

Félix wept.

As Libète comforted the boy, she whispered into Dorsinus's ear. You must awaken, dear man. You must come up out of this and regain yourself. He finally stopped his singing, and smiled. Was there some recognition there? He feebly handed her the half-finished bird. She took it. Her own eyes watered.

Félix ripped himself away and reclaimed his machete. He ran at the machine on the edge of the hole. He didn't know what its different components did, yet he started slashing at a set of hydraulic hoses, bursting some smaller tires at its base.

— Félix! Please, no!

He upended a boxy generator so that it fell into the deep wound drilled into the earth. The clatter rose and escaped. There were new sounds from outside: voices, barking. Lights played across the tarp cover. Libète looked on in horror.

She sprinted for him, pulling him away from the damage he wrought. They slipped out the other end of the tent and into the open night air, leaving Dorsinus behind to sing his endless song.

As they speed away from the checkpoint, Libète begins hyperventilating.
— What are we going to do, Dimanche? What are we going to-
— Calm down!

He cranks the accelerator hard, and it sounds as if the bike cries out in its exertion. The vehicles that had paused behind them at the checkpoint are distant, but moving again. Libète wonders if the men–*certainly not police*–have commandeered them.

— They'll be after us for sure! She had to shout to be heard. Maybe on those trucks!

Dimanche nodded. We need to get rid of the bike. And these guns. Here, up ahead. At the bridge, throw them over.

— All of them?

— Keep the pistol, he said. She nodded. He slowed, and she tossed them into a spindly, shallow waterway below. Libète saw two children watching from the bank as they washed. She worried they might retrieve them and hurt themselves.

— Don't worry. They'll be waterlogged. Dimanche said, reading her mind. He pushed the bike harder.

The taptap was still behind them. Its relative size neither grew nor shrank, meaning that it too was speeding. The other direction they saw a roadside market with a few passenger vans and some homes set back.

They pulled into the market, and women ran to them with their hands full of bushels of bananas, fried plantain chips, coated nuts, and sachets of water to sell to passengers through bus windows and the open rears of taptaps.

— Get some food. Water. Stuff that will keep. He gave Libète a wad of cash and sprang from the bike. The vendors encircled her like a pack of hungry beasts.

— Buy from me!
— My fruit is best!
— *Dlo se lavi! Dlo se lavi!* Water is life!

She could scarcely see where Dimanche had gone. She became paralyzed.

— Get away from me! she finally shouted.

— This young man has won the prize! Dimanche announced. Libète saw his arm wrapped around a confused youth.

The teenager was short, wearing a grease-stained apron. Dimanche had pulled him aside from a tent where he cooked meals dumped into Styrofoam takeaway containers. This one, he has won this fine motorcycle!

Libète's eyes widened. He *what?*

— Yes, he's won. He's won! But only if he claims it now. *Right now.*

— But, the youth said, I have my restaurant. I can't go.

Libète understood. Yes, go *now,* she said. Or some other soul takes your prize!

— Surely you have an associate here who can watch your restaurant for but a few minutes? Dimanche said. Even we can do so!

The youth was clearly conflicted.

— You really want to give me this?

— As we said, you won. Libète stood like a model showing off a gameshow prize. She let herself glance over her shoulder. The taptap truck was not far off, its front grill and bumper resembling a devious grin. Dimanche pulled his bag from the bike's seat.

— Here, take it for a spin. Dimanche forced a smile. It was utterly unconvincing, and Libète wished he had not tried. Dimanche placed the key in the youth's hand, and the young man looked at it stupidly.

And then he smiled.

— All right! he said, jumping in the air. All right! Everyone, look! I won!

— Yes, you did! Libète said, guiding him over to the bike's seat. Now be off!

The youth gave it too much gas as he shifted into gear, causing the bike to buck. He looked anxious, but once he did a quick spin in the gravel, his smile grew enormous. He putted away down a road perpendicular to the highway.

— I'm a winner! he shouted. A winner! A cloud of dust trailed behind. The crowd of sellers and customers split their gazes between the bike and the curious strangers.

Dimanche spoke. Come on. He and Libète ducked into the man's stall and hid. The vendors flocked toward the arriving taptap, but before they could surround it, it cut right in pursuit of the bike. The vendors cursed as the dust bathed them.

— What jerks!

— They didn't even slow down!

— They could have run us over!

Dimanche hollered at the sellers. Those vans over there. Where do they go?

— To Hinche, came a reply.

Dimanche clucked and started to fill a container with rice and *legim*. Stock up, he said to Libète. Libète filled another tub with fried chicken legs.

— You going to pay for that? one of the sellers asked.

— He got a motorcycle. That's worth two plates, he grumbled.

Food in their hands and their bags on their shoulders, the pair ran to the vans.

— When do you depart? Dimanche asked. The driver reclined in his seat, his legs propped up on the steering column. A cap covered his face.

— When the van's full, he said. He didn't remove the cap.

There was only one other passenger, an older man wearing a smart suit with a mismatched hat. How long have you been waiting? Dimanche barked.

— W-w-why, an hour, I'd say. The man's fingers tightened around his satchel.

Libète looked at the other van. It didn't even have a driver.

— How much is the fare?

— Three hundred goud each, the driver responded.

Dimanche ripped the driver's cap off his face. Here's money for twelve passengers. He dropped the cash into the hat. Now go.

The driver feigned indignity, taking his hat back. We pack eighteen into this van.

Dimanche dug back into his pocket and threw more notes at the driver. *Ale.* Go.

The driver sat up, looking at the cash. Yes, *sir*! He gave a mock salute. Dimanche and Libète climbed in.

The van reached Hinche without further event. Dimanche and Libète arrived at a hub of buses, vans, and taptaps. There were police at the station, and Dimanche eyed them carefully. They skirted around them in their search for another ride.

— Will you finally tell me where we're trying to go? Libète asked. 'Cap-Haïtien' was Dimanche's only reply. It was Haiti's second-largest city, coastal, and in the north.

— Why there?

— The air is clear, he said dismissively.

Libète grimaced. She followed Dimanche through the crush of people toward a bus that had Cap-Haïtien written on its side. How about this one? She moved toward it. Dimanche tarried.

— Our enemies will be on the main roads north. More checkpoints. He shuddered. No, we'll take a longer route. One they won't bother with. She probably knows where we're going by now.

Libète squinted. Who? Maxine? What makes you say that?

Dimanche didn't answer.

— Really, why are we going to Cap-Haïtien? We could hide anywhere.

— I'll tell you in time.

— Not 'in time.' *Now.* She slapped the side of the bus.

He grimaced. *Fine.* There is a boat.

— A boat?

— A boat. And it will sail soon. And you must be on it.

— Where is it sailing?

Dimanche looked dyspeptic. He looked over his shoulder and said the words: *Etazini.*

Libète gasped. The US? She leaned in and gritted her teeth. I never agreed to leave Haiti. Never. *Never.*

— Your way has been paid. And I am to deliver you. There's no choice.

— Says who?

— Ms. Stephanie.

— Bah!

— If you aren't on that boat, you'll die. You realize that, don't you?

— Then I'll die. Libète walked away from him.

He grabbed her elbow, and she tore it away. Please. These protests are unnecessary. It is the way things are, Libète. It is where we are.

She swept back toward him. If I am taken from this ground, I will waste away to nothing. Already, with all this time away from Cité Soleil, I can feel it. My soul. My heart. They're withering.

— Cité Soleil will move on.

— Don't you say that!

He spoke again. Cité Soleil doesn't need you. Haiti doesn't need you. You need them.

— How...*dare* you. How can you–you've never loved a place like me!

He held a pointed finger up to her face. You know nothing about me. You're not the only one to have bled for a place. But places, they're nothing. We float along, we never find a home. Not on this side of the water. Not on this side of life.

Libète didn't want to give the notion credence.

Dimanche reached out to touch her. The fingers he laid on her shoulder were surprisingly gentle. Every person in this world who loves you most is desperate for you to go and be *safe*, he said. Please. For their sake. You must go and do this thing. Dimanche searched her dark brown eyes. For my sake.

She looked at him, taken aback by his pleading. To have Haiti ripped from beneath her seemed unfathomable...

She found the details of the station fall away as the reality of things descended. Dimanche's hand hovered just behind her back, and she let him guide her toward another staging bus where a man called out, Sen Rafeyel! Dondon! Menard!–the knots in their coming journey's string. She boarded and Dimanche watched her climb the steps and find a seat. She hardly emoted. Hardly blinked.

He paid the caller the fare and grimaced. He knew he could not reach her in her sadness. All that was left was to guide her to where she must go.

Breathe. In and out. Out and in.

Félix and Libète hide on top of the axels of one of the thieving trucks.

The mining camp is roused. Boots on gravel tamp soft earth. Men holler at Dorsinus. He can give no explanation for the noise and damaged equipment. The camp dwellers' flashlights land on the severed hoses, the generator fallen down deep. Swearing erupts. Two pair of legs walk just past Félix and Libète's faces.

— Libète, Félix whispers. Prepare to run.

She glares at him.

— They'll find us. There's no way around it. But they don't have to find *both* of us.

She shakes her head fiercely. It aches with a dull, feverish pain.

— Get ready. I'm going to give myself up. When you see a chance, run.

— Don't you dare! Don't you leave me!

— You promised you'd do as I say. Get down the mountain. You'll be safe.

She longs to do this. To be rid of this moment and its fear.

They see a burly man on his hands and knees. He searches beneath one of the neighboring trucks with a sweep of his flashlight.

Félix lays his machete down and begins whispering prayers. He asks for protection, and for strength to take the blows he will soon bear.

It was she who dragged him into this. Why should he pay the consequences? But she had no choice. If she was taken, it would be the end. She would fall into Cinéus and Wilnor's hands and be passed to whoever had sent Lolo to find her. She would be given to the people who had killed her friends and pursued her across the country. They would likely torture her till she gave them those accursed Numbers, whatever they were.

She must do as Félix says.

She has to.

Heavy footsteps herald the approach of the man with the flashlight. The light pours from the cylinder in his hand and plays across the ground just under the truck. Félix's eyes are closed. He takes a deep breath, and a second, and a third. The man crouches.

Libète drops and grabs the machete. As she rolls out, she shouts: I surrender! I surrender!

A SPLIT SOUL

Ti kou ti kou bay fè mò.
Little blow by little blow brings death.

Fòk ou konn la pou ou al la.
You must know there to go there.

Dimanche and Libète arrive in Menard. The hour is late.

A group of men linger around a crank radio. They drink warm beer by candlelight. An old woman plaits a younger woman's hair, and they break into laughter. Pentecostals filter out of a late prayer service, heavy Bibles in their hands, heavy lids about their eyes.

Dimanche spins, taking it in, breathing in deeply. Libète watches him carefully. Do you . . . know this place?

He nods.

— These people. Some of them. The one with the radio, that's Daniel. He's a philanderer. And that woman, Magalie, I know her from her voice.

— This was your home?

— For a time. A gateway to other things.

— Better things?

He doesn't answer.

— Should you say hello, Dimanche? To Daniel? To Magalie? A reunion. That'd be nice, no?

— They wouldn't recognize me.

Libète is perplexed.

— No, he says. But there is one we need to see.

He started walking, stepping off the main road that bisected the town's thicket of homes. He struck a path among their fenced yards. Libète carried all their possessions and struggled to keep pace.

They came to a home–two floors, columned, covered in spackle–that even by night looked run down. It was the largest home she had seen in the town and it seemed sinister in its disrepair.

Dimanche knocked. Honor! he called out. His voice cracked.

A moment passed. Respect! came called back. The home's front door opened to a prudent width, and a white shock of hair poked from behind. Who's there?

Dimanche looked to Libète, and she noticed fear in his misshapen face. Dimanche, he called back.

The old man stepped out into the yard and took in his visitor. His hands lay limp at his sides. His mouth was agape. If he saw Libète, he didn't note it.

He came forward with tentative steps before embracing Dimanche wholly.

• • •

— Forgive me, but the generator, it's out of service, the old man said.

— Don't worry.

— Ah, and the fridge. I have no ice.

— It's not a proble–

— No delivery today. The sodas, they're all warm. Picot! he called. Picot! Get me ice! Ice!

A boy appeared from the shadows. He kept his eyes downcast and took a pair of crinkled goud notes from the old man's outstretched hand. The boy's defeated and tired movements reminded Libète of herself when she was a child servant. She thought to speak to the boy and acknowledge him by thanking him. Instead she floated to the entryway corner and watched the two men's ongoing awkward exchange in fascination.

— Sit. The man pulled out a chair for Dimanche. My boy, sit, he said. His hand ran through his bushy hair. You're here.

— I am.

They stared at each other. You're here, he repeated.

A clock ticked in the background.

— And did you–have you–

— Done what I set out to do?

The old man nodded.

— My task – he looked at Libète, suddenly wary of her presence – is complete. They're gone.

The man collapsed into his own chair. He stroked his cheek's stubble. My God. He turned to look upon her. And this one–I'm sorry, dear girl. Who is this one? He turned to her and spoke directly. Who are you? He gasped before she could answer. Your daughter, Dimanche? His face lit with a hopeful smile.

Dimanche shook his head, as if in shame. Like his life had been measured and came up lacking. She is a charge of mine, he said.

— My name is Lourd–

— In this house, Dimanche interrupted her, we can use real names.

— Libète, she offered. The old man came and knelt at her feet. So confused and taken aback, she nearly fell. He sized up her face before meeting her eyes. It's a pleasure to meet you. I'm called Celestine. He took her right hand and kissed it.

He rose as quickly as his rickety knees allowed. When Picot returns, he can take your things upstairs. You're staying? Of course you are.

— Only for a night, Dimanche said. If that's all right.

— It's been nearly twenty years, my boy! Celestine's hand met his forehead again. For only one night?

— We're off. To Cap-Haïtien. In the morning.

Celestine sighed. We have much to catch up on.

• • •

They spent the balance of the evening in the home's covered gallery, looking out on the yard and Menard, sipping sweating sodas, letting the crickets' songs fill the gaps in conversation. They talked in stops and starts about the weather, the failing soil, and politics in Port-au-Prince.

— So they're all gone, Celestine finally said as he rocked in his chair, circling back to an earlier subject and the one that most intrigued Libète. All gone...

Libète cradled the pigeon in her hands, stroking the creature. She sat up and inclined her ear. She didn't understand what topic these two tiptoed about. She decided to help them along and spoke up.

— Dimanche. Your accent–your ways–I always thought you were from the south, from the city. And you've not been back to Menard in all this time? Not in years?

— My work. It kept me away.

Celestine whistled. But this work is done? You're free?

Dimanche suddenly looked extremely tired. I've told you. Irritability claims him. Excuse me, he said. I can see by my manners I'm in need of rest.

Celestine stopped rocking. I'm sorry. I–I didn't mean to push–

— We'll talk tomorrow... been a long day. Dimanche's voice trailed off as he headed into the house, upstairs.

Libète *tsked*. He hasn't seen you in years, you show us such kindness, and this is his behavior? I'm sorry, Mesye Celestine. He can behave like such a... teenager.

Celestine showed a smile. No need, my dear, no need. My curiosity keeps me asking about what he's done rather than who he's become. That's my own fault.

Libète had so many questions. What's this work he's talking about? When he was an inspector?

— Ah, if you don't know, it's not for me to tell. A man at my age, I'd rather not think on it too much.

Libète nodded. Well, what about before then? How did you meet?

— Heh. I can remember the day well. Celestine nursed his soda. I can picture him as he was then. Fewer pounds, more hair. Ha. Ha! Did you see the rice fields on the way into town?

Libète searched her memory. With her thoughts consumed with the day's events, she noticed little on their hours-long journey to Menard.

— Yes, she lied.

— They're mine. They've been stolen out from under me over the years, though they're my heritage. All of my kids–a worthless lot–ran to Canada, France, the US. All of them dyaspora. He said the word like a curse. I'm no farmer. I'm not even smart! Bad deal after bad deal added up. He threw out the remainder of his drink into the yard. I'm just glad my ancestors can't see the mess I've made.

— Dimanche farmed?

— He has a gift! *Had* a gift, maybe. My only good years were when Dimanche was in charge of it all. Between you and me, he looks terrible these days. Like his spirit has been wrung out of him. He gestured. Like water from a sponge.

— Whatever's happened, he's still a good man. Libète said this begrudgingly.

— Maybe so. But hard to recognize these days, Celestine said. Hard to recognize . . .

The Son puts his parents into the ground.

He prepared the bodies himself. Dragged them on a makeshift sled himself. Dug the graves himself.

No one was willing to join in a burial for the murdered when the murderers still roamed about, meting out senseless death.

His father had been strung up on a tree before being shot. It was a villain's end. The type of callous murder slavers would commit to send a message beyond words. Today, though the method was the same, the message was different: to oppose the coup was to face this end. His father had not been a perfect man, but he had been good. As far as the Son was concerned, his mother had been a saint.

Day turns to night. He tamps the graves with his foot, slides the shovel into the earth beside the newly filled holes. The sweat and tears dampen him and make him cold.

He had climbed the mapou tree like he did as a child, when he would practice going up and down so that he could retrieve fruit from other trees that no one else was brave enough to reach. He climbed today to loosen the ropes that suspended his father's drained body in the air. The man's head slumped down as he spun in a lazy pirouette. The Son loosed the knot, watched the body slip. His father was at last returned to the ground that had given him life, sustained him, and would now swallow him.

He reunited his father and mother, laying them side by side.

Shots came in the distance, but the Son, he did not care. He fell to his knees and wept. For his parents, they were no more.

• • •

The murderers camped in the open, under a cloudless sky and slivered, silent Moon.

They slept soundly, as if judgment would never visit them for their crimes.

The Son watched their circle, lit by two weak fires. There was a watchman, but he was debauched. Before long he would fall asleep like the others.

The Son palmed his koulin's hilt, feeling its weight. He had grown up with such blades. He only thought of them as tools to help make life thrive. He never dwelled on their capacity to do the opposite.

His teeth gritted, he began slashing at the dark. He muttered exhortations. He riled himself from the weariness and exhaustion that dulled his senses.

Kill them
For what they did
End them
So they do no more

The blade was his father's. It was beautiful in its time-tested wear. Sharp. Faithful. It did not know whether it sliced through stalk or sinew, and did not care. It was an unthinking extension, willing to do its bearer's will.

The leader lay in the middle of them–eight men in total. He would be the first to go. If the Son could kill others, good. But this one, the head, would be chopped off the figurative body.

The blade arced silver with each cut of the air. The Son's heart throbbed. His mind clouded.

Jistis, he told himself. *Justice,* he nearly cried aloud.

He was tackled to the ground. He strained against the tackler's arms, but they were thick, and powerful. The Son screamed, but a hand clapped his mouth and trapped the sound.

— You will die if you do this! came the harsh whisper. They will kill you! Take it out on us!

The Son knew the voice. Knew it well. The clouds parted. Thought returned.

He rebelled against the lock-set arms out of obligation, but instead of raging, he sobbed.

• • •

— The leader's name is Pascal. The man handed the Son a cup of steaming ginger tea. They warmed themselves by a sheltered cooking fire.

— Mesye Robert, I have to do this.

— I didn't say I'd keep you from doing the thing. But you're going about it wrong. He looked at the steaming tea in his cup, swished it around, contemplated something. I'm trying to help you, Robert said. I didn't much like your father or his ideas–I'm sorry, but it's truth–though I don't want to see his son meet the same end.

— *I have to do this.*

— As I said, they'll kill many if you do.

— Then I'll kill them all.

— That's nonsense. One blade against half a dozen guns. Robert gave a derisive chuckle. His eyes followed the steam leaping into the air.

— You don't understand what they took from me.

Robert sipped and snarled. They took my wife in front of my little boy. Violated her. Made him watch. He glared at the Son. I understand a little.

— Join me then. We could get others. We could take them!

Robert sized him up. Revenge–proper revenge–takes planning. They took your father in an instant, but to make them truly pay, to snuff them out, it will take more time. That's the way these things should be done.

— What then?

A cry came from Robert's shack.

— Was that your wife? the Son asked.

Robert shook his head. My boy. He doesn't talk anymore–since the *vyolasyon*. He just cries out.

— Do you need to go to him?

Robert waved his hand dismissively. He'll learn to live with pain. It'll make him stronger.

They sat in uneasy silence.

— I ask again, what do we do?

— We will gather a certain group of men, Robert said. I will call them tomorrow night, by the drum. And wherever these villains lay their heads, we'll cut them off together.

Dimanche awakens late in the morning. Though not one to indulge his body and its pesky need for rest, the prior days have sapped him.

He came upon Picot and Libète and Celestine. Picot scrambled eggs over a gas cooking flame while Celestine and Libète sat at a square table dragged out to the gallery. It was a cool hour. The sky was gray and clouded, and this made the verdant greens of nearby trees and grass pop. He looked out in the distance and saw fields thriving. *The world as it should be. Not concrete and rebar. Not people living on top of one another in filth.* His hands itched for work. If they didn't have to run, he knew how he would spend the day: working in those fields.

Picot put a mug of piping hot coffee into Dimanche's hand without a word. The boy returned to his stove and eggs.

— Mèsi, Dimanche mumbled.

— Ah! Bonjou, bonjou, bonjou! Celestine said. He gave a small clap and rose from his chair.

Dimanche feigned a smile.

— I thought you'd died, Libète said plainly.

— I might have wished I had. His lips curled subtly, a genuine smile this time. Slowing down for a bit of rest, my memory caught up with me. My memory and I, we aren't always on good terms.

Libète tapped the table. Dimanche, Celestine and I were talking. Dimanche blew on his coffee. He told me some of your story, she said. Just a bit. About... about the loss of your family. I'm sorry.

Dimanche still looked out over the fields. He took a sip of his coffee, cringing at its tang.

— He shared about the men, those evil men, Libète continued. Those who took your parents from you.

— This coffee. It could use some milk, Dimanche said.

Celestine's eyes widened. Of course. Of course! Picot! Condensed milk! Go for it! He clapped twice.

— But the eggs, the boy protested.

— Now!

Picot killed the flame and grumbled as he slipped out toward the main road.

— Did you... kill some of them then?

— I tried. It would have been suicide to attack them on my own. My neighbor stopped me. He had another idea.

— Yes?

— We spread the word. That the murderers–they were paramilitaries, members of FRAPH–were dispatched to break us as a reprisal for our politics. The neighbor used his drum. Men gathered. I knew these men, but did not know them like this, not by night. We discussed and argued over what to do. In total, we had eight willing to attack them. We matched their number. We gathered our weapons and set out for their camp.

— Yes? Libète was sitting on the edge of her chair.

— They were gone.

Glad to hear he hadn't been forced to kill, Libète sighed unconsciously. Dimanche saw her. He wanted to both tell the truth and hide it.

— Gone? she asked. But to where?

— Pascal–that was the leader's name–and his pack of dogs fled. Slipped back to whatever foul place they'd come from. We thought they'd been warned we were coming. He chuckled. They were afraid, we learned, but not of us. It was the American soldiers come to liberate us.

— You lost track of them?

The words gave him pause. I never lost them. They've never left my thoughts.

Picot returned, slamming two small cans of condensed milk on the table. He struck a match and relit his flame.

— What manners, Celestine muttered under his breath. He reached for a bottle opener and pierced the cans, pouring the milk into both Libète's and Dimanche's mugs. The white swirled until it claimed the black.

Libète had a thousand questions but respected Dimanche's quiet. Picot soon came out with three plastic plates and placed a mound of eggs and a piece of bread on each.

— You should see the road, Picot said. Everyone is out. There's a truck–

— So what? Celestine said abruptly. Trucks always pass through.

— But the men in the truck. They have guns. They're asking all around. Looking for some man and some girl who have done something–

Libète dropped her mug. It cracked and shattered and spilled.

Their faces are pink, their fatigues are green, their guns are large.

They speak a language the Son knows is called '*Angle*' but that he's never heard uttered on that mountaintop he calls home. He watches them from the roadside. His few possessions are stuffed in a *djakout* bag slung over his shoulder.

The paramilitaries' disappearance consumed the Son. The desire to see them dead overwhelmed him.

Two days passed. Every moment he spent attempting to return to life as it was before his parents were taken he heard a nagging whisper fill his ears:

"*They got away. You let them get away, you fool. If only you had acted instead of letting fear and Robert keep you from killing them . . .*"

But the paramilitaries had left nothing behind. No clues. All he knew was a name–Pascal–and that the eight men who had ruined his life were not where he was. If he was to kill them, the conclusion was obvious: he could not remain here.

After nearly a day of walking down mountain paths, he reached an uneven road. He had heard gunshots, and when he did, he rushed toward them.

He found their source. The pink-faced men in green were parked on the roadside in a jeep. He watched them laugh as smoke climbed from their cigarettes, as smoke climbed from their gun barrels. Lying at the vehicle's wheels was a corpse, a black man, a paramilitary. He had a gun clutched in his lifeless hand.

After the cigarettes were spent, the Americans reluctantly got down from the jeep with a black body-length bag and prepared to use it to swallow up the dead man.

This man was one of the eight. The Son knew it. This was his only chance. He knew it.

From out of the shadows he sprang, shouting, Bonswa!

Guns leaped to the soldiers' hands. He dropped himself and his things to the ground and raised his hands high.

— Souple! Souple! he shouted, Please! Please!

One of the soldiers stepped down with his gun drawn and moved toward the Son. The American let loose a flood of gibberish. The Son trembled. The soldier lowered his gun and turned back around. All breathed in relief.

But the Son followed on his hands and knees. Souple, he said again. Souple. *Pèmèt mwen.* He reached out and touched the soldier's boot. The soldier spun and yelled another command, but the Son could not understand. He also did not care to understand.

— Souple. *Souple.* He gestured to himself and the dead man. Pèmèt mwen. *M ka ede ou.*

The soldier frowned and gave a sharp wave. The Son could not be so easily dissuaded.

— Souple. The Son ran to the dead man, picked up the body bag, straightened it. He looked up, nodding, forcing a smile. Pèmèt mwen, he said again. Pèmèt mwen. He saw the paramilitary's face up close. The bullet wound was on his forehead. It was small, above his right eye. His stare was vacant and his mouth pursed, like he died with a question on his lips.

The Son slipped the bag over the dead man's ill-fitted boots. He kicked the gun aside. He gave a servile smile as he ran his hands into the man's pockets and pulled out his effects: a photo of a white nude woman, some money, cigarettes, some hand-scrawled notes, a picture of a child. He stuffed them into his pockets. The three soldiers watched him, bemused.

The body bag was zipped, and the Son hoisted the dead man into the back of the jeep. He let the soldier handle the gun, and the Son eyed it, wondering if it was the one that ended his parents. The soldier in the back of the jeep with him gave a sort of smile, and the one in the road climbed into the driver's seat.

— *Anba,* the Son said.

— Huh? the driver said.

— Anba. The Son pointed down the mountain.

The soldiers said something, argued briefly, before the driver acquiesced. The Son rushed to grab his things before their minds changed, and soon they were trundling down the mountain's unforgiving road.

The journey into Menard passed in a blur, but he paid the changing landscape no heed. He heard pooled blood swish about the body bag and imagined the man's face and the bullet hole, all the while lamenting that he had not been the one to put it there.

Libète cannot move. Her mug is still on the floor in pieces. The eggs on her plate are untouched. She cannot move.

— It's a long way to Okap from here, Celestine says. Do you know the way?

Dimanche shoots from his chair. We'll have to stay off the main roads. They'll be all over them.

— There's a new road, Celestine says. Up the mountain. It goes all the way up.

— Byen, Dimanche says. He bolts upstairs.

Libète cannot move.

Celestine fills water bottles, orders Picot to throw together all the food he can.

She watches them rush about her. But her coffee. The mug. It spilled . . .

— Libète, get up and get your things. Dimanche's order stirs her.

— Yes, she says. Yes.

— We have a long journey ahead. By foot, unfortunately.

She doesn't know if she is up for it. As she climbs the stairs to her room, her eyes water. As she fills her red pack, those waters fall.

Within minutes she was back down. Dimanche and Celestine stood on the threshold of the yard and watched her come toward them.

Celestine looked to Dimanche as a father does his child. He clapped him on the back of the neck. He pulled Dimanche close, hugged him, whispered something in his ear. Dimanche stood limply, then hugged him back.

The pair left Menard on a trail to the east, through fields of cabbage. The ground started level and led to a grove that cast dappled shadows on the ground. She knew the mountains ahead meant their route would soon rise.

She spent a time thinking over his words.

He said they were gone.

From them, she pieced a story together.

He said they were all gone.

Her chest tightened.

Then he is a killer.

— Tell me, Dimanche. If it's a long road ahead. Please. Tell me all. To go from your village to being a policeman in Port-au-Prince? Leading some shadow life that saw you hunt these men along the way?

He walked ahead, not offering her a view of his face. Suddenly, he spoke.

— I got a ride with a group of American soldiers down the mountain. When their jeep reached Menard, I learned the paramilitaries had passed through the town. In all my life I had never even seen a town this size before. Pascal and the others fought the Americans there, those who had come after the coup. But those seven paramilitaries, they got away. I thought I was already at the end of my hunt. No money. No education. I was just an ignorant peasant. You heard it from Celestine, I'm sure. He took pity on me. Showed me kindness. Let me work his fields. In time, I became his lieutenant. In charge of his whole operation.

— How did you do it?

— I was *trè konsantre*. Very focused. Quite solemn in those days.

— More than now?

— The years have softened me.

They walked in quiet. The Sun had broken through the cloudbanks, and the first wave of sweltering heat settled over the valley. They reached the forest, and Libète picked a fallen branch from the ground to occupy her hands.

— You stayed with Celestine for a long while?

— Just over two years.

— He lives so simply now. Hard to believe he owned so much.

— His fortunes changed with the country's. You saw he was a bit scattered. Never had a head for business. Foreign rice flooded the land when trade barriers were lowered. That was a condition of President Aristide's return to Haiti after he was ousted. Celestine's family had farmed their own land for centuries, and *poof,* in a few years it was all but gone. I slowed the decline. But stopping it? Impossible.

— He didn't seem destitute.

— His kids send him money from abroad. He could have left Haiti, even back then. He's stubborn. To my knowledge he's never left the country.

— Why did you leave Menard, then? Having it so well after losing so much? She poked him with her stick. I saw it myself, he loved–loves-you. Like a son.

— I've only been a son once, Dimanche snapped, then sighed. His home could only be a waystation, he said. While with him I learned math, learned to read, learned to manage. With proper feeding my body thickened. I was able to keep track of details others missed. I proved my worth. In time the notes I took from the dead man's pocket came alive.

— What do you mean?

— Celestine helped me realize what they were. One was an address, in Port-au-Prince. As it turned out, one of his compatriot's homes.

— He wanted you to hunt these men down?

Dimanche looked only at the road ahead. Of course not. After I felt like I had repaid my debt to him – Dimanche swept his hands one against the other – I left. To Port-au-Prince.

— And you joined the police.

— If I was found to have killed men while standing on one side of the law, I could be taken easily myself. So I chose the other side. I was assigned to Cité Soleil after having success elsewhere in Port-au-Prince. I took the post. What difference did it make? It was a dangerous assignment. But I had no family and didn't care about the low pay. The hunt was the thing. Dimanche recalled it all with something like remorse.

— Seven men. Seven lives. She shook her head in horror. Her disappointment weighed on him, more than she knew.

— Not seven, he said. They spread out, but mostly stayed in Port-au-Prince. One was a cobbler. Another a shop owner. Another owned a café chain in Pétionville. One died in an auto accident. Another from a heart attack. One man even became a professor. All of them but one tried to live forgetful lives.

— So how many then? How many did you end?

— Four.

She threw her stick into the woods. But what of the law? Huh? The Dimanche I knew *worshipped* it.

— There is the law, and then there is justice. When the former denies the latter, justice must trump. He said it like a truism. Libète nearly launched into a sermon, parroting her old teacher Elize's admonition: "God is judge. Leave violence to him." She found her heart was not in the words. Maybe her belief was not.

— I tried to balance the scales. I killed, yes. I also fought the gangs. Kept innocents safe. Kept you safe!

She stared. I thought I knew you–not all the facts about you–but that I knew you.

He stopped, leaned back into a tree, and breathed deep to calm himself. I often feel the same way toward myself.

She couldn't look at him. She could only think of the tally. He killed four. Two died from other circumstances.

— You accounted for six. What of the last?

Dimanche stood up straight. Hesitation clouded his features. His story, he said, is your story.

The Hotel Karibe is dark. It is an unbearable hour.

Providence brings him to this moment and this purpose. Of this, Dimanche is sure.

He has shaved for the occasion and is dressed in average clothes. He looks respectable, like any of the exclusive hotel's guests. It had rained tonight, and his normally light guayavera stuck to his skin, but this distraction is no matter, not with what's before him. He brushes his hand over the pistol stuffed in his waistband, tactile reassurance for the work ahead.

After he arrested Benoit at Libète's leading, he was made to resign from the police. The only one who would have known of the bribe he accepted was Benoit, hence Benoit informed Dimanche's superiors. Clearly Benoit's part in the activity-being the source of the bribe-resulted in no prosecution, while Dimanche was out the door and on the street. Seventeen years' service, amounting to nothing.

He had a bit of money saved-not much, but enough-and along with the bribe's balance he was afforded the freedom to resume his hunt for Pascal. This pursuit had lain dormant ever since the earthquake.

The morsels of information he had gathered about Pascal over the years were few. One, the man used a number of false names and identities. These had thwarted Dimanche's search time and again. Two, he maintained a low profile. And three, he was involved in some sort of wide-reaching criminal operation of recent provenance, the subsidiaries of which seemed to dabble in most every form of vice.

He began calling in favors all around Port-au-Prince in pursuit of further information. By roughing up a street thug he had been pointed toward a local pimp who had led him toward a crooked mayor who happened to have a pair of unhelpful habits–addictions to sex and cocaine. A fair amount of pressure applied to the mayor–literally, resulting in the man's broken finger–led to a dockworker down at the city's port who had directed the mayor to where he could purchase cocaine. This worker knew another stevedore who was siphoning from illegal shipments that passed through a local straw business's storage containers. Dimanche relished this discovery: drugs were being stolen from the traffickers *by their own*. In and of itself, Dimanche didn't expect this chain of inquiry to lead to Pascal and thought of tipping off the police–the good police–to every link along the chain. But there was something the first dockworker said that stopped him. One of the traffickers was sniffing around, and this enforcer wasn't a low-level thug–he was reportedly older, well dressed, possibly senior. The volume of drugs purportedly being moved meant it had to be one of Haiti's larger operations. This prompted Dimanche to wait and watch.

With help from the dockworker, Dimanche timed his visit when the enforcer was at the port. The man posed as a customs officer. He interviewed. Took names. Eventually made threats. Got a man fired. Dimanche soon heard the thief turned up dead, but that was not his concern, not anymore.

Dimanche had actually laid eyes upon the enforcer. He was beardless, and the man's hair was peppered with white. He was of formidable size, though a gut slipped out and over his belt.

Trimming away the few decades of age, Dimanche was certain. He had found Pascal.

After the quake, the Hotel Karibe was one of Port-au-Prince's few luxury hotels still operating. That one could walk through a tent camp and wade through such human misery to pull up to the hotel minutes later and wade in the hotel's pool ate at Dimanche. And then there was the aimless nattering of the hotel's patrons, their glasses always filled to the brim, their plates heaped high. When cholera ravaged the countryside and began working its way through the bowels of Port-au-Prince, the indifference of it all was simply too much.

On this night, when he reaches Pascal's room, he pulls a magnetic key card from his pocket. It took a batch of half-baked lies with the concierge to get ahold of this prize.

The card slides through the door's reader. Green.

He cracked the door. A light was on. He inclined his ear, checked for movement. Hearing none, he drew his gun and crept into the suite. Sweat prickled on his skin, despite the cool, cool air inside. He felt it pass over his bald head, blowing from a vent over the door and throughout the room.

He scanned the suite. There was a central room with two connected chambers. A sliding glass door looked out on the hotel's palms and pool, a placid sheet of glass at this late hour. Not looking in front of him, he collided with an ottoman and cursed.

He was no spy, no expert in the clandestine. He had sat behind a desk much of his career, stood as a human barrier, interrogated the accused. He hated the character of a lurker slinking about under the cover of night. The justice he meted out shouldn't have to hide. It should do its business boldly, under the noonday Sun.

He examined the surroundings more closely. Bottles of wine, a solitary glass. A blister pack of pills sat beside them, most of the foil pouches punched. Next to the center table were shoes kicked off and a jacket carelessly dropped to the floor. The room, pristine and luxurious, was hardly touched otherwise.

Dimanche picked up one of the couch's pillows to quiet his pistol's inevitable report. He went to the first bedroom. No light showed inside. Cracking the door, he let his eyes adjust to the dark. No one had laid within the bed's sheets. He rubbed his tired eyes with a wrist as adrenaline surged through his system.

Dimanche had waited for hours in the outside corridor, trying not to appear conspicuous. Letting thoughts of murder run rampant in one's mind was no easy thing; summoning the necessary hatred and vengeance to kill in such a premeditated manner was exhausting.

He checked the other bedroom. It was the same situation: lights out, an untouched bed. He spun around, his gun sweeping the room wildly. The stakes involved with this encounter were unbearably high. If he succeeded, it was the end of a quest. The prior murders had never brought more catharsis than could last a day or two before he returned to his life lived by daylight, that of an upstanding officer of the law. It was a hypocrisy that ate at him: the officers surrounding him whom he chastised for laziness, an unwillingness to intervene in dangerous situations, and petty corruption had not looked into the void Dimanche found himself falling down.

Another deep breath, another attempt to recollect his thoughts. He had *seen* Pascal enter the suite. *Where could the bastard be?*

The only remaining room in the suite was a shared bathroom. He moved toward the door, saw it was ajar. Leaning toward the door, he could hear heavy breathing from inside. He raised the pillow to the gun's muzzle, steeling himself to pull the trigger.

— If you're here to kill me, Pascal slurred from inside the bathroom, at least let me do it myself. Let it be my sin rather than yours.

Dimanche hid behind the doorjamb.

The door opened. Before him, Pascal slumped against the tub's wall. He was in his underpants and undershirt, and he held a gun of his own to his ear, the pistol ready to shout death.

— Gun down!

— You caught me, Pascal said. He lays the pistol on the ground. No tricks. No tricks! You can kill me, s'il-vous plaît.

Dimanche didn't know what to do.

— Don't deprive me! I've wanted this for weeks. Months. The irony! You break in to do what I can't bring myself to do. God is at work! At work, indeed!

— Shut up! Shut up, you goddamned fool!

— Truth! Truth, truth, *truth*. I am a *fool*. I am *damned*.

Dimanche's gun flagged before reestablishing its true aim. Slide the gun over to me, he said.

Pascal sent it across the tiled floor.

— Which angel are you? Pascal asked.

— An angel? I am your judge, your executioner. Dimanche steadied himself. He found he liked this arrangement quite a lot. The culminating shot would not be the result of unthinking reflex but the deliberate bang of a gavel, the release of the guillotine's blade.

— Tell me everything! Every wrong! Don't let me escape! Pascal tightened his eyes and spread his arms with a grand gesture. Read the charges! We both know I'm guilty. But let me at least know the sins that are bringing about my end.

— You talk too much. Dimanche came close to him, certain that he could overcome this sad sack if he tried to swing. Open your mouth. Pascal did as ordered and Dimanche inserted his gun. He expected to get a surge of pleasure at seeing the fear he inflicted, but Pascal gave him no such satisfaction. He simply looked Dimanche in the eye.

— Northern Haiti. You and seven men came to my village. Killed and raped a host of my neighbors. Just to make us fear. My father, he was a good man. My mother, she was a good woman. And you all strung him up in a tree. Let him hang. Shot him. And her.

Pascal tried to speak around the gun's barrel, but couldn't. Dimanche withdrew it, letting him testify. Pascal squeezed his eyes shut.

— Honestly . . .

Nothing else came. Dimanche slapped him, and he opened his eyes.

— I don't. Don't remember. There were so many-

Dimanche slapped him again. You took things of–such–*value*.

— I know.

— And you don't even care.

— It's vile. He shook his head. I'm vile.

This time a punch. Pascal didn't protest, just rubbed his jaw. I'm sorry. He sat there dazed. No one tries to recall their sins but the penitent, Pascal said. And I've not been one to bow low.

Dimanche lifted the butt of his gun, and finally Pascal lifted a hand to block the blow.

— Please. Pascal lifted his index finger. A proposition. We know how tonight ends. How I will end. But help me remember. I know I don't deserve such a thing, but let me. This is no ploy. I have no phone. No backup outside. Let me look at you by light, in the eye. Let me be made to remember what I've ordered. What I've done.

Dimanche–the part of him still governed by procedure and rules and law–agreed. Get up. Put on your pants.

Within minutes, they faced each other on opposite sofas.

Dimanche had held his gun at the ready as he recounted the day his father died. Pascal simply sat, nodding as Dimanche told him about the years spent preparing for this very encounter. Dimanche recounted the deaths of the other squad members he had killed. Pascal gave a *tsk tsk*. Truly a villain, he said several times.

The telling took over an hour, and as Dimanche neared the end he spoke of the dock, of the hotel, the card sliding through the door lock, the green light bidding him come.

Pascal sighed, looked at his watch. I suppose it's about that time. Dimanche grunted. May I–may I taste wine, just once more? Pascal signaled toward the bottle on the table between them.

Dimanche considered. Let me pour it.

— Of course.

Dimanche drained the remnants of a bottle worth half of what he made in a month as a policeman. He slid the trendy wine glass across the table. Pascal drank.

— What's your name? I realize I don't even know it?

— To the world, I'm Dimanche. I've been that since I left home. But my real name is Marcel.

— What are you going to do after you leave, Marcel?

— He shrugged. Not a question I've been concerned with. I was booted from the police.

— Oh? Corruption?

— There was some of that, yes. I'm not proud of it. I accepted money to help me believe what I wanted to believe. It was a mistake. No, I'm glad to say my dismissal was persecution.

— Really? Pascal swished the wine about his mouth and wore a look of supreme pleasure on his face.

— For standing up. To another villain, one just as base as you. Jean-Pierre Benoit.

— Pascal nearly spit up. Jean-Pierre Benoit? Ha! We have a mutual enemy, then. I can't stand the man. He's pathetic. Ruining Haiti.

— Says the murderer and drug-trafficker.

— You. You're . . . the officer, then? The one in those videos who tackled him to the ground?

Dimanche nodded.

— Good Lord. He set his wine on the table and clapped, a smile leaping to his face. Unbelievable. He shifted in his seat, and Dimanche lifted his gun. The girl, Pascal said, fidgeting with excitement. The girl there with you. The one who cried out. Who accused him. Do you know her? The one called Libète?

Dimanche stood up. What about her?

— I've followed her. For a number of reasons.

— *What are you talking about?* Dimanche looked as if he might reach across the table and strangle Pascal rather than shoot him.

— None of *those* reasons. I met her once. Before that night. I was told to stop her from getting away from us, from our island. She stirred up a whole ferry. We had guns. We had all the power. And these people, these—ordinary people—they stood up to us anyway. I could have ordered my men to kill every person on that dock. But—I couldn't. There was something there, a power—I couldn't trespass against it. I let her go, thinking I'd apologize to my boss. I mean, she was just a girl, the child of some enemy of his, and he had many enemies. A few weeks later I saw the video of Benoit, of you. Of her. The same girl. Seared in my memory. I never told my boss I realized it was the same girl. Didn't see the need.

— That's incredible. Unbelievable.

— It is. Pascal laughed. Tell me, Marcel. You care for the girl?

Dimanche wasn't prepared for such a question. She is... Dimanche struggled.

— An intangible thing. I know, it's hard to pin d—

— She is hope.

Pascal was quiet. Finally quiet.

He spoke again. What if... yes. What if... Pascal's mind seemed to be running. Dimanche—Marcel—whatever—I have a proposition for you. My choices have made me money, more than I can spend. I deserve death, I know. You can kill me tonight if you wish, absolutely you can, but what if—what if I tried to undo some of my wrong?

Dimanche's pistol stayed fixed on him.

— I see Libète is important to you—what if you were to keep her from harm?

— From harm?

— Benoit will strike at her. That's how he and his ilk work. I know. She needs protection. You've lost your job on account of her; what if she *became* your job? Pascal was effervescent. Yes—yes, yes, yes. Dimanche. I know I'm damned. I know it. But I'm tired of rolling around in my own filth. Help me - Dimanche balked - help me redeem *some* of my wrongs.

— You're past redemption.

— I know, I *know*. He sipped his wine again, worried at the sudden turn this might take.

Dimanche sat suddenly and laid his gun down. If I resurface, I'm a dead man.

Pascal couldn't stop nodding. Then stay in the shadows!

— I won't be fooled by you.

Pascal raised his hands again, red sloshing out of his glass. Then kill me. But if you had any idea what's coming to Haiti, what I've been a part of orchestrating–the drugs we move, they're nothing. Nothing at all. A means to an end.

— Tell me that, then.

— No. I can't. Then I'm dead tomorrow. Look. Protect her. You get paid. I'll slow what's coming. Those are the conditions.

— What difference could she possibly make in all this?

— In reality? None, I fear. None of us can stop this.

Dimanche scowled. He would not speak as he thought the offer over. He slammed the gun down on his seat cushion and paced. Finally, he turned and leveled his index finger at Pascal. This is a reprieve. For her sake. It changes nothing. You're still a dead man.

Pascal's face emptied. If you don't put me out of my misery someday, I'd be most disappointed. Most disappointed, indeed.

Libète lets Dimanche finish his tale. At its end, she can stay quiet no longer.

— Why-why didn't you tell me these things? She is trembling, trembling fiercely. Her hands are twined behind her head, and she cannot help but crouch. She wretches.

Dimanche is shocked. Libète, I don't understand.

— Pascal. I know who he works for. I know! If what he said is true, the only one he could work for is named Dumas.
— How did you... know that name?
— Oh God, oh God, oh God...
— Libète, stop!
— Dumas, he's a shadow. I've tried to forget the name, tried to forget. She looks up at Dimanche, dumbstruck. He's my father, Dimanche. My father!

Dimanche can't come to understand.

— God, Pascal doesn't even know. Not even Dumas knows what I am to him. He thinks I'm Limyè's child but–

— But, Dimanche stammers, your last name–

— It's Limyè, yes, a name I took from a man who loved my mother. Dumas, he *violated* my mother. I'm the... the result of his crime! She pinches the bridge of her nose, cringes.

— What a thing. What a thing.

Her mind careens. Pascal's money has made this possible? He sustained you all along?

Dimanche nods. But that's at an end.

— What do you mean?

— I am certain he's dead.

— What? You?

Dimanche sighs, shakes his head.

— By whom, then? As soon as the words escape, she knows. The radio, she says. That night on the radio show. The man who was killed. The man who gave Jak and I the Numbers. That was Pascal.

Dimanche nods. I heard the broadcast from the street while I kept an eye on the station. I recognized the voice immediately. He must have been listening for you. I communicated with him just a little after the night at the hotel. He followed you. Your work. I'm not surprised. Dumas must have finally come after him for whatever obstruction he told me he was going to create.

— But why give us the Numbers?

— He must have known they were coming. That he had no other way, in that moment, to transmit what had been locked safely in his head. So he had to share it with the world to share it with you. He trusted you to do something with them. To protect them.

— Dimanche, that means–that means Dumas is the one hunting me and Jak. The one behind Maxine, in pursuit of the Numbers–it's all been him! And he–he doesn't even know who I really am to him . . .

Dimanche reaches for her, his hand outstretched feebly.

Libète closes her eyes, breathes slowly, counts to three. She starts walking again, and her face is a veil hiding a grating anger. Let's keep going.

• • •

In the time before night fell, Libète and Dimanche had exchanged no other words. They climbed along waterways with gleaming white rock underfoot and along treacherous backwoods paths, up and up.

It was almost as if he could see inside her, her every synapse sparking bitterness, a tainted heart pumping hatred throughout her body. Libète was trapped in a prison-like realm of thought that Dimanche recognized; he'd inhabited the same place for so very long, and still knew no way to lead her out. For her, the villains who had set her on this mountain path were now labeled, lined up in a row like targets at a carnival game, ready to be plinked into oblivion if only she was given the opportunity to end them.

In the past years he'd had hours of solitude to reflect on whom he'd killed and what he'd done. But vengeance helped him trap and eliminate any trace of guilt. Visions of a gun, in his hand, exploding, watching his victims–men, fathers, sons–leak their blood. *They took. I took back.* It was simple transactional thinking. He told himself this over and again. Yet seeing Libète this way spurred change within him. The lies he'd built a life on could no longer stand.

Darkness descended and storm clouds gathered. He stopped. They were not so far from a river. He laid out a blanket for himself. Handed her another, and she took it.

They slept.

Hours passed.

They awoke.

It was the puttering of a dirt bike. The incongruence of its man-wrought engine grated against the woven songs of running water, birds' nighttime calls, and coded crickets' chirps.

This sound in this place was an uncommon thing, he knew. Springing from the ground, they gathered their things and hid behind the trees. The bike advanced deliberately down the same path they had traveled, casting a wide light over the forest floor. When the rider reached the ground where they had been sleeping, he paused to inspect the earth. He took out something boxy. Dimanche's eyes widened. Before Libète understood what was going on he had dashed from the shadows. The rider was already speaking.

— I've found them. The man rattled off some other details about his location.

Libète watched in horror. Dimanche ran at the man full bore. Ripping the device from the rider's hand, Dimanche sent his elbow into the man's face. The man shouted out in alarm and pain. Libète trailed, her hand to her mouth. The rider, reeling but still straddling the bike, leaned forward and placed his hand on the bike's accelerator. Dimanche's fist was midswing as the bike lunged to life and the surge of gas caused the bike to fishtail. Dimanche's punch landed but the spin of the bike's back end collided with Dimanche and sent him sprawling. The wheel, twirling fast, finally clenched the earth and shot forward. Dimanche cried out. Libète watched the bike and rider shoot toward a nearby tree. The man slammed headfirst into the trunk. Now in a tangle with the bike on the ground, the rider did not stir.

Libète ran to Dimanche's side.

— My leg, he whimpered.

She looked down. His left pant leg had been ripped away by the tire's mad spin. But it was worse than a friction burn. The bike's back wheel had driven over his leg.

Dimanche's ankle was broken.

And Maxine, and Dumas, knew where they were.

THE FALLEN SEEDS

Pye bwa ki wo di li wè lwen, gren pwomennen di li wè pase l.
The tall tree says it sees far, the wandering seed says it sees more.

Nèg di san fè, Bondye fè san di.
Man talks without doing, God does without talking.

Libète stands on the remnants of the fort, looking down over the whole of Haiti. She sees fishermen cast their nets. A child slave cower in fear. Merchant women laughing and laughing and laughing.

She sees couples in love, making love. She attends university graduations. Christenings and first communions, All Saints' Days. Concerts in stadiums and nightclubs. She walks through streets full of rubble on the day of the earthquake.

She moves further through time, back to the start of her island.

She is able to see the Taíno Indians and watch as Anacoana holds court. She dines with Papa Doc, plays ball with Baby Doc while he is still a toddler, before his innocence was lost. She swims with mermaids, toils alongside slaves. Paints with Frankétienne, reads Jacques Roumain's first drafts, takes to the stage to play duets with Ludovic Lamothe. She sees the blood shed over many long years. She sees good men devoured, evil men prosper. Mothers give birth, and die in birth.

It has been a long day. She finally returns to the fort and surveys it all, every last thing. A wind blows. Twigs and branches and grass and weed and corn and beans and carrots and leaves swirl together until they make up a body, a living thing. *Didi.*

They stand facing one another. I've seen it all, Libète says. Every moment. Every detail. There is much good in this land. So much. But the *wrong* of it. Millions of blotted hearts. The pain they cause one another . . .

Didi grabs her shoulder and unfurls her other arm, as if to say, But the Land! The Land is good!

— This Land? It is barren. Dying. Just another sign this country is forgotten, forsaken.

Libète turns back. Why doesn't he *speak*? If he's there? If he's love? All of her pained memory comes forth, and she is nearly crippled. Didi is there to support her. Why is God silent in the face of it all?

Didi cups her knotty hand and brings it to her ear.

Libète does the same.

And in it, Libète listens.

She inclines toward the storm and hears nothing.

She inclines toward the quake and hears nothing.

She inclines toward the fire and hears nothing.

And then finally, she stops, turning away from all the furious sound and inclines toward the quiet, and it is there she hears a gentle whisper.

She awakens on the floor to a banging outside. The Sun has arrived for the day, and she can see its rays like tendrils reaching through the narrow gaps where the daub has fallen away from the wattle. She registers her surroundings. The bucket. The flies. She's in the jail.

She winces. Her head rebels against thought–*such pain!*–and her body falls into shivers and weak coughs. She tries to speak, but words are vaporous things.

So thirsty.

The pounding on the door continues.

— Libète? The voice is familiar. A man's. The call is followed by shallow breathing.

— *Wi?* she chokes out.

— I brought this for you. He walks around to the side, slides a squat brown bottle through a hole chipped away at the level of the jail's floor. *Dlo*, he says.

Across the floor she goes, desperately. She grabs the bottle, lifts it, drains it. She catches the last drops on her tongue and slides back down onto the ground, nursing her aching temples. Her thirst remains unquenched.

— Mèsi, she croaks.

— You're welcome.

She cracks her eyelids, and looks at the eyes prying through the hole. They are Lolo's.

She feels new pain. *Why . . . why . . . why . . .*

— Libète, I'm sorry. I'm sorry. I had no choice.

She cannot speak.

— Maxine's coming. On her way. Whatever you know, whatever they want, you must give it to them.

Libète gives him no reaction.

— Benoit wanted to kill me. I had to do what he said or I'd be dead. I didn't want to . . . to do any of it. Then Maxine came, like a miracle. Promised me protection from Benoit. Promised me new drugs to treat my disease. But they said I had to look for you. These two guards, they heard from their bosses to keep their eyes peeled for a girl like you. They thought you might be here and Maxine ordered me to come, all the way across Haiti. Like some sort of scout or something. To make sure it was you. In that moment, I refused. I said I couldn't hurt you anymore. They, they hurt me, Libète. Hurt me bad. They took my medications.

She looks away and curls into a ball. Her sympathies are unstirred.

— They will level Foche. I've seen enough of them to know. This, all of it, will disappear. Just give them what they want so that all the suffering-yours, Foche's-*ends*.

Coughs overtake her, a furious bout, and the blood, it comes. Lolo cannot watch. He cannot stand to see his condition reflected at him. He departs, staggers away, down the hill and soon down the mountain, pulling the tears from his eyes and cursing the storm that gathers.

Libète fashions a splint for Dimanche. He endeavors to tolerate the pain.

He winces as Libète wraps a branch to his fractured ankle.

— Ah*hhhh*.

— It will be okay, Dimanche. She bites her lip. All will be well. She speaks as Dr. Françoise, her nun friend, would to a patient.

— Check the bike, he groans. See if it can run.

— Right. She ran the fifteen feet to where it lay. The rider lays mangled, unmoving. *No helmet. Not good.* She examines the bike's front wheel, but the fork is bent and wheel misshapen.

— *Li kase*, she says as she shakes her head. She pries into the man's backpack. There are foil-wrapped things, military rations by their looks. Two flares. There must have been a weapon too, but it was lost in the dark. *He didn't expect to be out searching for us for long.*

She hustled back to Dimanche, sliding the food and supplies into his duffel bag.

— Maybe if we hide someone will pass and they can help us. You said this path leads to a mountain road? Someone with a mule might come through-we could get you on that, go up the mountain and down its other side.

— Yes, he sighed.

— All right! It's decided. Yes, we're in good form. Let me help you up. Libète strained. It was like lifting a boulder. He let his good leg bear most of his weight.

He took a step, or at least tried.

He bit his bottom lip and grabbed Libète to regain his balance. He reminded her of an injured street dog.

— It's all right, she said. It's all right. Plenty of time. No rush. You'll be fine, we'll be fine, when we get to Cap-Haïtien there will be a hospital. Here...

She helped him hobble toward a tree. He leaned against it and exhaled. Maybe a cane, he muttered.

— Right! Of course! She scanned the ground for a hearty branch, finding nothing suitable. She saw a low-hanging bough and hopped up and let her free weight tug it down.

Crack!

It and she fell to the ground. Once in hand, Dimanche tried using it as a sort of crutch. He took a few labored steps. It held.

— Let me get your bag, Libète said.

— It's too heavy for you.

— *Give it here!* Her composed veneer cracked. He handed it over, and she slung the strap over her shoulder. He was right. She wondered how long she could manage to carry it.

They got off the main path. The sky remained grim, filled with swirling clouds that foretold rain. Dimanche struggled with the uneven terrain.

— They'll be following. Probably on bike. Or something similar. Dimanche said the words between winces. A truck couldn't come along this way.

— Put them out of your mind.

— The flares you grabbed. Light one.

— Won't that show where we are?

— I need the light to see the ground. They're trailing us. Time is short and we need to make the most of what we have.

She withdrew a flare from the bag. She pinched one of its ends and held it away from her, as if it was a stick of dynamite. How do I light it?

— The tab at the top; pound it hard. Be careful! Keep it away from yourself.

She yanked the tab, and it burst into a red flame.

— Good. Now, hold it close to the ground for me.

— Like this.

— *Parfait.* Perfect.

— Dimanche...

— Yes, Libète?

— Are we going to be okay?

Without a moment's hesitation, he answered: Yes.

They walked without speaking for some minutes. Dimanche focused on the ground before him, grunting with each step. The recovered walkie-talkie chirped and cracked periodically. They must have changed the frequency, he said. Or are keeping quiet.

The burden on Libète's shoulders felt like a thousand pounds. She let her gall fuel her as her other reserves of energy were depleted. The feelings of hatred for her enemies gave her new clarity and sharp focus. Words seeped from her mouth.

— Justice demands it... when I get the chance...

— What are you saying, Libète?

She muttered more, but Dimanche couldn't hear the words.

She stopped. I'm going to kill them. Those who sent me down this path. Just like you did.

Dimanche nearly tipped over. No.

— I'll do it. I'll hunt them down. And I will hurt them. I will make them bleed. Benoit, Maxine, Lolo – she shuddered – Dumas.

Lightning arced through the sky. Dimanche glimpsed her twisted features. He was terrified.

— I . . . need to rest, he said.
— We have to keep going.
— I need to rest! Dimanche roared. To hear you say these things . . .
— Hypocrite.
He collapsed to the ground and rubbed his face. He dripped sweat. He spoke.

— The night I nearly ran at those who killed my father with a machete, Robert, from my village, warned me they would kill me if I killed them.
— And?
— He was right, but in the wrong way. No matter what I want to believe, I see now: killing them did kill me.

She listened with arms crossed. Her nostrils flared with her every breath.
— That kind of justice costs, so very much. I know what you're feeling, I do. You think hatred is the cure for your pain. But it's a poison. One you take, thinking it will kill another.

Lightning flashed again, closer.
— My life could have been different. There could have been happiness. I could have lived on the land, in my home. I could have healed there. Instead, I ripped myself away from what was good–
— I've already lost everything good.
— There is a further cost! And you will pay it!

She sneered. You would go back, then? Undo what you've done!
— Yes. Yes! God as my witness! His own words surprised him.
— Then you're a *kapon*. A coward. I can't join you there, Dimanche. My loss, it has no answer, at least not that you can give.

He could not speak. The thought of her following in his steps sickened him. Oh God! The waste . . . Oh God. He covered his face with his cupped hand and trembled. Oh God.

Libète disdained seeing this tower of a man brought so low. She turned away from him.

The clouds rumbled, or so Libète thought. They heard the sounds at the same time. More engines. Like dust in a swirling wind, fear was whipped up anew.

Dimanche snapped to, wiping his tears. Up ahead, he said. Those rocks. We can hide there.

She strained to take up the bags again and trudged to a place where they could watch the road. He continued sweating profusely.

— Libète.

She didn't answer.

— *Libète.* Dimanche seemed himself again. Steely. Resolved. You trust me? he asked.

She nodded.

— We'll survive this. We'll get you to Cap-Haïtien. We'll get you across the water. You'll be safe.

She nodded again. Don't lose sight of this, he said. Now, we need to have a talk. It's a difficult subject–

— Then keep it to yourself.

— Libète–

— Don't say it!

The fear was changing her into something she was not.

— We will be safe, but aren't now. If something happens, look for Dieudonné. If we get separated, go to Dieudonné. You hear? Tuck that name away. We'll meet up there. But no matter what–*no matter what*–do not tell anyone who you really are, or where you come from. *Anyone.* It will endanger you. It will endanger them.

— Go to Dieudonné, she repeated.

The engines were growing closer.

— We need water, Dimanche said. Go to the river. It should be that way. Take your bag with you, fill up all our bottles. I'll keep watch.

— Dakò. Her mind lingered on what had just been said. *Dieudonné.*

— Libète–

She paused to look at him. I would do anything for you, he said. Anything.

A tear slipped down her cheek. She knew this was the closest he could come to saying he loved her. With all the feelings coursing through her, she didn't know what to say back. She turned toward the river, and he reached to tug at her bag's hanging strap.

— Whatever happens, don't lose hope. His eyes felt as if they were boring into her. The end of hope is the end of us all, he said.

She nodded and rushed down the quiet path toward the river alone.

Libète lies sweating on the jail's floor, her mind set on hate.

Cinéus and Wilnor keep watch with their dog on a nearby shaded boulder. She knows their voices well, their cackling. They discuss their reward for trapping her, how they will spend the money. Their dreams are quite small. They want to return home to open a butcher's shop in Gonaïves.

— You hear that, ti fi? Cinéus calls to her. You're our future!

There is singing now, two women's voices, and the sound rises up the hill. Libète rolls over, squints through the wall's cracks. It's Magdala with Délira, and her baby. Magdala carries a basket on her head.

What are they doing?

— Hey, you two. Yeah, you! Let us in the jail. We need to give the prisoner some food.

— No. No visitors. Cinéus threw a stick, and his dog coursed after it.

— Aw, come on. Aren't you men? You don't have to be cruel to do your jobs. She has a long journey ahead of her! Let her at least have a full stomach before she goes.

The dog dropped the stick before Wilnor, and he patted the animal's head. He looked to Cinéus, who shrugged. Wilnor got down from their boulder and hustled over.

— It's the least we can do, said Cinéus. You can fatten this calf today for our fattened calves tomorrow. He snickered as Wilnor came over and inspected the basket. Magdala didn't understand the joke and scowled anyway.

The lock came off the door. Libète cringed at the light. She sat up and dusted herself off. The door swung open, and Magdala swooped in. She gave Libète the most powerful of embraces despite the blood soaked into Libète's shirt. My dear, my dear, my dear.

— Give her the food and get going, Wilnor said.

— Bite your tongue, Magdala snapped. If this is good-bye, at least give us a few moments.

— Whatever. He locked the door behind them and left.

Délira looked very tense, even more so than Libète. She approached Libète and gave her a small kiss on the cheek.

— Sophia, take off your clothes, Magdala said.

— What?

— Take them off. Your headscarf too. Délira had already handed her baby to Magdala and was following the same instructions.

— What are you both doing?

— They're coming for you, but we won't let them have you.

— Why?

— Ah! What a silly question. Because we love you.

— Youn ede lòt, Délira said. One helping another. This is my thanks. For delivering me, for saving him.

Libète put her leaden limbs into action and began to swap her clothes. I'm sorry they're a mess, Libète said. Délira nodded warily and put them on anyway.

When the clothes were switched, Magdala handed Delivrans to Libète. Libète didn't feel good about using him as a prop in the deception, and certainly not when she was ailing and likely contagious.

— It's the only way, Délira said, answering Libète's concerns. She wrapped Libète's headscarf about her own head. He'll be back in my arms soon enough.

— Ah, the *transfòmasyon!* Magdala remarked. It's complete!

Libète's eyes watered as she looked at Délira. You are so incredibly brave, Libète said. As soon as they realize the ruse, we'll have problems.

— Of course. But we will deal. Délira, lay on the ground and face away. Ah, that looks perfect. Sophia, hold the baby close. And hide your face; act like you've been crying.

Magdala breathed deep and forced a smile. Guard! she called. We're done!

• • •

Libète and Magdala rushed over the hill, taking a back route to reach Janel's home. Libète felt the babe cooing in her arms. Such an immense responsibility wrapped in such a small body.

— Janel must be made to know what you discovered about Dorsinus– about the Sosyete and their involvement with these, these miners! She spit. Rapists is what they are!

— How did you know I'd been taken? It dawned on her. Félix reached you?

— In the middle of the night.

— He's safe, then?

— For now, as far as I know. He told me how you gave yourself up to protect him. He escaped as soon as he could. He woke me wildly, like one possessed. Said he needed to talk to others.

— And you're here already? To rescue me?

— At first, I was paralyzed. I didn't know what to do. I've never been very brave, you know. But I thought of you. Saving Délira. Helping Jeune. Protecting Félix. You remind me of my father. He was a good man. She dabbed at her eyes. A very good man.

Libète reached out to touch her. Tell me about him. I need inspiration to face what's coming our way.

— He's a hard subject. She sighed, collecting her thoughts. Whenever we were crushed by life–maybe a bad crop, maybe a dead baby–he would say, 'The end of hope is the end of us all.' And so we would hope, and pray.

— He said that, did he?

— And he stood up for what was good. There were endless dark days, as far back as I remember. We weren't always from this place. He and my mother, they chose to come here. To raise the consciousness of the people. But the opposition, it was strong.

First the *chef de section* and *tontons macoutes*. Then the military. Then the paramilitaries. Oh! This mountain has suffered. He would say, 'We are seeds, fallen on the ground. If we go through our days laying ourselves down for others, we'll see a big harvest. A big one. Nothing can stop such seeds from growing into strong trees.' He heard the old preacher who used to come through here say that, and he planted it right in his heart. For me, he'd always say, 'I love you.' Many fathers wouldn't say things like that so openly. To my brother, he had to phrase it differently. He was a man, after all. 'I'd do anything for you,' he told my brother.

Libète stilled. What happened to him?

— Men with guns came. When I was about your age, thereabouts. I ran, but he stood his ground, along with my mother, to keep them from pursuing me. 'Peace!' he shouted. 'Peace! Aren't we brothers?' The men with guns, they hit him. Brought him to his knees in front of her. I hid. I watched. Until I couldn't.

Her eyes watered. When faced with evil in those men, he and my mother gave themselves up. He was loved by most everyone. But there were always divides in the community. Hardship sucks away generosity. But his death, it changed things.

It was terrible for a long while, it really was. Crops stayed bad year after year. So many left the mountain to try to survive in the city. I moved in with a man to get by. He was bad. He left me when Félix was a baby. And my brother, my *marassa*, my twin–he was lost to the city too. Never heard from again.

— You had a twin?

— I did. But you know what? After all that heartache, Hearts United formed. The organization, it was the harvest collected from my father and mother's planting. My parents had dreamed of a unified community ever since they came here. The Good Lord takes evil and uses it for good. I've seen it. I've seen it time and again.

— And what about a man, oh, what did he call him? Libète asked herself. The man who convinced him to wait?

Magdala was confused. Who do you mean? A man?

— Robert! That's it! Do you know a man by the name of Robert, living here in Foche?

— Why, that's old Jeune's name. But nobody calls him that anymore.

The color from Libète's face slipped away. Magdala. I have a very important question for you. Your brother–was he named Dimanche?

— My brother? No.

Libète paused, sighed. It felt like a revealing curtain had been pulled back halfway and then dropped.

— But my father, yes.

Libète's eyes widened. She shifted Delivrans and his swaddling to her other arm.

— Cheri, what in the world is the matter?

— What is his name? Your brother's true name?

— Why, Marcel. Marcel Dieudonné.

With tears in her eyes, Libète spoke. My dear friend, I know what became of your brother.

⁂

Libète returns from the river. Her pack is full of water bottles positioned carefully so as to let the frightened pigeon rest on top.

It was hard to find her way back. New lances of lightning slashed across the sky, making shadows shift and slide. The thunder that followed was a series of delayed explosions, paralyzing in their strength. The fear encroached on her.

She heard the same unnatural sounds as before, but closer now. They were like the dirt bike, but lower.

The motors cut. Dogs barked.

It dawned on her. *Dimanche knew they would find him! He wanted me far off!*

Libète saw flashlights sweeping over the woods. She ran.

I have to save him! I have to–

She lost a shoe – *no time to stop!* – up and down, tripping on roots, stubbing a toe. She threw out the bottles of water–they weighed her down, made too much noise. She wanted to scream but kept it in. When she was half a football pitch away, she slowed.

It was already too late. The dogs' barking stopped. The lights rested. They had found Dimanche.

She crept closer. She heard orders, mostly clipped, and two men in fatigues left their ATVs and kept Dimanche on the ground. They searched his bag and his person. They collected his gun – *why didn't he shoot them?* – and bound Dimanche. Had the fight left him entirely?

And then Libète saw. Maxine came forward out of the dark and shined a blinding light in Dimanche's face. Where is she? Maxine asked.

He didn't respond. She kicked him in the stomach, and Libète cradled her own as if she had received the blow. Dimanche gasped.

— Talk. I'm tempted to let my dogs eat you. After what you did to poor Remus back in Jacmel...

She kicked him again. They're hungry, she said. One dog gave a sharp bark, almost as if in agreement.

— I told Libète to run. To leave me, he wheezed. To get across the border. Maxine looked at his splinted ankle. She stepped on it, and he screamed.

She circled him, observing his misery like a dispassionate scientist.

— Working for a man like Dumas, Dimanche said, is dangerous. He's like one of your mutts, liable to eat you up whole when you turn your back. Just ask Pascal. Years of loyalty-

— Please. Maxine stood. You know why Pascal died.

— All I know is he died for a few digits.

Libète couldn't see Maxine smile but heard the woman force a laugh. The inspector still inspects! So that's it? Trying to get clues, even till the very end? She stepped on his ankle again. Just tell me where she is. She'll live. I promise. I have no reason to hurt her.

Libète unconsciously folded her hands before her face and waited for his answer.

— You don't realize how hope spreads.

— What? Maxine said.

— You try to cut the plant, but you spread the seeds. You try to crush the seeds but you only plant them deeper. I've sinned. Done terrible things. But I would never violate the trust of that girl. If you think I would betray her for my own safety-

Maxine pulled a gun from her side and shot Dimanche.

Libète cried out, and fled. The dogs heard, and followed.

Magdala has to sit, has to sit *now*.

She collapses at the telling of the thing, not comprehending it all, and weeps.

Libète cries too as these terrible memories breach their containing walls and flood everything. She falls to the earth too and clutches the baby. *New life, new life. Live for that.*

— To know he's gone . . . Magdala says.

— When I arrived, in your home, I said my people would come for me. I knew Dimanche–Marcel–would not, but I couldn't face what his death meant then. I realized I didn't want to be Libète anymore–the exiled girl, the abandoned girl, the girl who sees her friends die.

— A fallen seed, Magdala whispers. That's what he is. She whimpers. On to Janel's. Our best hope, she chokes out.

Libète's fever makes it hard to stand again and push on, but Magdala's hand rests on Libète's shoulder. Moans continue pouring from her. She needs Libète to lead her on.

When they crest the hill, they see Janel tending beans in her yard. Janel looks up and becomes stone-faced at recognizing Libète.

— Sophia? Magdala? What's going on? How are you here?

It seemed an odd question.

— There are problems, Libète said, evenly.

Janel blinked. Come in. Yes, come in. She led them inside her home, drawing two chairs together for them to sit. Isn't that–Délira's child? Janel asked.

Libète nodded. Magdala was still despondent, and Libète placed a bracing hand on her friend's knee.

— But why do you have him?

— I was captured last night. At the dig. Cinéus and Wilnor trapped me in the jail. Madanm Janel-Félix and I discovered something terrible. Those men are *not* recovering our history. They're mining!

Janel sat up straight. Magdala was inert.

— If this is true... excuse me. I need to call the people together. Janel reached for her nearby conch shell and rose to step outside. She paused and gave out one long, sustained blow followed by three short bursts. She repeated the signal.

Libète felt an excruciating pain behind her eyes. But Janel–it is worse than that. The Sosyete is in league with the miners. Dorsinus–Félix and I–*we found Dorsinus*. He's been made a–a zombie.

Janel braced herself against the doorframe.

Libète pressed on. We need to rise up against these people. The community must stop this. Disarm the guards. If you know who the members of the Sosyete answer to, especially the one who is above this local group, you have to go to him. Convince him of the wrong being done.

Janel's shoulders sank. She spun to look out her doorway and peered out. Her eyes searched for something.

— Madanm Janel–are you hearing me? They are tearing up *our* land. If they continue, they'll pollute our water, ruin our crops, give us sicknesses.

— How are you so sure?

Libète blinked, cocked her head. If these men are doing what they do under the cover of a lie, it has to be because their methods are fast and rough and wrong. It's just a matter of time before–

Janel looked outside again, and seeing something, sighed in relief.

— Who's there? Libète asked, annoyed at Janel's distraction.

— It seems there are two trucks coming our way. Full of armed men. Paramilitaries, it appears.

Magdala suddenly rose. They're coming for Libète? Magdala whispered. Then we must hide her! They can't have her!

Janel's face was an empty slate. It's too late for that.

Libète nearly wretched, and the coughing began again. Magdala was horrified. What are you–

— You must both go with them.

— Go . . . *with* them? Magdala wailed.

Libète closed her eyes, shook her head. She tried to stifle the scratch at the back of her throat that made not coughing an impossibility. You sold us, Libète choked out.

Dear God.

— You made Prosper go out with Cinéus and Wilnor last night. You ordered him.

Dear God.

— You know they've been mining all along. And you helped them hide it.

Dear God.

— You don't fall under the Sosyete's authority. They fall under *yours*.

Libète stood, holding the baby tight, tight, tight. You ordered Dorsinus to be handed over to the Sosyete. You ordered the Sosyete to make me leave. Your lies – her voice fell to a whisper – they're endless.

— You talk of lies? Janel said. Your name isn't even your own.

— No! Magdala exploded. She pulled at her hair. No, no, *no.* We trusted you, Janel . . . above all others! Her cries rose.

— It was all to protect Foche, Janel said. The land was dying. Our youth were leaving. *We* were dying. The university–the miners–came with an offer. They would give us seed, fertilizer, and water. And the results? We haven't seen yields like these in years! Parents are eating, as are their children. The community, it has *hope* again.

— At what cost? Libète murmured. Her arms tightened too much, and Delivrans began crying. You traded everything for a good season. You're about to let them rob the common plot. This child–this child in my arms–will not have a *home.* You understand? They have bought you, and fooled you, and you've led this community headlong to its destruction.

Janel trembled. She reached for a nearby mug and threw it. It nearly hit Libète and the child and shattered against the wall. Get *out! Now!*

The trucks had come close. The men jumped down, their guns at the ready. Magdala forced Janel out of the doorway and screamed and Libète came close behind her. From behind Magdala's flailing she glimpsed a terrible figure step from the lead truck. Libète dropped to her knees.

Maxine.

The woman, bedecked in military garb, walked cautiously toward Magdala, toward Libète, toward the child. At *last*, she said.

Magdala's tears stopped for a moment. Is this woman–is this the one you told me about?

Libète could only stare at the ground, only cling to the child mewling in her arms.

Magdala knew her answer. You *murderer.* Her wails began again, climbed higher, spread all across the hills.

Janel watched the scene with fear and trembling. Take them, she gasped. You can pass word to the big shots running the mining operation that with them gone, all is not lost.

— Tell them yourself. They just hired my people for security. The girl is all I'm here for. She advanced toward Libète.

Bursts of gunfire in quick succession erupted from not far off, echoing throughout the mountains.

All looked in the direction of the sounds. A silence followed that no one would break.

— What the *hell* was that? Maxine finally asked as she drew a pistol. No answer came. Those were shotgun blasts. These peasants wouldn't have their hands on them. She barked at the man next to her, Drive up the mountain with your squad and see what's going on.

The leader and six other men piled back into the second pickup and set off, kicking up dust in their wake. Maxine turned to Janel. Woman, if there are problems here, everything is off. You understand?

Janel fidgeted.

— Get these two in the back, Maxine ordered. The men laid hands on Libète first, and Magdala flared up in a furor. Don't touch her! Don't you touch her! She pushed one man away and pivoted back toward Maxine. Though the men reached to restrain Magdala, she let lose a wild round of blows against Maxine. Caught off guard and shielding herself with her wrists raised, Maxine fired her gun reflexively.

Magdala collapsed.

— No! Libète screamed. It was a piercing, anguished sound and made all pause.

The men pulled Libète from Magdala's side as the woman clutched her wounded chest and shook, her mouth gaping and afraid. Maxine backed away slowly.

— I didn't mean to, Maxine said, so quietly no one could hear her words.

Libète cried and cried, Magdala! Magdala! Maxine, you bitch, you devil, you–

— I didn't mea–

— Janel! Libète roared. Take Délira's child at least! She thrust out her hands and held the frightened and confused boy in the open air. Take Delivrans!

Janel didn't respond. She couldn't comprehend the horror unraveling before her. She looked away as Libète was forced into a truck bed.

— *Magdala*, Libète cried. *Mag-da-la!* she shouted.

Already, the dear woman was gone.

Maxine trudged slowly toward the truck's bed, slipping her pistol back into its holster and fastening it with a snap. With the help of one of the soldiers, she climbed into the bed, and the truck started down the mountain.

Through tear-clogged eyes Libète saw Prosper run into view. He held a machete in his hand. Sophia! he shouted. He dropped the blade and went to Magdala's side while his mother hovered with her hand held to her mouth.

— All for numbers, Libète moaned. All for some damned numbers! Her lip trembled. What makes them worth killing and ... and ... *destroying*?

Maxine looked emptied. She chose her words with care. A new, old Haiti. That was all she said.

Libète could not ponder riddles now. All she could comprehend was despair and the child screaming in her arms.

A new, old Haiti. A Haiti I don't want to live in.

Libète looked at the world rushing past: the road and its narrow shoulder, and just beyond, a vertiginous drop to lower ground. In the blur of color and emotion, she had an epiphany of such tremendous clarity it staggered.

This could end.

Her muscles tensed throughout her body.

Just a leap. All it would take. The Numbers would be no more. My sacrifice. For Haiti ...

This was how it would be. She flexed her legs, ready to push herself backward over the side fender, hoping that her collision with the ground might snap her neck before experiencing that terrible, terrible fall.

But the child in her arms–would she take him with her? End his life too?

There is a Land

The thought made her tremble. Her shoulder, through which a bullet passed long ago, ached anew with phantom pain.

It is here

She was entrusted with his fate, this babe of today, boy of tomorrow, man of not yet. Could she leave him behind with these villains? Could she throw herself toward her end when a life of such unknown potential and hope pulsed in her arms? Could she?

And it is coming

She could not. New tears slipped into Delivrans's hair, and she held onto him and all that he was and all he could be and all that Haiti could be.

They sped past the market's plane. She glimpsed hundreds of eyes on them, and half as many faces turned up, wondering what new curse was descending on their mountainside. Libète felt Maxine's hollowed eyes locked on her. Libète shifted, and Maxine's hand sprung toward her like a lunging serpent, her fingers coiling about Libète's wrist.

She does not know I have no fight left in me. None at all.

The careening truck rounded a bend and skidded to a halt. Everyone in the back was thrown in a crush toward the cab. The baby cried out among curses. Libète craned her neck to see what obstructed the road.

It was one of the miners' large Mack trucks. Inexplicably, Jeune's son Junior stood toward the vehicle's rear.

The men with guns streamed from around Libète like hornets from an injured nest. They yelled and let loose a shout of bullets, but Junior ducked, ran around the side of the truck, and avoided the deadly spray. Maxine kept a firm grip on Libète. Libète kept a firm hold on the child.

The paramilitaries advanced toward the dump truck with their guns still drawn. In their haste they failed to notice the small flame brought to life by Junior as it subtly climbed up a cloth and into the truck's gas tank.

The truck erupted in shock and flame, and all became chaos.

New and poorly aimed gunfire spilled out from behind boulders above. The soldiers caught in the open fired up at the concealed shooters above, but they had wasted too many bullets on Junior. Soon they were robbed of life.

The pickup began a mad reversal. Libète, in a rush of adrenaline, tried to pull away from Maxine, but the woman was stunned and refused to let go.

Shots pierced the pickup and its cab, and suddenly the vehicle's course no longer tracked the contour of the mountain road–the driver was hit! The pickup began to push backward on a path that would take it straight off the cliff.

— Let go! Libète tried again to rip herself from Maxine, this time with success. Maxine finally stirred, and both fell from the truck bed haphazardly.

The tumble was all sharp pain and spin and a hollowing of breath. Libète rolled and rolled, enveloping the child to soften the blows he might sustain. Maxine landed even harder.

The pickup slid off the road and plummeted.

Libète was stunned. She sucked in dirt and dust in her attempt to trap breath, her every cough making her newly bruised body shout in pain. The pickup collided and rolled, and black smoke began spiraling into the sky. Libète cried out as sense of herself and her injured body finally returned.

Delivrans. Dear God!

She feebly lifted her neck to examine the boy. He did not cry. He did not blink.

Oh God! Oh God! Magdala. Didi. Laurent. Dimanche. And now him!

But then, he breathed.

And Libète cried out:

Mèsi

Mèsi

Mèsi

THE VIOLENT BEAR IT AWAY

Sa ou plante se sa ou rekòlte.
What you plant is what you harvest.

Moments after her landing, the men with guns – the men from Foche – were upon her. One took Delivrans. With their help, Libète stood, but just barely. As soon as she could, she reclaimed the child.

After taking Maxine's weapon, the men tried to force the woman to stand, but she could not. She collapsed, and two men had to lift and carry her by the arms as her whole body hung limply like a broken reed.

Jeune, weak as he was from his heart attack, acted as the group's leader. A cane in hand, he led the assembly's march back up the road to the bustling marketplace with his hand clapped proudly on Junior's back. Libète noted the faces of these other men: they were those she had toiled alongside in the fields, sold mangoes to in the market, sat next to in church. *All members of the Sosyete*, Libète realized.

But how could that be? They had just fought with her *against* Dumas's private security and paramilitaries. She now knew that at Janel's leading they been aligned with the miners all along. What had changed?

In the moment, Libète couldn't help but think of the Maroons, the bands of slaves who had taken to the mountains and defeated the French and British troops sent to put down their rebellion. These men in the

Sosyete shared blood with the rebels who likely laid waste to the mountaintop fortress years ago. Libète felt a swell of pleasure at the retribution meted out against those who had come to steal her away. That feeling passed as soon as she saw Félix.

They came upon a second group of Sosyete members. Félix stepped down from among their ranks with a smile on his face. He rushed to her, enveloping her in his arms. Libète could not help but cry.

It was him. He organized this. After she had been taken from the mine, he must have sought the Sosyete out and convinced them to act. The distant gunshots heard while at Janel's home were this troop dispatching Cinéus and Wilnor. They stole the dump truck, drove it into place, planned the roadblock. They used their weapons on the soldiers in the second pickup sent to check on the disturbance and stole their guns. *It was him.*

He pulled back from the embrace confused.

It was only then that one of the other men came to him and whispered the terrible news about Magdala. The word was soon whispered among the other men.

— Bondye!

— Not her!

Jeune went to Félix and laid his hand on the back of the boy's neck. Félix tried to dam the tears as he looked at Maxine, who still hung feebly between two men. The exertion made him tremble. For the first time he lived in a world in which his mother did not.

Their assembly continued toward the market with a crippling sense of sadness.

There were sounds of mourning in the marketplace as they approached. People made way so that Jeune could walk to its center. To Libète, it was a sea of eyes and gaping mouths she could not meet. She felt exposed, as if all her secrets had come to light. From the corner of her eye, she noticed that men from the mining encampment sat on the ground, each with their hands tied behind them. Dorsinus was there too, staring into space. His eyes were clouded and his senses dimmed, but at least he had been pulled from the edge of that maw in the ground that had seemed ready to devour him the night before.

Children everywhere clung to their parents, and their low crying hovered over everything. Délira approached and slipped the infant from Libète's arms. Tears traced the lines of her cheeks. Other neighbors propped up Libète as she hobbled toward the market center, or consoled Félix. Maxine was bound with ropes around her hands and neck and was led as if she were a beast. Some spit on her or struck her as she passed. Prosper watched it all, his face a tangle of inscrutable thought. He stood while Janel sat on the ground beside him, hiding her face in her hands. Before them both lay Magdala's body, covered with a blood-stained sheet.

In the bustle, Libète didn't notice the chair set on a seller's cleared table. A man took Jeune's cane while three others helped hoist him up and into the seat. He tried to speak to all, but he could summon little more than a rasp. The members of the Sosyete looked among themselves, before each one's stare landed on Junior. Knowing their intent, he shook his head, but they prodded him on. No, his whole body said. They lifted him to stand next to his father anyway. Jeune whispered something to his son, and his son, the mute, opened his mouth.

— This is not a time for lies, Junior said, repeating Jeune's words.

And with that Libète knew all. There he was, Papa Legba, the head of the Sosyete. And beside him stood the brilliant dancer with the powerful voice.

Many gasped at the minor miracle of his speech. Junior proceeded timidly before his words surged in confidence. He continued parroting Jeune's words: they were a confession. They announced Magdala's death, Janel's terrible bargain with the miners, and the Sosyete's complicity in handing over Dorsinus to be a slave. Yes, the Sosyete had been involved, but, according to Jeune, had been used by Janel. She was the town's leader and the Sosyete's higher authority. They trusted her and believed the community's interests were served by the men who came from outside.

— The Sosyete was meant for the protection of this community, Junior repeated. That was its purpose, going all the way back to the beginning. But we failed. We saw it corrupted. And we stand before you. Though I cannot speak for the others involved, I lay down my leadership, and would call for its abandonment. Its secrets have divided us, cost us dearly. Jeune's stare lingered on Félix, whose own gaze was locked on Maxine.

— We must decide how to deal with our sins, Junior said. These miners surrendered without violence. They were employees doing a job. But this woman – Jeune signaled to Maxine – she is different. She is the sole survivor of those who brought guns to use against us. We must go and tell the police, tell the country, what has happened here. We must make it known that the digging was taking place. And we must even be prepared for more trucks filled with more men carrying more guns. Jeune turned to Libète.

— And Sophia, it seems you are known by these people. Somehow wanted by them?

Libète was not prepared to speak. I . . . I am so, so sorry for my part in this. They have been after me for a long while. When they come again, they will be after me, and . . . I won't stay in Foche any longer. I'm sorry for bringing this on you all. Her chin quivered. On Magdala . . .

She buried her face in her hands, and everyone respected her quiet tears. When Libète finally looked up, she expected to see harsh stares. Instead she saw sympathy. Kindness. Compassion.

— And yet, this one remains. Jeune pointed to Maxine, who seemed nearly catatonic. She is guilty of making war against Foche, and now Foche must decide how she will die.

Jeune forced himself to speak the next sentence himself: Who will kill her?

Libète's heart leaped. And though she hated the thought, she knew what she must do.

— We will, she said. Félix and I. Félix looked up at Libète in surprise, seeming to shrink from the responsibility. Libète's eyes stayed trained on Maxine. She walked up to Prosper, her stomach fluttering, and took the machete from his hand. It's his and my right, Libète said. This woman took his mother and was trying to steal me. We'll take her to the mine pit. Drop her in. And after she's gone, I'll leave Foche for good.

Félix, resigned, took Maxine's gun from her guard, the same gun that had killed his mother. The guard handed over Maxine's rope, and Félix yanked it hard. She choked and winced, but rose. The two children led her away from the crowd.

It was a long walk up the mountain, and no one spoke. Strangely, the ghostly improvised music emerged again, its notes rising and falling with Libète's own breathing. Finally, Libète knew what this symphony was. Emanating from deep within her, it represented powerful yearnings beyond the boundaries of conscious speech. They were, simply put, prayers. Libète let the music play even as she proceeded toward a moment not long from now when she would do the previously unthinkable.

Maxine said nothing. Her expression floated between anger and resignation.

Félix trudged without speaking. Libète noticed his finger did not leave the gun's trigger.

— Where are you from, Maxine?

The question caught Félix and Maxine by surprise. She looked up at Libète.

— I'm from Léogâne.
— Do you have family?
— A mother.
— Does she love you?
— I hope.
— Will she mourn you?

They walked in silence as they passed Magdala's home. Its open door creaked in the breeze.

— How did you start your work?

Maxine didn't answer. Félix gave a stiff tug on the rope, and she choked her reply.

— I had a gift. For putting things together.

— Did you always work for criminals?

— Not always, she murmured. Not always.

— What will you miss?

Maxine's face tensed.

— When you're dead–

— I understood the question, she said icily. My dogs.

— Not another single person?

— The ocean. Waves coming in. The thrill of the chase.

— What else?

— My body.

— Do you believe in God?

— No. I . . . hope he's not there.

— And what about regrets? Have any?

— I . . . do. The woman. Magdala. Magdala's son, I want you to know I'm sorry for her. I'm . . . not who I want to be. Félix refused to look at her. He was set upon the land ahead.

Maxine's face clouded. Stop torturing me with these questions, she whimpered.

The quiet returned.

They walked through the large iron barrier that had kept the mine obscured from the community for so long.

— What are the Numbers?

— They're nothing . . . not now.

Félix pulled her to the edge of the principal pit. The network of plastic sheeting had been pulled down, allowing all of the injuries to the earth to be seen. By day, the deepest penetration was even more ghastly. It had been Dorsinus's prison and very soon would become a tomb.

Libète tapped Maxine's kneecaps with the blade's tip. On your knees. Now.

Félix crouched low and watched.

— Can you – Maxine trembled – make it quick?

Libète did not answer.

— What. Are. The. *Numbers?* Libète repeated the question, lifting her blade to Maxine's throat.

Maxine stared into the pit and contemplated its depth, its darkness. They're the location of money, money that Pascal hid away from Dumas, right before Dumas had him killed.

— How much? What's the price for all this misery you've handed out?

— Nine million. But it's not just money. It's what it buys. These men. Their food. Their guns. You've kept Dumas from his private army.

— Why would he want an army? Nausea came in waves at what the man, the one with whom she shared blood, was after. *A new, old Haiti.* The words played through Libète's mind. What was he going to do with his army? Libète asked.

Maxine's eyes tightened into slits. Please. Just end this.

Libète loosened the rope about Maxine's neck.

— Put out your hands.

Maxine doubled over. Please, don't take my hands–just a bullet. Please, don't torture me. I know I deserve it, I know, but please, please . . .

Libète felt possessed by a hatred that was pure and unadulterated. She lifted her blade. Félix looked away. Maxine cried out.

Libète slipped the machete between Maxine's wrists and sawed at the rope. Maxine gasped.

Félix raised his gun. What are you doing, Libète? What are you doing?

— I won't kill her.

Félix balked.

— I won't do it. My hands, I held Delivrans in them not half an hour ago. What world . . . what world do we make for him if you and I take her life?

He rushed at Libète and pushed her aside, pointed his gun at Maxine's temple. The woman moaned. What about my mother? he asked. Huh? How can you say you loved her if you let her go?

— Your uncle. Your mother's twin. I knew him, Félix. I saw his life. He lived to kill those who took your grandparents, and it ruined him. And Félix, I can see it now. You're so much like him. And your uncle, he gave himself up for me, hoping I wouldn't make his same mistakes!

Félix kept the gun pointed at Maxine, unable to understand what Libète explained. I can't let what she did go!

— Neither can I, not yet! But we must! There is a land, coming but not yet here. When I look out, not through eyes of hate, but those of hope, I can see it. The land flourishing. Trees growing, bellies full, the sick healed, tears wiped away, joy replacing sadness . . .

Félix shook with quiet sobs. The barrel of his gun was still fixed on Maxine's temple.

— I believe. I believe it's arriving, even now. And I won't let her take it from us, Libète said. The words flowed smoothly and calmly. I won't choose to live in the dying land. I won't let her and her kind drown everything in blood. Enough have died. The innocent, and those misguided men who lived by the gun. They were children of parents, fathers of children . . .

Libète approached him. Laid her hand on his. Lifted the gun so it pointed into the air. She pulled on his trigger finger, until the gun offered up its terrible report. Félix let her take the weapon from him and fell to the ground. He buried his face in his hands and grieved for his mother, the land, his home.

— Maxine of Léogâne, who has done great evil, who has stolen more than you can ever repay. We've killed you. The two of us. And now we release you.

— Some trick? the broken woman whispered.

Libète shook her head, the ethereal music playing loudly in her ears. Go, Libète commanded as her own tears fell. *Go.*

Maxine rose and looked at her freed hands, withdrew the rope from her neck. She ran, as best as her battered body allowed, and ran far, from what had nearly claimed her, from what she could not understand.

Libète fell at Félix's side and joined him in mourning all that was gone, counting the high cost of the humanity they retained and staring into the pit before them as noonday light pierced the dark and wrestled it for control.

And that is the story
Of the Boy's Seeds that were planted
And the Girl's Fire that was extinguished
Who left the Land
And found it again
For the Land
It is here
It is coming
It is where we stand
And nothing can hold it back

EPILOGUE

Lespwa fè viv.
Hope gives life.

Eleven months later

Dusk arrives in Deschapelles, and Gervilen Marcelin rushes along the rutted road with a board tucked under his arms as he tries to beat the Sun's disappearance. It had been a very bad day.

Firstly, his wife was caught out in the rains the night before and fell ill with a fever. Her care and all of today's domestic work fell to him. He got to work in the fields in the blazing afternoon Sun, and everything took a turn for the worse when his trusty pickaxe snapped as he tried to remove tree roots. His mule that normally would have aided in such work had died not a week before. His best friend Dorsainvil thought the creature's abrupt end was due to a disliked neighbor's nefarious act, but Gervilen knew better: the creature had been ancient. Without another axe, Gervilen had to begin the half-hour walk home, and his rheumatism clamored for attention every step of the way. When he returned home he found the neighbor's goat had broken into his yard and ate all of their budding *pwa chouk*. This despite his cacti fencing *and* the goat's wooden A-frame collar *and* that the beast had been tied to a spike! The hellion had apparently eaten the rope. As he pulled the goat from his yard, he was certain the beast's bleating was some kind of taunting laughter.

— This day, Gervilen muttered to himself as the sky's color began to drain away. He sighed.

Their only daughter had died several years back–the damned cholera at work–and he and his wife were left to age into oblivion alone. At least that's how he felt. They were already in their forties, and the girl had been a welcome, late surprise. His treasure. Whip-smart, she had finished first in her school in Verettes in the national Philo examinations. She even had a scholarship lined up to study business administration in Port-au-Prince. What a future she had in store! He wiped away a tear. Oh, how he missed his girl!

With dinner complete, dishes washed, and his sick wife placated, the one thing left for him was to sit and sip and play dominoes with Dorsainvil.

He found the man in his usual spot along the road. Dorsainvil was rocking back on his stool, his can of dominoes sitting at his feet. Dorsainvil ran a *boutik* out of his house, and they'd while away the hours sitting by a solar-charged light while talking, usually reminiscing, interrupted only occasionally as someone arrived to buy a pack of crackers or cigarettes or a bit of rum or Bongú milk to be added to tomorrow morning's coffee.

— I thought you weren't coming.

— This day, Gervilen said. This day . . .

— What happen–

Gervilen held up a silencing finger. We can talk about any subject–politics, lost loves, regrets, or sins–but what we will *not* do is talk of this day.

Dorsainvil shrugged and unscrewed the cap to a fresh bottle of rum taken from his display. He handed it to his friend. Gervilen took a sizable draught before handing back the bottle. Pulling up his own stool, he sat and unfolded the hinged table he carried and locked it in place. They laid the table on their laps, spilled the dominoes, and began their first of many games.

It was not long before a young man approached, leading a donkey. When he lingered without speaking, Dorsainvil spoke.

— Take what you want and put the money in that container. I'm busy.

The boy was unsure how to proceed.

— I'm not buying. I'm selling.

— And what would you have that I might be interested in?

— This donkey.

Both men looked up from their game.

Dorsainvil squinted, trying to assess the beast in the low light. That, son, is a sorry bourik. It's older than me.

— He's faithful.

— He's ancient.

— He's faithful, the boy repeated.

— Fidelity isn't everything.

— It's enough.

Gervilen spoke. Then why sell him?

The boy paused. That's my business.

Gervilen raised an eyebrow, sipped from the rum again. He needed another beast of burden for planting, but he could always rent one rather than buy again. That was the only way to go with how his luck had been running.

— Sorry, son, Dorsainvil said.

— Not interested, Gervilen said, laying down his second-to-last domino.

A girl stepped from behind the wall. Out of the corner of Gervilen's eye, the way she caught the wash of light made her seem otherworldly, maybe elemental.

— Please, monsieurs, she said. We've been struggling these last months. This creature has carried us through every difficulty we've faced. We've worked hard, but no matter what, we've struggled. And now we need to travel, to the city. Urgently. We're unable to scrape the money together to pay the way back home, and we need money when we arrive.

Dorsainvil turned back to the game and gave a perfunctory apology. Gervilen kept looking at the girl, burrowing into her eyes. There was something so very familiar there.

— How much? Gervilen asked suddenly.

The boy stood up straight. Seven thousand goud.

After a moment's consideration, Gervilen upended the board and their game.

Dorsainvil cursed. What the hell are you doing?

But Gervilen was off, lost in the dark. Within ten minutes he'd returned. He forced the money into the boy's hand. He went to the girl, took both her hands in his, and searched her eyes once more. They teared up, and she pulled her hands away to wipe at her eyes and smiled. He smiled back.

— Where's home?

— South, she replied. We're going to Port-au-Prince.

— If you two hurry, you can pile on one of the last produce trucks heading there tonight.

— We'll do that, she said.

The two youths approached the donkey. The boy looked so very sad as he stroked its mane. The girl came close too, and drew up the beast's face to her own. I'll miss you, Saint-Pierre, she whispered. She turned to Gervilen. His name is Saint-Pierre, she said.

Gervilen nodded soberly. Dorsainvil chortled. Madness, he said under his breath.

The girl and boy took their djakouts from the donkey's saddle bags. The boy handed Saint-Pierre's lead over to Gervilen.

— Mèsi.

— Mèsi, Gervilen replied.

The girl and boy walked down the road.

— You're going to regret this, Dorsainvil whispered.

— This, Gervilen said as he turned to his friend, is the best thing I've done in a long, long while.

On the very fringes of the light's reach, the girl turned and waved to Gervilen, who still watched. He waved back. The youths disappeared into the dark.

When Libète and Félix reemerged by a lamp's light near the produce truck, Félix spoke.

— Parting was hard.

Libète nodded.

— Are you sure you're up for this?

Libète took a deep breath. The air felt like it entered her lungs and exited as it should. The intervening months had been long, and hard.

— Yes. It's time.

— I don't just mean your sickness. With the money from the sale, we could wait–

— You're worrying again, she said.

— Am I?

They negotiated the price for the ride with the truck's driver and threw their packs up high on its bed already burgeoning with large sacks full of produce. Félix was attentive and helped boost Libète so that she could ascend the pile first. There were already two others there, situated closer to the truck's front.

— Are you sure it will be safe where we're going?

Libète reflected. It definitely won't be.

— Then why go? He asked. Help me understand.

— It's...

There were so many reasons to return to Cité Soleil. What they had discovered these past months about Dumas's plot, and what they had discovered about each other. There were truths that had to be testified to publicly, and there was a truth buried deep inside her that couldn't be ignored, known only to her and to God.

Libète smiled sadly and nestled her head into Félix's shoulder. She took his hand and wove her fingers into his and kissed his cheek. Home, Libète said, finally finishing her answer.

And with that he was satisfied, for in the uttering of that single word there may have been sadness, regret, and fear, but more powerful than those, and more enduring, and more indomitable, was hope.

ACKNOWLEDGMENTS

Many helped with the writing and publishing of this book. Michael Benson, Kathy Colvin, Corrigan Clay, Ben Depp, Alison Dasho, and Danielle Marshall deserve many thanks for contributions both large and small. I'm grateful to Jennie Smith-Paríolá and Stephanie Munson at Cornell University Press for permission to reproduce lyrics to the songs *Come join us, come on, you'll see where we are* and *I must give the good Lord thanks*. Neil and Christy Miller merit a special note for generously sharing their experiences in rural agriculture and midwifery, respectively.

I'm indebted to so many since relocating to Haiti. The staff of Mennonite Central Committee (MCC) and MCC Haiti in particular have shown me tremendous kindness and care. It's an honor to work with you. To my Pub Church family, thanks for letting me grow with you.

To readers and friends who have encouraged me in my writing, you have blessed me tremendously.

To my family, I thank you for your support and love.

To Katharine, you are precious.

Bibliography

A number of published works and articles were helpful in the writing of this book. They are named below:

Berlinksi, Micha. "Into the Zombie Underworld." *Men's Journal.* Sept. 1, 2009.

Davis, Wade. *The Serpent and the Rainbow.* New York: Simon and Schuster, 1985.

Danticat, Edwidge. *After the Dance: A Walk Through Carnival in Jacmel, Haiti.* New York: Crown Journeys, 2002.

Smith, Jennie Marcelle. *When the Hands Are Many: Community Organization and Social Change in Rural Haiti.* Ithaca: Cornell UP, 2001.

Sprague, Jeb. *Paramilitarism and the Assault on Democracy in Haiti.* New York: Monthly Review, 2012.

"Ti Zwazo." *Mama Lisa's World of Children and International Culture.* Trans. Maggy Paraison. Web. Apr. 18, 2014. http://www.mamalisa.com.

The Holy Bible: New International Version, Containing the Old Testament and the New Testament. Grand Rapids: Zondervan Bible, 1978.

Turnbull, Wally R. *Hidden Meanings: Truth and Secret in Haiti's Creole Proverbs: A Collection of over 1,200 Haitian Creole Proverbs Featuring English Translations and Interpretations.* Durham, NC: Light Messages, 2005.

ABOUT THE AUTHOR

Ted Oswald is an attorney. He lives in Port-au-Prince, Haiti, with his wife, Katharine.

He is also the author of:

Because We Are: A Libète Limyè Mystery #1
No Bad Bush: A Tale of Sierra Leone
The Bloodied Birds (A Because We Are Short Mystery #1)
The Kings of Nothing (A Because We Are Short Mystery #2)

If you wish to receive an automatic e-mail when Ted's next book is released, sign up at *tedoswald.com*. Your e-mail address will never be shared and you can unsubscribe at any time.

Word of mouth reviews are crucial for any author. If you enjoyed this story, please consider leaving a review on Amazon or Goodreads, even if it's only a line or two; it makes a tremendous difference and is greatly appreciated.

Connect with Ted by email or on social media by visiting
tedoswald.com.

CPSIA information can be obtained at www.ICGtesting.com
Printed in the USA
BVOW08s1204240816

460042BV00002B/18/P